| | | – – JUN 2014 |
|---|---|---|
| 4/8/14 | **2 7 DEC 2017** | |
| 15/8/14 | – 2 NOV 2018 | |
| 2 8 AUG 2015 | | |
| 1 8 SEP 2015 | – 2 NOV 2018 | |
| – 5 OCT 2015 | | |
| 1 6 DEC 2015 | | |
| 18/10/16 | – 7 MAY 2019 | |
| 21/10/16 | | |
| 2 0 SEP 2017 | | |

Please return this book on or before the date shown above. To renew go to www.essex.gov.uk/libraries, ring 0845 603 7628 or go to any Essex library.

# Past Chances

Bernardine Kennedy

**headline**

First published in 2007 by
HEADLINE PUBLISHING GROUP

First published in paperback in 2007 by
HEADLINE PUBLISHING GROUP

5

Cataloguing in Publication Data is available from the British Library

ISBN 978 0 7553 3538 1

Typeset in Bembo by Palimpsest Book Production Ltd,
Grangemouth, Stirlingshire

Printed and bound in Great Britain by
CPI Group (UK) Ltd, Croydon, CR0 4YY

Headline's policy is to use papers that are natural, renewable and
recyclable products and made from wood grown in sustainable forests.
The logging and manufacturing processes are expected to conform
to the environmental regulations of the country of origin.

HEADLINE PUBLISHING GROUP
A division of Hachette Livre UK Ltd
338 Euston Road
London NW1 3BH

www.headline.co.uk

*For my father, mother and brother. R.I.P.*

# Chapter One

*Hampstead, North London, 1971*

'Eleanor!' The deep voice bellowed full power through the closed bedroom door, making her jump despite the fact that she had known it would only be a matter of time before he crept up and listened at her door, the way he always did whenever she was in there.

'Change that station now or turn that wireless off. You know I won't have that sort of so-called music in my house.'

With a heavy sigh Eleanor Rivington stretched out her hand and turned off Radio Caroline; the transistor radio was the only mod con she had in her room; she had bought it herself when she had first started work. Although she knew her father wouldn't enter her bedroom if she was in there, she nonetheless did as he demanded or he would just keep on and on from the other side of the door until she gave in.

He never allowed his adult daughter a single moment of privacy, even to the extent of going in there while she was at work to seek out anything that he deemed unsuitable for

1

her to own, and then confiscating it. Modern magazines were his pet hate and he would ceremoniously shred her precious copies and then burn them in the kitchen boiler in front of her.

After one very brief and unsuccessful attempt at assertiveness several years before, Eleanor had decided that it was better to go along with his demands while at the same time making sure that anything he would disapprove of, however innocent, was stowed instead in her locker at work.

Smiling wryly as she heard the familiar heavy sighs that always accompanied his receding footsteps, she stretched out on the lumpy mattress that had seen many better days and, with her hands clasped under the back of her head, she wondered, not for the first time, what it would be like to live somewhere other than the old-fashioned, poorly maintained mausoleum of a house that was, and always had been, her home.

Eleanor's favourite way of going to sleep was to close her mind to the dingy bedroom that she was actually in and picture herself somewhere normal; somewhere away from her elderly and controlling father with his Victorian ideas of how a young single girl should live her life.

Especially she loved her fantasy of being in a bedroom that was pretty and feminine, that didn't smell musty and didn't resemble a prison cell; somewhere she could listen to any radio station she wanted, watch the programmes on TV that she chose, not the ones dictated by her father, and play records. But more than anything, she wanted to make friends and bring them home for coffee and chats, and go shopping for clothes that reflected her age.

In fact, she wanted to be able to do what the other girls she worked with seemed to do as a matter of course – to just be normal instead of the constant outsider.

Because he was her father, she loved Harold Rivington – and he certainly cared for her in his own way – but most of the time she didn't like him. He had always scared and intimidated her, and she hated his overbearing regime as much as she hated the guilt that he laid on her every single time she stepped outside the front door leaving him behind.

Eleanor had known for a long time that their way of life was stuck very firmly around forty years in the past instead of in the 1970s, but it wasn't until she had finally been allowed to leave her cloistered school at eighteen and had started working, that Eleanor Rivington had seen just what life could be like in the real world. Now, at twenty-one, she was starting to rebel in her mind if not in her body. She wanted to be a part of that world and have some fun.

Her friend from work, Marty Cornish – her only friend, in fact – would constantly make her laugh with his tales of the disasters of flat-sharing, and Eleanor would fantasise about it being her in the leaky, decrepit hovel with drunken visitors and the aroma of tobacco smoke and marijuana drifting down the stairs.

But her father had other ideas and she could see no way of breaking free without mortally wounding him and exacerbating her own feelings of guilt; however much of a bully he was, there was simply no way of getting round the fact that she was all he had.

Out of loyalty to her father she always pretended to Marty that she was perfectly happy living at home, but she knew he could see through this. In fact, she was as unhappy and restless at that moment as she could possibly be, but as she drifted off she tried to keep happy and positive thoughts in her head. Falling asleep happy was the only way she could keep the nightmares at bay . . .

As she began to relax, the footsteps came back. 'Eleanor! I've made us some cocoa – it's on the table in the kitchen.'

'I'm too tired, Dad. I just want to go straight to sleep,' she replied without moving.

'Eleanor, it's ready for you. Now come down and drink it; it will help you sleep better. Those silly nightmares are going to make you ill.'

Eleanor sat up. She knew he meant well. 'Okay, I'll be down in a few minutes.'

'Good, because I want to talk to you.'

*I want to talk to you* used to mean that she was in big trouble and was about to be punished, but now it meant that he intended to warn her about something or other that was immoral and unseemly, some perceived failing in the wicked world from which he had to protect her.

Snatching her dressing-gown from the hook on the back of the door, she wrapped it around herself tightly and at the same time pushed her feet into her slippers. Trying to feel

4

enthusiastic about a hot cup of cocoa and two digestives, she made her way down to the chilly kitchen.

Harold Rivington always said he only had her best interests at heart, and his daughter Eleanor believed him.

Several weeks later, at the Regency Hotel in Bayswater where she and Marty both worked, it was Eleanor's tea break and, rather than go all the way up to the staff room, she walked over to the hotel bar and watched surreptitiously from the doorway as Marty, the resident barman, did what he did best and put on a show. She loved watching him at work and had been standing there for several minutes before he glanced across and saw her.

'Lennie,' he called out, 'come into my inner sanctum and paste a happy smile across your pretty little face for my revered customers. They like that, and the wider the smile, the bigger the tip – well, that's what I reckon. Look at my teeth, everyone – ear to ear great big gnashers flashing at you!' Marty grinned happily and bared his very white but slightly uneven teeth from behind the bar where he was putting on his usual show of juggling bottles and cocktail shakers with the easy grace of a circus performer.

'Stop calling me Lennie,' Eleanor hissed at him, coming over to the bar – but she was used to being his foil and didn't mind playing the game. 'My name is Eleanor and, as you very well know, I don't get tipped, I get a salary. Sort of.'

'Well, my little honey-bee, smile wider and learn to juggle

as per moi and you might pull in a few extra quid to top up your takings!' Marty turned to his audience and theatrically reached for another bottle. 'Am I right, folks? Or am I right? How would you all like to see the lovely Eleanor up here on the bar-top beside me, doing this with that happy smile on her face . . .'

As they laughed appreciatively, the handsome young man threw the bottle high into the air and in one agile move, vaulted up onto the bar to catch it behind his back. As everyone clapped, Eleanor shook her head affectionately. Folding her arms across her chest, she leaned back against the wall and continued to watch Marty, wishing she had just a portion of the self-confidence that he displayed, dancing around his territory night after night.

She loved the flamboyant Liverpudlian showman who was as extrovert as she was painfully shy. He knew he was attractive and he also knew exactly how to make sure he was the centre of attraction. His trademark work outfit of tight black shirt and matching flared trousers complemented his shoulder-length blond hair that was carefully tended and trimmed to look unkempt. He had befriended Eleanor on her first terrifying day at the hotel and she adored him. He was the first real friend and confidant she had ever had.

Marty Cornish was a very personable young man who always had a semicircle of admirers grouped around the sweeping bar in front of him, many of whom, both male and female, passed him their phone numbers along with the tips. But beneath the display of supreme confidence there was a secret insecurity and a strong desire to be both liked and loved by everyone.

As Marty juggled, Eleanor glanced around at the public areas of the Regency Hotel. It had obviously once been quite luxurious but now the building was rundown, with peeling paint and tired coving, bits of which regularly dropped off. The whole place would benefit from a complete refit, but as long as the tourists continued to enjoy the old-fashioned ambience and kept on coming to stay and spend their cash, the new corporate owners could see no reason to spend any money on it. If the guests thought the threadbare carpets and faded gold leaf were all part of the history of the place, then that was just fine with them.

When Marty had first attempted to enliven and modernise the ground-floor bar, resistance had been fierce, but once the profits started improving he had been allowed almost free rein, and the Crystal Chandelier Bar had been invented. It was still a tacky old bar underneath the glitz, and there was neither crystal nor chandeliers in sight, but Marty knew that if he could get the punters in and then amuse them, they would keep coming back.

While Marty put on his own show in the bar night after night and enjoyed himself, Eleanor worked sedately behind the antiquated reception desk, dealing with every problem that the clientèle of mostly foreign guests could throw at her. She liked her job and enjoyed the constant flow of different nationalities that passed through the hotel daily, but she had little ambition or motivation. It was just a job to her, a stop-gap, nothing more. Eleanor had been trained by her father to accept that she would possibly work for a few years and then marry someone of his choosing.

And, of course, she would continue to live at home and look after him.

It was what all the women in her father's family had done and, because of the sheltered way she had been brought up, it had never occurred to her to question it until recently. Throughout her life she had been brow-beaten to such an extent that she automatically fell straight into the role of submissive daughter when she walked through the doors of the family home. It was second nature.

'Venita!'

Deep in thought, Eleanor physically jumped as Marty shouted the name and looked out past her into the lobby.

'This way, gorgeous,' he continued, still playing to his audience. 'Come on through and meet my best friend, Lennie – she's tucked away over there in the corner trying to be inconspicuous though I doubt you know the meaning of that particular word, do you, Ven?' He winked mischievously at the group of both regular barflies and hotel guests who were perched on the chrome and faux-leather barstools in front of his territory watching the show.

'Not that the lovely Lennie deserves to be in the corner, of course. Only naughty girls get sent to the corner and our Lennie is a good girl. A very good girl, in fact, so apologies to all you red-hot males lusting in her direction.'

Again the laughter rippled, and although Eleanor smiled

along with it she also reddened as she always did when Marty focused the spotlight on her, but as she spun round to hide her embarrassment, she walked straight into the young blonde woman who had crossed the lobby.

'Oh excuse me,' she murmured, sidling past with her eyes down. 'I wasn't looking where I was going.'

'Nah, it was my fault but don't rush off. I'm sure you know Marty just can't help showing off, as long as there is an audience of at least one or probably even none. This is a man who has been known to entertain himself in front of the mirror for hours. I'm Venita.' She held her hand out. 'And I know you're Lennie – Marty's talked a lot about you. I don't understand how we've not met before, although Marty don't half like to be secretive and mysterious and keep his mates apart. Divide and conquer, that's his game, I reckon.' Her smile was open and generous as she shook Eleanor's hand.

'He's spoken a lot about you too.' Eleanor's eyes moved around, searching for an escape route. 'Look, I'm really pleased to meet you but I do have to get back to work. I only came over to the bar to deliver a message, and I can sense the bad vibes winging over from my boss, Mr Reception, already. He really hates seeing staff hanging around the public areas.'

'What time does your shift finish? I'm meeting up with Mart as well as my mate Megan later tonight. Are you joining us? Marty said he was going to ask you.'

'I doubt it, I really have to get home—'

'Oh come on, we can get to know each other. Any friend

of Marty is a friend of ours and he said he had something to tell us. God knows what it might be, but he seemed over the moon about it!'

Eleanor smiled nervously; she could handle difficult guests but she found social conversations and occasions a trial.

'Okay, I'll see what I can do. I'm off at eight tonight if all goes to plan.' As Eleanor spoke she knew there was no way she would really go to meet them, but it just seemed easier to go along with it than have to deal with friendly persuasion.

'Oh, that'll be great. See you in here just after eight then?' Venita's South London accent grated on Eleanor but still she smiled.

'Fine, but as I said, if I can get away on time,' Eleanor murmured and lowered her eyes. 'Now I really must go, it was nice to meet you.'

Putting her favourite polite, almost subservient, expression on her face Eleanor again took up her post behind the dark solid wood reception desk and wondered why on earth someone like Venita would want to socialise with *her*. Leaning forward surreptitiously, she looked through the doorway to the bar and observed Venita, whose loud throaty laugh was turning all heads in her direction.

The young woman, probably about the same age as Eleanor herself, was wearing a canary-yellow shift dress that was scooped dangerously low across her breasts and barely reached the top of her thighs at the hem, along with a pair of chunky knee-high black suede boots. A matching wide black belt with laces instead of a buckle was slung low around her shapely hips and her false, over-blacked eyelashes fluttered furiously at Marty and his customers.

To Eleanor's critical eye, subconsciously influenced by her father, the whole look was tarty, especially combined with the long platinum-blond hair that fanned out over her shoulders framing a pushed-up cleavage of near mammoth proportions.Venita! she thought to herself with a slight mental sneer. What sort of a stupid name is that? Definitely made up by someone whose real name is probably something like Edna, who wants attention from anyone and everyone, and well suited to someone who happily takes their clothes off in public! And no doubt Megan is the same. On that ungracious thought, she turned back to the impatiently rustling queue that was building in front of her.

But well after her shift had ended, Eleanor found herself nervously pacing the empty staff room drinking a cup of muddy coffee instead of just grabbing her coat and bag from her locker and heading for the underground station as usual. Lighting a cigarette, she drew on it fiercely. Pacing and smoking, she thought long and hard and tried to figure out why she hadn't just said no. Maybe it was because, deep down, she wanted to go with them and have some fun with people her own age. They seemed to love their lives. Maybe she was secretly envious of them . . .

Just then, the door swung open and Marty bounded in.

'Jeez, Lennie, five floors. Five fucking floors! Why we can't use the lifts is beyond me; all that wasted energy is going to be the death of me. I'll drop down dead one day, I swear it.' He struggled to get his breath back. 'I wondered if you'd shot off home already and forgotten about us. What's keeping you? The girls are dying to meet you properly, we're going to hit a club but I still have to hand over to that twat Olivier who seems to think I'm trying to screw his tips. Just because he couldn't juggle an empty tin can and gets a couple of bob short of fuck all because of it . . .'

'I can't go to a club, Marty, you know I can't.' Eleanor stared at him in horror and then looked down at the clothes she had changed into – neatly pressed pale blue slacks and a prissy white blouse with a bow at the neck. 'I've got to get home. I don't mind a quick drink in the pub up the road, but that's it. Dad's expecting me . . .'

'Come on now, Lennie, I didn't climb five flights just for a bollocking and a rejection!' Marty threw his hands up in the air. 'Though I must admit I was surprised when Venita said you were up for it.'

'I said I'd think about it but I didn't say I'd go to a club, that's for sure. She said you were all meeting up – I just thought we were going for a coffee or something.' Eleanor could feel her panic levels rising rapidly.

'Okay, okay, how about a compromise? We'll go to the pub for a quick jar and you can make up your mind once you've got to know the girls.'

'I've made up my mind already, Marty. I have to get home.'

Marty leaned against the wall and grinned. 'I know you

think you have to, my darling, but I'm sure I can change your mind. Now give us a drag of that fag – I need it to get my energy levels back up after those stairs.'

Handing her half-smoked cigarette to him, she sighed, 'Come on then, one drink and then I have to get home, I really do. I hate the underground in the evenings and my father will worry.'

'Then you'll be even more interested in the conversation we're about to have. Come on, chop chop, back down five fucking flights and while we're at it undo that fucking bow! Let it all hang out, eh? That's my girl!' Laughing, he reached out for her hand and pulled her through the door.

# Chapter Two

Eleanor and Marty walked into the bar together to see Venita perched on a stool with her legs carefully crossed to just about cover the tops of her tights and holding court in front of a crowd of open-mouthed admirers. On the adjoining stool, posing in almost the same wide-eyed provocative position that exuded sexuality and naughtiness, was a very similar-looking young woman.

Venita smiled brightly as soon as she saw Eleanor. 'Hello again. This is my friend Megan. Megan, this is Lennie, Marty's friend. Come and join us.'

'I really can't, not here, hotel policy bans staff from the bars.' Suddenly scared, Eleanor shook her head vehemently. 'They're quite strict – they don't even like friends coming in. Marty's already been told off about it. I'll just wait outside until he's handed over to Olivier.' She knew she sounded childish, but she couldn't help it. She felt corralled and nervous.

In tandem the two young women smiled and slid off their stools, tugging furiously at their hems.

'No way, we'll all just head straight to the pub. Marty

14

can catch us up.' Venita turned back to Marty. 'Okay, Mart? We'll see you in the Bull as soon as.'

As the three of them left the hotel Eleanor blushed a deep crimson; she couldn't remember the last time she had felt quite as mortified as when Venita and Megan homed in on either side and looped arms, almost marching her along with them. Passers-by paused and stared and Eleanor knew without a doubt that not one of them was staring at *her*.

Whereas Venita and Megan were both blond and around five feet five inches, with deeply tanned and voluptuous figures on full display, Eleanor was nearer to five foot ten, with shoulder-length brunette hair tied back with a piece of black velvet ribbon, slender almost to the point of skinny, and dressed from top to toe in clothes that were far too old for her.

Marty had often boasted about his friends Venita and Megan, and although she had never actually met them before, Eleanor felt that in a way she already knew them. And disliked them.

He had told her often that they were both glamour models who had featured in the tabloid newspapers and men's magazines, and that their dizzy-blonde act was in constant demand because they always modelled together under their adopted name 'The Saucy Sisters'.

They weren't sisters, of course, they weren't even vaguely related, but when they had met by chance outside a glamour model agency that had turned them down individually, and realised how similar they could make themselves look, they had immediately hatched their plan.

Three days later, the same agency, after seeing the new portfolio of photos taken by a backstreet wedding photographer who hadn't been able to believe his luck when they'd asked him to take the pictures, had immediately signed up 'The Saucy Sisters' and their new careers had instantly taken off. Marty loved being on the periphery of the excitement.

'Where do you live, Lennie?' Venita asked curiously after they were settled with their drinks. 'Mart said you're out of town a bit.'

Eleanor cringed at the familiarity of the nickname Marty had given her but she couldn't bring herself to object.

'I live with my father out Hampstead way,' she replied. 'It's on the Northern Line, not bad during the day but I hate the late journeys. Sometimes I stay in a staff bedroom but it's so claustrophobic up there in the eaves. I'd really hate to have to live in at the hotel like the chambermaids do.'

She caught Venita and Megan exchanging slightly amused glances. 'It's no problem, you know,' she snapped defensively. 'I don't mind living at home with Dad. I've always lived there. It's my home and he's always been there for me—'

'Oh God, Lennie, I'm not criticising. I wish I had close family, and as for Hampstead, I've never even been out that way,' Megan interrupted apologetically. 'We're from the other side, south of the river. Ven shares a dump with an old boyfriend and his mate, and I'm sort of with my ex-foster mum, when her old man's not around to grope me at every opportunity.' Eleanor gasped without meaning to. 'Oh, it's okay,' the other girl said, noticing her reaction. 'Par for the

16

course really, with tits like these. Me and Ven learned to live with it long ago. There's a lot of frustrated old bastards out there who get their kicks from copping a quick feel whenever they can.' Megan and Venita smiled at each other knowingly, making Eleanor suddenly feel very naïve.

'What's more of a bugger is that our work is in Central London – and, of course, so are all the worthwhile parties. Taxis cost a fucking fortune. We've been looking at sharing somewhere cheap and cheerful . . .'

'Mmmm,' agreed Eleanor politely, 'I can see that would be convenient for you, but it's so expensive in the centre of town.'

'Not if you get the right place, the right people and enough of them,' Marty put in as he appeared behind them and dragged a chair across from another table. 'And I reckon I have. That's what I wanted to see you all for.' He looked at each of them one by one, savouring his moment. 'Now this rich bloke I know, no name so don't ask, who swears he's straight but I reckon secretly fancies the pants off me, is going to Australia for a couple of years to screw sheep instead . . . or did he say shear sheep?' Marty feigned puzzlement. 'Anyway, he wants to head off to the outback to find himself, or something equally fucking stupid.'

Marty tutted and shook his head affectedly while at the same time raising his eyes to the ceiling once again. 'You know, the sort of thing you can do when you have wads and wads of filthy lucre handed to you on a plate from the parents. So, he's offered to rent me his house, a gaff in South Ken somewhere back of the High Street. Thing is, even on my tips I can't afford the rent although it is a total bargain on a par with anything else.'

Leaning across, he wrapped an arm around Eleanor's shoulder. 'So there it is, girls, the offer of a lifetime for you. I haven't seen it but it sounds good to me. How do you feel about a four-way share? Between us all we could afford it and we'd all get on, I just know it. You girls can walk round starkers and with no make-up on, safe in the knowledge that I don't fancy any one of you anyway!'

Marty adored being the centre of attention so as they all laughed, he batted his long silky eyelashes at them and continued loudly, 'Though I do have to warn you, you'll have to keep an eye on your boyfriends! I do have a reputation to keep up!'

Eleanor laughed along with the others but it wasn't quite as hearty. It was all so unexpected and, much as she'd fantasised about it, suddenly she couldn't imagine leaving the security blanket of her closeted life at home, let alone going to live with the weird threesome of Marty, Venita and Megan. Three people all so very different from her in both upbringing and outlook.

But more importantly, she couldn't even imagine a way of telling her father, who she just knew would out and out forbid it. However, as the evening wore on and she started to loosen up and enjoy herself in their company, she wondered whether it might actually be fun to give it a try.

Just for a while.

# Chapter Three

'Oh I think not, Eleanor!' Harold Rivington glared at her across the breakfast table. 'You are not going to live in a backstreet in London and you're definitely not going to share a slum with dropouts and yobs.'

Eleanor watched his face carefully but didn't respond; his various expressions had always been her barometer to his mood.

'In fact,' he continued to rant, 'under the circumstances, you are forbidden from even going back to that bloody ridiculous job in that bloody ridiculous hotel.' He paused before continuing and she could see him getting visibly angrier with each word. 'It's not even a real job and as we don't need the pittance you earn, you can now stay here and keep house.' He frowned and shook his head. 'I'm getting fed up with doing everything around here while you play at going to work. I allowed you to go there on certain conditions. Now I'm withdrawing my consent.'

Eleanor stared at her father who was wearing his *I'm very disappointed with you* expression. She had known he would forbid her to move into the shared house and she had put off telling him for as long as she could. But the time had come and she knew she had either to tell him or just stay at home under his rule for the rest of her life. She had psyched herself to stand firm for once, was trying to remember Marty's advice to be strong.

'What do you mean?' she said. 'I'm only going to share a house in London to be nearer to work, and it'll only be for a while. I'll still come and see you all the time.' She laughed nervously to try and lighten the mood. 'I'm not eloping off to Katmandu with the milkman, Dad, I'll just be up the road. You can come and visit me as well.'

Her father shook his head slowly. As he glared at his daughter, his badger-coloured bushy eyebrows descended towards his tortoiseshell glasses until they nestled on the frames like two fat caterpillars, so wild and woolly, they looked decidedly at odds with the shiny bald pate that gleamed brightly in the sun's rays streaming through the window. She could see he was irrationally furious and knew only too well his power to intimidate and browbeat when the mood took him.

'Do not backchat me, Eleanor, you weren't brought up to speak to your elders like that.' He paused and studied her closely. 'You know, I'm becoming very concerned about you. You never used to be disobedient – I'm worried you're getting into bad company and bad habits. And you keep coming home outside of your curfew hours in taxis.'

The way he sneered the word *taxis*, Harold Rivington

made it sound as if that alone made her guilty of a heinous lapse in morals.

'Bad company? What do you mean by that?' Eleanor smiled again to take the edge off her words but it was limited to the corners of her mouth. 'If you've never met my friends, how can you say they're bad company? And as for bad habits, I get a taxi from the station to save disturbing you when I've had to work late. I didn't realise how much you enjoyed driving to the station in the dark.'

Eleanor was starting to feel uncomfortable under her father's dark glare. Other than listening to pop stations on the radio and reading teenage magazines, she had never done anything for him to disapprove of – and yet he still didn't trust her. She constantly made allowances for the fact that he was of a completely different generation and now in his seventies, but regularly the childish thought that she hadn't asked to be born to aging parents flashed through her mind.

'Well, of course they're bad company, you stupid girl,' her father continued angrily. 'They can't be nice people if their parents are allowing them to live in a house together without supervision. And with a man there as well! Is that why you keep staying out late?' Suddenly he spluttered on his toast and his eyebrows shot up his forehead. 'Are you going out with him, Eleanor? Is he a secret boyfriend? Are you behaving like a slut behind my back?'

Irritated that she was, once again, having to defend herself against his outrageous assumptions, Eleanor replied, 'Dad, he's just a friend, I promise. He's a friend to all of us. There's nothing going on, Marty is truly just a work colleague. And he's a genuinely nice, kind person. It is possible to have friends of the opposite sex, you know.'

'A pervert, more like. Only a pervert would want to live with three young girls.' Her father screwed his face up in disgust. 'I dread to think what could happen. He'd be creeping in and out of all the beds like a thief in the night. None of you would be safe. None of you.' He shivered and wrinkled his nose up in distaste at the thought, again making Eleanor even more frustrated, even though part of her wanted to laugh. If only he knew the truth about Marty Cornish . . .

'That's not fair, Dad,' she said calmly. 'Marty really is a nice chap – I work with him so I know him well by now. He's been so good to me at the hotel, helping me fit in. I told you, men and women can be friends. Come on, you're friends with Ruby, your partner at the Bridge Club and *she's* married – what does her husband think of that?'

The red-knuckled fist slammed down on the table, causing the crockery to jump and Eleanor to stop mid-sentence in shock at the ferocity of it.

'Don't you dare insinuate things like that about me! Ruby is the wife of the Club Secretary, not that it's any business of your filthy mind. You see, Eleanor? That's what happens when you mix with people like that. Now we will not discuss this any more. You are under strict curfew and will not leave this house again until I say so. Do you understand? I'm not having you influenced like this!'

'Oh Dad, come off it,' Eleanor interrupted crossly. 'I'm

twenty-one, I can do whatever I like. You can't make me stand in the corner any more. I don't want to fall out with you but I do want to live and socialise with people my own age for a while. I want to have some fun before I settle down and I'm going to do so.'

'Settle down? Do you seriously think any half-decent man is going to want you after you've lived with another man? No man wants someone who's been touched by someone else; no man can be expected to accept that sort of disgusting behaviour.' Harold Rivington's face was suddenly so red with anger he looked on the verge of exploding.

Eleanor was torn. She wanted to explain that Megan and Venita were just two girls of her own age, she wanted to be able to tell him that Marty was queer and not the least bit interested in her sexually, but she knew that would send him into even more of a frenzy. The idea of heterosexual men around his daughter was bad enough, but a homosexual man would really send him off into orbit.

'It's not like that, Dad, you're twisting everything. I'm not going to *live with a man*, I'm going to share a house with three other people who are all the same age as me, more or less. We'll all have our own rooms and our own lives, but if you think about it, Venita and Megan – the other two girls – and I will be heaps safer with a man in the house to ward off any unwanted advances.'

'Enough, I said.' Her father stood up and focused on her, leaning heavily on the table with both hands. 'We're not discussing this any more, Eleanor. You're not going and that's the end of it. Now clear the table like a good girl and then we can do the washing-up together.'

Eleanor sighed. 'Look, Daddy, I'm sorry, but this time I'm not giving in. I am going to move. I love you and don't want to fall out with you, but I also want to have some independence. You can trust me, I promise you, but then I thought you knew that already.'

'Well, obviously I can't trust you or we wouldn't be having this conversation. Now go straight to your room and stay there until I say otherwise,' her father responded, making sure Eleanor was, as always, aware of her place as his daughter.

'Sorry, Dad, I have to go to work and make the arrangements. I'd like you to be happy for me but I am going regardless.'

'NO! Never again will you see those people. Go to your room now.'

Quietly, Eleanor pushed back her chair and walked out of the room enveloped in the familiar guilt that he planted in her regularly, wondering if she would have the strength to follow the move through, especially as it was all arranged for the following week.

She hated it when he shouted; she instantly flashed back to the nightmares that she had suffered for so many years. The nightmares where he was always shouting at her mother and she could hear him beating her; she could hear the sounds of fist on skin, interspersed with the sound of her mother whimpering and begging him to stop. Every sound had been real, but then when she had eventually cried out, her mother had rushed to her room to soothe her and re-assure her that it was all just a nightmare, that nothing at all had happened; then the next day her father would berate her for having an over-active imagination.

And now he was shouting and she was palpitating and trying not to remember anything at all.

*True or false.*

Rebellion was not in her nature, but the reiteration that her father didn't trust her upset her far more than she could have anticipated. How could he possibly think that of her, she mused sadly, especially after all the years when she had been there with him constantly. His only companion.

Although it was way past time to get ready for work she didn't go straight up to her room on principle; instead she went out of the side door that led into the small walled section of the rambling, overgrown garden that had always been her haven. Climbing ivy and honeysuckle covered the brick walls that were edged with tall evergreen shrubs and an assortment of hardy plants that needed little tending. Eleanor maintained the walled garden as best she could by herself; she loved the time she spent out there alone weeding, pruning and trying to get it back to how it was. When her father allowed her.

Eleanor had been well into her school years before she had realised exactly how much her parents had cloistered her away from the outside world. An only child born to older parents who had long given up hope of having any children, she had been smothered and loved, although both her parents had a strange way of showing it.

She had never been allowed any freedom. Her father had always denied her even the tiniest bit of that.

Her classmates at the small local private school had soon realised she was different and homed in on her as a suitable target for bullying. They tormented her about everything, from her immaculate but over-large, long-skirted uniform, her mother always meeting her from school and, of course, the obvious age of her parents. The bullies delighted in picking away at her and excluding her from as much as they could, but Eleanor had never been able to tell anyone. She had hated every moment of her schooldays, and her home had been her comfort blanket where her mother had wrapped her up, hugged her and protected her from the outside world and also, as much as possible, from her over-bearing father.

But then, the day after her thirteenth birthday, Eleanor had come out of school and her mother hadn't been there.

The minutes turned into hours as Eleanor had waited quietly first at the school gate and then later, on the doorstep, unaware of what to do or who to talk to. Then her father had come home from work at his usual time and the hours had turned into days, then into weeks. Without a word of explanation to anyone, including her beloved daughter, Rosetta Rivington had disappeared from the family home that day, leaving no note and taking nothing with her apart from her handbag and the clothes she was wearing.

On that defining day in her life, Eleanor's mother had just quietly vanished.

Her father had professed to be unsurprised and had told Eleanor quite callously that her mother had run off with another man and abandoned them for the sake of her own lust. He had also stated adamantly that her name was never to be mentioned again. In the beginning Eleanor hadn't believed any of it, had been convinced that her mother would suddenly return in much the same way as she had left. But by the time a year had passed, father and daughter had settled into a routine that would eventually become custom and practice.

It was as if her mother had never even existed.

As soon as his wife had disappeared, Harold had taken on the role of housekeeper and carer, ruling the household, and his daughter, with the rigidity of a Commanding Officer. It wasn't long before Eleanor had stopped trying to talk about her mother because her father would become so angry, but she never stopped thinking about her and wondering how she could have done such a thing to her only daughter, whom she had professed to adore.

Perching on the edge of the weatherbeaten wooden bench, Eleanor glanced sadly now at the centrepiece of the small walled garden, a beautiful magnolia tree that would soon be in full bloom. At the same time, out of the corner of her eye, she could see her father blankly staring at her from the kitchen window.

The girl had a sharp flashback to how much her mother

27

had loved the tree and how her father had sadly become focused on it and tended it so very carefully after his wife had left. Or was it the other way round? She couldn't remember; all she knew was that the scent of magnolia both soothed and upset her still. Dejected, she wondered if leaving home was a possibility after all; she just didn't know if she could go off and leave her aging father all on his own after everything he had already been through.

Brushing the moss from the damp bench off the seat of her dressing-gown, she went back indoors and, bypassing the kitchen, she headed instead straight up to her room to get dressed for work.

As she pulled on her clothes and tied her hair back, she made up her mind to tell Marty straight away that she wouldn't be joining them; that way he would have time to find someone else for 'her' room. She knew she couldn't do it to her father. She just wasn't strong enough.

'I'm off to work, Dad,' she shouted with her hand on the front door. 'I'll be home early tonight – I finish at five and I'll cook dinner when I get in.'

Turning the catch, she pulled at the door but it didn't open as normal. It only took her a split second to realise that her father had deadlocked the solid oak door that led to the securely enclosed porch, and removed the key.

'Dad!' she shouted as loudly as she could. 'Dad, come on, I have to go to work – they're expecting me. Give me the key and we'll talk when I get home. I won't leave you, I promise, I won't move out. Just open the doors . . .'

When he didn't respond Eleanor decided to try the back door which had a different lock, but found she couldn't get through into the kitchen either. Running frantically from door to door throughout the house, she soon realised that he had locked nearly every single one and taken all the keys out of the old-fashioned locks. The only rooms she could get into were her own bedroom and an adjoining bathroom, although she still had access to the stairs and landings. She glanced at the shelf where the telephone normally stood and saw it was empty. The phone had been stretched to the length of its cord across the floor and tucked under the door of the kitchen where she guessed her father was. She could picture him sitting bolt upright in his favourite chair right beside the old grey kitchen boiler with a threadbare tartan blanket tucked over his knees.

'Dad? Dad! Come on, you can't do this to me. You have to let me out sooner or later. Let me out now and we'll talk about it again. Dad? I'm so sorry I upset you. Open the door and we'll talk.'

But the silence continued.

Running round again she hammered on every door, one after the other, becoming increasingly hysterical as she got no response. He must have sneaked around behind her locking all the doors as she was getting washed and dressed.

'Dad! Dad! Let me out now! You can't do this – you can't lock me in here like this. Open the door before I break it down.' She could feel the panic rising up from her chest.

29

'Come on, Dad, please. I know you don't mean it – just unlock the doors and we'll forget all about it.'

But still he didn't reply.

The Rivington family home on the borders of Hampstead was a large detached property with both an attic and a cellar, and secure within its own grounds. Although superficially clean it was also old fashioned, very sparsely furnished and poorly maintained to the point of being decrepit, but it was the only home she had ever known.

When she was young it had been her haven and bolt-hole where she was secure away from her tormentors at school and happy to be smothered by her mother's unconditional love. But now she didn't know what was happening and suddenly felt very scared, and despite trying to force them out of her mind, the flashbacks were hovering in front of her.

# Chapter Four

Because Marty had again been warned by the manager about having friends in the hotel, Megan had tucked herself away in a corner at the far end alongside Venita. Both were trying to be unobtrusive as they listened to the barman muttering almost to himself.

'It doesn't make any sense. One minute Lennie's all for moving in with us then the next she takes off without a word? Something's happened, I know it.' Speaking out of the corner of his mouth, Marty ferociously chucked bottles in the air with his working smile still pasted firmly on his lips.

'Well, like I said just now, maybe she didn't want to do it and didn't know how to tell you,' Venita hissed at him in a stage whisper. 'Come on, Mart, we can find someone else, maybe someone who'll fit in better. I mean, you only have to listen to her for five minutes to realise she's an old-fashioned stay-at-home Daddy's girl, but you insisted on pushing her to do something she didn't want to do just to make up the numbers.'

'Don't be such a hard-nosed bitch, Ven.' Cleverly, Marty managed to glare at her sideways while still smiling for the customers. 'Lennie just seems shy, but when you get to know her she's a really good person. Genuinely caring and a true friend. She just needs you two to be fucking nice to her instead of looking down your noses. I just want to get in touch with her . . . I hope she hasn't had an accident or is ill or something. It's been five days now.'

Venita and Megan exchanged raised eyebrows. 'Had an accident?' Venita laughed sarcastically. 'Oh come on, Marty, she's chickened out. I told you she wasn't right for us. We'll manage with just the three of us until we find someone else. I mean, maybe this is a blessing in disguise. She's not one of us and it wouldn't have worked.'

'Take no notice, Mart,' Megan suddenly joined in, worried that Venita would really irritate him and sour their opportunity to be part of the move. 'You found the gaff so it's up to you who you have in the house. Maybe you're worrying over nothing. Maybe she'll still show up. Look, if something had happened, then surely her father would have phoned in? She doesn't live alone.'

As Marty carried on doing his show on auto-pilot, Megan could see that he had actually stopped listening to them. Although she found it hard to understand in a chalk and cheese kind of way, it was obvious that he had a huge soft spot for Eleanor and would hate to think of her letting him down.

The first time she had met Eleanor in the bar and then seen them together, Megan had noticed that Eleanor and Marty, although polar opposites both in personality and background, were similar in that they both functioned slightly on the periphery of life, albeit for completely different reasons. Eleanor, probably because she had been so sheltered, stayed back, unsure how to interact, and Marty, because he was basically very insecure about his sexuality, rushed in headlong and tried too hard to make everyone love him.

'It just isn't like her to let anyone down – she's the most reliable person I know.' Marty still sounded distracted. 'She hasn't told the boss why she's not here and she isn't answering the phone. He reckons she's going to be fired as soon as she does ring in.'

Venita started to say something but Megan kicked her foot and glared. They both let Marty continue his mutterings.

'I just don't understand this at all. I'll get her home address from Porter George. He's got access to the filing cabinet and he'll give anyone anything for a bit of a backhander.'

'Okay, okay, I give in.' Megan held her hands up in front of him. 'If you get the address, and if of course you pay my fare, then I'll go and visit her and see what's what. Just out of interest, Marty, love, why haven't you already got her address or phone number?'

'Because her father's an old tyrant by the sound of it, but that's by the way at the moment. Thanks for the offer but it had better be me, she doesn't really know you.'

'You're not off for hours, Marty, and also you're a bloke. If her father is as you say then that'll just make it worse. No, get me the address and I'll go and see what's occurring and put you out of your misery.' She looked at his expression and sighed. 'Marty, I'll be nice and tactful, I promise. I quite like the girl actually, and let's face it, she'll hardly be competition in the house!'

Marty smiled appreciatively and shot straight off into the reception to seek out George and get the information.

An hour later, Megan found herself at the top of a long wide avenue edged with established trees and carefully trimmed hedges and verges, and suddenly she wasn't as keen to seek out the missing Eleanor. She could almost smell the affluence of the area as she counted down the numbers on the houses which were nearly all detached and set well back in their own space, protected by swathes of greenery from each other as well as the road.

Megan had spent most of her twenty years in a variety of care homes, and the houses she was now looking up at were the kind of properties that her former children's home housemates regularly went out to burgle. She herself had survived the system and stayed mostly out of trouble because of her burning desire to be rich and famous, and she was intelligent enough to realise that a criminal record would hinder that.

Despite her malnourished and neglected start in life, Megan Murphy's voluptuous breasts had erupted out of her skinny body when she was barely twelve years old. Then she had wanted to curl up and die of embarrassment; she hated them and they caused her such grief that the priority in her life for several years had been to cover them up as best she could. Quickly she had perfected the art of hunched shoulders and baggy tops to try to disguise them while at the same time learning how to skip out of the way of the groping hands of teenage boys and grown men alike.

But that had all changed the day that Ted Burnett, one of the care home staff, had offered her a fiver for a look when she was without a cent in her purse. Megan had quickly realised that Ted had a fetish for big breasts, and in her last two years in the home she had saved enough to buy a complete new wardrobe of sexy clothes and a set of black and white scanty glamour photographs that just about passed as a portfolio. As soon as she had the basic necessities, as she saw them, she was out of the system and perfecting her already acquired skill of using the opposite sex to get her where she wanted to be. Famous, independently secure and as far removed from her own mother's situation as she could be.

Megan looked again at the piece of paper Marty had given her and double-checked that she was standing outside the right house. It wasn't the largest property in the road but it was certainly the most rundown. There was an air of neglect about it, even from the crooked gate, but it was still impressive to Megan as she stared at the Crittall-framed leaded glass and a gnarled old wisteria clambering all over the walls and partially obscuring the windows.

Lifting the latch on the creaky wooden gate, Megan walked up the path to double porch doors and, taking a deep breath, pressed the doorbell. When there was no sound of a bell ringing she waited a few minutes before pulling back the handle that edged the letterbox and rapping it loudly.

When there was still no answer she tried the porch door, but it was locked. Stepping back, she glanced around before knocking firmly again, but when there was still no sign of life in or around the house, she cursed under her breath at the wasted journey, turned and started to walk back down the path.

After a few steps a noise stopped her in her tracks; pausing, she stood for a moment with her head on one side and listened. She was sure she could hear muffled sounds coming from the direction of the porch that enclosed half of the front of the house – but she could see through the grubby glass that, apart from several empty flower-pots and some post on the floor, it was empty. Again she listened and again she heard it.

Turning, she went back to the porch and tried the door again, rattling the handle. 'Hello?' she called tentatively as she pressed her ear to the glass. 'Hello?'

'Help! Help me! Who's there? Can you get me out?'

Megan could barely make out the words or the voice. 'Hello?' she called. 'Can you shout louder? Is that you, Lennie? I can only just hear you. What's the matter? Why can't you open the door?'

'I can't get out, I'm locked in!'

As Megan pushed her ear close to the glass, a figure appeared at a run from the side of the house, brandishing a garden fork in front of his body and pointing it towards Megan.

'Get off my property now!' he shouted. 'Get away, you're trespassing. Go on – get out! Get out before I call the police.'

As she hesitated, he moved towards her and rotated the fork in the direction of her stomach. Megan backed up a little then paused, more out of shock than anything else. The man snarling at her was grubby and dishevelled, his worn corduroy slacks and threadbare jumper several sizes too large. As she continued backing off, Megan guessed he could be either the gardener or a passing tramp.

'I'm sorry, but it sounds like there's someone trapped inside. I can hear a voice calling for help. I wondered if it was my friend, she lives here . . .'

The man looked her up and down, making no attempt to disguise his distaste, before starting towards her again, the fork aimed straight at her neck.

'Get off my land, you slut – go on, clear off. I don't want the likes of you here contaminating my daughter. Slut, slut, slut.'

'Okay, okay, I'm going.' Megan held out her hands submissively in an attempt to calm the man who she was sure was completely nuts and turned to leave, but then she again heard the faint voice.

'. . . police . . .'

Megan hesitated only a second longer before walking quickly down the path and out of the gate without even a glance back. The man with the fork and the mad eyes had put the fear of God into her, and as soon as she was through the gate she broke into a run, her inbred instinct in the face of trouble. But it was that same worldly-wise instinct that told her something was very wrong in the house behind her, so she slowed and went looking for a phone box.

The response to her garbled 999 call was rapid, and when the police car arrived, Megan was hopping from foot to foot on the edge of the pavement, chewing nervously around the edge of her long pale pink nails.

Two men stepped out of the car and walked over to her. Megan suppressed a smile at the familiar double act. The older man was more rounded and looked slightly bored; the younger one was lanky and self-conscious.

'I'm Sergeant Anderson and this is PC Wicks,' the older officer grinned into her cleavage. 'Was it you who called us, miss?'

'Yes, there's something strange going on inside that house there.' She pointed towards the front door. 'I came to visit my mate 'cos I was worried, as she hasn't turned up to work for several days, but this old boy came after me and threatened me with a garden fork. I could hear someone inside shouting for help, but he chased me away. I think someone might have fallen over in the hall and can't get up. I dunno, but I need you to find out.'

As she paused for breath the young policeman smiled and put his index finger up to his lips. 'Sssh, slow down, love, I can't understand what you're on about when you're chattering along like a runaway train. Now, take a deep breath and start at the beginning, telling us first of all what you were doing at this property in the first place . . .'

After Megan had gone through it again, the two policemen looked at each other and nodded.

'You stay right here and we'll go and check it out.' The younger officer, PC Wicks, straightened his shoulders importantly as he spoke. 'Do you want to sit in the car for a minute or two – get your breath back? If the man you described is still there we can talk to him and see if your friend is okay.'

Despite her concern at what was going on in the house, Megan still allowed herself a secret smile. She could see he had tried his best to focus on her face but his eyes kept flickering back to her chest. He was young and good looking, if a little boyish for her taste, and his face had reddened because he knew that she had noticed.

'Thanks, mate, I will sit in the car if you don't mind. I'm worried about my friend and it might be her in some bother in there.' She smiled at his embarrassment. 'I'll just wait until I'm sure everything's okay, then I'll get off.'

She watched curiously as they made their way through the gate and out of sight. The man with the crazy eyes and a garden fork in his hands had freaked her out far more than she would admit, and she had no intention of seeing him again if she could avoid it, but at the same time she was genuinely concerned about Eleanor.

However, just as she was starting to relax and think about getting out of the car and making her way back to Marty before she had to give her name, a sound like a car back-firing echoed through the still, early evening atmosphere, and made her jump in the seat.

Sitting in the police car with her hands folded carefully in her lap, Megan felt the terror rising up in her throat as she tried to convince herself that the sound really wasn't what she dreaded it might be.

It seemed like for ever before anything happened, but it was actually only a few minutes before the normally quiet Hampstead road was awash with noisy police cars and Megan was being firmly ordered to stay exactly where she was. Not that she had any intention of leaving the security of the car, even if it was a police car, but she did push the door open wide and try to listen to the staccato shouting that echoed all around the outside of the house.

It wasn't long before Megan found out that the explosion of sound hadn't been a car; it was the man with the garden fork, the same man who a few short minutes before had been threatening her, forcing a double-barrelled shotgun up into the roof of his mouth and pulling the trigger before collapsing under the magnolia tree in the garden.

# Chapter Five

The sound of the gunshot reverberated through into the hallway where Eleanor was standing waiting and hoping that someone was going to rescue her. The noise sent her racing up the staircase three at a time to look out of her bedroom window, which overlooked the back of the house. Scanning the garden, her eyes quickly settled on the still figure of her father lying on his side with what she could see was a gun clasped in his hands. Frozen to the spot, she tried to figure out exactly what was going on, what had happened. During the previous week, it seemed that everything familiar and normal in her life had been turned upside down.

Bewildered, she watched as, after a pause, several policemen ran up to her father, and then one of them leaned down and moved him over before reaching for the pulse point first on his wrist and then on his neck.

She was still fixated on the scene unfolding below when she heard the echo of splintering wood and breaking glass followed swiftly by footfalls pounding up the polished wood staircase in her direction. A sudden terror swept over her and she hurled herself down the side of her bed and cowered up against the wall.

Hearing what sounded like scores of heavy feet entering her room, she shrank back even further, too scared to look up, fearing what they might want.

'It's okay, miss,' a deep voice soothed, 'we're the police. It's okay, you're safe, you can come out, we just want to talk to you, to help you . . .'

As the voice registered with her, a hand reached out but she folded herself into a ball, tucked her hands up under her armpits and stayed where she was with her chin on her chest. Her natural instinct for danger was fixed in overdrive.

'What's going on?' she whispered fearfully as she eventually looked around vacantly without making any eye-contact. 'I don't understand. Was my father attacked? Why is he lying out in the garden? Who did this? Have we been burgled?' Her eyes continued to dart around as the two officers at the foot of the bed exchanged querying glances with each other.

It was at that point that PC Wicks, who had been standing back in the doorway of the bedroom, his face white and damp with nervous perspiration, spoke up. 'There's a friend of hers out front in the car, I'll go and get her. It might be better if there's someone she knows in here.' Without waiting for a response he took it upon himself to run back down to the car to fetch Megan.

'Oh God, whatever's happened? Is she hurt?' Megan's hand flew up to her mouth as she walked into the room where Eleanor still sat crumpled in the corner.

The sound of Megan's voice drew Eleanor's eyes and she stared up and looked at her, even more confused to see Marty's friend standing in her bedroom alongside the police.

'What are you doing here?' Eleanor shook her head as she tried to take in something else out of the ordinary. Megan wasn't her friend. Megan was Marty's friend and there was no reason why she should be in the house.

'Oh Lennie, God, I thought you'd been hurt as well.' Megan sighed, her relief almost palpable as she held out her hand. 'It's me, Megan. Come here, come on – stand up . . .'

Cautiously, Eleanor pulled herself up and looked around before focusing again on Megan as the only familiar face around. Then, as the panic took a complete hold on her senses, she reached out and grabbed Megan's shoulders with both hands. But she couldn't speak straight away. She just trembled from head to toe.

'Ssshh, it's okay, you're safe,' Megan murmured, stroking her hair and trying to reassure her.

'I d-don't know what's happened,' Eleanor stuttered as a bright red blanket was wrapped around her shoulders by unseen hands. 'Dad seemed to flip when I said I wanted to move out. He locked me in the house and wouldn't let me out, and now he's out there on the ground. And there's a gun – I saw a gun. I think someone's shot him.' She sobbed between each word as she struggled to tell Megan as much as she knew. 'I have to see him, I have to find out who's done this.'

'It's okay, Lennie, just come with me, you're safe now,

43

we'll find out what's going on.' Megan looked around and her eyes settled again on the young policeman who looked as bewildered as the two women at the situation he was caught up in.

'Can I take her downstairs? She needs to get out of here.'

'Yes, no, I don't know!' He looked completely over-whelmed and glanced towards his senior officer for help.

'You'd better go and wait downstairs,' Sergeant Anderson decided. 'Someone will probably want to speak to you, to find out what this is all about.'

At that moment, one of the other officers who'd first entered the room appeared but then stood back to let Megan through. 'I think we should send you to hospital for a check up, miss,' he said gently. 'You look as if you're in shock. There's an ambulance outside. We can talk to you later.'

'No, I'm all right,' Eleanor said quickly, scared she was going to be packed off away from her father. 'I have to stay here. I have to see Dad and find out what's happened. This is all crazy, crazy, crazy.'

'I take it you mean the man in the garden? Did you see him properly? Can you confirm he's your father?'

'Yes, of course he's my father – I saw him lying on the ground from the window. How is he?' Eleanor's initial confusion was turning to anger as her mind started to clear and she took in all the people standing around her bedroom. 'Why aren't you down there doing something for him? He could be bleeding to death!'

'Someone's with him. If you go downstairs with your friend, I'll go outside and see what's happening, but I want you to stay indoors while I check. The ambulance may actually have taken him already.'

'I have to go with him – he'll need me, he has no one else.' Eleanor's voice rose several octaves as the panic restricted her vocal cords. 'I want to see him. I have to know what this was all about. I don't understand what's happening to us.' Eleanor's eyes, wide with alarm, darted back and forth as she stuttered the words out. 'I d-don't know what to do. Megan, what do I do?'

Equally wide eyed, Megan looked at her and said, 'I really don't know, Lennie. Maybe we'd better just wait until the police tell you exactly what happened; if we go downstairs they can come and find you when they know something. I tell you what, just come with me. I'm going to ring Marty, he'll know what to do.'

Megan led Eleanor down the stairs by the hand as if she was a child and pushed her gently onto a chair before taking the telephone back into the hall and calling the hotel. Just as she replaced the receiver, the officer came through and beckoned her to follow him as he approached Eleanor, who was perched stiff backed on the edge of the old-fashioned velour upright chair in exactly the same position as when Megan had left her.

'I'm really sorry to have to tell you this,' he looked at Eleanor sympathetically, 'but I'm afraid your father died at the scene. It appears he shot himself, although we'll have to wait for confirmation from the Coroner. Can you give me any reason why he might have done that?'

As Eleanor jumped up and made a run for the door, he moved over and blocked her path with a large but gentle arm across the doorframe.

'You don't want to go out there. I'm sure you don't want to see him as he is – just let them do what they have to do.'

Eleanor looked around the room, feeling as if she was in an alien place, somewhere far away from her familiar home. More than anything she wanted to run, but her legs wouldn't do what her brain was telling them; instead they crumbled under her and she slipped like a dead weight onto the linoleum-covered floor.

# Chapter Six

The weeks surrounding the investigation into her father's suicide and the subsequent funeral passed in a surprisingly unemotional blur. Despite the level of the tragedy, Eleanor had forced herself to detach from it to such an extent that it no longer seemed real. She just went through the correct motions, dealing calmly and efficiently with all the formalities of death that were thrown at her. Various estranged relatives and friends came to try and help but she instantly ordered them all away. It was Marty, along with Megan and Venita, who proved to be her main support, the only ones she allowed to help her through it all.

Marty was the one who tried to help her make sense of everything; he brought her tasty snacks and sweet drinks to try and tempt her absent appetite and then, when the dreaded day came, the three friends grouped around her at the funeral, forming a protective barrier against the bickering relatives from both sides of the family whom she barely knew.

As part of her detachment, Eleanor focused obsessively on mentally acting out the scenario where, during her father's funeral, her mother would be spotted hiding guiltily in the shadows dressed from top to toe in black and wearing dark glasses and an all-encompassing black headscarf. Maybe even a face-covering widow's veil. But regardless of her disguise, Eleanor fantasised that she would recognise her immediately and would run over and demand, 'Why? Why did you run off and leave me alone with him? Why did you never come back for me?' Then they would fall into each other's arms and everything would be all right again. She and her mother would be reunited and get to know each other once more.

Over and over she played the potential scenario in her head, until she managed to convince herself that it was a real probability, that it was in fact a premonition of a real event that was about to take place.

But when the day finally came, nothing untoward happened.

It turned out to be an ordinary uneventful funeral that was all over in a flash. Her father's suicide had split the families into completely separate factions, but there was little expression of emotion from either side and no outpouring of grief; just a stunned silence as everyone tried to understand how such a tragedy could have happened.

As the final mourners drifted away from the stark atmosphere of the crematorium and back to the cars, to attend the funeral lunch, Eleanor stood silently and gazed at the dozens of wreaths and flowers that were neatly laid out on the grass with their cards on show, and wondered again at how her whole life had been turned upside down in such a short space of time.

★  ★  ★

'I don't think I'll ever be able to thank you enough for every-thing you've done for me,' Eleanor said to her three friends. Everyone else had left the private function room of the bland restaurant that she had chosen as neutral territory for the funeral lunch. It had all been so excruciatingly awkward for everyone; once they had finished eating, the first people started to leave, and the others followed shortly after.

Just Marty, Megan and Venita hung back as everyone left, all three looking uncomfortable in their formal clothes.

'How are you doing, Lennie?' Marty asked as the door swung closed on the last mourner.

Throughout the whole proceeding Eleanor had forced herself to bite back both her anger and her tears. Inside, she was outraged and furious at her father, but she knew she had to hide it or she would fall apart.

'I'm fine, Marty, just fine,' she lied. 'I can't believe how much you've done for me and I truly appreciate it, but now I just want to get on with my life and I don't want to talk about it any more.' She looked around the table. 'That life is over. Today has to be the first day of my new life; it has to be like that otherwise I know I'll never stop asking ques-tions and wondering why, even though there are no answers.'

Leaning across the table she touched a hand of each of them gently, but as she got to Marty he quickly reached back across the table and took hold of hers.

'Can you really shut out the past just like that? There were people at the funeral who seemed genuinely concerned for you and your future. They are family – family who really want to get close to you, but haven't been allowed to. Maybe you should accept their support. You're not used to managing everything yourself, are you?'

Pulling her hand back defiantly, Eleanor said crossly, 'Of course I can manage. Just remember, they're the family who didn't bother before. I didn't know them then, why should I know them now? None of them bothered to check out how I was doing after my mother went off. Bloody cowards. I'm too old to be the family orphan now.' Her voice was bitter as she pursed her lips around the end of her cigarette and puffed it nervously. 'Funny how they all want to look after me now, isn't it? Especially obscure Cousin Janet who lives in a council flat in Dagenham and has never sent me so much as a birthday card. Now she wants to move in and look after me and the house. Huh! Two-faced bitch.'

Marty and Venita exchanged amazed glances.

'It's okay,' Eleanor sighed as she spotted the looks. 'I suppose I can understand it and I'm not really criticising them all. I'm sure they mean well, but now I'm going to look after myself for the first time – and I've already decided what I'm going to do. I'm never going back to that god-awful hellhole of a house.' She glanced around at them all, gauging their re-actions. 'I've made up my mind, I'm going to share with all of you. If you still want me to, of course? I promise not to wander the house at night weeping and wailing.' Although her words were for all of them, it was Marty she looked at.

'Well, of course we want you to! But we thought you might not want us after . . .' He hesitated and looked to the others for help. 'Well, you know. With that . . .' He continued to fumble for the right words and glared at Venita and Megan, but neither of them made a sound as they studied the tablecloth.

Eleanor knew exactly what he meant and what Megan and Venita were thinking.

'You mean with that great big house sitting there empty? It's okay, Marty, it's not a taboo subject – you can say it out loud!' She shrugged dismissively. 'And anyway, apparently there are debts to pay and because he topped himself, my father's life insurance isn't valid. But that's not the point; the house is tainted and so would the money be if I sell it. It's just blood money, it's poisoned and I don't want anything to do with any of it.'

Eleanor had spent her whole life being protected from real life, firstly by her mother and then by her father, albeit in a different way. She had little idea about bills and everyday finances, and knew nothing of the cost of anything other than groceries and the chainstore clothes that she always wore because her father told her to.

'Yes, but couldn't you sell it and live where you want – do what you want? I don't know,' Megan said haltingly. 'You could do anything you bloody well like, so why would you want to share a house with us when you could live in your own?'

'I know what you mean,' Venita joined in. 'I'd be off like a shot from a gun if that was me. "Barbados, here I come," I'd say. "Find me on the beach," I'd say – "biggest umbrella under the biggest palm tree".'

For the first time in weeks, Eleanor laughed heartily. 'I

want to because I like you all and you've been such good friends to me!' she said. 'And I like my job as well, so why would I want to go off anywhere else? All I'd like now is some normality. I've never had that, you know.'

'But you don't have to work at all, let alone in that dung-pile of a hotel.' Venita still didn't get it.

'Well, as I said, I want to, so that's it. Now I don't want to talk about any of it any more.' Almost defiantly, Eleanor looked from one to the other. 'So if you're going to let me share with you I have to go back to the house just once more, pack up the last few bits I'll need and have a meeting with Mr Meacham, my father's solicitor. After that, it's all down to him. He's volunteered to take it all on.'

'I'll come with you.' Marty jumped up.

'Thanks, Marty, I appreciate the thought but I need to do this on my own. I'll be fine. I need to be alone for a while, especially today.'

Since the day of her father's suicide Eleanor had been staying at the hotel in one of the guestrooms. She hadn't been able to think about committing herself to moving into the house-share, but at the same time she hadn't been able to bring herself to sleep alone in the creaky old house either, with all its accompanying ghosts and nightmares. Several long weeks of enquiries and questions had occurred before the funeral could take place, and that was the day she had focused on for starting over.

In the run up to the funeral, Eleanor had gone back to the house a few times and forced herself to go through the sparse personal belongings that needed checking, and then she had left everything else to the house clearance company that was due to arrive and strip it bare of everything that was so familiar to her.

Back at the now depersonalised house that had been her home all her life, Eleanor walked slowly around it and studied it as if she was seeing it for the first time. Because she had known no different, she had never realised quite how dark and depressing it was, but as she looked she could also see how lovely it could have been.

As it should have been.

Sadly, she walked through the old-fashioned kitchen with the now extinguished boiler and out into her beloved walled garden for the last time. Gazing at her mother's blossoming magnolia tree, she realised it was the one thing that she would miss, despite her father soiling it with his grotesque suicide. It was the strongest link to her mother, and yet it was the only thing she couldn't take with her.

Maybe one day, she thought as she studied the tree. Maybe one day Mum will come and find me and explain why she did what she did.

With the tips of her fingers, she gently pulled off a bloom and flattened it before placing it carefully between the pages of her diary. She wanted nothing else from the house that had been her home all of her life.

Closing the front doors, she resisted looking back; she also refused to give in to the urge to shout, scream, cry and dissolve into a hysterical heap.

'Thank you, Mr Meacham. Now I'm leaving it all to you to deal with, even though I feel I'm taking advantage of your friendship with my father. I just don't think I'm ready to sell up completely yet. I mean, supposing my mother did come back? She wouldn't be able to find me.'

She smiled politely and held out her hand to the stout middle-aged man who was waiting outside looking as if he was about to burst into tears himself.

'I'm so grateful for this,' she went on, 'especially as there's no money to pay you with until some rental money starts coming in. I wonder how my father got into so much debt? I mean, he certainly didn't spend it, did he?'

'Stocks and shares, I think. He liked playing the markets – it passed the time for him. But you know I'll do anything for you, Eleanor. I don't want paying! I've known you since you were born, and my wife and I are both so sad this had to happen to you.' The elderly man's eyes filled as he gazed at Eleanor. 'As you know, Hettie was a friend of your mother. It's such a shame that she wasn't able to do more. Maybe if we'd tried harder to stop Harold locking himself – and you – away . . . And, of course, what he did to you – we should have intervened . . .'

'I know you did your best, Mr Meacham, but it wasn't so bad. At the time it was normal to me,' she said, interrupting him gently. 'And I'm so very grateful for everything you've done since. Could I speak to you at some point about my mother? This isn't the right time, but maybe once everything is finally sorted out? I couldn't find one single thing in the house that related to her; he'd thrown everything out.'

The man smiled at her sympathetically. 'Of course. You can come and talk to us anytime, my dear. In fact, you have to come round for dinner, Hettie would love to see you. She always wanted to talk to you about Rosetta but your father could be very stubborn. She has photos, you know.'

Impulsively, Eleanor leaned forward and kissed the man on his cheek. 'Thank you. I'm not ready now, but soon. Really soon. Give your wife my regards in the meantime and thank her for the flowers.'

'Can I give you a lift to your new home, Eleanor?'

The girl hesitated for a moment, then said, 'No, thanks, I'm fine. I've already phoned for a taxi. I'll be in touch, Mr Meacham. In a little while.'

She walked down to the gate and placed her suitcase on the pavement beside her feet. It was the end of an era. The end of her childhood. At twenty-one she was on her own for the first time.

She didn't dare turn around and look at the house, knowing she would never again see her mother looking down at her from the arched window on the turn of the stairs. Never again.

# Chapter Seven

Stepping out of the taxi, Eleanor paused for a moment then took a deep breath and walked across the pavement to the front door of the house that was to be her new home. It was flung open instantly by Marty, who she guessed had been watching from the window.

Just like her father used to. And her mother before that.

Her funeral outfit was already in the dustbin and she was back in her trademark slacks and shirt, though without the grips her hair hung loose around her face and she'd swiped a touch of colour across her lips. After all the traumas of the previous weeks it really felt as if a weight was lifted off her as she walked into her new home with just one old leather suitcase and her handbag.

When she had been going back and forth to sort out the family home, Eleanor had surprised herself with her single-minded approach to the situation. While Marty and the girls had worried round her constantly, she had quickly determined to put it all behind her as soon as possible and get on with a new life.

'Never look back,' she had said with obvious bravado

when Marty had continued to try to talk to her about it before the funeral. 'Nothing I do can change the situation, so I'm not going to think about it any more. They didn't think of me, did they – either of them? My mother ran off without a goddamned word to me, and my father killed himself in a fit of selfish pique at not getting his own way for once. Why should I let their selfishness ruin the rest of my life? Why?'

The house that Marty had been so enthusiastic about was as different to the decrepit and rambling Hampstead house as it was possible for a house to be. It was also as different as it could possibly be to the house Marty had so persuasively described to the girls.

The back of South Ken High Street had turned out to be a dodgy side street in Notting Hill, and Marty's friend didn't just own that house he was renting to them, he owned half of the street. Marty had found out he was an entrepreneurial and ruthless slum landlord who was elusive when repairs or renovations needed doing, but he always managed to find a rather large debt collector with a cricket bat if any rents became overdue.

Centred in a dark-bricked terrace and opening directly onto the street, it had originally been a two-up two-down workman's cottage built in the late 1800s with only the very basic necessities. Since then it had been renovated and extended to include a utilitarian bathroom and an extra bedroom.

The idea was that Marty and Eleanor would each have

their own rooms and Megan and Venita would share. 'Tastefully furnished' to the landlord meant a mish-mash of secondhand furniture from the Portobello market, but there was something appealing about the place nonetheless. And, of course, it was in the centre of London near an underground station with easy access to the party zone – a must for Megan, Venita and Marty.

'I guess I was conned by His Lordship; he must have decided I wasn't good enough for the classy gaff in South Ken! Maybe he thought I'd be having drug-fuelled orgies every night.' Marty shrugged his shoulders theatrically and lightly touched the utility hallstand. 'Huh – he knows me so well!'

Eleanor looked at him sharply, momentarily unsure if he was joking or not until he nudged her with his shoulder and winked.

'Marty, why are you friends with me?' she asked curiously. 'Honestly – why do you want to be friends with me? I'm not your sort of person. Venita and Megan, yes, I can see that. They're outgoing, funloving people and they know the ways of the world as well as where the best parties are – but me? Why me?'

''Cos you and me click, my darling – we match.' Marty pulled her by the arm and kissed her cheek. 'You and me, we're birds of a feather but with different plumage. Both orphans of the storm, as my old ma used to say back in Liverpool – odd ones out. Now let's get you settled in while it's quiet; the girls are down the pub.' He reached across her. 'Give me your bag.'

Eleanor pulled her arm back so he couldn't reach the handle of the case and waved a finger at him. 'Marty, I love you dearly and I need you so much as my friend, but I don't need a bloody surrogate parent. Now I can settle myself in! I know where my room is, so you go off and do whatever you're doing and I'll be down in a while. I haven't got a lot with me, as you can see. I've still to collect my other stuff from the hotel.'

The two friends' eyes met and suddenly they were both laughing.

'I reckon we'll all of us be okay, Lennie.' Marty pulled Eleanor close and hugged her before dancing up and down the room and pretending to swing from the narrow door-frame. 'Four crazy, mixed-up weirdos all in here together. Never mind the swinging sixties, they've gone; we're going to enjoy the silly seventies in our own little doll's house near *the* part of London. But . . .' he paused dramatically, 'before we can do that we're going to go shopping and get you into something more trendy. Marks and Sparks is out, and that little boutique round the corner is in. We are going to dress you like you've never been dressed before . . .'

By the time Megan and Venita arrived back, Eleanor was watching TV and Marty was fast asleep on the couch, snoring contentedly with his mouth open.

'Oh my God, Ven,' Megan gasped dramatically and took her head in both hands. 'Just look at this frightening scene of domesticity at its worst. Is this what we've got to look forward to?'

'We're in the wrong house. This is Mr and Mrs Pipe and Slipper's house, the old married couple . . .'

The three of them grinned, the uncomfortable post-funeral atmosphere gently broken.

'How did it go at the house, Lennie?' Megan asked. 'Did you get everything done?'

'It went okay.' Eleanor shrugged dismissively. 'Everything considered, and now I'm here and that's it. How was your evening?'

'We only went down the Prince Albert. We went because we thought you might be upset and need some time . . .'

'Hang on there!' Eleanor interrupted, holding up both her hands. 'I do appreciate the thought but I really don't want you to feel you have to pussyfoot around me. I'm a big girl now and I'm a damn sight more clued-up than I was a few weeks ago. Normal life starts *now*.'

Her emphasis on the word *now* woke Marty.

'Oh shit! Did I drop off? Are you okay, Lennie?'

Eleanor glared at him.

'Okay, okay, I won't ask again – well, not in that context anyhow. Now, girls, what are we going to do about dinner tonight? I'm famished.'

'That's solved,' Eleanor said immediately. 'We're eating out and it's my treat as a thank you for everything you've all done for me. Let's take a walk and see what we fancy, unless you've sussed out all the trendy places already.'

\*   \*   \*

Later that night, Eleanor sat on the edge of the bed and looked around at the room that was now her home. It was at the back of the house, perched precariously on the flat roof of the downstairs extension. It was tiny and sparsely furnished, but she already had an image in her mind of how she wanted it to look. Pretty. She wanted it to be the polar opposite of her old bedroom, the same as she wanted her life here to be the opposite of her old life, with nothing to remind her of it. Ever.

As her mind started to float back, she panicked and deliberately forced herself to focus on the present. Looking out of the small sash window, she glanced along the line of back-to-back yards. Several of the houses had lights on inside and Eleanor could see some of the inhabitants moving around, getting on with their everyday lives – all oblivious to their neighbours and especially oblivious to Eleanor Rivington the orphan.

As she watched, fascinated, a knock on the door made her jump.

'I've not come to check up on you, Lennie, just to bring you a cuppa.' Venita's voice came through the closed door. 'Can I come in, or do you want me to leave it outside for you?'

Eleanor opened the door and stood back to let her friend in.

'Thanks, Ven. I was just imagining how I want this room to look. I've never been able to do up my own room before, and as there's so little furniture in here I can buy some of my own stuff to make it more like mine. What do you reckon?'

'Yeah, I suppose you could do quite a lot in here, although maybe not swing too many cats! But then I'm hoping you're not going to spend too much time in here alone.' Venita slumped down onto the bed and swung her legs up. She had changed into a psychedelically patterned purple kaftan that made Eleanor smile. She had only ever seen Venita and Megan wearing clothes that were short and tight and empha-sised their voluptuous figures. It was also the first time she had seen either of the girls without full make-up. Suddenly she could see how young and vulnerable Venita really was.

'I love that colour.' Eleanor pointed to the silky purple fabric. 'Marty says I have to get myself some new clothes but I don't really know where to start. He said he'll take me to a boutique.'

Venita rolled her eyes up to the ceiling. 'Do yourself a favour, Lennie, don't let Marty push you too quickly into changing everything. I love him dearly, but he can be a bit like speedy Gonzales when he gets going. You need to move into your new skin, so to speak, at your own pace. Also, when you do go clothes shopping, take us, not Marty. Please, please don't let him take over your wardrobe. Christ, I can just imagine what he'll put you in. Promise me.'

They both laughed.

'I must admit, I had wondered about that. Maybe when you've got time, you, me and Megan could all go shopping together? I'd love you to help me.'

'It's a date! Now I'd better get myself off to bed. Meg and I have an early shoot down on Brighton beach, and we're being picked up at four-thirty by Big Dean, our so-called manager. The forecast says it's going to piss down very shortly. And they call it glamour modelling?' Venita reached over and hugged Eleanor. 'It'll all be okay, you'll see. We'll eventually have the best time together, but first you really have to let yourself grieve, you know.'

Eleanor felt her eyes prickle but she was determined not to cry again. Her new life was about to begin and she didn't intend to start it with tears.

# Chapter Eight

'Marty!' Megan shouted up the narrow staircase. 'I've already called you twice. There's someone here for you. Come on, I'm waiting to go out; get a bloody move on, you drunken arse.'

'Who is it?' Marty's voice was thick with sleep and his throat hurt. 'I'm knackered and hungover, I can't move.'

'Some bloke called Jamie,' she shouted impatiently. 'He says he was with you last night. Now just get down here!'

Marty forced himself awake. His eyes felt as if they were on fire behind his face and his head thumped alarmingly. At that moment he seriously wanted to die. *Jamie.* He tried to remember who Jamie was, but he couldn't; the night before didn't even exist in his memory.

'Ask him to come back this afternoon,' he croaked as best he could.

'Too late,' she replied sharply. 'He's already in the back room.'

As Marty fell out of his bed and crawled into his jeans and T-shirt, he cursed his weakness when it came to alcohol and any assortment of dubious substances he could get his hands on. It only needed a couple of drinks and then his promises to himself, along with his inhibitions, flew out of the window. He must have told the bloke hovering downstairs where he lived.

He truly hoped he hadn't had sex with him. Or bought any drugs from him.

As his feet hit the bottom stair Megan flew at him and snarled venomously, 'About fucking time, you piss-artist. I shouldn't have to stand around babysitting your dodgy mates. And trust me, this one is dodgy. Looks like he needs a good wash, but he's not having one here. And don't feed him, either! Bloody strays.'

With her coat flung over her shoulder she marched to the door. 'You owe me for this half hour of my life. If I can't get a taxi right now I'll be late and you will die.'

Marty shook his head and staggered through to the sitting room at the back of the house where the windows to the small paved yard were wide open and the breeze fluttered the curtains. Screwing his eyes up at the brightness he tried to focus on the young man who had made himself very comfortable on the sofa. His feet, in chunky well-worn shoes, were crossed on the coffee-table. And he was nonchalantly flicking cigarette ash on the carpet. His blue jeans were grubby and worn and his shirt was creased.

'Hey, man. You look rough,' he grinned as he saw Marty. 'Good night though, wasn't it?'

Marty had no intention of admitting to a memory loss so he ignored the greeting. 'Feet off the table, mate.' He looked pointedly at the cigarette hanging loosely between the other guy's fingers. 'And I'll get you an ashtray, shall I?'

Still standing, Marty studied him openly. Although he couldn't remember the face, the vibes told Marty that Jamie wasn't gay so he guessed he hadn't pulled him, though he knew it was a possibility that he might have tried. Was it drugs? he asked himself as he continued to study the young man. He was very scruffy, indicating to Marty that he was possibly short of cash and probably jobless, and his dark hair hung lankly to his shoulders. Marty stared at the dishevelled clothes and tried to remember.

He wished he could but he couldn't.

'I need a caffeine fix to get me started and clear my head,' he mumbled. 'You want tea or coffee?'

'Haven't you got anything stronger? Scotch would suit me better.'

'Nope! No alcohol here. Tea, coffee or a glass of water. That's it.'

'You're kidding me, mate.' The young man looked towards Marty and sneered openly. 'No fucking booze? Give me some cash and I'll shoot up to the offy on the corner and get something.'

'No.' Marty paused and looked at him suspiciously. 'Look, I'm sorry but I've got a lot on today. It's tea, coffee or nothing – and then I've got to get going.'

'Hey, don't give me crap. Five minutes ago you were in your pit and you'd still be there if it wasn't for your mouthy mate with a gob bigger than the Blackwall Tunnel.' He

grinned lasciviously and licked his lips for Marty's benefit.
'So now just be cool, man. I'll have a black coffee, plenty
of sugar.'

Marty escaped into the kitchen, put the kettle on and
tried to gather his wits. He remembered leaving the Crystal
Chandelier at eight and then going on to the club, and he
also remembered knocking back some whisky and possibly
popping a couple of pills of some sort. Was it Jamie who
had given them to him, he wondered as he tried to trawl
through his brain. But he couldn't remember a thing after
that.

Shit, he thought. And then he was saved.

'Hello, Jamie, what are you doing here?' He heard Venita's
surprised voice in the distance and raised his eyes gratefully.
Someone else knew him. He picked up the two mugs and
wandered back in as if he hadn't heard.

'Hiya, Ven.' He forced himself to sound bright and
surprised. 'I thought you were off somewhere with Megan.'

'No, she's got a date as far as I know. So, you two know
each other already?'

Venita looked from one to the other expectantly but
Marty concentrated on the mugs he was holding and let
Jamie answer.

'Met last night in Shadows. Your mate here was off his
head and dancing on the tables. He was so out of it I thought
he was going to do himself a mischief,' the man grinned
and winked at Marty, 'or else do someone else a mischief,
so I dragged him home and dropped him off safely on the

doorstep. Lots of dodgy people around at that time of night if you're off your face.'

'I know – thanks, mate. Appreciate it. How did you know where I lived then?'

'Er, you told me?' This time Jamie winked at Venita.

She looked at Marty and sighed loudly. 'So, yet another hangover. No wonder you look so bad, but exercise is good for a hangover so how would you like to make your favourite housemate a coffee also? Do you know, I've got the whole day off with bugger all to do except clear out my wardrobe.' Plonking herself on the sofa beside Jamie, they both put their feet up on the coffee-table and started talking like old friends.

Marty shrugged and went back to the kitchen, relieved that nothing worse had happened the night before. I have to stop drinking, he told himself. This is a warning.

Because he was from Liverpool, Marty Cornish's insecurities meant that he felt continually obliged to act up to his Scouser Scally image in public. He could play the part of a streetwise 'Jack the Lad' to perfection, pretending he'd ducked and dived all his life, lived on the streets and got by on his wits alone, whereas in reality he had been brought up in a strict family in a very political, working-class area of the city where there was a correlation between the doorsteps being polished daily and everyone knowing everyone else's business.

His mother had always proudly boasted how their gentle and studious son was a genius destined to be the first in the family to go to university, but his hated father, ever handy with a belt, hadn't been impressed; he simply viewed him as work-shy because the boy had no urge to follow him into a lifelong job working in the docks. Neither of his parents had any inkling that the young Martin locked himself away to study because it was easier than trying to understand his blossoming sexuality. He did, however, know instinctively that if he found the school playground hard then he would never be able to survive Liverpool Docks.

Then, in the summer holidays between the end of his A-levels and university entry, Marty had volunteered to help out at his school on an extra-curricular assignment. Before the end of the holidays he had become involved in an intense gay relationship with Harry Anderson. The man he called 'sir'.

A teacher on the assignment. A *married* teacher.

It was during those summer weeks that Marty felt he had found his true self. After a bewildering adolescence, he had finally discovered that he was homosexual; but although he was relieved to admit it, he was at the same time eaten up with guilt at what he knew his parents would categorise as evil and perverted.

There was no question in his mind that they would disown him and be mortified by the thought of anyone finding out – if of course, his father didn't beat him to a pulp first. It was because of the guilt that Marty also discovered the dubious pleasures of alcohol and drugs, and by the end of that summer of excess, both were a habit to him.

As of course was Harry.

Despite his young age Marty had known that the relationship couldn't possibly carry on, despite Harry's protestations of love. If the affair were discovered, the teacher would lose everything – his marriage, career and even his freedom. Marty couldn't risk any of this happening to the man he loved, so instead of heading off to university in Scotland as planned, he had packed a few basic necessities, jumped on a train to London and never gone back.

On the spur of the moment, he had simply switched off his old life and switched on a new one as an openly gay young man in the big city.

As he prepared a mug for Venita now, for the first time in years Marty thought about Harry and wondered if it was possibile to find out what had happened to him. Especially now that he was beginning to feel dissatisfied with his mad lifestyle – of which the previous night was really just another example.

'Marty, where's my coffee? Get a move on, I'm gasping in here.'

'Sorry,' he said as he went back through, 'kettle's slow. So tell me, how do you two know each other?'

'We met a few weeks ago in the Albert. Jamie was covering a shift when they were short of staff and we got talking.'

'Yeah, but I didn't know Ven lived here when I dragged you home last night,' Jamie put in. 'Small world, huh? How many of you are there?'

Venita turned to him. 'There's four of us – me, Megan,

my partner in crime I was telling you about, Marty here and Eleanor who works with Marty. I'm sure I mentioned her and her tragedy. We call her Lennie.'

'Bit cramped though, isn't it?'

Before Venita, who could chatter for England, had a chance to hand over too much more information, Marty jumped in defensively.

'It suits us fine and we all get on okay as a group. I'm the girls' guardian angel. I protect them all from unwanted advances and dodgy dates with scheming bastards.' With a challenge in his eye Marty stared at Jamie. 'I'm sure you've guessed I'm gay. Yep, I'm queer, bent as a nine-bob note and therefore safe as houses around the girls.'

Jamie laughed out loud. 'You reckon I'd find that a problem? If it was a problem I'd have left you to fend for yourself last night after you tipped all that crap down your neck and lost your senses. You're being paranoid, mate. Gay – not gay. Who gives a toss?'

Marty relaxed and smiled. 'No one, I guess. Sorry, just feeling a bit rough. I think I might have to go back to bed for a while and sleep the alcohol off.'

'Me and Ven are off to the Albert now for a drink and a snack. I'm meeting some mates there. Wanna join us? It'll be a laugh.'

'Thanks, but no thanks. I'd chuck up if I even saw food right now.' Turning on his heel, Marty waved backwards in their direction. 'We'll catch up another time. Oh, and thanks again for helping me out last night. I've decided I have to stop drinking. From now. This is it! I'm going on the wagon right this minute.'

As he staggered back up the stairs he heard Venita laughing hysterically and shouting after him, 'In your dreams, Marty! You're no more likely to give up the booze than I'm going to give up getting my tits out for the photographers.'

Marty felt his resolve strengthen as he heard Jamie join in the laughter a little too heartily for his liking; he couldn't wait to discuss it with Eleanor. He knew she would understand.

# Chapter Nine

'Sshh,' Eleanor giggled. 'If Marty knows you're in here he'll go ape – 'cos he's given up drinking, you know. He's being very good now he's sober. He looks after us and he cleans and cooks for us instead of going out. We get lovely dinners.' Still giggling, she rolled over clumsily and stretched her arm down to grab the nearly empty bottle of wine that was on the floor beside the bed. 'Have you got the glasses down your side?' she whispered loudly, slurring her words just a little.

Jamie reached down into the narrow gap between the bed and the wall for the glasses and then held them steady as Eleanor poured a little into each one before waving the empty bottle over her head.

'That's it, all gone unless you want to creep down and get the other bottle out of the fridge. But you must not get caught.' She hiccuped. 'Oh dear, I think I'm a bit tipsy!'

'Just a bit, sweetheart, but who am I to criticise? I know you're a grown-up even if Marty thinks you're actually his twelve-year-old daughter. Doesn't it drive you bonkers, having to account for yourself to him all the time?'

Puffing up her pillows and automatically pulling the top sheet up over her naked breasts, Eleanor said, 'Don't start on about Marty again. He loves me and he is like my big brother. He looks out for me and he's been so unbelievably kind, I can never ever repay him.'

'If he's that much of a friend he wouldn't want repaying!'

'Leave it, Jamie. I can't explain, but he'll always be my best friend. Always.' She glanced sideways at the young man lying in bed beside her. She was completely besotted with him.

Jamie Kirk had a louche, long-haired, bad-boy charm about him that had attracted her instantly. He was the kind of boyfriend her father would have hated on sight, and that added to the attraction – though she would never have admitted it. At first she had been convinced he was after Venita because they were often together and he would call round to see her, but it was Eleanor who, a few weeks after their first meeting, he had asked out.

Her first reaction had been surprise, followed by a certain wariness. She had forced herself to say no, unsure if she was treading on Venita's toes, but also unsure of what to do because she'd never had a boyfriend. But Jamie had gone out of his way to reassure her that he and Ven were just friends and, to keep everyone happy, he had even suggested keeping their first date under wraps. Eleanor had gone happily along with the idea because it was easier than explanations.

Especially to Marty.

But then she had kept on seeing him and, as time passed,

she found it harder and harder to tell the others she'd been deceptive, mainly because by then she had fallen desperately in love with him.

'Okay, let's forget about Marty for now.' With one swift movement Jamie threw back the sheet and pulled her towards him. 'I'm sure you and me can think of something far more exciting to do than lie in bed talking about Saint Marty of Notting fucking Hill.'

Confidently, he nuzzled the inside of her ear before gently taking her lobe in his mouth and rolling it around the tip of his tongue. Wrapping her arms around his neck, Eleanor felt the familiar tingle ripple through her body as he reached down to her breast and took her nipple in his hand.

Suddenly he stopped and leaned up on one elbow. 'Again?' he asked her with a smile.

'Yes, please,' she sighed.

'Ask me then.' His fingers hovered on her rock-hard nipple like a butterfly. 'No, beg me! I want you to beg me. Beg me to fuck you again.'

'Please, Jamie, fuck me again. Please.'

'On your knees and beg for it . . .'

And of course she did.

The soporific effect of the wine, combined with the confident movements of Jamie's hands and mouth took her away once again to places she had never been to before she had met him.

Eleanor had learned a lot about sex by reading the soft porn magazines that Venita and Megan received regularly through the post because they were starring in them. When no one was around she would sneak them up to her bedroom and study the letters and features in much the same way as she used to study her school textbooks. Some of it shocked her and some of it turned her on just reading about it, but none of it had prepared her for the shockwaves that came with the experienced hands and phenomenal staying power of Jamie Kirk.

'Oh God,' Eleanor sighed much later as she turned over towards the bedside clock. 'It's six o'clock, Jamie, it's getting light. You'd better go now, while everyone is asleep. I can't believe we've been at it all night. You don't think I'm a tart, do you?'

'Oh my, Miss Eleanor, how could you even think that? That is one thing you could never be! Gorgeous, sensual, sexual, classy, yes. Tarty? No.' He stroked her hair and then lightly touched the end of her nose with his index finger. 'Again?'

'No!' Eleanor laughed and curled herself up into a ball under the covers. 'I can't take any more, I really have to sleep. If you creep out now you can come back later for breakfast and pretend you just appeared by chance. It's my day off so I'm free all day.'

'I'll try and get back,' he said as he rolled over to the edge of the bed and grabbed his jeans, 'but I need a bit of kip as well and, as I'm not allowed to stay here and get it, I'll have to trog all the way back to my manky bedsit in the land of the Oz backpackers and do the best I can.'

Eleanor felt her mouth go dry the way it did every time Jamie was about to leave. The fear that he might never return was always there hovering around in her mind. Her feelings for him scared her, they were so intense, and thoughts of him were in her mind constantly.

'Okay, I'll tell Marty and the girls today. We're all around this morning. I'll tell them at breakfast and you can come by after. I'll ring you.' Her tone was positive as she looked at him but he shook his head.

'Well, girl, that depends on if you're prepared to take some stick. They're all so bloody protective of you, you can bet your life they'll try and talk you out of it. Especially Marty, he acts like you're his property and he can't stand me. He'll be fucking furious that firstly we're seeing each other and secondly you didn't tell him about it in the first place. Can you deal with that? Can you really deal with a very angry Marty?' Jamie stared at her with his deep dark brown eyes piercing into her so sharply she was sure he could read her mind.

'Be fair, Jamie. It was your idea not to say anything about us in the first place,' Eleanor replied hesitantly.

'Ah yes, but you were happy about it, and also that was when it was only going to be a couple of fun dates. Now it's more than that. If they go all loopy and parental, would you give in and chuck me? Would you side with them over me?'

'Oh God no, Jamie. I wouldn't do that, I couldn't. I love you!'

As soon as the words were out she panicked that she'd overstepped the mark but he turned back to her. 'Wow. That's something else. Do you mean it?'

'I suppose I do, but I never meant to say it. I don't want to put any pressure on you.'

He leaned over again and kissed her long and hard. 'That sort of pressure I can take.'

It was only after he had gone that she realised he hadn't actually said how he felt about her.

But Jamie had been right about one thing: Marty didn't take it very well at all.

The room they used as a kitchen-dining room was small and cramped, so if they were all in there at the same time, it was shoulder to shoulder. Eleanor had waited until everyone was squashed around the pine table sitting on the matching benches tucked in an alcove and then she made her short and sharp announcement.

Megan and Venita merely exchanged amused glances with each other and raised their eyes, but Marty went straight up into orbit.

'You *what*? You're kidding me, Lennie – you and that little shit drug dealer Jamie?'

'Don't you dare talk about Jamie like that, Marty. I've just told you, we're in love and he's certainly not a drug dealer, he's a musician, he plays guitar—'

'Musician my arse. He's vermin, you can do so much better than that.'

78

Eleanor opened her eyes wide and said sarcastically, 'Well, well, Marty Cornish. Do you know, suddenly you sound just like my father. He reacted like that when I said I was moving in with you. He called *you* all those names. I never thought you were like him. Maybe Jamie was right—'

Before she could finish the sentence Marty jumped up so furiously he jogged the corner of the table, spilling his mug of tea everywhere; Eleanor had never seen him so angry.

'Jamie knows that I know exactly what his game is and he's trying to pre-empt me. He's after your house, plain and simple. He wants somewhere to live and someone to keep him and you're it, Lennie.'

It was Eleanor's turn to jump up, angry tears welling up in her eyes. 'Oh, don't talk such bollocks, Marty. He doesn't know anything about it – I've never said a word to him about the house. Same as I don't talk to anyone about it because in my mind *it doesn't exist*. And anyway, that's not very flattering to me, is it? Aren't I attractive enough to pull a bloke without a few bob to lure him in?'

'That isn't what I meant and you know it.'

'Well, that's the way I took it and I want an apology.' Standing face to face with him she glared fiercely and then turned to the girls. 'And what about you two? Do you agree with Marty? Am I really just a stupid thick bitch who's too ugly to get a boyfriend unless I lure him in with promises of riches he's never dreamed of?'

Noticeably embarrassed by the unexpected confrontation Megan and Venita shrugged their shoulders in unison.

'Up to you what you do, Lennie. You're a big girl, you can choose your own bloke. Just be careful is all I'd say,' Megan said as she tried unsuccessfully to wipe the floor and then the table with the threadbare floor mop.

'Yeah, that's right,' Venita agreed, but Eleanor could see she was more interested in watching Megan wrestle with the mop. 'Whatever turns you on, babe! I reckon Jamie's okay so long as you keep your eye on the ball. He's a bit of a wheeler dealer but he seems good company and harmless enough.'

Marty shook his head. 'You're just plain fucking stupid, the lot of you. Cook your own breakfasts.' Visibly upset, he smashed the frying pan down onto the cooker and stormed out of the kitchen.

'He'll get over it,' Megan said. 'Our Marty has always been a bit of a drama queen.'

'I wish he wasn't upset,' Eleanor sighed.

'He just thinks Jamie is usurping his position as your guardian angel. He'll get over it in a few days. You'll see.'

But Eleanor knew that something had changed in her relationship with Marty and it worried her because she loved him dearly. Deep in thought, she walked out into the backyard. The first months in the shared house had been very strange for her. Apart from sleeping at the hotel on the odd night when she was working, she had never been away from home for even a night, and suddenly she was in a new home, in a new area and living with people she barely knew.

But from the start she had been determined to draw a veil over everything that had gone before, and life had soon become bearable and Eleanor was starting to feel content with her lot. Not happy, exactly, but content enough to look towards her future. Deep down she knew that at some point she would have to resurrect her feelings for both her mother and her father, but she still couldn't face that and she had no idea when she would be able to deal with it so she had just shut the door on it.

Eleanor Rivington was determined to make a success of her life and to make it on her own merits, on her own salary. Everything to do with her father's finances had been ably dealt with by Mr Meacham. He had even arranged for the house to be rented out unfurnished in the short-term to pay the outstanding bills that Harold Rivington had left behind. There was a little left over each month and the solicitor had put it straight into an account that Eleanor pretended didn't exist. It was too soon and still too painful for her to have any part of it. Despite knowing she should, Lennie hadn't even been able to go and visit his wife Hettie, her mother's friend. 'Soon,' she had told him with a smile when she last saw him. 'Soon I'll be able to, I promise.'

Then her new life had really started and for the first time ever, Eleanor tasted freedom. The four of them had set about manically living life in London to the full, but they also all worked really hard as well; Megan and Venita were trying desperately to make it, Marty was still off the booze and drugs, and Eleanor was looking around for a better hotel to work in.

And then along had come Jamie Kirk.

Marty was all too aware that the moment Jamie had wormed his way into the middle of the equation was the moment when the dynamics of the house had started to change. The changes were so subtle that the girls didn't seem to notice but Marty noticed it every day, and it niggled away at him constantly.

He remained convinced to the point of obsession that Jamie was a conman who was only after Eleanor's money, and it rankled with him that none of the others believed him. He even went so far as to ring Mr Meacham, Eleanor's solicitor, to alert him, but as the older man pointed out, Eleanor was an adult who was entitled to make her own decisions, even her own mistakes. Much as he would like to protect Eleanor . . .

Despite Jamie Kirk's protestations of innocence Marty knew with certainty that although he did occasionally strum the guitar in a grubby backstreet pub, he was also an opportunist drug dealer. But although Marty had seen him sneaking around in clubs and pubs doing deals and pocketing cash, he knew that he couldn't mention any of it to Eleanor again as it would be playing right into Jamie's hands.

Jamie had not only succeeded in sweeping Eleanor off her feet, but he had cleverly charmed Megan and befriended Venita. Now all three of them thought he was an okay guy and they dismissed Marty as being jealous at having another man around the house.

So while on the surface everything was much the same, the easygoing camaraderie that had been so comforting when they had all first moved in together had faded, and slowly they all started to move away from each other. Marty had thought that if he played it cool, Jamie would inevitably trip himself up but it didn't happen like that. It was Marty who had gradually become the outsider. Frustratingly, there was nothing he could do about it and he was unhappy.

He was so unhappy that he had fallen off the wagon quite spectacularly the day Eleanor had announced her relationship with Jamie, and then stayed off it. Every night, whether he was working or not, he was out and about being the life and soul of the party somewhere.

Marty Cornish had once again lost control of his life, and once again he thought about Harry, his first and only love, and wondered how things could have been if they had run away together.

# Chapter Ten

His brain banged within his head and he felt as if his body had been run over by a lorry. Every single part of him ached and he didn't have a clue where he was, other than that he sensed he wasn't in his own bed. Scared to open his eyes, he lay still and tried frantically to remember what had happened the night before. He heard curtains being opened and was aware of the accompanying daylight on his face.

'Good morning, my handsome boy.' A voice penetrated through the fug and jogged his memory a little. 'How are you feeling after our little games last night? Tired, I'm sure, so I've brought you a tasty breakfast, to revitalise you.'

Cautiously, Marty reached a hand out and touched the satin sheets that were over and under his naked body, before forcing his eyes open and focusing on the man who was standing beside the bed stark naked and holding a large breakfast tray at arm's length.

And then it all came back to him in a rush. The bar, the new customer with a penchant for the most expensive champagne, huge tips, a gold Rolls-Royce and chauffeur waiting outside, a private elevator, pills . . . pain. So much pain.

Oh fuck, he thought. How did I let it happen? Why didn't I get out in time? 'Good morning,' Marty muttered in the direction of the naked man. 'Got any Alka-Seltzer? I've got the head from hell. In fact, everything hurts.'

The man smiled and laid the tray on the vast bedside table before climbing into the oversized bed himself. 'On the tray beside you, fizzing in the glass already. I guessed you'd feel bad – too much of the very best champers can do that, you know. Especially if you're not used to it.'

Marty snatched the glass and greedily drank the fizzy water while at the same time planning what to do next. The man beside him was singularly repulsive. Marty tried to look at him without making it obvious and assessed from his receding hairline and drooping eyes that he was well into his fifties. He had a large white paunch that hung loosely from under his grotesque man-breasts down to his genitals, and several podgy chins that enveloped the heavy gold chain and medallion around his neck.

'Sadly, I haven't got time to stay for breakfast.' Ignoring his pain, Marty put on his best smile. 'I have to go now, I'm due at work.'

'No, my gorgeous boy, you're not. You told me last night you were free all day today. That was part of the deal.' The man slapped him sharply on the thigh and smiled lascivi-ously before grabbing hold of Marty's hand and placing it firmly over his penis. 'Five hundred pounds bought me your company until tonight so there's still many hours of our agreement to go. Now eat up, you're going to need all your strength for what I've got planned for you and me, today.'

'Sorry, mate, no can do. I gotta go.' Marty threw back the sheet and jumped out of the bed. 'But you can keep your cash, last night was on the house.'

'Anthony!' The man didn't actually shout, he just raised his voice. 'Persuade young Marty here to stay for the fun.'

As Marty started to gather up his clothes the bedroom door flew open and an ugly gorilla of a man, over six foot tall with no neck and weighing about twenty stone, appeared in the doorway with a smile on his face and a gun in his hand.

'Get back in the bed, pretty boy, and do as you're told. If Mr Smith says stay, you stay. If Mr Smith says bend over, you bend over, and if Mr Smith tells me to shove this gun right up your pretty-boy arse then I shove it. With pleasure. And I'll also fire it with pleasure and watch you writhe in agony as your bowel slides out before you slowly bleed to death. Comprendez?'

'Thank you, Anthony.' Mr Smith smiled and nodded. 'I think young Marty here may just have misunderstood his situation. After all, a deal is a deal. Now, as he doesn't want any of the breakfast we lovingly prepared for him, you can send the others in.'

Anthony stood back and two naked men appeared in the doorway. They were of a similar age to Mr Smith and similarly grotesque, but their faces were gruesomely masked with black leather. One held a long thin riding crop and the other a wooden paddle.

Grinning, they approached the bed.

That evening, Mr Smith informed Marty, again with a smile, that they were honest businessmen who sincerely believed a verbal agreement was as important as a written one. He had agreed to take part and he was being paid. It was a done deal.

After the other two men had left the room he called Anthony to help a battered and bleeding Marty put his clothes on. Then Mr Smith pushed five hundred pounds into Marty's pocket and told Anthony to drop him back at the hotel.

Leaving, he was more aware of his surroundings than when he had arrived. The be-mirrored personal elevator took them directly down to the underground car park beneath the apartment building where Anthony immediately put a forceful hand under Marty's elbow and pushed him towards a car.

It wasn't the impressive gold Rolls-Royce that he had arrived there in, but a run-of-the-mill and very unobtrusive Ford Cortina that had definitely seen better days.

During the short car journey, Anthony was fiercely persuasive as he warned Marty that Mr Smith and his friends should never be mentioned to anyone; he reiterated the warning as the car pulled up sharply in the quiet side street alongside the hotel.

Anthony nodded his head. 'Right! Out now, and

remember, nancy boy, not a word or you'll have me to deal with and I'm not as gentle as Mr Smith and friends.'

Marty stumbled out of the car; he was in agony and scared to even put one foot in front of the other. As he started to straighten up, Anthony leaned over and pulled the door shut. Gingerly, Marty took a few steps along the pavement and as the car drove away he could hear Anthony laughing manically through the open window.

Marty tried to look normal as he walked cautiously into the familiar hotel lobby. His initial focus was on getting a drink but he only made it as far as the reception desk, where he was relieved to see Eleanor busy filing guest cards into a small filing box.

'Lennie, have you got a minute?' He leaned forward and spoke quietly, not wanting anyone else to notice him. 'I need to talk to you – now – it's urgent.'

Barely glancing up, Eleanor sighed heavily. 'If this is about Jamie I really don't want to know. This isn't the time or the place.'

'It's not about fucking Jamie.' Marty struggled to talk and keep his balance at the same time. 'It's about me. Something really bad has happened and I need your help. I don't feel too good.' As a wave of faintness overcame him, he leaned both his elbows on the desk. 'Please, Lennie . . .'

Before he could say anything else, his head fell forward and he banged his forehead on the polished wood. Eleanor's hands flew up to her mouth and she automatically looked around to see if anyone was taking notice.

'What is it, Marty?' she hissed. 'Have you taken something?'

Before he could reply, Marty felt so weak he had to let himself slide down to the floor. Sitting with his head on his knees and his hands flat on the floor he tried desperately to stay conscious. Eleanor saw him disappear so she ran around to the front of the desk and crouched down. 'What's happened to you, Marty? What's wrong? Tell me! Oh my God!'

# Chapter Eleven

Without even thinking, Eleanor dialled 999 for an ambulance despite Marty's protestations that he'd be okay in a moment. He was sitting on the floor with his back against the reception desk and his knees up to his chin. His face was as white as paper. As Eleanor knelt back down beside him he reached over and grabbed her hand. The porter had rushed off and found a blanket so Marty was covered but still he shivered uncontrollably and there was a group gathering, trying to see what was going on.

'I don't want an ambulance, Lennie, just put me in a cab and let me go home. I'll be okay, really I will. I can't go to hospital. I'll go to the GP later, I don't want everyone to know about this.'

'Don't be ridiculous, Marty, you're bleeding – you have to go to hospital. You're injured, even I can see that.'

'They mustn't know who I am.' He looked into her eyes pleadingly. 'Tell them I'm a tourist, tell them you don't know me, anything, but don't give them my name and address. I'm begging you, Lennie. The people who did this will kill me.'

Eleanor was in a state of shock herself as she looked at her friend and tried to figure out what was going on.

'Who will? What are you talking about? I don't understand. Are you involved in something illegal? You have to tell me what's going on!' Her voice was getting higher and her speech faster as her distress increased. 'Where's all the blood coming from? Have you been stabbed or mugged? What?'

She could see Marty was trying to speak but she couldn't understand what he was saying. As he continued to mutter Eleanor moved her head closer to hear him. 'You mustn't tell anyone at all, promise?' he gasped.

'I promise,' she found herself saying.

'I mean it, Lennie. This is between you and me, only you and me.'

'Okay. I've already promised.'

'I was raped,' he whispered painfully, 'by three wealthy old bastards – they'll kill me if I tell anyone. I'm in big trouble, but I'm in such pain. Help me, Lennie . . .'

As she took in what he was saying, Eleanor felt as if she was once again back in the place she had been when her father killed himself. She could feel the same anger starting to build and she had to make a conscious effort to keep hold of herself for Marty's sake.

'Marty! You *have* to tell the police. I'll ring them now.'

'*No!* I mean it. These are bad people and one of them comes in here – he'll know if I've said anything.'

'I'll come with you to the hospital. I'll explain—'

'No! You can't. Don't come in the ambulance, they'll ask questions. Keep away from the hospital. I'll get patched up and then go home. I'll see you there.'

Barely had he finished speaking when Eleanor was up and running behind the desk, barking orders.

'I have to go with Marty,' she told her new assistant, who nodded but looked completely bewildered. 'I'll just get my bag. Don't let the ambulance take him without me.'

Eleanor had no intention of letting Marty go off to hospital on his own but at the same time she wanted to respect his wishes. He had done everything possible for her when she had needed it, now it was her turn to help him. Facing the wrath of management, she jumped into the lift, shot into the staff room, grabbed her bag and coat and was back down in a matter of minutes, arriving at the front desk at the same time as the ambulancemen.

The only problem was that Marty was no longer there.

'Where is he?' she shrieked. 'Where did he go?'

After much shrugging and headshaking, the porter walked across. 'He said he was going home, said he was feeling fine and didn't need any help, thank you very much. Apparently it was a bad curry. Huh! I'd say it was more like a really bad hangover, myself!'

'Shit!' Eleanor snapped, craning her neck every which way. The small crowd had dispersed, losing interest once the centre of all the attention was up and walking, leaving Eleanor and two impatient ambulancemen.

In an instant she had a grip on the situation. Marty was her friend and she had to be his friend 100 per cent.

'I'm really sorry. He looked so ill, but perhaps he just fainted?' She smiled winningly from one to the other. 'We have to be so careful here, just in case. This is a hotel.'

'I can understand that, but if we can just have his name for our records . . .'

Eleanor lowered her voice so the staff couldn't hear her. 'I don't know who he was. He just came in off the street and collapsed in front of me. I guess we overreacted, eh?' She smiled apologetically with her eyes wide. 'I'm so sorry for wasting your time.'

The two men nodded grimly at Eleanor before marching out, leaving her to lie through her teeth to her manager about what had happened.

Because Marty had claimed to be okay and then disappeared, Eleanor had no reason to leave so she had to finish her shift and then, as soon as she could, she was out of the door and in a taxi.

Back at the house, she flung the front door open. 'Marty? Marty, where are you?'

After checking through the downstairs rooms she took the stairs three at a time and tried the door to Marty's bedroom but it was locked.

'Marty, open this door right now or I'll get the police to do it. Marty?'

She heard the click of the lock and tried it again. The door swung open. The room was in darkness and she could just make out Marty crawling back into his bed. She flicked the bedside light switch on and gasped as she looked at him in the half-light.

Marty was so pale his face looked translucent, apart from the vivid red and purple marks around his mouth where he had been gagged. He was sweating so heavily his bed was drenched, but as she looked in frozen horror at the lash-marks on his body he quickly dragged all the covers up to his neck.

'My God, Marty. You have to go to hospital. You're injured and ill . . .'

He opened his bloodshot eyes and looked at her. 'I can't,' he whispered flatly. 'If this gets out, I'm a dead man – you didn't see the goon with the gun and what he threatened to do with it. Just call the doctor, will you? He can't tell anyone, can he?'

'I guess not, he's your doctor. I'll go and phone him now but I'm scared you need more than that.'

'Lennie, please don't say a word to the others. Just say I have flu, but especially don't tell Jamie. Swear to me you won't tell Jamie.'

'I won't tell anyone, Marty, I swear, not even Jamie. I just can't believe this, those perverts are dangerous.'

He grabbed at her arm but his grip wasn't there so his hand fell back down limply onto the covers.

'I'm such a fucking idiot, such a stupid fucking idiot. I asked for it, didn't I? I got pissed and let my guard down . . . he bought champagne and I glugged it down, he gave me pills and I took them without a thought. I was acting like a two-bit whore, going off with someone because he had a gold Roller and offered me five hundred quid. This wasn't worth five grand. You must despise me so much, Lennie.' His voice broke.

'Of course I don't. We all make mistakes.'

'Well, I despise me.' His voice faded and he shivered violently.

'I'm going to ring the doctor now. You can tell him whatever you like about what's wrong, but you have to see him.' Eleanor squeezed her friend's hand and swallowed back tears at the sight of him in this shocking condition.

It took Marty many weeks to get over both his external and internal injuries, but Eleanor knew that it would take far longer than that for him to get over the psychological damage.

She kept her promise and told no one the real reason why Marty stayed in his room for so long. She just murmured the words *flu*, *virus*, *infectious* to the others over and over, and had to bite her tongue when they laughed about how long it was taking him to recover just because he was a bloke.

The main culprit in the teasing was always Jamie and Eleanor hated it. She hated that he was so spiteful and she hated that he was using Marty's illness to score points over him.

But no matter how mean he was, it didn't stop her feelings for him. Eleanor was addicted to Jamie Kirk.

# Chapter Twelve

One late-August evening, Eleanor was sitting on the bench in the backyard enjoying the warm rays of the sun on her bare shoulders as well as savouring the break from the warring men in her life. She had put the new Beatles LP on the turntable of their shared record-player and was humming along to her favourite tracks.

Several stressful weeks had passed since Marty's attack and Eleanor was at breaking point appeasing both Jamie and Marty and trying to keep them apart. Marty was her best friend and she couldn't imagine not having him in her life, but she was completely and blindly in love with Jamie and couldn't imagine life without him either.

Especially at that moment in time.

She desperately wanted to keep them both happy and for them to be friends but instead, each of them hated and resented the other. No matter how hard she tried she just couldn't resolve it; each was as bloody minded as the other.

After Marty's *illness* as it was always referred to, when Eleanor had spent so much time with him, Jamie had become obsessively jealous to the extent that he had taken to constantly checking up on her. He would either phone or turn up randomly at the hotel to make sure she was there; he would ring her whenever she said she was at home, even in the middle of the night, and if she wanted to go out with the others then he would inevitably turn up and push his way in.

Especially if Marty was there.

One night, when no one in the house had heard the phone ringing at two in the morning, he had shinned up the drainpipe and she'd woken with a start to find him staring in through her bedroom window.

Jamie ensured that Eleanor had no life of her own and it reminded her of the way things had been under her father's regime. She went to work and she went home unless she was out with Jamie – and even those occasions were few and far between. It was as if he was scared she was going to run off with any passing bloke. Fun nights out with Megan and Venita and their new friends were no longer an option. It just wasn't worth the hassle of the interrogation afterwards, as every moment of Eleanor's life away from Jamie had to be explained and justified.

But she loved him nonetheless and because of that did exactly as she was told, just as she had with her father. She convinced herself, as she had done with her father, that it was because he loved her so much.

Marty meanwhile had sunk into a deep depression. Unable to cope with the possibility of *Mr Smith* appearing on the other side of the bar when he was working, he had given up his beloved job at the Crystal Chandelier and spent his time at home cleaning obsessively and cooking for the others. He chainsmoked day and night, nervously lighting one cigarette from the end of another and despite the constant, time-consuming food preparation for everyone else, a lot of which went in the bin because they were out, he himself had stopped eating. From being the life and soul of the party, always up for anything, Marty had turned into a nervous wreck, rarely sleeping and taking no interest in his appearance.

Eleanor was worried sick, but as she was the only person who knew what had happened to him, she wasn't able to talk to anyone else about her concerns.

Because it was Marty who had signed the lease on the house, he had always dealt with all the bills and rent payments, and the others paid him a quarter each. None of them realised that after Marty stopped working, and when the £500 he had been given had all been used up, Eleanor started subsidising Marty's share of everything; and although she paid it happily, she was terrified Jamie would find out. Instinctively she knew that he would go raving mad and then use the information to demoralise Marty even further; she could imagine the gossip that would follow as Jamie badmouthed him to everyone.

Once again in her life she was feeling imprisoned and claustrophobic.

'Cooee . . . can I join you?'

Glancing over her shoulder, Eleanor saw Venita peering through the back door at her.

'Of course! Come and sit here.' Eleanor patted the seat beside her. 'It's so warm and peaceful and I'm topping up what's left of my tan.'

Venita perched uncomfortably on the very edge of the battered garden bench alongside Eleanor.

'Lennie, have you got five minutes for a chat?' she asked nervously.

'Of course.' Eleanor leaned forward and, putting her hands above her eyes to shield them from the sun, she peered at Venita who wasn't quite looking at her. 'What's up? You look worried. Is it to do with your spat with Megan this morning? You two were really going at it.'

'God, no.' Venita shook her head vigorously. 'That was forgotten the second it ended. She thinks I'm a tight-arse with money and I think she's a mad spendthrift. And of course she wants her long-lost — but reappeared now she's earning — father to be our manager. No way. End of! We agreed to disagree on that one, for the moment anyway. No, it's to do with Jamie actually, and of course Marty.'

Eleanor sighed and offered the packet of No. 6 cigarettes that she was holding. She had been fully expecting something to be said by either Megan or Venita; the situation was so bad that she was worried they would ask her to move out and take Jamie out of their lives. Nevertheless, she didn't want to hear about it, or have to face it.

'Oh God, I know, it's awful, isn't it? I do try and mediate. I wish they could just get on but they're each as bad as the other. Two male egos locking horns and I really can't figure out why. Why do you think there's so much animosity? Why is Jamie so jealous of Marty? It's a bloody mystery to me. Suggestions on a postcard, please!'

Venita took one of the proffered cigarettes, lit it and drew the smoke in deeply.

'It isn't a mystery to me, Lennie. Oh bugger, look, there's no easy way to say this. I have a confession to make. You remember before you started seeing Jamie? I knew him from the pub and then I met him here again when he came to see Marty?'

She looked at her friend questioningly, waiting for a reply but Eleanor remained silent for a few moments before responding, the furrows in her brow the only sign that she was listening.

'I remember hearing about it all, he brought a very pissed Marty home from some club. I didn't meet him till later and then I thought you were seeing him. You said he was nice enough but you didn't fancy him and that's when I started seeing him.' Eleanor peered suspiciously at her friend. 'Hang on, were you lying to me? Did you fancy him really? Is that what this is about, Ven?'

Eyes wide, Venita said immediately, 'No, of course not. It's just that . . . well, you know how I chatter away without really thinking. As Marty says, I engage my mouth before my brain instead of the other way round. Well, I'd chattered in the pub and told him about you.' She paused again and started twiddling the ends of her shoulder-length blond hair. 'I'd also stupidly told him all about the house. Your house.

I know you think he doesn't know about it but he does, and lately he's been asking me a lot of questions. He wanted to know all about it, like what it's worth and whether you're going to live in it or sell it. And if you do sell it, will you have the money to do what you like with.'

She stopped, waiting for a response from Eleanor but when she didn't get one she continued, with the words tumbling out far too rapidly.

'He even wanted to know the name and address of your solicitor. Lennie, I'm with Marty's way of thinking now. I don't trust Jamie and I think that's why he wants to fence you off from the rest of us. I just know he thinks he's found Easy Street. I'm sorry.'

It took a moment for Eleanor to realise exactly what Venita was saying, and then suddenly she felt quite sick. She wanted to deny it all, to accuse her friend of lying, but there was also the niggling thought that it might just be true. Her love for Jamie was intense and passionate, and she couldn't imagine life without him, but there was a tiny part of the old cautious Eleanor that didn't like him very much as a person – the same part that didn't trust him completely. Deep down she knew he was bad news but she didn't want to accept it and anyway, she couldn't help herself.

'I've wanted to tell you for a while but I didn't want to upset you,' Venita continued softly. 'I wasn't sure if you'd believe me either, so I've asked around a bit, like I should have done in the beginning.'

Eleanor managed a hint of a smile. 'Why? Why should

you have? *I* didn't ask anyone. I trusted him and I'm not your responsibility.'

'Anyway, the gist of the whole thing is that Marty's right,' Venita went on, still spitting the words out rapidly in her nervousness. 'Jamie is a dealer and a thug who beats up people who don't pay on time. He hospitalised a young girl last week in Hackney, apparently because she wouldn't go out on the streets to get him his money. I know you're madly in love with him, but he is a nasty piece of work. I'm so sorry, Lennie.'

Eleanor didn't say a word. She leaned back on the bench and closed her eyes. She wanted to cover her ears and not hear a word, but she knew that would be childish. She wanted to scream and shout and accuse Venita of lying, but she knew that would be childish also.

'So,' she spoke carefully and slowly, 'what you're saying is that the only reason Jamie's with me is because of the bloody great wreck of a house that I own, courtesy of my nutcase of a father blasting his brains out? If that's the only reason, then why isn't he hanging round you? Or Megan? You've both got far more money than I have. I'm still paying my father's debts with the fucking rent money that's a pittance anyway, because the house is about to fall down.' She looked closely at her friend, willing her to say she'd got it all wrong.

'You must be sitting on quite a nest egg now, Ven,' she pointed out, 'with all that work you've been doing. Megan told me how much you both got paid for that car show in Germany alone.'

As soon as Venita lowered her eyes and hesitated Eleanor knew the answer. In one moment all her old insecurities came streaming back. Her mother didn't love her enough, her father didn't love her enough, now Jamie didn't love her enough. If at all. In that instant she knew she and Jamie were over. He too would be gone from her life.

There was a resignation in her voice as she said tiredly, 'This is such bad timing, Ven, do you know that? You really should have told me before and given me a chance to make up my own mind over it. Have you told Marty and Megan? Do they know about this?'

'No, I haven't said a word to anyone, but I just knew I had to tell you. I mean, Marty has always said it about Jamie, that's why he hates him so much, but he doesn't actually know what I know.' Reaching over, she took hold of Eleanor's hand. 'I know I should have told you before, but I suppose I was also hoping I was wrong, or even that you'd split up and then I wouldn't have to say anything.' She smiled a little tearfully. 'Plus, of course, I knew everyone would be absolutely fucking furious with me for blabbing to Jamie in the first place!'

Eleanor's expression was pensive. She could hear what Venita was saying but it was almost as if the words were jumbled.

'I mean it – now is such a bad time for something like this. In fact, it couldn't be worse.' She turned sideways and looked directly into Venita's eyes. 'I'm pregnant, you see, Ven. I'm having Jamie's baby.'

Venita stood up quickly and turned to look down at

Eleanor, who was still speaking very normally and calmly, as if they were discussing the weather.

'Pregnant? How? I mean, I thought you said you were on the pill? Oh Lennie, you didn't do this on purpose, did you? Did Jamie do it on purpose? Tell me it wasn't planned.'

'Of course it bloody well wasn't – well, not really. I knew I'd missed a couple of pills but I didn't think it would matter – and anyway, by the time I realised, it was too late so I've ignored it.'

'How far gone are you?'

Eleanor answered sheepishly. 'I don't know – nine or ten weeks maybe? I didn't realise for a while because I felt like shit anyway. I've never felt so sick and ill as I have lately.'

'You are kidding me, Lennie!' Venita shrieked. 'How the fuck did you cover that up?'

Eleanor smiled wryly. 'I didn't cover it up as such, but I'm surprised you never noticed. No one noticed, not even Jamie. Actually it made me realise that no one looks at me at all. I'm basically invisible.' It was at that point that it all became too much for her and a long wide teardrop ran down the edge of her nose. She didn't bother to wipe it away. Or the next one.

'This is all so unfair,' she said in a quivering voice. 'Why didn't you tell me about Jamie before? You should have told me, it's too late to do anything now.'

'I know, I know,' Venita shrugged helplessly, 'but we can sort this out between us, I'm sure. We'll all help you with whatever you decide to do.'

Eleanor's eyes opened wide. 'You can't tell Marty, he has enough to cope with at the moment. He's still not got over—' She stopped herself just in time.

'I know he's had a pretty rough deal but he's all right now; yes, he's just a poor weak bloke but blimey, all these weeks off work for a virus.' Venita snorted, but then she stopped and looked at Eleanor curiously as if something had suddenly clicked in her head. 'Or was it something else? I've often wondered if something happened to Marty that day he took to his bed. No virus lasts this long. What happened? Tell me.'

'Can we leave Marty out of it for the moment, Ven?' Eleanor sidetracked Venita's question. 'I have to think about this Jamie stuff; please, please don't say anything to the others yet. Promise me?'

'If you don't want me to then I won't, but I think you're wrong not to involve them. We all care about you.'

'I'm not saying never, I'm saying not now. I have to think and I have to speak to Jamie.'

'I'd say don't tell him, but if you do, please don't let him know I told you about that other stuff, will you? I've seen him when he's crossed and he can be a madman.' Venita looked really concerned as she tried to make Eleanor understand.

'I won't say anything. Anyway, I'm going up to my room – I have to go and think. I'll talk to you later.'

Eleanor forced a weak smile and, leaving Venita in the yard, she went up to her room, pulled the curtains over and lay down in the bed. She was completely calm and emotionless as she stared at the ceiling. So calm, in fact, that she surprised herself. No matter how hard she tried to convince herself otherwise, she knew she was desperately and painfully in love with Jamie and often fantasised about a future with him and having his children. A little voice sometimes whispered in her ear telling her to beware, and on the whole she blocked it out, but just occasionally when Jamie was being controlling and jealous and shouting the way her father had, she would wonder.

Closing her eyes she carefully thought back over all the conversations she and Jamie had had in that room, in that bed, about their future. The plans they had made that she now realised were all instigated by Jamie had always involved a lot of money.

She didn't want to believe that his motives were purely mercenary, but her well-honed instincts told her that Venita was surely right.

# Chapter Thirteen

After her talk with Venita, Eleanor had stayed closeted alone in her room pleading a migraine. She didn't want to see anyone, including Jamie. She knew he would be steaming mad but she just wanted to lie very still and quiet and be able to think clearly.

Alone.

The way she used to analyse everything in her life when she was a child.

She loved her bedroom at the back of the house; she even had a strange affection for the damp patch on the wall, the leaky sash-window and the dodgy light switch that their no-longer-friendly landlord refused to fix.

She loved it purely because it was her room.

When Eleanor had first moved in, she would lie in bed and try to imagine the lives and loves of the people who had lived in this house when it was built – their routines, their clothes, their relationships.

It was the first time in her life that she had been able to do what she wanted with a room and so she had, even though the others had laughed affectionately at her choices.

Ignoring its faults, she had turned it into a cosy haven; she loved it, but Venita and Megan, whose shared room was a pigsty, thought it too girly for the 1970s. Eleanor had carefully chosen the multi-shades of pink and mauve chiffon that were draped over the curtain track, around the wooden bedhead, and even over her table lamp, which cast a warm glow on the room. But especially she loved the deep purple bedside rug that she knew would have sent her father into orbit.

But now, in light of her conversation with Venita, it all seemed less attractive. As she looked around dispassionately, Eleanor wondered if it was now tainted because of the highly charged and very sexual relationship that she had experienced in here with Jamie Kirk.

When Eleanor had asked, Venita had been more than happy to phone Jamie to pass on the message about the migraine and then to give him exactly the same answer when he phoned again and then again and again.

Through her open bedroom door she also heard Venita forcefully but oh so politely denying Jamie access to her after he had turned up on the doorstep.

'No, Jamie, I'm sorry, but Eleanor doesn't want to see anyone at all.'

'Well, I can understand that, but she doesn't mean me, I know. What have you said to her? If you've made trouble for me then you're one dead bitch, I promise you,' she heard him snarl nastily.

Jamie had quickly realised that it was the wrong thing

to say to Venita so he changed tack and tried apologising; then he tried saying again that he knew Lennie didn't mean him. Eleanor even heard a scuffle as he tried to push past but he failed. Venita on a mission was not someone to be messed with.

She couldn't sleep at first but then again she didn't want to; she wanted to figure out what she was going to do about her relationship with Jamie and her pregnancy. She knew there was no point in asking him for the truth because he was a very accomplished liar and, to even come close to getting him to admit to his deception, she would have to tell him Venita had been talking and she couldn't do that to her friend.

And of course she also knew that he would touch her, kiss her, stroke her hair and tell her how much he loved and needed her, and she would fall for it regardless. If she told him she was pregnant he would want to marry her. However well she thought she now knew him and his ploys, she was all too aware that she would fall for that as well.

That was why a gentle flicker of commonsense told her she had to stay away from him while she thought it all through. Was it possible that Venita had been exaggerating? Had she misinterpreted an innocent remark? Or was she just plain jealous? Eleanor tried every which way to justify it all but she couldn't. Jamie Kirk had, at the very least, been dishonest. At worst he was taking her for a total idiot and trying to manipulate her. Just as her father had done all her life.

It was in the darkest hour of the night that Eleanor fell into a restless sleep and her childhood nightmares returned with a vengeance. But this time, instead of dreaming of hearing it all through the walls, she dreamed she was by the door to her parents' bedroom, watching.

*Harold Rivington was standing in his pyjamas with his fists raised and his face scarlet with fury as his wife cowered back on the bed with her arms wrapped around her head and body. The punches rained down on Rosetta's curled-up arms and legs as she protected herself as best she could.*

*'You're a whore, a filthy slut. I know you've been with other men, I can smell them on you. Whore, whore, whore!' He snarled every word with hatred in his voice.*

*'I haven't, Harold, of course I haven't. Look, I'm not well, please don't . . .' Her sobs were muffled by her arms.*

*'You try to refuse me my conjugal rights because you're out prostituting yourself!'*

*'I don't, Harold, I promise you, I only went to the shops. I'm sorry.' Rosetta could barely get her breath.*

*The man paused for a moment in his onslaught then removed the narrow leather belt from the loops of his trousers that lay on the chair by the door. His wife curled up tighter.*

*'Stand up and stop grizzling!' he ordered her. 'You have to be punished, you know that. Whores and prostitutes must be punished.'*

*'Please don't. I haven't done anything, I haven't been with anyone. Please, please, not again . . .'*

*'Stand up or I'll call Eleanor in to watch what happenes to sluts like you. She should know her mother is nothing but a filthy dirty whore.'*

*Defeated, Rosetta slowly uncurled and, still sobbing quietly, she slid off the bed and stood in front of her husband.*

*'You know what to do,' he said in a choked voice. 'Turn round and bend over.'*

*Again she did as she was told. Tears streamed down her face but there was acceptance in her movements. As she bent over with her hands tightly gripping the footboard of the wooden bedstead, Harold pulled her ankle-length nightdress up to her waist and thrashed her six times on her bare buttocks, counting down as he did so. As he said, 'Zero,' Rosetta stayed where she was, knowing exactly what was to come next. She could see his penis was already grossly enlarged and poking obscenely through the front of his pyjamas.*

*But then she heard a noise and turned her head to see her daughter watching silently through a crack in the door, which was ajar.*

*'Eleanor . . .'*

*Rosetta pulled down her nightdress and flew to the door, opening it wide.*

*'Mummy, Mummy, what's happening?' the young girl cried, her eyes wide with horror at what she had witnessed.*

*Rosetta bundled her daughter back to her own bedroom and hugged her tightly. 'Nothing's going on, darling, nothing at all.*

*You're having another of your nightmares. Nothing's happened at all, now back to sleep, Mummy will stay with you . . . Mummy and Daddy love you.'*

*The next day, Harold and Rosetta both convinced their daughter that the whole episode was nothing more than a bad nightmare.*

Eleanor awoke with a start in a muck sweat. Her hair was stuck to her head and she could feel her heart palpitating as if it was operating independently of her body. It was only a nightmare, she told herself, just the same old nightmares coming back because she was stressed.

The pain started at around three in the morning as a vague cramping low down towards her groin, and then gradually it increased to an ache. For a while she wondered whether she had mistaken the signs of pregnancy and maybe there was something really wrong with her, like appendicitis, but she continued to lie calmly on her bed, still fully clothed, flat on her back with her legs stretched out and her hands under her head.

Her thought processes had become so detached from her emotions that she found herself again being completely rational.

The way she had been after her father's funeral.

The way she had been after her mother had run off without a word.

It was just as she decided that, baby or no baby, Jamie and his controlling behaviour would have to be similarly removed from her life that the pain worsened to an excruciating knife-like stabbing and she could feel a dampness between her legs. Suddenly she was doubled up in agony.

Forcing herself from her bed she staggered out onto the tiny landing and hammered on the door of Megan and Venita's room.

'I'm in such pain,' she gasped. 'I think something's going wrong here.' With tears streaming down her face she hugged her stomach with both arms and sat down quickly on the stairs for a moment before realising that she was bleeding heavily.

'The carpet,' she muttered as Venita came out and sleepily tried to assess the situation.

'Fuck the carpet,' she said, wide awake now. 'I'm calling an ambulance right this minute.'

Megan appeared behind Venita, then a few seconds later, Marty's door opened.

'What's going on, Lennie?' he asked. 'What's up? Is the migraine worse?'

Eleanor could feel herself drifting away, along with the blood loss. 'I think I'm losing the baby.'

'You're what?' Megan and Marty cried in unison.

'Ven is calling an ambulance. I need to lie down, I think I'm going to faint . . .'

Marty put his hands under her arms and tugged her back from the stairs before lying her on her side and crouching down beside her, gently stroking her forehead.

The last thing she heard as she was being carried down

the stairs in a stretcher was Marty ranting madly in the background.

'I'll kill him – I swear I'll fucking kill the bastard if anything happens to Lennie . . .'

# Chapter Fourteen

First she heard strange sounds in the background and then someone calling her name from far, far away.

'Eleanor, Eleanor. Can you hear me, Eleanor? Open your eyes for me . . .'

The voice came closer and, forcing her heavy lids to open, Eleanor found herself looking up at the blurry face of a nurse who was leaning over her. And then she remembered.

'Did I lose it?' Her tongue felt three times its normal size and her throat ached; she also had trouble stringing her words together because her mouth didn't want to function. 'The baby, is it gone?'

'I'm so sorry, my dear, but yes, you lost the baby. You've also had some surgery but you'll be okay. Now I want you to relax and go back to sleep; you need to sleep off the anaesthetic. We'll take you up to the ward in a minute and pop you in a side room, then you can rest. Doctor will talk to you later.'

After that original awakening Eleanor lost all track of time. The regular strong painkilling injections made her so light-headed she couldn't distinguish between day and night, fact and hallucination. She wasn't sure if she had imagined her friends visiting; she thought they were there at times but it seemed that whenever she managed to open her eyes she was alone in the small side ward.

At one point when she felt more awake, she gingerly reached under the sheets to touch her tummy where her baby had been and realised that her abdomen was heavily bandaged. *Surgery?* she thought as the nurse's words came roaring back to her. *What surgery? And why?* But then she was given another injection and drifted back to her new safe place of cottonwool dreams.

Marty was pacing the floor like a newly caged tiger. Back and forth he marched, clenching and unclenching his fists until Megan could take no more.

'Marty! For fuck's sake, sit down. You're driving me nuts. Let's talk about this. I know you're worried, but this is really over-reacting in a big way. Lennie got pregnant, she had a miscarriage. Absolutely traumatic for her, but not totally Jamie's fault.'

Marty glared angrily at Megan and then kicked the door with his booted foot.

'Traumatic? Is that all you can come up with? I'm going to kill him, the little shit.'

'No, you're not,' Megan stated forcefully. 'You're going to save your energy for supporting Lennie when she comes home. Jamie is just a pain in the arse who is best ignored.

But remember, it takes two to tango – he didn't exactly force himself on her, and I'm sure he didn't force her to get pregnant either.'

Venita had remained wrapped in a guilty silence until that moment.

'Well, I think he got her pregnant on purpose! Marty's right to be furious with him, even if it is for the wrong reason,' she blurted out suddenly. 'Look, I promised Lennie I wouldn't say anything, as she wanted time to think, but I can't keep quiet now this has happened. I just have to tell you.'

'Tell us what?'

'About Jamie and Lennie. But first I want you, Marty, to promise that you'll not do anything. Lennie has to deal with this herself. We've no right to take over her life; she's a grown-up and needs to make her own decisions about him.'

Eleanor tried really hard to focus but she couldn't take in the information the surgeon was impatiently trying to give her. It was over two days after her surgery and, although the pain was still intense, her head was clearer and the doctor was being very matter-of-fact with the medical details of her surgery.

'I'm sorry, I'm not with you,' she sighed. 'Can you explain it again with small words? My brain isn't functioning and I don't understand all these medical terms.'

'I wonder if it might be better if we wait until your . . .

your husband or whatever is here? Maybe he could help you understand the situation more fully.'

She looked at the man standing at the end of her bed surrounded by students and nurses. Tall and slender, with round wire spectacles on the very end of his nose and an outrageously bright patterned tie, he was obviously a surgeon at the top of the tree, but Eleanor could see that his people skills were down at the bottom.

'I don't have a husband, or anyone else for that matter, but I'm not stupid, just groggy. Please explain exactly what you mean in non-medical terms.'

Eleanor hated herself for not being able to control her emotions, especially in front of a group of strangers, but she couldn't help it. She wanted to jump out of bed and batter the arrogance out of him but she didn't. Instead the floodgates suddenly opened and she started crying uncontrollably.

The surgeon had the grace to look a little sheepish before turning and walking away from the bed. 'Nurse will explain it to you again when you feel better,' he muttered over his shoulder.

And the nurse did.

Sitting alongside her and holding both her hands firmly, Staff Nurse Cathy Hart explained very carefully to Eleanor that something had gone wrong with her pregnancy and she had lost the baby, but there had also been the extra complications of haemorrhaging during the surgery.

Eleanor was told she had been given an emergency

hysterectomy in order to save her life. They had completely removed her womb.

'Has anyone else been told about this?' Eleanor asked as she tried to take it all in.

'No, my dear, there was no next-of-kin listed for us to tell. There have been some phone calls and of course questions from visiting friends, but we only ever say you're as well as can be expected.'

Eleanor cried quietly as she tried to take in the devastating news. Not only had she lost the baby she had already become attached to, she would never be able to have any other children. As she sobbed, the nurse sat quietly beside her stroking her hair until the tears stopped and her heaving shoulders stilled.

'Is there anything you want? Anyone I can ring for you? There must be someone you can confide in.'

'Can you ring my friend Marty Cornish, please?' Eleanor shuddered as she spoke. 'He's the closest I have to family. He's like a brother.'

'Would he have been the father of the baby?'

'Oh God no, the father doesn't know, but that doesn't matter now anyway; there isn't a baby any more. There's nothing to know,' Eleanor murmured sadly. She was all cried out and overwhelmed with weariness.

'I'll go and ring Mr Cornish now . . .' Cathy paused mid-sentence and both women looked round together as they heard the door, which had been ajar, creak open wider.

'It's fuck-all to do with Marty the poofter. It's me. I would have been the father – if anyone had bothered to tell me about it, that is.' Jamie stood framed in the doorway with a face like thunder.

'Do you want him in here, my dear?' Cathy Hart asked her.

'Yes. Just for a moment.'

'Don't you be upsetting her, young man; she's very poorly and needs lots of rest.' The nurse glared her disapproval of Jamie. 'Just you remember, I won't have any bad language on this ward and if you upset my patient your feet won't touch the ground as I have you thrown out head first.' She turned back to Eleanor and said, 'I'll be just outside at the desk if you want me.'

'How did you know I was here?' Eleanor asked Jamie curiously as Cathy left the room. She was beginning to drift away but Jamie's next words brought her awake again.

'Nothing gets past me, Lennie. Remember that.'

# Chapter Fifteen

'So, Lennie, why exactly didn't you tell me you were pregnant? What right do you have to keep that from me? That's if this mysterious baby you're talking about *was* mine, of course.'

Jamie was leaning casually against the wall beside the bed with his head on one side and his arms crossed. His small pointy face was framed by slightly greasy shoulder-length dark hair and he needed a shave. Although his bearing was casual and his voice level, Eleanor could see he was as dangerously tense as she was weak and immobile. However, despite feeling so ill, she was determined to confront the issue with him.

'Of course it was yours, as you bloody well know, but I didn't want to tell you because I had to decide on my own exactly what I was going to do.'

'No, Lennie,' he snapped, '*we* should have decided what *we* were going to do. This wasn't your decision to make.'

'Yes, Jamie, it *was* my decision! Anyway, it's been taken away from me now. There is no baby any more so it really doesn't matter.'

'How can it not matter? I thought we were a couple.'

Eleanor looked up at him sadly. Lying on her back, unable to move, and with an intravenous drip in the back of her hand she felt so very vulnerable even though the man in front of her was Jamie Kirk, the father of her dead baby and the object of her love. But she knew with certainty that however much she loved him, she just had to cut him out of her life. He wasn't good for her.

'No, Jamie, we're not a couple,' she whispered. 'We're two people who had a fun relationship, but there's no future for us. If we were a true couple then you might just have noticed I was pregnant, wouldn't you? It's over, Jamie. Too much has happened for anything else.'

As she spoke, Eleanor watched his face closely. Although in severe pain she was scared that any painkillers would muddle her mind up again, so instead of calling for the nurse she breathed deeply in and out and held her tender abdomen with her hand. The bandages reminded her again of everything she had lost but she was determined not to let Jamie know she had suffered far more than a miscarriage.

'Of course there's a future for us! We could get married, we could have another baby . . .' His voice was husky, pleading.

'Don't be silly, Jamie, we can't possibly afford to get married, let alone have a baby.'

'If you . . . I mean, you could . . .' Eleanor watched as he stuttered over the words then threw his hands up in the air. 'Oh, for fuck's sake, I know you own a bloody great house in Hampstead that would set us both up for life if you flogged it. And I'm hurt you didn't tell me.'

To Eleanor's surprise, he actually managed to look hurt.

'I didn't want to mention it,' he went on self-righteously, 'I wasn't interested in your money, but now it's all out in the open maybe you could sell the house, we could buy a half-decent flat and use some of the money to live a bit, to bloody enjoy ourselves.'

At that moment Eleanor knew with absolute certainty that Venita was right about Jamie, but she also knew that it didn't alter the way she felt about him; she was still in love with him. It was going to take all her willpower not to let him back into her life.

'No can do, Jamie, you must have got it wrong. I don't have a penny that I can access until I'm forty. Right now I'm just a boring old hard-up hotel receptionist who lives in digs.'

Speaking as casually as she could, she watched his naturally expressive face tell its own story. The nervous tic that she only ever saw when he was really stressed was vibrating under his right eye, the veins were starting to stand out on his neck and every muscle in his body was taut. She could see he was making a massive effort to look as if he was calm but it wasn't working.

Again she touched her empty belly and the waves of pain were as mental as they were physical.

'But surely no one can stop you from having your fucking money. It's yours, you can do whatever you want, you just have to tell them, tell them we're getting married.'

Then he started to rant and rave as she had anticipated. Jamie always believed that attack was the best form of defence and, as he carried on, Eleanor just closed her eyes and concentrated on breathing her increasing pain away until he stopped.

'No, Jamie, that's not how it works and even if it was, it's nothing to do with you. I told you. It's over.'

'I don't believe you, you're just being difficult because your hormones are up shit creek. Come on, we love each other, don't we? Think of the life we could have.' He pulled her hand towards him and gently kissed the back of it. 'You'll be out of here in a few days and we can start arranging it. A wedding, a new home, a decent honeymoon, maybe in the Caribbean . . .'

'Without any money?' She managed a sarcastic laugh.

'If we get married we can go to court. They'll give us the money – they have to – and as your husband I'll be entitled—'

He paused as he saw Marty walk in the side room, his fists clenched.

'The only thing you're entitled to, shithead, is a smack in the mouth. Get out of here! Now!' Marty snarled the words deep and low. 'If you don't, I'll break your balls with pleasure. Now *get out*.'

'Not for you to say, Marty, you sad old poof – sorry!' Jamie leered and wiggled his backside provocatively at Marty.

'Go away, Jamie. It's over, I told you,' Eleanor whispered as her energy levels dropped off the bottom of the scale.

124

Jamie looked from one to the other and then his eyes rested on the nurse who was hovering near the doorway.

'We'll talk about this later, Lennie.' He smiled at her, his winning *I'm a lovable rogue* smile. 'I'll come back when you're feeling more together.' Turning sharply on his heel, he left but not without sticking two fingers up at Marty on the way.

Eleanor looked up at Marty and her chin started to wobble. 'Leave it, just let him go,' she said shakily. 'Can you just check he's not still hanging around outside and then close the door?' Shutting her eyes tight, she managed to hang on to herself for a few seconds until the door clicked close. 'Marty, I've had a hysterectomy, they've taken everything away. I'm twenty-two and I'll never be able to have any children. I'll never get pregnant again. That was it.' She started to wail softly. 'What am I going to do? Why did this have to happen to me?'

Marty hugged and comforted her as best he could, as they cried together.

It was over three weeks before Eleanor was able to leave hospital; it had been a long hard time for her and both physically and mentally she was at her lowest point ever. However, she had found a new friend in the constantly supportive Cathy Hart.

When the nurse had been working the night shift she had often sat with Eleanor when she couldn't sleep and the ward was quiet, and they'd talked for ages. It was the first time Eleanor had spoken in depth to anyone about her old life and her parents, and it was cathartic to discuss it with someone completely uninvolved and non-judgemental. Especially at that moment in time when she was trying hard to come to terms with her latest loss and feeling that everything was against her.

But it wasn't only Eleanor who talked. At forty Cathy Hart was old enough to be her mother but the age gap wasn't a barrier between them. Eleanor learned that Cathy and her husband Paddy lived on a rundown council estate near to the hospital where they both worked. The couple were originally from Ireland, Paddy was a hospital porter and they'd been married for ten years. Ten frustratingly childless years, which made Cathy a sympathetic listener in the long dark hours of night-time when Eleanor was doing her best to come to terms with the news of her own future childlessness. A bond was forged between the two women – a link that helped to make both of them strong.

The day of her discharge eventually arrived, and as soon as the consultant she had nicknamed Dr God proclaimed her fit to go home, Eleanor started to gather up her belongings and mentally prepare herself to leave the cocoon of the hospital. Though pleased to be going home, she couldn't help wondering how she would react once she was back in the outside world. She just knew that Jamie would be on the doorstep as soon as word got to him that she was out; Jamie Kirk didn't take kindly to rejection.

She had also become dependent on Cathy Hart, who understood how confused and demoralised she felt about everything and who came in to say goodbye, despite it being her day off.

Because she had never seen her out of her unflattering blue and white striped uniform, it took Eleanor a few seconds to recognise Cathy in her civvies; her bright auburn hair that was usually twisted tightly inside her starched nurse's cap hung wildly around her shoulders, emphasising the smattering of freckles across her rounded face, and the flattering beige trouser suit made her look much taller and slimmer and ten years younger.

'Wow, I nearly didn't recognise you, you look fantastic!' Eleanor said as the other woman hugged her. 'How did you know they'd let me out today? I thought you were on a few days' holiday and well away from here.'

'I asked Sally to ring me when you were given the all-clear so that I could be here to say goodbye and wish you well. Now you take care of yourself, young lady,' she said affectionately. 'Make sure those lovely friends of yours look after you well for a good few weeks now. Though I'm sure they will without me saying anything! You're really lucky to have them for support.'

'Oh, I know I am – I don't know what I'd do without them. Or you, for that matter, Cathy. I couldn't have got through it all in here without you to help me along and keep me sane.' Eleanor was again close to tears. 'We will keep in touch, won't we? I really want to.'

'Oh, come on now,' Cathy laughed, her gentle Irish accent flowing melodiously over the words. 'As soon as you're back in the swing of your exciting young life you won't want an old biddy like me hanging round you. But I'll give you my number then you can ring me if you need to. I know from experience that it helps to talk about all these things. No good bottling it up inside.'

'I won't ring you when I need to, I'll ring when I want to.'

Marty arrived at that moment and they all walked down to the exit together where there was a taxi running on the meter.

'Do you want a lift?' Eleanor asked as they climbed in.

'No, I'm going to the shops on the way home. But ring me tonight and let me know how you're settling in back home.'

They all hugged and waved and then the taxi pulled away.

Eleanor was on her way to start yet another new phase in her life. A life with the knowledge that she would never ever have a child of her own.

# Chapter Sixteen

As they made their farewells on the steps, none of them noticed the shadowy figure standing just around the corner from the well-worn porticoed entrance to the old London hospital. With a smoking joint held loosely in a hand behind his back, Jamie Kirk watched and listened.

Most days, Jamie had gone to the hospital and checked with his source, a naïve young nurse on the adjoining ward, whether Eleanor was still there. But that day he had luck on his side and had arrived just in time to see Marty go in with a small suitcase in his hand. Realising that it had to be going-home day, he hung around for about an hour waiting patiently until he saw them come out.

Lifting the joint to his lips, he inhaled deeply, then put it back out of sight. Did they really think that he wouldn't stick around to keep an eye on his investment? Did they really think that he was going to let Eleanor Rivington and her inheritance slip through his fingers after all the work he had put into ensuring that she really was his – hook, line and sinker?

There was absolutely no doubt in Jamie's mind that, just

129

as soon as he had the opportunity, he could talk her round and, if needs must, he would just have to make sure that he got her pregnant again. Immediately.

He was about to take a bus back to the house so that he could blag his way in to see Eleanor when it occurred to him that there might be more immediate mileage to be had from finding out a little more about the saintly nurse who, from the affectionate farewells going on, seemed to have befriended her.

He hadn't recognised her at first, but as she had turned her face in his direction he had remembered instantly and also been quite surprised to see that she was actually a very attractive woman. He skulked around the other side of a wide pillar and listened to the distant conversation. It irritated him to hear the meaningless promises to keep in touch; everyone did that when they left hospital or prison, and then they never did. But maybe the nurse would? Maybe the nurse was also after a taste of Eleanor's inheritance?

He stayed back until the taxi pulled away, by which time the nurse was almost out of sight, then, pulling his jacket collar up and tucking his hair inside, he caught up enough to keep track of her but not enough to be noticed and then started to follow her. She wandered in and out of a few local shops until her large straw shopping basket was almost overflowing with muddy vegetables and a chunky loaf of bread, and then she headed towards what Jamie knew very well as one of the roughest estates in the area.

Not only did he know it like the back of his hand but,

when he could get away with it, he also liked to trade his dope and pills in the numerous anonymous stairwells and alleyways. But even though it was a lucrative area, it was also very dangerous territory that was marked out into invisible grids by the resident dealers. Hence Jamie's surprise at seeing the saintly nurse take an alleyway short-cut without even a sideways glance. He guessed she was visiting a patient but then he saw her stop midway along one of the long narrow balconies that fronted a grim block of flats and let herself in a front door with a key.

After making a note of the address he turned and started to head away from the area as quickly as he could. He had nothing on him to sell so it wasn't worth the chance of getting caught.

But then something stopped him and he turned back.

Although Jamie knew the estate inside out it wasn't only because of his wheeling and dealing, it was because it had been his home for much of his life. But unlike a lot of the kids brought up here, his family life had been reasonably normal back then. Well, as normal as it could be on the 'Rat-Trap' as it was known almost affectionately by the residents.

Jamie had never admired his parents' ethic of hard work and honesty, he just despised them for not doing anything to break out of the situation they were in. From a young child, Jamie had been determined that, whatever it took, he wanted better. No way would he end up on the same estate like his father, who worked long hours in a grimy factory unit for a pittance because he was uneducated and honest.

Jamie wanted both money and status and he wasn't too fussy about how he got them.

However, his exit from the family home hadn't gone quite the way he had planned, and because of that the Rat-Trap had a hold on him. Every so often he gravitated back even when he didn't want to. Just to try and change things.

Rapping loudly on one particular door, he waited until he heard the familiar clonking of a walking stick heading up the hall.

'Who is it?' the elderly voice croaked.

'It's me, Jamie. Open the door,' he shouted.

'Go away!'

'Oh, come on. I just want to talk to you.'

He could hear her fumbling around noisily in the hallway; the opening of the door took a while because of the dead-lock and the chain, but he waited, albeit impatiently.

'Hi, Nan.' He grinned at the woman as she opened the door and peered at him through milky eyes. 'You should put your glasses on when you answer the door, then you could check the spy-hole first and see who it is. You just never know who it might be.'

'What do you want, Jamie?' the old woman asked. 'You know you're not allowed here, not after what you did. Your father told you never to come back.'

'Oh, come on, Nan, I know you don't really mean that. This crap has been going on for too long. Can't we get over it? I've said I'm sorry so many times. It wasn't my fault and it was ages ago. Please, Nan. You know deep down it wasn't me.' He didn't want to show his desperation but it was there in his voice.

'Just go away and leave me and my pension alone. You're not wanted here. Your mother doesn't want you and your father will skin you alive if he catches you.' Using her large, well-padded body to block the front door off she sucked the cold air in and shivered before continuing. 'You're not welcome here, Jamie, you know that. Your dad'll come straight round if I ring him and tell him you're here bothering me again — and I will ring him, I swear it.'

A wave of frustration swept over him. It had been several years previously when Jamie had taken a friend with him to visit his ailing nan, who had been provided with a studio flat close to her son and his family. Although he had often helped himself to a couple of quid when she wasn't looking he genuinely hadn't realised that his so-called 'friend' had pilfered her purse from her handbag, and also stolen her savings from inside the old metal teapot, along with some assorted worthless but sentimental jewellery and her precious diamond engagement ring.

Because of that, and thinking he was in on it, the whole family had turned against him, and from that day on none of them would have anything at all to do with him. He had broken the family code of morality by stealing from his own. Even his mother slammed the door in his face if he tried to visit. There were few crimes on the Rat-Trap worse than stealing from your own grandmother. No one believed that he was innocent and it hurt. It really hurt.

'It wasn't me, I told you it wasn't me, I keep *telling* you it wasn't me – it was that bastard Danny – and I tried to get it all back for you.' He felt like a ten year old again and he hated it. He may not have been the perfect child but he had never been as bad as they made him out to be.

'You told me that, Jamie, but you brought him into my home and then afterwards you left him half-dead in the canal. That was nearly as bad as what you both did to me. The pair of you came in here and robbed me. Now bugger off.'

'I beat the shit out of him because of what he did to you, can't you see that?'

She hesitated for a second, her expression softening, before she suddenly slammed the door in his face, leaving him seething afresh at the injustice of it all.

What he wanted most in the world was to be able to go back to the Rat-Trap as a success and show his family he'd made it – and Eleanor Rivington was the key to that. If he married her then he could have some cash to spend on some decent clothes and a fancy car, and he could also buy his grandmother a new diamond ring.

Then the Kirk family would look at him differently.

# Chapter Seventeen

Eleanor surprised everyone by recovering remarkably well from her surgery. Once again she had successfully exercised her ability to switch off and mentally dismiss traumatic events in her life; she was determined not to think about any of it so she didn't. 'Never look back,' she kept saying to anyone who questioned her lack of emotion.

'Do you know, I sometimes think the others are a bit disapproving of me for not cracking up and going completely loony, but what else should I do?' she asked Cathy as they sat together on a bench in the park during the Staff Nurse's lunch-break. 'I'm a firm believer that what you can't change you have to accept. There's absolutely nothing I can do to bring back my womb, any more than I could bring back my mother and father so I have to let it go and get on with my life.'

Cathy murmured supportively without passing comment or judgement. As she always did.

'I'm so glad I was put on your ward that day, Cathy. I think it was Fate making us friends.' Eleanor gave the woman beside her a hug. 'I really appreciate your support. You've helped me so much just by listening and not fussing and flapping around, especially as it must be so painful for you in a sort of similar situation.'

Cathy shook her head. 'Oh, it's not painful to me at all, apart from empathetically. I can feel your pain but it doesn't make mine any worse, and I know it makes you laugh when I say it, but I do enjoy fantasising about you being the daughter I might have had.' Preening herself, she flicked her hair back theatrically and pouted. 'Though naturally I would have had to have been a child bride!'

They both laughed easily at the idea for a few seconds before Cathy stopped and then carried on thoughtfully.

'Actually, my dear, it's when I think about that – when I think that I could easily have a child, children, the same age as you and your friends, that I wonder if Paddy is right: maybe it really is too late for me to have a baby. Maybe I should just be grateful for a marriage of sorts, a roof over my head and a job I love; others that I see every day in my job here in London have far less than me.'

'Never ever are you too old! You're still young enough at heart to be a fabulous mum. I take it he's still resisting everything you suggest?'

''Fraid so!' The edges of Cathy's lips turned down as she looked off into the distance. 'I keep trying to persuade him but I doubt he'll change his views now. The trouble is, time is racing on and if we don't do something soon it'll be too late and the options won't be there. Sometimes I wonder whether he really wants a family at all, maybe because his own childhood was so unhappy. He ended up an orphan at the age of nine . . .' Her voice trailed away.'He won't consider any medical help. He reckons it's God's will and if God wants us to have a baby He'll give us one. I did try and tell him that the Immaculate Conception trick is old hat. It's been done already.'

'Cathy!' Wide-eyed with fake shock, Eleanor smiled widely. 'That is so bad of you!'

'Yes, I know, but it gets to me that that's how Paddy really sees it. I can't make him understand that sometimes, when nature is playing up, we have to give her a helping hand. Especially at my advancing age.' Cathy smiled but it was forced and Eleanor could see that the woman beside her was hurting even more than she was.

'Well, you know the answer: come out on the pull with me, throw your inhibitions out of the window and have a one-night stand. You're a nurse, you could time it right and you might just get pregnant. Paddy needn't ever know it wasn't truly a miracle!'

They both laughed as they always did when Eleanor offered her regular solution to Cathy's baby problem – caused, it appeared, by Paddy having had mumps as a child.

'If he wasn't gay I'd offer you Marty. Now he's a good-looking young man, and if Jamie wasn't a con artist who'd rip you off at the same time, you could give him a try, but then thinking about it . . .' She stopped mid-sentence and put her head on one side. 'Of course! Thinking about it, you don't actually need the person, do you? Just some random sperm from someone who looks a little bit like either you or Paddy.'

They both stared wide-eyed at each other.

'Now that's an idea worth considering,' Eleanor continued. 'Paddy need never know, and if he queried, you could, with hand on heart, state that you had never been with anyone else and it was just nature's way.'

'Hardly,' Cathy smiled. 'Medical artificial insemination is one of the options I've tried to get Paddy to consider. I mean, that's bad enough, in hospital with a strange doctor and a syringe, but imagine doing it to yourself! Ugh – that is really too awful for words. And anyway, I'd know it wasn't Paddy's and I have a big enough problem with guilt anyway. I'm an Irish Catholic, remember!'

'Oh well, it was worth a mention and maybe a little thought?'

'Right, on that note I have to get back to work,' Cathy said, changing the subject. 'I'll see you soon, my dear. You take care and don't let them work you too hard at that hotel of yours.'

They hugged and then went off in separate directions.

Cathy was going back to work and Eleanor headed off to the doctor's to sort out her sickness certificate. She knew that after three months she was physically better, and she was definitely ready to go back to work and try to search out some kind of normality.

Jamie was still being a problem; in fact, he was intimidating her far more than she would admit to anyone, with his constant stalking – he popped up everywhere and always seemed to know where she was going to be. But so far she had stood firm and not given in to the charm, the friendly persuasion or even the veiled threats of harming himself.

She still had to achieve her aim of indifference towards him, but she felt she was getting closer. Sometimes she could go a whole day without thinking about him and wishing things had been different. If Venita hadn't told her, if she hadn't lost the baby. If if if . . .

Walking home from the bus-stop, Eleanor's mind was miles away as she pondered her future and thought about what she could do to make it all more bearable. Going back to work was one step forward, but apart from that she didn't have a clue.

Turning the corner towards home she wasn't surprised to see a police car parked up. Even in the short time they had all lived there, the place had degenerated from a none-too-nice area to a dump, with three of the neighbouring houses boarded up to prevent more squatters and the pavements and gutters littered with rubbish.

Their landlord appeared to be deliberately letting all his houses fall into disrepair so that he could pull them down and redevelop the land. Not that Eleanor cared – she just hoped that when they eventually had to move, they could all still stay together. In the meantime they had taken a joint decision to sit it out until the millionaire landlord offered them a better financial incentive than he had already suggested.

Clicking her key in the lock, she threw the door open.

'Marty!' She called out. 'Look, I've decided – I'm going back to work on Monday. I'm fit and able, and this proves it, so you don't have to mollycoddle me any m—'

She stopped in her tracks as she saw Marty, looking as if he was about to burst into tears, standing over by the window with a policeman on either side of him.

'What's going on? Marty? Have you robbed a bank again?'

'Lennie, it's you they want to see. They have something to tell you . . .'

'What about? I haven't done anything wrong. Never. Never ever,' she joked as she looked from one to the other and then stopped when no one joined in. 'Why do you want to see me? Is it something to do with Jamie?'

'Are you Miss Eleanor Rivington?'

'Yes, I am.'

'Do you own the property, a house, number twenty-four Ashton Gardens? In Hampstead?'

'Yes, I do. Why? Has there been a break-in or something? My solicitor deals with all that – I don't have anything to do with it and I don't want anything to do with it, but I'll give you his details.'

'No, miss, it's you we need to speak to. As the owner and a previous resident, I'm afraid I have to inform you that there was a body found in the garden of the property and we need to ask you some questions.'

Eleanor laughed with relief. Nothing to worry about.

'Oh, for Christ's sake, you scared me for a minute. I know

full well there was a body in the garden. It was my father – he committed suicide earlier this year and I was there. I saw it. There's been an inquest and it's all been sorted out, it's nothing we don't know about.'

'No, miss, we know all about that, but that isn't what we mean.' The office speaking cleared his throat. 'The remains of a body have been found buried there; the body appears to have been there for some years. It was buried under a tree in the secure part of the garden, the part surrounded by a wall. We think a fox must have disturbed the remains; the current tenant went to investigate a noise and found bones. Human bones . . .'

Eleanor felt as if she had been hit over the head with a mallet. Her room spun and lights flashed brightly behind her eyes.

*The nightmares. Her nightmares. The noises, the muffled screams . . .*

In that instant she had a far too vivid image in her mind of her father constantly tending the magnolia tree and standing beside it for hours with his head bowed. She had always thought it was because it was her mother's favourite tree, but in that instant she knew that wasn't the reason.

It was because he had killed his wife, her mother, and buried her there. Of course it was. She knew that was what had happened, but she must have blanked it out for all those years.

*Her father had murdered her mother.*

She knew instinctively that she was right, and suddenly

141

all those strange lonely years locked away with her father made sense. He didn't want her to remember.

Straightening her shoulders, she forced herself to think clearly and unemotionally.

'Was it under the big magnolia tree?' she asked. 'The one in the centre of the walled-off part of the garden?'

'That's right, miss, and how do you know that, might I ask?'

She could see suspicion instantly flash across his previously neutral expression.

'By adding up two and two, of course. It's so obvious,' she answered coolly with barely a flicker as if she was reciting a monologue. 'I think you'll find that the body is that of my mother. She went missing nearly ten years ago. Her name is – was – Rosetta Rivington. At a guess my father killed her, although under what circumstances I can't imagine. He told me she'd left home, disappeared without telling him. Of course, he murdered her – and if I hadn't been so very stupid I'd have realised that years ago. It's so obvious. So absolutely fucking obvious.'

Again the two policemen exchanged questioning glances; they were probably thinking that if she knew about it, she must have had something to do with it.

'In that case, miss, I shall have to ask you to come down to the station and make a statement, and then we'll have to go about identifying the remains and ascertaining what happened and how she came to be there. If it is her.'

Eleanor nodded politely; it was as if they had invited her for a cup of tea.

'Oh, I'm sure you'll find it's my mother, and naturally I'll come with you, but I have to ring my solicitor first, purely out of courtesy, and have him meet me there. He was a family friend who knew both of them.' She looked at Marty, who had been shocked into silence by the turn of events. 'Will you come with me? If you're not doing anything, that is.' She turned back to the policemen, who looked completely bewildered by her bright-eyed lack of emotion. 'Which station are we going to? Shall I come with you or make my own way there?'

Marty seemed to suddenly come to his senses. 'Of course I'll come with you, Lennie.' He went over and held his arms out to her. 'I can't believe this, I just can't believe it. Maybe you're wrong? Maybe some random stranger, a tramp or someone like that, went in there at some time for shelter after you'd left there and passed away in his sleep . . .'

She shrugged him off gently. 'And then found a spade and buried himself under a tree? Marty, I just know I'm right. It would explain everything. I knew deep down she wouldn't just go off and leave me, I knew it. And then there was the way Dad flipped when I told him I wanted to move out. I reckon now that if Megan hadn't turned up he'd have done the same to me. My nightmares weren't nightmares at all – those dreadful things really happened. They lied to me. Both of them. Those nightmares were real life and my father and mother made me believe I was imagining it all.'

'You're just making assumptions, Lennie,' Marty said softly. 'Get your head back to where we were when you first came in and don't say anything else – you never know what they're thinking.' He gestured with his eyes to the two officers, who were chatting to each other.

'Who?'

'The police, of course,' he murmured. 'Say nothing. They were looking at you so suspiciously.'

Eleanor sighed. 'Marty, trust me, I know. I just know and I've got nothing to hide, have I? I was only just thirteen when Mum disappeared.'

'No, of course you've nothing to hide, Lennie – I know that, but they don't.' He pulled her into the kitchen. 'Don't say anything else, not without talking to your solicitor. Now you go with the police, I'll phone your Mr Meacham and meet you there asap. In the meantime say nothing till this Meacham gets there. Okay? Promise me?'

# Chapter Eighteen

Eleanor looked across the grubby wooden table at Aaron Meacham. Although she had known him all her life, he had only ever been around on the periphery, with her father. His wife Hettie would visit with him occasionally and she and Rosetta Rivington would closet themselves in the kitchen while the men would talk business, as her mother used to say, in the lounge. At those times, Eleanor had always taken refuge in her bedroom away from boring adult stuff. Hence she had no idea of the topics of conversation in either room.

'I can't believe all this, Eleanor, it's beyond me. I knew your parents for so long and even though it was a difficult marriage I could never have imagined this in a million years. Never. I'm shell-shocked. How could he do it? *If* he did it, of course. Poor Rosetta. I wonder what could have happened to have pushed him to do something like this?'

His voice was breaking as he rambled and he held his head in his hands. For a moment Eleanor wanted to laugh at the irony of the situation. Aaron Meacham was her solicitor and he was with her at the police station to support and help her, and yet *he* was the quivering wreck. She also felt strangely relieved she wasn't in any real trouble because at this moment he wouldn't have been capable of doing anything constructive to help her.

'I know just how you feel, Mr Meacham – Aaron.' For the first time ever she used his Christian name as she reached out and took his hands in hers across the table, trying to comfort him. 'I don't pretend to understand, but in a way it will be a relief for me if it is found to be her. It would take away all the doubts I've had about myself over the years since she disappeared. I used to think it was all my fault that my mother had gone off and left us.'

Her eyes wandered off into the middle distance as she tried to figure out how she really felt about it, but Aaron Meacham just kept talking.

'No, Eleanor, no, whatever happened, it was never your fault. The police want to talk to you now. I'll be present but I wanted to see you alone first. You're going to have to go back to that time when your mother disappeared. Do you think you can do that, Eleanor?'

The young woman laughed humourlessly. 'Oh yes. I can remember every second of that day perfectly, but I haven't a clue why it happened, or how it happened, so I doubt I can tell them anything interesting. Maybe they can give *me* some clues instead of the other way round?'

He shook his head back and forth and Eleanor watched fascinated as a big fat tear started to grow in the corner of first one eye then the other before escaping and rolling down his cheeks together.

'I'm sorry, I'm so sorry,' he wept.

'It's okay.' She tried to reassure him but she didn't know how. 'I can deal with all of this, no problem. I'm not worried about it at all. Let's just get it over with and then we can both go home.'

Like a child he sniffed loudly and then flicked his perfectly starched white cuff across his face leaving a damp stain before standing up, his back instantly ramrod straight. 'I'll tell them we're ready for you to be interviewed.'

In the event, the actual interview wasn't anywhere near as bad as Eleanor had anticipated. The questions she had dreaded seemed mainly formalities and the policeman taking the statement was professional but kindly.

She wanted to tell them about the nightmares that she now knew weren't nightmares at all, but when it came to it she just couldn't; with both her parents dead there was little to be gained by bringing it all into the open, to be disseminated at another inquest.

To be discussed at another funeral.

Within a couple of hours it was all over and they were on their way back out. As they reached the front office of the station Marty, who had been waiting there, jumped up and ran over to them.

'Lennie! Oh my God, how did it go?'

'Fine really.' She shrugged quite calmly. 'They just wanted some information. It now has to go to the Forensic Department while they try and establish identity. There'll be more questions, of course, and hopefully some answers, and it's going to take a while but I know in my heart that it's her, it's my mother's remains in the garden.'

'No, you don't. You don't know that, you're pre-empting.'

Eleanor tutted and pushed his hand away from her arm impatiently.

'Oh, for fuck's sake, Marty, just for once *listen* to me! I'm telling you I know and it's okay. I know now she didn't go off and leave me, she didn't abandon me after all. Do you know what a relief that is? It all fits into place. She *didn't* leave me.'

'But Lennie . . .' Marty looked bewildered at her composure.

'Don't but me. Don't you understand? SHE DIDN'T LEAVE ME! Now I know what you're going to say yet again, but just don't. I don't want to talk about it right now. Any of it.'

She nodded her head in the direction of Aaron Meacham who was still looking alone and lost. His face was grey and it struck her that he was just a little old man. She felt the need to comfort him, to reassure him that he didn't need to feel guilty. No one could have foreseen any of it.

'Do you mind if I visit Hettie tomorrow?' She took his arm as they walked outside. 'I feel I need to speak to her now, now that things have changed. Maybe it's time for some closure for all of us. I shouldn't have left it this long and I'm sorry.'

'Of course, my dear. Do you remember where we live?'

He handed her a card. 'We'll expect you at around eleven, but then I'll leave the both of you to chat. Hettie will like that.' He paused and looked confused, as if he was unsure where he was all of a sudden. 'I don't know what you want to do about the house. I think it'll be hard to let it again after this. I mean, two bodies in one garden? And it's falling into disrepair. Who's going to want to live there now? Do you want me to try and sell it? What do you want me to do? It's just an albatross around your neck.'

Eleanor was lost for words so she just smiled and kissed him on the cheek. 'We'll talk about all that another time, there's no urgency. You go home to Hettie and let her take care of you and I'll see you both tomorrow.'

Back at the house, Marty started fussing round her and Eleanor could feel herself becoming increasingly agitated by it but she tried not to let it show. He wanted to call Megan and Venita who were away on a shoot, then he wanted her to go back to the doctor and stay off work; he also wanted to call Cathy. Once again, Marty had a caring purpose in his life and it was exactly what he needed. But it was certainly not what Eleanor herself needed.

'Okay, Marty, this is it. You and me, we need to have a little chat.' She grabbed his hand, pulled him forcefully over to the sofa then, placing both hands on his chest, she pushed him backwards on it and sat down beside him.

'Now I love you, you're my best friend in the world and I don't know what I'd do if I lost that friendship, but you're

149

not my carer. This is yet another hiccup in the truly fucked-up life of Eleanor Rivington. I can deal with it. Really I can. I've learned how to detach myself from things like this, bad things. But I can only do it if you let me.'

As he tried to interrupt she held her hand up.

'No, Marty, enough. I don't want to talk about shit any more, I want us to just go out and go mad together, like we used to. A night out on the town is what I really need more than anything. I want a few drinks, some loud music and mad dancing. Loads of noise and loads of crazy people. You up for it?'

Marty looked at her curiously for a few moments and then laughed. 'Do I have a choice? You know, you're one strong woman, Eleanor Rivington, and if I wasn't gay I'd marry you tomorrow. If half of what's happened to you lately had happened to me, I'd be on the floor, a gibbering idiot.'

'Yes, well, I'm not going to let that happen to me. Ever. I'm going back to work on Monday and I really think it's time now that you got over everything that happened to you and found yourself another job. Sometimes life is a real bitch but that's no reason to give up.'

She reached out her hand and pinched him gently on the cheek.

'You're a handsome, caring young man who deserves far better than to be in this place all day being nursemaid, housekeeper, cook and dish-washer to three crazy women. Not that we don't all appreciate it, of course!'

Marty's face sank visibly. 'Oh God, Lennie, I don't know.

You're right, of course you are, but it's so hard to face up to it after that night. I'm so scared it might happen again, that I might bump into Mr Sadist Smith, but I'll try. I promise.'

Although he had agreed at that moment to go out with her, it surprised her that he didn't try to back out. It would be his first time to a club since the incident with Mr Smith and she knew how desperately hard it would be for him, but she was determined to help him break his self-imposed isolation.

She was equally determined not to think about her old home, the walled garden and the magnolia tree with her mother lying underneath it for all those years. Freezing cold and all alone. It was enough to break her heart.

And she certainly wasn't going to think about her own, permanently lost motherhood.

The next day she would go and see Aaron and Hettie Meacham and put the final touches to her memories before locking them away, but in the meantime she wanted to go out and have some fun.

Together, Eleanor and Marty mucked around like teenagers as they dressed up ready to go out on the town, both chucking clothes all over the place and fighting over the tepid bathwater and the hairdryer.

'God, Lennie, you look just like Cher,' he laughed as she put the finishing touches to her poker-straight nutbrown hair. 'And I just lurve the velvet trousers – purple is my fave colour right now. I may just have to borrow them.'

'Thank you, kind sir, and you look pretty good also. If I didn't know you I'd fancy you myself. Next time we go out you can wear the trousers and I'll borrow the shiny shirt and that oh so sexy belt!'

There was no getting away from the fact that they were a beautiful couple. He was as blond as she was dark, both were tall and slender, and both were fashionably dressed to impress.

The club they went to was one of those spit and sawdust dives down in a dingy basement that had somehow become very trendy, and the queue was backed up round the block. The self-important doormen had total discretion on who was allowed in and who was firmly barred.

It was a chore but they finally made it in after being given the once-over. Eleanor spoke quietly to Marty out of the corner of her mouth as they were allowed through.

'I just want to be so sarky and say what I think to those macho gorillas. I hate having to smile and look grateful to Neanderthals, but if we don't then we won't get in, will we?'

'No, and we wouldn't get in anywhere else either because they work a system between them all.' Marty sighed. 'However, I'm also shit scared I'll see that other gorilla Anthony moon-lighting in here or somewhere.'

'Then just tell me and we'll leave immediately. No probs. Now, we're agreed? No pills and no dope. Just alcohol but not too much, and no champagne cocktails; you've been dry for so long you probably only need one G and T to be pissed as a parrot! In fact, me too!'

She slipped her arm in his as they made their way down the winding staircase into the cavernous underground room that was already in full disco swing.

For the first couple of hours in the darkened dungeon-like room the couple stayed close together but after a few drinks Marty relaxed and soon started chatting to a man who was sitting alone at the end of the bar watching rather than participating; they had locked eyes a couple of times and when the man finally smiled Marty responded. At first he tried to keep Eleanor by his side but, as soon as she sensed him feeling comfortable she moved a few paces away to the railings that encircled the dance-floor. She feigned interest in the dancers moving rhythmically together to the throbbing beat, but she kept an eye on her friend nonetheless because she knew he was still so fragile that it would only take one more bad experience and he would disintegrate completely. Marty wasn't as strong as she was.

She just hoped that his radar was correct this time.

Suddenly she sensed someone close beside her but she didn't look round.

'Hi there. I know this sounds like a well-used line – heck, it *is* a well-used line – but I promise you I really do need a light for this cigarette and I noticed you're smoking . . .'

Eleanor reached into her bag and handed over a box of matches before letting her eyes take in the owner of the friendly voice with an American accent.

'Thanks,' he smiled as he lit his cigarette and then offered the box back to her.

'It's okay, you can keep it, I've got spares. Always a good idea in these places, I find.'

'Are you with someone? Boyfriend?' He glanced over at Marty and she knew immediately he had been watching her.

'No. Just a very good friend. We watch out for each other, just in case.'

'I'm pleased to hear it.' He held his hand out politely. 'I'm Greg.'

She offered hers back and noted he shook it firmly with a strong grip. 'And I'm Eleanor.' She studied him in the semi-darkness that was interspersed with coloured lights flashing off the huge mirrored disco ball hanging from the ceiling. She could just make out a tall and muscular man with collar-length fairish hair and clear hazel eyes who was several years older than herself and leaning towards conservative in his clothes and manner.

He looked decidedly out of place in the throbbing basement.

'Can I get you a drink?' he asked politely.

'Thank you! That would be great. I'll have a brandy and Coke, with ice.'

As he fought his way to the crowded bar Eleanor looked over and caught Marty's eye. He raised his eyebrows in a query. Eleanor raised hers back.

They both grinned.

★   ★   ★

That night, as she lay in bed alone and the events of the day started to sink in, Eleanor finally fell apart and sobbed into her pillow at the tragedy of it all. So much had happened in such a short space of time but she had no intention of letting anyone know how she felt. How she wished her father was still alive to pay for what he had done. How she longed to apologise to her mother for not realising, for believing the reassurances that all was well. That it was all 'only a nightmare'.

When she did fall asleep, just as dawn was breaking, the nightmares were violent and terrifying as her sleeping brain brought her mother back to her.

*Pleading, Rosetta Rivington held her hands out to her daughter. 'Help me, darling, please help me. Make him stop . . .'*

*But Eleanor stayed where she was, safe behind the doorframe. Harold Rivington, stark naked, was laughing and stabbing at his wife's naked back with a garden fork. As he laughed, he stabbed harder and harder and the blood started to flow from the wounds.*

*'Eleanor, please, please do something! I'm your mother – stop him!'*

*But Eleanor continued to watch as her father kept stabbing Rosetta, and then she collapsed on the floor, but still he stabbed her, over and over until her skin had almost disappeared. When he eventually stopped, the young girl watched mesmerised as he dragged the remains of her mother down the stairs and out into the garden.*

*Deep in shock, Eleanor watched from the window as he carefully dug the hole and then kicked the bloody body down into it.*

*When he walked back in and saw his daughter, Harold Rivington beamed.*

*'It's just you and me now, Eleanor. Won't that be nice?'*

*His bloody hands reached out for her but Eleanor started screaming . . .*

When she opened her eyes, it took her a moment to realise that this time it really *was* a nightmare – that wasn't how it had happened at all – but this time her mother didn't come to reassure her. She couldn't, because Harold Rivington, her husband, had murdered her and buried her in the garden.

Eleanor tried to sort fact from fiction in her mind but the lines just became even more blurred and her feelings of guilt soared.

# Chapter Nineteen

Eleanor staggered barefoot into the kitchen with her shocking-pink wrap pulled tight, runs of mascara under her eyes and her hair unbrushed. Marty was already there, fully dressed and looking bright-eyed and pleased with himself.

'My oh my, missy, you look like shit! You have to learn to pace yourself when you're out drinking. Moderation is the key.'

'Fuck off, Marty, everyone in the whole wide world hates reformed drinkers and born again non-smokers more than they hate politicians and nuclear weapons!'

'Okay!' He twirled around the kitchen with one hand on his hip and waving a tea-towel over his head. 'So Lennie Lennie, we both pulled last night. How's that for good luck? Mine's called Jon, and he's actually a barman at the club – he was off-duty last night. I'm seeing mine again tomorrow. And yours?'

'His name's Greg, some big bank-type company in the City. I can't remember the name but I'd never heard of it anyway. And I might see him again, I'll see – I've got his phone number. Marty, I'm so pleased it went well for you. You deserve it after everything.'

'And you too. That Jamie was a first-class shit; you definitely need to find yourself someone who is more of a gentleman. Yep, you need a gentleman in your life, same as I do.'

'Shall we start a mutual appreciation society?' Eleanor laughed. 'This time I'm taking it casual and slow. I want fun, nothing serious at the moment.'

'Well, I really want serious. I can't face any more of the hassle of partying. But anyway, talking of Jamie, which I wish I wasn't, has anyone, meaning you, seen anything of him lately?'

Eleanor loved Marty so much she couldn't be angry with him for bringing Jamie up once again.

'He's still around and still professing his undying love for me to anyone in the pub who'll listen, and of course going on about the miscarriage. He even suggested he thought it was an abortion gone wrong. He's a dick so I don't care.' She shrugged and pulled a very convincing face.

'Do care, Lennie, and keep one eye out for him all the time. He's dangerous.'

'Oh, I'm aware of him, but I don't want him to take away my freedom so I'm being cautious but not paranoid.' She put her arm around his waist. 'I must have something to eat and then I'm off to see Mr and Mrs Meacham. Duty calls.'

★   ★   ★

Eleanor could feel the trepidation building inside her as she walked up the crazy-paved path to the Meachams' house. It felt scary but she knew it was something she had to do before she could come to terms with the past and properly close the door on her childhood.

As soon as she neared the front door it flew open and Hettie Meacham ran out and threw her arms around her, despite being about a foot shorter and whippet thin.

'Eleanor, my darling girl! I'm so pleased you came and I'm so sorry this has all started again. I am so unhappy for you, just as it was all going away, I can't believe it. When Aaron told me I said no! Surely not! Not beautiful Rosetta, surely Harold couldn't have done a terrible thing like that . . .'

Eleanor tried to tactfully prise herself away from the iron grip of the tiny woman who looked like a small exotic bird with her dyed orange-red hair piled high on the top of her head and fixed with a clip, and layers of bright make-up outlining her eyes and lips.

'It's okay,' Eleanor told her affectionately, 'it really is. I don't deny it was a shock but I can deal with it. I'm getting good at dealing with things now, Hettie – in fact, I'm the expert.'

Hettie took her hand as if she was a child and pulled her along the path. 'Come in. I'll make tea and we can talk. Aaron has gone to the office. I didn't want him to, he's taken it very badly because he thought of your father as a friend and he feels so bad we didn't realise, but he insisted. I rang all the children and they said let him do what he wants so I have.'

As they got to the door Hettie stood back and Eleanor walked ahead of her into the wide and pristine hallway that was overcrowded with ornaments, knick-knacks and photographs of the couple's six children at various stages of development. The atmosphere of the house instantly struck Eleanor as naturally warm and homely; it smelled of home baking and furniture polish, and the smell took her back to the time before her mother had disappeared.

She would come home from school to the aroma of cakes and scones and hot chocolate wafting throughout the house, and the smell of 4711 eau de cologne on her mother. Then they would huddle together beside the sooty old kitchen boiler and talk about her day.

But now she wasn't even sure if her memory of it was real.

Real or not, the atmosphere and smell of Hettie and Aaron's house made her feel so bereft she just wanted to turn around and run. But she didn't; instead she smiled.

'I can understand your concern, Hettie.' She stopped and looked at the tiny woman in front of her. 'I hope you don't mind me calling you Hettie. I too was worried about Aaron yesterday – he was so upset by what had happened.'

Hettie was busily making the tea with carefully meas-ured tea leaves and a warmed pot before setting up a tray with a lace cloth and matching milk and sugar pots.

'We're both so upset, Eleanor dear, and in shock. In fact,

we both feel guilty about not realising exactly what was going on.' She looked round at Eleanor sadly. 'Your mother used to pop over sometimes and we'd have a cup of tea and a gossip, but she always made sure she was back in time for you coming home from school. She used to watch the clock and then dash back in time to have tea ready before going to meet you. That's why I couldn't believe that she just ran off.'

'I know how you felt about my mother, but what did you think of my father? Really think of him?' Eleanor watched her closely.

'Well, it's not good to speak ill of the dead, but he was always a strange one. I never really got to know him and I don't think Aaron did either, even though he tried. Harold was so cold and unemotional and, forgive me, Eleanor, but I have to say it, he was mean.' She searched for the right words. 'He could be mean with money, according to Rosetta, and he could also be mean-spirited – but a *murderer*? I don't know. You and your mother were all that he lived for. Something awful must have happened to push him over the edge so far that he killed her. Though maybe she died accidentally and he didn't want to admit to it? Maybe she turned on him? It's possible.'

As she carried the tray through to the sitting room Eleanor followed her. She knew there was no point in suggesting she didn't stand on ceremony because Hettie loved doing it. And it really was a ceremony. A hand-embroidered cloth was carefully laid across the wooden tea-trolley, tiny petits fours were geometrically placed on a two-tier cake stand decorated with paper doilies, and a selection of biscuits was piled high on a serving plate.

Eleanor stirred her tea in the dainty matching bone china cup. 'You see, the problem I have, Hettie, is that I could possibly have forgiven him if he'd killed my mother by accident, in temper, if he'd admitted to her death, but to tell me that she'd run off and abandoned me, had an affair with another man, and then ban all talk of her in the house?' Angry tears burned Eleanor's eyes. 'And all the time she was out in the garden where I went every day! I used to sit on the bench no more than a couple of feet away from where she lay. Now *that's* evil. He should have called the police and confessed.'

Hettie's eyes filled in sympathy and she reached across and patted her arm. 'You're right, my dear, that would have been the right thing to do, but then he was always strange – surely you must have noticed? Rosetta had no life outside of the house; she was only allowed to come here because of Aaron. Harold didn't even want her to go to the shops alone, he was so possessive. After she disappeared, your father wouldn't let me help look after you.'

'But why? Wouldn't it have been easier for him?'

Hettie Meacham looked at Eleanor curiously, as if she wasn't sure of what to say. 'I don't think he wanted it easier. He wanted you all to himself, the same as he had wanted Rosetta. If he could have locked you both up and kept you away from the rest of the world, then I'm sure he would have done so.'

Eleanor forced herself not to cry at the unfairness of it all.

'It all seemed normal to me at the time. It's only since his death that I've realised that some things maybe weren't as they seemed. I suppose my mother must have shielded me from a lot. The first time I truly saw his madness was the day when I said I wanted to leave home, then of course he killed himself, but I think he would have killed me first if Megan hadn't called the police.'

'Oh, your mother protected you like a lioness,' Hettie interrupted her reassuringly. 'You were a late and unexpected bonus in her life. She used to say that you alone made her life worth living. I don't think her marriage was what she would have chosen, but right or wrong she stuck it out as long as she was alive.'

Eleanor screwed her eyes up as she tried to remember more about her life with her mother, but it was hard because she had deliberately not thought about it for so long.

'I do know that I loved my mother in a completely different way to how I loved my father, but then when he told me she had abandoned me, that she had put herself first, it all changed around.' Eleanor raised her thumb to her mouth and started nibbling around the edge of her nail. 'He even got rid of all her belongings. Everything. Do you know, Hettie, I don't even have a photo of her? It scares me that I can't remember what she looked like, especially now.'

Hettie Meacham jumped up and rushed over to the ornate oak sideboard that dominated the room and pulled open a drawer. She rifled through it for a while, piling envelopes and pieces of paper on the top as she dug deeper.

'Here!' she cried triumphantly. 'I have several photos. I love taking photographs – I even have some of you with her somewhere, but I'll have to carry on looking for them. This house is so tidy on the outside but inside the cupboards and drawers is a hidden chaos.'

Eleanor took the photos from a smiling Hettie and looked at them slowly one at a time. A surge of emotion swept through her as she looked at the image of the mother she had adored for thirteen years, the mother who had disappeared in an instant, never to be seen or mentioned again.

'She doesn't look like I remember, is that silly?'

'Of course not, you had the brain of a child and now you have the brain of an adult. You see things differently. Do you want to see the photos of your parents together or is that too painful?'

'No, it's okay. I was explaining to Aaron yesterday, I'm really fine. And no, I'm not in denial! I just feel as if a great weight has been lifted – although of course I want to know how it happened, but with the only two witnesses both dead we're never going to know that, are we?'

'Probably not.' Hettie hesitated. 'But maybe that's best? I would guess they had a row and your father lost control. He did suffer a lot from depression; your mother told me that he sometimes had the highs and lows of mania. I suppose that's why he killed himself and of course, where he did it is poignant.'

'I never knew he was depressed – I thought that was just how he was. How could I not have noticed when it was just him and me for so long?'

'That's precisely why, my dear. All I want you to remember is that your mother loved you with a passion and so did your father in his own way. Nothing can ever take that away.'

Hettie went over and gently kissed Eleanor on the top of her head.

'Now, you put those photos away safely in your bag, and I'll keep any more I find aside for you. Would you like me to make you a sandwich? Just look at you, you're so thin, I've seen fatter matchsticks. You need feeding up if you're going to have fit and healthy babies one day for me to be granny to.'

Eleanor thought for a moment about confiding in the woman but she couldn't take any more emotion, however well meant.

'Oh Hettie, any more to eat and I'll explode. No, let's just chat. Tell me all about the family. I understand from Aaron that Joshua is getting married? And that Debbie has a new baby?'

'Oh yes. It's all so exciting . . .'

# Chapter Twenty

After many crazy thoughts and ten days of dithering, Eleanor finally decided to take the bull by the horns and ring the man she had met in the club. There was something about him that had attracted her, a calmness combined with casual normality that she found very appealing in her confused life as she waited for news from the police. She knew that there was still the trauma of another inquest and another funeral to go through, but she wasn't going to think about that.

Eleanor was convinced that if she didn't think about all those things then they would go away and no longer be a problem.

It was because she didn't want to talk or think that she made a conscious decision not to tell Greg anything about her past – not about her parents, Jamie, her miscarriage and hysterectomy, nothing emotional at all. She wanted a clean slate to start from; it wasn't the right time for anything deep and meaningful and she didn't want any more sympathy from anyone.

She loved all three of her friends but they were constantly

walking round her on eggshells and all refused to accept that she was okay with it all.

Once again she retrieved the card from her bag and studied it. *Gregory Casheron* was the name on the personal card along with two phone numbers, one for work and one for home. Before she could change her mind again she glanced at her watch and quickly dialled his home number.

'Hello,' she spoke cautiously, 'is that Gregory Casheron? This is Eleanor, we met in the club last week. Do you remember? I gave you matches for your cigarette. I won't be offended if you don't remember and I—'

'Of course I remember you,' the friendly voice at the other end interrupted quickly. 'I've been thinking about you and hoping you'd ring, and also cursing myself for not getting your number.'

They chatted easily as if they were old friends and Eleanor felt as comfortable talking with him on the phone as she had done in the club. This was a man who, unlike Jamie Kirk, wasn't an emotional threat to her.

'Can I persuade you to come out to dinner with me tonight?' he asked. 'If you're free, of course. If not, then some other night – or would you prefer lunch?'

Eleanor smiled to herself. She certainly didn't need any persuading.

'Whereabouts in London do you live?' she asked, as casually as she could.

'I have an apartment near to Hyde Park. Sounds better

than it is and it isn't mine, it's a company flat. Where are you?'

'In a truly scummy house-share in Notting Hill that couldn't be any worse than it is. The whole block is going to be demolished to make way for flats and we're on notice to quit. It's a bit like a war-zone. Right now it's us against the big guys, on principle.'

'Sounds grim. How about I call for you at eight and I'll have made a reservation in the meantime. Italian okay for you?'

'Italian sounds just right. I love Italian food.' And she gave him the address that she had so carefully withheld at their previous meeting.

After Marty's horrific encounter with the mysterious Mr Smith, Eleanor had realised that she herself needed to be more cautious with strangers, however seemingly safe and sensible those strangers appeared to be. But Gregory Casheron was okay, she just knew it.

Eleanor spent as much time getting ready for her date as she had when she went out with Marty, but this time she was aiming for smartly dressed down. From what she had seen, Greg seemed like a tidy, slightly conservative kind of man as opposed to high fashion like Marty.

Because everyone always complimented her on her hair she left it to hang naturally on her shoulders and put the emphasis on her eyes. Fishing a light beige skinny polo neck out of the depths of her untidy wardrobe she teamed it with chocolate brown hipster flares and a wide black leather belt that was designed to sit loosely round her hips. Her new platform boots made her look even taller and slimmer than she was anyway.

Marty was out so she poured herself a drink and waited, at the same time hoping she wouldn't be stood up. She was looking forward to a night out with someone who knew nothing about her.

Cathy Hart hadn't been in from work long when the doorbell rang long and hard. Someone had their finger on the bell and was keeping it there. Automatically she looked through the spyhole on the door and saw the young man Jamie whom she recognised from when Eleanor was in hospital. She opened the door on the chain.

'Yes?' she asked brusquely through the gap, feeling very uncomfortable at seeing him on her own ground.

He smiled. 'Hello, Nurse Cathy. I wanted to talk to you about my girlfriend Eleanor Rivington.'

'Well, that's tough, young man, because I can't discuss a patient with you. You must know that. Now if that's all? I've just got in from work and I have a lot to do. You shouldn't be at my home.'

One swift high kick and the chain was broken, the door was open and Cathy was momentarily stunned and bleeding from a graze on her forehead where the door had flown back onto her.

'Oops.' He grinned at her without humour. 'Lousy chain,

that. You'll have to get a stronger one next time. Perhaps get Paddywack to do it?' He put his foot inside.

'Don't you dare try and come in here. Get out now or I'll call the police . . .' But as she spoke he shouldered past and turned to face her.

'Shut the door, bitch, and put the bolts on. I just want to talk to you without interruption and then, if I get the right answers, I'll go.'

'My husband is due home, he'll go crazy.'

Jamie laughed, hopping from foot to foot like a boxer. Cathy could see straight away that he was high on drugs and out of control. She quickly assessed that he had only recently taken something.

'Give me a break, Nursie Nurse, I've seen your old man and he couldn't fight his way out of a paper bag. Now, let's make this easy for both of us. I've seen you out and about with Lennie and I want to know what she's said about me. I want to know what's happening with her house and why she won't see me any more.'

'I wouldn't have any idea about that – why don't you just ask her? Or one of her friends? I'm guessing you know them all.' She tried to speak calmly, aware of how unpredictable he was, especially if, as she suspected, he was high enough to not know what he was doing. She closed the door quietly but didn't touch the bolts.

'It is for you to say.' He grinned madly at her with his face so close to hers it looked distorted. His hand reached over her shoulder and flipped the bolt. 'Tut tut, Nursie

170

Nurse, you're not trying to put one over on Jamie, are you?'

When she didn't reply he continued, 'Come on then, tell me all about it.'

'Eleanor has never discussed her private life with me. Really, all I've done is counsel her over the miscarriage. It's all been very professional.'

Quickly his forearm was across her neck, pinning her to the wall. 'Don't give me professional, bitch, I've seen you with her. You're friends, and friends tell each other things, don't they? She's told you and I want you to tell me.'

Cathy tried to think on her feet. She was scared but she knew she had to find a way to appease him and get him out of her flat.

'I don't discuss any personal things with Eleanor and she doesn't discuss them with me.' She looked him in the eye and tried to project some compassion even though she was scared. 'Our relationship is purely professional, and we meet outside of the hospital to make it more relaxed. That's all, Jamie. I'm a nurse, you know that, I deal with medical things. Eleanor has suffered a trauma and I'm helping her get over it.'

'Yeah, a nurse after a quick buck. I bet you're fucking brain-washing her, getting ready to fleece her, to rip her off, to take what's mine. I've been watching you both for weeks, I know what your game is.'

Cathy tried to assess the situation as, wide-eyed, Jamie continued to move from one foot to the other and wave his hands about with little co-ordination. She noticed his clothes were grubby, as if he had been sleeping in them and hadn't changed for days. His long hair was tangled and unbrushed, and he smelled of stale tobacco and sweat.

'Jamie, I really don't know what you're talking about. Now I think you should leave before you get into real trouble, before you get caught here.' Cathy used her best soothing voice to try and calm him but she could see he was becoming psychotic and about to lose control.

'I tell you what, Jamie, I'll ring Lennie, shall I?' she went on. 'See what she has to say? Mind you, this time of day she's probably at work, but I'll give it a go for you if it'll help.'

He looked at her suspiciously. She could see he was getting confused by her amenable manner. Slowly, and with a smile, she walked over to the phone and picked it up from the cradle, then, hoping he was too off his head to notice, she dialled a colleague's number. The colleague who, because she was feeding her cat, she knew with certainty was away on holiday.

As the phone rang and rang she shrugged and held it out to him. 'There's no one in – I reckon they must all be at work. I tell you what I'll do, Jamie love, next time I see Eleanor, which will be . . . um . . .' she made out she was thinking, 'her next appointment with me is on Wednesday week. I'll have a chat with her then and ask her to get in contact with you. How about that? Might that be a help to you?'

'I'm not waiting that long. I want to know now, right

now!' Without warning he started to calm down; his shoulders slouched and he leaned back against the wall. It was as if someone had turned a switch off and he was no longer wired. He was coming down.

'I do think a lot of Lennie, you know,' he said. 'I know I was crap to her and the money was part of it, but she was good for me. And she loved me, I know she did. We could have been okay together; if she hadn't lost the baby we could have got married, been a family. I'd really like that. My own family have disowned me, I haven't got anyone any more.'

In a strange way she felt sorry for him but she knew she had to get him out of the flat as quickly as possible.

'I know that, Jamie, I can see you really want to sort things out with Eleanor. I'll do what I can for you, I promise.' Her nursing training allowed her to lie easily to someone who was presenting a threat to her.

But he wasn't listening any more, he was gabbling furiously. 'My gran lives round the corner, and my mum and dad. None of them want anything to do with me. Bastards. Me and Lennie, we're two of a kind. We both had shit families but she has the money to make it better. I have fuck all . . . we could help each other, me and Lennie.'

He looked at her closely, his expression one of pure bewilderment, as if he'd only just realised where he was. Cathy took her chance.

'Listen to me, Jamie. I want you to go now, and if you do go right now I won't call the police about the door, I promise. But my husband will be home in a minute and he

173

really will contact the police if he finds you here and his door battered. He'll raise merry hell. Go now and I'll talk to Eleanor. I promise.'

As he hesitated she smiled. 'Go on. Away you go.'

'You will talk to her?'

'I will talk to her.'

As Jamie Kirk left her flat, she closed the door gently behind him to avoid any more confrontation and sighed deeply. Her instinct was to call the police but she could see that he was one very troubled young man who probably needed help more than anything else. She went through into the kitchenette and put the kettle on the gas stove.

She wondered if she could help him. After all, guessing the age of him, he could just about be her son. The same as Eleanor could be her daughter. Both of them were the right age, although of course she had never known if her baby would have been a boy or a girl. Immediately she was back in the dark place where she spent so much of her adult life. The place where she blamed every minor misfortune on herself and her previous sins, and where she saw her childlessness as her punishment for what she had done all those years ago.

She had always thought there would be retribution for the secret abortion she had suffered when she was an eighteen-year-old nurse alone in London with no one to turn to. No one in the world knew about it other than the elderly nurse who had 'helped' her, and her own conscience.

But now the craving for a baby was getting worse. It was

a constant ache that was bringing her down and slowly driving her mad, and as the months passed, and she felt her fertility fading more rapidly, she was becoming more and more obsessed with her guilt. She was also starting to hate Paddy for not being honest with her in the very beginning.

Cathy turned the kettle off and poured herself a glass of cheap, rough sherry from the bottle at the back of the kitchen cupboard instead, before going into the lounge, sinking into her favourite armchair and putting her feet up on the worn velvet footstool.

Downing the tumbler of sherry in one she thought about Eleanor's joking suggestion of DIY AID. She laughed as she said the letters out loud. Suddenly she was excited as she saw the possibilities. It was worth a try. Anything was worth one last-ditch try. The thought of the rest of her life with boring Paddy Hart and no child was unbearable.

Cathy and Paddy had married ten years before. As a dedicated career nurse, which was the reason she had had the abortion in the first place, she had dismissed marriage, even children, as not for her, but there came a time when she wanted to marry and have a family, and Paddy had come along, seemingly at just the right moment. It hadn't been a great passion for either of them but they had got married and jogged along companionably enough until she realised she wasn't going to get pregnant. All the examinations had reassured her that, despite the previous 'miscarriage' there was nothing wrong with her but still nothing happened.

She just couldn't get pregnant.

It had been five years before Paddy had finally admitted it might be — in fact probably *was* — his fault, thanks to that awful teenage bout of the mumps. He had broken down and cried, and although she felt compassion for him, she also felt a blackness for the lack of a child.

And now she knew she would never have the baby she craved unless she did something about it, even if it was dishonest, unethical and immoral. But then surely God couldn't punish her any more than He already had?

# Chapter Twenty-one

*. . . the body found buried in a garden in North London has been formally identified as that of Rosetta Rivington, who had previously lived in the house and went missing ten years ago. Her husband, Harold Rivington, recently committed suicide at the same spot. The cause of Mrs Rivington's death has not been established, although it is believed that she was unlawfully killed. The police say they are not looking for anyone else in connection with the death. Rosetta Rivington had never been reported missing. The couple had a daughter, Eleanor, now in her twenties. Her solicitor made a statement but said that she had no comment to make.*

*'And now here's the weather . . .'*

Eleanor was very aware of Cathy Hart watching her face as the news was being read. She had already been told in advance about the result of the forensic tests by Aaron Meacham and was expecting it, but still it was a shock to see the familiar newsreader looking at her from the television screen, his voice sombre, declaring it on the local news alongside the sports results and the weather forecast.

'It seems strange to hear about something so tragic, the deaths of two people, being condensed into ten seconds of local news just before the weather. Quite bizarre really, I think I'll watch the news through different eyes from now on.' Eleanor sighed and walked over to turn the TV off.

'Do you realise, hundreds of thousands of people have watched that piece of news and thought, Oh what a shame, but, after those few seconds, they have already forgotten it because it doesn't actually affect them?' Still standing, Eleanor folded her arms and looked at Cathy. 'Already they're up from their chairs and putting the kettle on and thinking about what to have for dinner or something similar. It's a very strange thought, isn't it?'

Cathy shrugged her shoulders. 'I suppose that's the way we all keep going, by not taking every single bit of bad news on ourselves. I doubt we could survive if we did that every day.'

Eleanor studied Cathy who was perched right on the edge of one of the armchairs looking uncomfortable.

'What's the matter?' she asked. 'You look as if you're about to pee yourself.' She laughed. 'I know you hate coming round to this den of iniquity . . .'

'No, I don't, Lennie. To be honest, it's you. You worry me. I think you're kidding yourself if you believe you can just ignore all that's happened to you.'

'Nonsense.' Eleanor brushed away Cathy's concern. 'I'm fine and you know that, really. It's happened – nothing I say or do can change any of it. Death is pretty much irreversible, isn't it? I mean, I can cry and shout and kick kittens, but it won't bring either of them back, will it?'

'Yes, I know that, but you've lost your father, your mother again, and your baby . . .'

'But that wasn't like a baby to me, Cathy,' Eleanor interrupted sharply. 'You and I see things differently. I didn't want it, I hadn't humanised it, so how could I possibly need to grieve for it? The disappearing womb is a bit of a bummer, but who knows? I might never get married or want children. Maybe I could adopt if I had the urge – anything. It's not the end of the world to me. I'm not fussed about children anyway.'

Eleanor did an exaggerated little dance in front of Cathy.

'See? Everything that matters is in working order. I can walk and talk, I can eat and drink and I can have sex without worrying about taking the pill. Now, enough about me – what else shall we talk about? I'm bored with me and my lack of womb!'

Cathy sat even further forward on the chair with her elbows on her knees and studied the floor.

'What? You look as if you've swallowed a lemon whole. Come on – what's bugging you?' Eleanor asked kindly.

'Nothing specific. I just feel a bit pissed off with life in general right now and whenever I come over here I feel quite jealous of you. It makes me wish we could move off that awful estate. I think it would do Paddy good to live somewhere more communal. He's got no interests outside of the hospital. I'd love to move to somewhere like this with a bit of a garden and half-decent neighbours.'

'But this is such a dump! I mean, look out of the window. Why would you want to live somewhere like this? It's a demolition zone. They're going to pull the lot down and we've got to move. The noise has already started.'

'Try living on the Rat-Trap for a day and you wouldn't think this was so bad. Anyway, it's okay for you, you're here by choice, you and your friends, all slumming it for a laugh with the rest of your lives in front of you to go wherever you want.' Cathy pulled herself up. 'I'm sorry, I'm being stupid. It's not your fault and anyway, we can't afford to move unless we move right out to one of those New Towns like Harlow, and change hospitals, but I can't see Paddy ever wanting to leave London. His whole life is at that frigging hospital – the social club, the union, all his equally boring friends, everything that is important to him. I'm way down the list of priorities in his life.'

It was the first time Eleanor had heard Cathy sound bitter about Paddy.

'Oh Cathy, that's not true, he's just a bit sort of . . . I dunno, maybe stuck in his ways?'

'What? Like you told me your father was stuck in his ways? Same as that, eh? Would you go back to that? Being ruled and regulated and not allowed a choice?'

'You know I wouldn't, and that's not fair.'

'Well, life's *not* fair, as you'll discover for yourself twenty-odd years down the line when history comes back to bite you like it has me.'

'Fancy another cuppa in the meantime?' Eleanor asked

ever so meekly, making Cathy laugh. Just as quickly the mood lightened.

'God, I'm being a bitch right now! But there is something I really do want to talk to you about.' Cathy lowered her eyes and her voice at the same time as if she was scared of being overheard. 'Lennie, I wanted to ask you about what you said, about – you know – DIY insemination. I can't stop thinking about it. I wondered if it might just be a possibility.'

'Heavens, I'd almost forgotten about my flash of inspiration.' Eleanor smiled. 'Good idea, huh?'

'I don't know about that, but you opened the door just a chink for me. Oh God, I feel so weak but sometimes I want a baby so much it's a physical pain, it really hurts and it makes me so irrational.' Opening her eyes wide she moved them around to stop herself from crying. 'I suppose it's my age; it's now or never time and I can't face it being never. I guess in a couple of years it will start to get better, but right now my hormones are leading me a merry old dance. All I want is a baby. It's all I think about now, and Paddy can't give me one.' She tried to smile but it didn't quite work and it turned into more of a grimace.

Eleanor sat down on the sofa and put an arm around her shoulder. 'I really don't understand Paddy not wanting to try all the options for you. It's so selfish. Does he know how strongly you feel about it?'

'I don't think he wants to know, although he too is suffering from the lack of a child. He just finds it impossible to talk about it. But I suppose I can kind of understand why he doesn't.' Cathy shrugged. 'He would then have to face the confirmation that it's his sterility that's the problem. He's a middle-aged macho Irishman, it's a lot to ask of him.'

'Well, if you're really interested in my suggestion I'll talk to Marty. I bet he's got loads of friends who would oblige, and I'd ask him to make sure they were okay. You can do the rest. You're a nurse – I'm sure you know better than me how to achieve maximum . . . er . . . you know what!'

'No, no, no, I don't want you to arrange anything.' Cathy jumped up in panic. 'I just want to see if it's a possibility. Then I'll think about it. It seems so immoral, yet I'm desperate. Is it so very wrong to try something like that?'

'Of course it's not, Cathy. It's logical. I'll do what I can to see if it's a poss.'

'Marty won't tell anyone, will he?'

'Nope. He's good at keeping secrets is my Marty, but I won't tell him it's for you anyway,' Eleanor promised.

Cathy looked at Eleanor and grimaced apologetically. 'Lennie, am I allowed to talk to you about Jamie, or is his name still taboo around here?'

Eleanor froze momentarily and Cathy could see her wondering exactly what was going on. 'What about him?' she asked cautiously.

'He came to see me. In fact, he forced his way into my flat and terrified the life out of me. He says he wants to get back with you and he also thinks I'm after your money. Have you been holding out on me about something?'

182

'Oh, he's obsessed with the fact that I may have a few bob. As soon as he got wind of it, he saw me as an insurance policy for his future. Or maybe a means of funding his drug habits – I don't know and really I don't give a fuck about him now, Cathy. It's over and I'm seeing Greg, a real gentleman who doesn't treat me like shit.'

'I just wanted to warn you that Jamie is convinced you are still in love with him and he's not going to give up on you without a fight.'

'Of course I'm not in love with him and Jamie isn't in love with me. He just thinks I have money which I don't, not really. Just a decrepit old house that's nearly falling down and worth bugger all. Everything else went on my father's debts.'

'Tell him that and then he might leave you alone.'

'I did, and he didn't believe me. Anyway, no more now, that's enough about Jamie Kirk. He's another part of my history!' Eleanor took hold of her friend's hand. 'Just stop being a caring nurse for once in your life, Cathy love. I keep telling you – I'm fine, fine, fine!'

After Cathy had gone, Eleanor put her feet up on the sofa and tried not to think about Jamie. Instead she concentrated on Greg who she was going to meet up with again that evening. It would be their fourth date in a month and although she enjoyed his calm company, she had kept him firmly at bay romantically. Jamie was always in the back of her mind; deep down she was still in love with him and probably always would be, but he was bad for her. He was her addiction but she'd already done the cold turkey. Now she had to work hard on maintenance.

So determined was she never to be in a relationship like that again that she was keeping Greg at arm's length physically and her emotions well under wraps. The most they had done was kiss on the doorstep, almost like old-fashioned courting teenagers. Never again, she kept telling herself. The next time she became involved with a man it would be with one who loved her more than she loved him. That way she would be able to keep emotional control.

It suited her also that Gregory Casheron was a workaholic who was busy nurturing his career in the money market and always put work first; he worked six long days a week and often had to fly back and forth to the company offices all over the world. His long hours, combined with Eleanor's often erratic shifts, meant that their relationship was more on the telephone than in person and, for the time being, she was content with that.

'Hello you!'

Eleanor had been so deep in thought she hadn't heard Marty come in. 'Hello you too. How's it going?'

'Great, I'm happy happy.' Marty bounced across the room, a wide grin on his face. 'Someone has been fired at the club and Jon has recommended me. It's lousy pay, probably crap tips but, because the shifts are so long, I'll get heaps of time off to spend with Jon. But it's a start; a step back onto the old work treadmill.'

'Oh Marty, that's great news. When do you start?'

'Next week. I can't wait.' Marty threw himself into a chair. 'I just hope I can do it okay. I haven't worked evenings since you-know-what happened. Hopefully, if Jon's there it'll be okay and I'll cope with it.'

Eleanor jumped up from the sofa and hugged her friend enthusiastically before perching on the arm of the rickety chair. 'It'll be just fine, really, I know you're ready for it. Anyway, while you're in such a good mood, can I ask you a favour? A really big favour?'

'Of course you can, precious. Anything for you. What is it you want?'

'Are you ready for this? It's really bizarre, I don't want you to be shocked or offended . . .'

'How intriguing, Miss Rivington, do go on.'

'Okay. Do you or Jon know someone who would be prepared to donate some of their sperm to a friend of mine? It's someone I work with at the hotel, she's desperate for a baby but her husband can't quite manage to hit the spot, if you know what I mean. He wouldn't know anything about it; it'll appear to be a wonderful accident, and she wouldn't know who it is who's donating so it will all be really anonymous for everyone. Except me.' Eleanor scrunched her shoulders up and grinned like an excited child.

'Okay, Lennie. This time you win. I really am shocked and yes, it's really bizarre. It's a joke, right? You're winding me up.' Laughing hard, Marty threw himself off the chair and rolled dramatically around the floor.

'Actually, Mr Smartarse, I'm deadly serious. She is just so desperate for a baby and, to be fair to her, it was my suggestion, not hers. I think it's such a good idea. A nice healthy bloke just has to you-know-what into a pot and then she'll do the rest. It's worth a hundred quid to the donor and she'll be so happy if it works.'

Eleanor threw the hundred quid in without thinking. It had suddenly occurred to her that money would be a very good incentive, and if necessary she'd pay it herself. Cathy had been good to her and she deserved it.

'A hundred quid? Are you sure this isn't a big set-up? Seems crazy. And supposing it works, will she appear on the doorstep sometime in the future and expect whoever it is to play Daddy?'

'Of course not! If AID is done at the hospital it's all anonymous but she can't have it done like that because her husband won't agree. If by any chance it does work then she'll tell him it's his own little miracle and everyone will be happy.'

'You're absolutely bloody crazy, do you know that?' Marty was still on the floor shaking his head as Eleanor continued laughing happily.

'Of course I'm not crazy. It's called business. You have something she wants, she has the money. It's just buying and selling and you and me are the brokers. Just like flogging your car or whatever. The only thing I ask is that it's someone with sandyish hair who's fit and healthy with no obvious inherent problems to pass on!' She paused.

'Oh – and not you or Jon. That wouldn't be fair to me if it works.'

'Not asking a lot then, considering we're talking about my friends who all have obvious inherent problems! Do I get a finder's fee?'

'Ooh, I don't know about that. Where's your charitable spirit? Why not pretend that Christmas is coming early this year?'

# Chapter Twenty-two

Megan and Venita were sitting opposite each other in the overcrowded café feeling decidedly bored and pondering why they were there.

'What do you reckon this is all about? I mean, it's obviously to do with Lennie – she said so – but what it can be that's got anything to do with Cathy the super-nurse, I don't know.' Venita looked sideways at her friend.

'Me neither.' Megan frowned and folded her arms over her expansive chest. 'I can't imagine what it can be that Lennie mustn't know about. Some sort of surprise party? I dunno, that Cathy is a strange one. I mean, she's getting on a bit, so why is she so friendly with Lennie, who's young enough to be her daughter? I think it's weird.' Pausing, she looked around to check if Cathy was there. 'Still, Lennie likes her so I suppose it's none of our business. We'll find out soon enough: she's already twenty minutes late though, daft bitch.'

'We'll give her till half past and then we'll go . . .'

At that moment the door swung open and Cathy Hart rushed in and looked around.

'Over here, Cathy – we're over here!' Megan shouted across the room and waved wildly.

'Cut it out, will you. We're trying not to be noticed, remember? You jumping around screeching and bouncing your tits is a bit of a giveaway, don't you think?' Venita muttered out of the side of her mouth.

Megan and Venita, as The Saucy Sisters, were hot property and easily recognised if they were together in character, so if they didn't want that recognition they had to dress and act down.

Both were wearing jeans and loose-fitting tops. Venita's hair was pulled back into a stern fifties-style ponytail and Megan had tucked hers up under a plain brown beret. Without the heavy make-up and huge cleavages on show they looked like two teenagers and not in the least recognisable in the small café located up a side street behind the hospital.

Cathy waved back and made her way over to them through the closely packed tables.

'Hello! I'm so sorry I'm late. It's good of you to come, and even better of you to wait. Do you want a refill? Something to eat?' She indicated their empty cups.

'Coffee, please,' Venita said. 'Black, no sugar – for both of us. Diet diet diet, that's all we hear from our manager these days. That bloody word, diet.'

As Cathy moved off to the counter, Megan sniped, 'My dad doesn't think like that. He reckons, we're great just as we are. If he was our manager . . .'

'Not an option, Meg. Sorry, but your dad is an opportunist and he thinks we're his opportunity.' Venita shrugged. 'Not going to happen – we signed a joint agreement and joint it stays until The Saucy Sisters divorce each other.'

A moment or two later, Cathy came back from the counter with a tray. 'Here you are. Hope you don't mind watching me have this enormous cake, though. I'm starved – it's been a long hard shift and I haven't had a break at all since breakfast.'

Megan and Venita exchanged impatient glances. Both were wary of Cathy and her motives so neither of them wanted to be there being friendly with her, but after the cryptic way Cathy had put it on the phone they had felt they had no choice. And of course, they were both naturally curious.

Megan plonked her elbows on the table and put her chin on her hands. 'What exactly is it that you want to talk to us about? We're a bit bewildered – it all sounded so secretive.'

Cathy looked from one to the other. 'Well, obviously it's about Lennie. I'm worried about her and I know you're her best friends. So much has happened to her lately but she pretends everything is okay. She makes out she's as happy as Larry but I don't think she is.'

'Nonsense,' Megan snapped defensively. 'She's strong, she can deal with these things – it's how she is. She's a natural survivor. We were all so impressed by the way she handled her father's suicide and all that other shit that followed.'

'That's right, and I'm not sure I feel happy talking about

her behind her back like this. She'd hate it, I know,' Venita joined in, her tone slightly more conciliatory than Megan's. 'Maybe you just don't know her like we do. She'll be fine if we give her time; she said she's okay and I think we have to believe her.'

Cathy looked from one to the other and shook her head. 'I'm concerned it is all bravado and I *don't* think Lennie is coping very well. She seems to be getting almost high on her grief and she has to let it out eventually. It's like steam in a kettle – if you don't give it an escape it explodes.'

'And?' Megan's expression was defiant. 'What do you suggest we do? Kidnap her and deliver her hand-wrapped to the nearest psychiatrist? Or maybe to you?'

Cathy frowned at Megan's aggressive stance. 'Well, yes, actually. Me. I really am trying to help her but I don't want to offend either of you. I don't agree with you but I accept you know her best; however, if she does blow I really do want you to call me first. I understand her frame of mind and—'

'And we don't?' Megan queried sharply. 'We appreciate your concern, but Lennie will be okay. We know her and we'll look out for her.'

Cathy shrugged. 'Okay. I just thought I'd let you know that if you do get worried yourselves then give me a call and I'll do what I can.' She handed over a slip of paper with a phone number on it. 'I am a nurse, you know. Now I just have to eat this cake. I hope you don't mind, I'm salivating just looking at it.'

'Have you finished for the day now?' Venita asked curiously.

'Oh God, yes. I've been on the ward since seven thirty this morning and I'm done in. That's it for three days, in fact. Three wonderful, wonderful days off. I can go out to the pub and get pissed and then take to my bed the next day with a guilt-free hangover. Heaven!'

The three women made small talk for about five minutes before Megan and Venita made their excuses and left.

'That woman gives me the creeps. I think she reckons she's a bit of an amateur psychiatrist and she's practising on Lennie. All that crap about Lennie not coping . . . she just wants to be a part of our lives because it's more interesting than hers. She's bored with her husband and her marriage.' Megan looked sideways at Venita as they waited on the corner for a taxi to come along.

'I suppose there is something a bit clingy about her, but it doesn't bother me like it does you. Do you think it's because she's a nurse? The sort of authority figure you seem to hate on sight?'

'Possible,' Megan admitted. 'I've had that phobia about all things medical ever since the time when I was a kid and the doctor had to examine me because of the abuse. The butch nurse from hell held me down gleefully as he stuck that light thing up inside me to have a good old look round. Sadistic bastards. They made me feel it was my fault I'd been raped over and over, like I'd happily let him do it.'

'That must have been so scary.' Venita looked at her friend sympathetically. 'I can't even imagine it. Although my family never gave a toss about me, at least none of them ever did anything to me – other than ignore me completely, of course. I might as well have not existed. I was just The Invisible Child!'

Megan smiled wryly. 'Wish I'd been invisible. Isn't it strange how four dysfunctional people, all about the same age, seem to have found each other? I mean, for fuck's sake, there's not a normal one amongst us! You, me, Lennie, Marty. Nutters, the lot of us.' Megan laughed as together they clambered into the taxi.

Venita joined in the laughter. 'And if you add in Jamie and Cathy hanging around . . . well! But then look at you and me now, we're doing fine despite all that shit. Or maybe because of it. If we'd been part of normal families we'd probably be working behind the sweet counter at Woolies or getting fat arses in the typing pool and boasting about our tacky garnet engagement rings.'

'Mmm . . .'

When Megan and Venita had first met and formed their 'Saucy Sisters' alliance, it had been purely because of the physical likeness between them. But as time had gone on they had become friends and had quickly found parallels in their lives.

From as far back as her memory went, Megan had been sexually abused by her mother's most regular on-off boyfriend Rick, whom Megan had always known as Daddy Rick. It had been custom and practice, and for a long time Megan had just accepted it. Rick had told her repeatedly that that was what daddies did, and although she didn't like it she believed him.

It had only ended when he had accidentally broken her leg. The young girl had tried to intervene as Rick had drunkenly battered her mother, and both Megan and her mother had ended up at the bottom of the stairs. The social workers were called in by the hospital, and when Megan was discharged she had been taken straight to a children's home miles away, despite the fact that Daddy Rick had instantly disappeared and she could have safely gone back home.

As Megan herself had often said, it had been from the frying pan straight into the fire. This was the start of several years of shuttling between foster homes and children's homes, some good, some bad, but none that could give Megan the one thing she craved, a normal family life. And then the father she had never known had turned up and, despite all his faults, he offered her that feeling of belonging.

'Venita,' Megan said slowly, 'there was something else, something I've never told anyone . . .'

'Here will be fine,' Venita said to the taxi driver and fumbled in her bag for her purse as the car turned the corner.

Once the car pulled away, she turned back to her friend. 'Sorry, you started to say something.'

'Did I? Oh well, it can't have been important – I've forgotten already.' Megan shrugged. She decided that Uncle

Rick was best left in the past. There really was no need to drag it up and analyse it.

After Megan and Venita had left the cafe, Cathy ordered another coffee and an even larger cake, then moved across to an empty window seat and pulled a newspaper out of her bag. She wasn't intending to read it but she didn't want to get caught up in conversation with Mama Maria or one of her offspring, who she had noticed earlier eyeing Megan and Venita suspiciously.

Cathy loved the homely atmosphere of the spotlessly clean café that, over the years, had become almost an extension of the hospital canteen. It was owned and run by a large Italian family who treated all their regulars as part of that family, which was nice, but it also meant that everyone, especially Mama Maria the family matriarch, wanted to know everyone's business.

That day, Cathy didn't want to be part of Mama's extended family so she opened her newspaper at the crossword, fumbled in her bag for a pen and then feigned interest in the clues.

She felt quite pleased with the way she had handled the meeting. With her professional eye she could see that Eleanor was teetering on the brink of a breakdown. Her whole demeanour pointed to it – the insistence that she was coping fine and the almost manic good humour. Cathy guessed it wouldn't be too long coming and she wanted to be there to try and contain it until she had achieved her aim.

By whatever means, Cathy Hart wanted a baby and she

didn't want to throw her one opportunity away. She was caught on the horns of a moral dilemma. As a nurse she had a duty of care to anyone who was ill, but as a frustrated mother all she wanted was a baby and she didn't care how she got it or who she trod on, on the way. She knew that, under normal circumstances, the person who was Eleanor Rivington would never have come up with the outrageous notion of DIY AID, let alone offer to facilitate it for her. It just wouldn't have occurred to her. It was a crazy idea but it was also the one and only chance that Cathy had left, and the more she thought about it, the more desperate she was to at least give it a try.

But she knew that if Eleanor cracked up too soon and went over the edge, then her best chance would be gone.

For many years Cathy had kept her craving for a baby under control but lately it had become an obsession that was taking over her life. She would find herself walking round the shops for the sole purpose of looking at babies in prams and fantasising about what it would be like to have one of her own to hold and love. She had even taken to wandering from the gynaecology ward where she worked over to the busy maternity block in her lunch-hour so she could stand and gaze at the tiny newborns in their cribs and pretend that she herself was going to be taking one of them home. As she noted the number of babies passing through the ward day in and day out, many of them born to totally unsuitable mothers, she was incensed at the unfairness of it all.

In her darkest moments she even thought about taking one, maybe one that was going home to a life of neglect. One where the mother already had several children. It would be so easy. Just pick it up, walk out and disappear forever. Just her and her baby. Just the two of them. If she chose it carefully, she rationalised in her fantasy, no one would miss it.

So far she had managed to resist the urge to snatch and run.

So far.

As a well-qualified nurse, Cathy knew all about Artificial Insemination by Donor, and she knew how it worked – if, of course, it did. She also knew she could easily do it herself, but timing was crucial and her optimum time for conceiving was two weeks away. She had already booked several days off from work in anticipation.

Cathy had worked hard to convince herself that another fortnight would make no difference to Eleanor and her mental health; all she had to do was sit tight and hope that it all went to plan. She knew she had to keep a close eye on the girl nonetheless, which was why she'd alerted Megan and Venita just enough so they would call Cathy and she would be the first medical professional to see her; then once the insemination was done it would no longer matter whether Eleanor was compos mentis or not.

As she left the café intending to head home, she saw a bus pull up that was going in the opposite direction. On impulse she jumped on it and headed towards the Regency Hotel where Eleanor worked.

Squaring her shoulders she walked straight in through the revolving doors and cautiously looked around the dingy interior. Her eyes settled on the reception desk where, to her relief, she spied Eleanor standing on the guest side deep in animated conversation with a young couple holding a map.

Cathy felt uncomfortable and out of place in the cavernous lobby of the hotel. Ever since she had met him, Paddy had continuously banged on about his 'them and us' idealism. 'Not our sort of people,' he would say. 'We're not like them.' He said it about everyone who wasn't what he called '*real* working class' and that included Eleanor and her friends. He called them all snobs without even knowing that much about them.

The only time he had met Eleanor, she had made the mistake of mentioning that she had gone to a private school. Paddy had gone on and on for hours about Cathy getting above herself and betraying their working-class roots by consorting with a different class. It was his favourite soapbox stance on his favourite topic, and could be very wearing. Cathy sometimes wondered whether their lack of children was making her husband embittered; he did seem to be a lot more angry about everything these days. She sighed inwardly.

Just then, she managed to catch Eleanor's eye and the girl appeared in front of her with a professional smile on her face. 'Can I help you?' she asked briskly, before leading Cathy by the elbow away out of earshot. Then: 'Is something wrong?'

'I'm sorry to bother you at work,' Cathy said hurriedly. 'I just wanted to say that if you can find someone who can do the business in two weeks' time then I'm up for it. I've decided I want to give it a go, but I don't want anyone to know.'

'Oh, that's great.' Eleanor's eyes glistened with excitement. 'I'll get going my end and see what I can do. Oh, this is such good fun,' she squealed quietly, 'but now I have to get back – the new manager is one nasty bastard. I hate him and he hates me so he's always watching me and waiting for me to slip up. That man deserves a carving knife in his shoulder blades, fat, slimy, sexist pig.'

Cathy smiled at Eleanor's muttered vehemence. 'I don't want to get you in trouble so I'll be off,' she said. 'I just knew I couldn't ring you tonight when Paddy's around. Tell me when you know something, won't you? Two weeks today exactly is when I'll need the you-know-what.'

Cathy turned on her heel then and scuttled out with her head down, hoping no one would notice the wide crazy smile that she could feel spreading across her face.

# Chapter Twenty-three

Eleanor was flying on an emotional high just at the thought of being able to help Cathy, whom she considered her friend and saviour. Cathy and her fertility problem had become her focus, a complete distraction from everything else that had happened in her life.

Now the day they had been planning for two weeks was about to arrive and it was her role to co-ordinate the actual event and make sure Marty's friend – who she was sure was Jon's workmate – and Cathy didn't find out about each other. *Anonymous* was the key word Eleanor kept repeating, mantra-like. It all had to be *anonymous*.

The magic ingredient would go from the Donor to Marty, Marty to Eleanor, Eleanor to the Recipient. And it had to happen in the shortest possible time. For Eleanor it was all so thrilling, the plotting and planning; she had been awake all night thinking excitedly about the 'Event' as she had taken to calling it, that was to take place that very afternoon at three o'clock in a borrowed room in the nurses' accommodation at the hospital.

The planning gave her something to think about and she desperately needed that distraction from the demons that tormented her wired brain in the dark of the night.

During the day she could focus on her job, and of course on Cathy's Event, but as soon as she fell asleep, her subconscious would go into overdrive. Eleanor couldn't remember the last time she had had a night of unbroken sleep. It was always the same routine: after forcing herself to stay awake as long as possible she would eventually fall asleep and that would be when *they* would come to visit.

First her mother, dressed as she was the last time Eleanor saw her, in a mid–calf-length cotton floral frock with a flared skirt and cap sleeves, would appear at the end of her bed clutching a tiny baby. *'Look, Eleanor, look what Mummy's got here. It's your baby daughter. Isn't she lovely? Mummy's going to look after her for you; just until you can come and look after her yourself.'*

As her mother spoke, she always smiled happily and rocked the bundle in her arms back and forth, and a feeling of calm would sweep over the sleeping Eleanor at the realisation that her mother was happy and that her own little lost baby was safe. The baby was always a girl and always wrapped in a big shawl, so big and fluffy that Eleanor could never quite see the baby's features, no matter how hard she tried. But she knew it was her baby.

Then, just as she relaxed and was enjoying being with them

both, her father would appear beside them waving a shotgun and screaming about sluts, whores and bastard children. In her nightmare he was about seven feet tall, and as he shouted at them, his face would contort into the devil's likeness.

'*Kill the bastard child and whore. Kill them. Kill. Kill. Kill.*' Then he would slowly raise the shotgun and take aim at his wife and the baby.

Eleanor would try to reach them before he could fire, to protect them, but her legs were always leaden and she could never move fast enough. Her mother would turn sideways to try to shield the baby and then, just as Harold Rivington was about to pull the trigger, Eleanor would wake up palpitating and unable to breathe because of the sickly-sweet smell of magnolia that invaded her nostrils.

In her confusion, it never occurred to the girl that it was her poor, overwrought mind playing tricks; she truly believed that her mother brought her lost baby to see her every night. She wanted to see her mother and her baby but not *him*, so she would then have to force herself to stay awake for the rest of the night.

In the middle of those long lonely nights when she was too scared to go back to sleep, she deliberately blocked out all thoughts of her parents; she trained herself to think of other things. She would often think of Greg and their growing relationship that seemed to be going from strength to strength. It didn't have the fire and passion of her mad affair with Jamie, and Greg certainly didn't make her heart flip or excite her in the same way, but he was gentle and well mannered and treated her like a lady – the very opposite of Jamie, who had used her and caused her such heartache.

Gregory Casheron. She would roll the name around out loud and then she would add the next one. Eleanor Casheron. Greg and Eleanor. Mr and Mrs Casheron.

The second Mrs Casheron.

It sounded good to her. Not fantastic, not exactly the love of her life, but good enough.

When Greg had told her he had an ex-wife and a teenage son in the States, she had been taken aback, but when she had thought about it, she realised she had been naïve to expect a man of his age not to have some sort of past. And of course she had her own secrets.

Eleanor was aware that the time had come to tell Greg everything. She knew she would be able to tell him about her parents because it was an okay thing to confide; she knew he would be sympathetic because he was certainly that kind of person, but being barren was a different matter altogether. She still wasn't sure what, if anything, to say about that. After all, she kept telling herself when she thought about it, lots of women just don't conceive.

Like Cathy Hart.


The day of the Event finally dawned. For once, Eleanor had had no trouble staying awake, and she hadn't given a thought to Greg or Jamie. Her focus was totally on Cathy.

She jumped out of bed and banged furiously on Marty's bedroom door. 'Wakey wakey, Marty! Today's the day and I want to make sure everything goes to plan. Come on, up. I want to discuss it with you.'

'Lennie!' he shouted back through the closed door. 'It's six o'clock in the fucking morning! Just how long do you think this is going to take?'

'I want it all to be perfect, so up you get and I'll cook you breakfast just this once, as a thank you for being so kind and going along with this. It means so much to me.'

'The only thank you I want is my finder's fee of hard cash. I hope your mate coughs up, I'm skint,' he muttered sulkily from the depths of his room. But still he did as he was told and went downstairs to where Lennie was juggling frying pans and singing out loud and out of tune.

'Come on, Lennie, I can't listen to this racket, not at this time of day. You have to calm yourself down a bit, you know, you've been flying without drugs for weeks now.' He ran his fingers through his long blond hair instead of a comb and joked, 'Well, I *hope* it's without drugs. Maybe you could bottle whatever it is and I could flog it down the club. We'd soon be rich.'

'I'm just so happy,' she explained. 'I feel I'm doing some-thing really good for someone else – and so are you. We're being completely selfless and charitable, and I feel over the moon about it.' She laughed madly. 'So I sing. And you should sing as well – we should sing together.'

'Well, I'm not feeling that charitable and I don't want to sing – and I certainly don't want to listen to you singing off-key.'

'Oh, you are such a miserable old man. An old-man-before-your-time old man.' Lennie dished up the breakfast with a theatrical flourish of slices and serving spoons.

'Lennie, you know I don't eat bacon.' Marty looked at her curiously as he took the plate. 'Please don't take this the wrong way, Len, but don't you think you're getting too involved in this baby-making project? I'm worried about you: you should step back and see it for what it is, especially as the chances of it working are practically nil.'

'Is this negativity and concern just because I gave you bacon?' She looked back at him and they locked eyes. 'Bacon is good for you, you need it.'

Marty looked away first. 'No, it's not because you gave me bacon, it's because you're going over the top with all this. Anyway, what time's the handover again? What time does my mate have to perform his charitable masturbation?'

'There's no need to put it quite so crudely, Mr Cornish!' She banged him firmly over the knuckles with a large serving spoon. 'As near to two forty-five as possible. You give me the container and I take a cab to the hos— to where I have to go. Three o'clock is the handover time. Now, coffee? Or tea? Come on, Mart, take advantage of this golden opportunity to be waited on. It won't come around again too soon!' Again she laughed then reached over to the radio and turned it up full blast before dancing around the kitchen and waving her arms in the air to the rhythm.

Just as quickly she stopped and took his face in both hands. 'Listen to me, Marty, I want you to take this seriously.

It's important to me.' She moved her face closer to his to emphasise her words. 'I'm going out soon, I have things to do this morning and I won't be back – and that way, I won't see your friend. I really don't want to know who it is so I'll meet you on the corner at around ten to three. I'll already have the taxi and then I can rush straight off. Okay?'

'For the three-hundredth time, yes okay, I understand your instructions. Though it may take a bit longer; you may have to wait if his human body parts don't obey instantly.'

'That's okay, so long as you get it to me immediately. This is so important, Marty, nothing must go wrong.' The expression on her face was deadly serious, and as she reached down and grabbed his arm hard, he could feel her finger-nails digging deep into his flesh. 'Nothing can go wrong, do you understand?'

Marty gently peeled her hand off him. 'It's okay, Lennie, we'll get this done and then perhaps you and I need to go somewhere and relax, maybe take a holiday. We both need it. And I want you to promise me you won't get involved in something like this again, eh?'

Eleanor looked at him with surprise. She couldn't understand why he was always being so intense recently whenever he spoke to her; after all, they were just having some fun.

Once the countdown started, everything went like clock-work, and after Eleanor had delivered the plastic pot wrapped in a brown paper bag to a nervously excited Cathy she went straight home and, exhausted, flopped out on the sofa.

However, as soon as her body relaxed, the adrenaline rush seeped away and as her mood sank, she could see nothing in her future except for the nightmares and a relationship with someone she didn't really love. The artificial high was replaced by a depression so profound that, without really knowing what she was doing, she phoned the pub round the corner and asked if Jamie was there.

Within half an hour they were back in bed together.

# Chapter Twenty-four

Eleanor Rivington's descent into complete meltdown was alarmingly spectacular, because although the clues were there, no one, apart from Cathy, realised just how detached from reality the girl had become. Even Marty didn't understand just how bad things were. Eleanor had presented herself as strong and capable for so long, everyone believed that she could get over everything that had been thrown at her. On the surface, she appeared to function normally, but everything she did at the hotel was on auto-pilot, and outside of work she survived by isolating herself as much as possible in her own world that revolved around her mother and her lost baby.

And Jamie Kirk.

The final eviction notice had been served on the house-mates; this had thrown the others into a panic and they were all concerned with finding alternatives, but Eleanor would just smile beatifically when they asked her what she was going to do.

'I'll be all right, I'm going home, I'll be fine,' she'd say. And they would believe she meant to the house in Hampstead and bitch about her selfishness in not inviting them all along to live there as well.

But actually, the group were already starting to separate emotionally. Marty was absorbed in his relationship with Jon and, thanks to Megan's father, Pete, who had finally wheedled his way in as their manager, Megan and Venita were getting sucked into the seedier side of glamour modelling where the big money was.

After the 'Event', Cathy had swiftly withdrawn into herself as she prayed constantly for success and forgot about her concerns for Eleanor.

Without Cathy's problem to focus her mind on, and with Greg away on an extended business trip to Canada, Eleanor was left with nothing but the twilight world of the dreams and nightmares that haunted her constantly day and night, and Jamie – who was more than happy to take advantage of the situation without asking any questions about her very strange personality change.

It was during this decline into confusion that Eleanor found herself being pulled towards religion. It had started when, in pure desperation, she prayed one evening for the dreaded nightmare not to come. She wanted so much to sleep and switch off her hyperactive brain that she put her hands together and prayed as she used to when she was a child. She prayed over and over again for her mother and her baby to visit but not her father, who scared her so much.

And one night it happened.

She had the dream without her father spoiling it, and it

was so soothing that when she awoke she squeezed her eyes tightly shut again and prayed for it to come back. She then discovered that if she tried really hard and focused her thoughts, it was possible to conjure them up anytime. She could even have conversations with her mother who always stood in the same pose with the baby swaddled in her arms.

Just like the statue in the church.

Just like Madonna and child.

She would creep into the local Catholic church as often as possible and just gaze at the statue, willing it alive. Willing her mother and baby alive again and back with her.

It was during one of these vigils that she suddenly had an irresistible urge to see the sea. She could hear her mother directing her down to the coast, to the same place where they had all gone for a holiday when Eleanor was young.

As soon as the idea entered her head it became her next obsession and she could think of nothing else. She had to go to Eastbourne.

She could remember a little about the town, something to do with the long-ago holiday, although in the beginning she wasn't clear what it was. However, one Sunday morning as she sat quietly on the wooden pew and let the regular service wash over her, she looked up at her mother holding her baby and remembered.

Instantly she knew exactly where she had to go and why.

Without telling anyone what she was doing or where she was going, she caught a train down to the south coast.

★　　★　　★

'Anyone know where Lennie is?' Megan asked. 'I thought she was in her room but when I went to say hello it was empty but so untidy, clothes spread everywhere, and that's not like her.' She glanced at the two others lounging around the sitting room in front of the television. 'Any ideas, anyone?'

'Nope,' Marty replied. 'I've not really seen much of her, lately. I was a bit worried about her a while back, but she says she's fine and I've been so involved with Jon . . .' Marty looked from Megan to Venita and grinned but the girls didn't react.

'That Cathy, the nurse that Eleanor is all pally with, told us she thought Lennie was going a bit loopy but we told her to take her nose out of our business,' Venita said.

'I didn't know that – you never told me.' Marty looked puzzled. 'I know Lennie was a bit wound up about things, but whatever gave her that idea?'

'Dunno.' Venita shrugged dismissively. 'Interfering cow reckoned Lennie's not normal because she's not weeping and wailing and throwing things. We told her that that's how Lennie is and she left it at that. I mean, we're the ones who know her.' She looked at Megan for back-up.

'Yeah, that's right. Lennie deals with things in her own way. She doesn't make a fuss, she just copes. She's stronger than all of us put together. She's probably at work – none of us were around this morning.'

'Or last night for that matter,' Marty grinned and they all laughed.

As they were sitting chatting, the phone rang and Marty went off to answer it.

'She won't be far away anyway,' Venita yawned. 'It's the funeral, day after tomorrow, isn't it? For her mother? They've finally released the body now the inquest is over.'

'God, yes, I'd forgotten – but I don't think she's had much to do with the arrangements; and the reception thing afterwards is going to be at that solicitor's house. All she has to do is turn up this time. Are we all going with her?'

Both girls were sitting on the floor leaning against the sofa and painting their toe nails shocking pink. Part of being The Saucy Sisters was ensuring that the minor details matched, as well as the more obvious hair and clothes.

'Dunno. I think it's all so spooky, a funeral for a load of old bones; the body's already been buried for ten years, there can't be much of it left.' Venita shivered dramatically. 'I don't want to go but I suppose we have to show poor Lennie that we care.'

'I don't want to go either but the poor woman's entitled to a proper funeral as opposed to being dumped under a fucking magnolia tree by a psychopathic old man!'

Marty came back into the room scratching his head and looking worried.

'What's up? Been dumped again?' Megan looked at Venita and grinned.

'Don't take the piss. That was the hotel. Lennie's not turned up for work two days running and they asked me what's going on. I didn't know what to say. I said I'd ring back.'

'Well, where can she be then? She's certainly not here

212

and I know for a fact that super-boring Gregory Casherwhatshisname is away at the mo 'cos she told me,' Megan said.

'Maybe we'd better ring and ask Cathy the nurse then,' Venita suggested. 'She might know – they've been sort of close since Lennie was in hospital. If she's not on duty I haven't got her home address. I just know she lives on that crap council estate near the hospital.'

Marty spun round. 'I'll go to the hospital and see her – I'm not working today. Maybe you girls could have a check through Lennie's room and see if there's any hints?'

Venita and Megan went up to Eleanor's room together and then, a short while later, came down again.

'You're not going to like this, Marty.' The two girls grimaced at each other.

'Not going to like what? Come on, tell me.'

'Looks like she's been seeing Jamie again,' Megan said. 'There's an overflowing ashtray under the bed with the remains of several joints, and half a bottle of whisky. And his filthy rucksack is also under there with some clothes and stuff in it.'

'How do you know that it's his?'

'Firstly because I recognise it, secondly because it's got his fucking name on the label and thirdly because it smells just as shitty as he does. She's back with him, I bet you.'

'I'll kill him.' Marty threw his arms up in the air.

'Oh, give the macho act a rest, Marty. You're not her keeper. Look – if you go and see Cathy, we'll go and find out where Jamie might be. Okay?'

'I suppose so.'

'And remember, we're just checking to see that she's all right. I don't want you trying to frogmarch her home like a teenage runaway!'

Marty took a taxi to the hospital and went straight to the ward where he knew Cathy worked. With a charming smile he gave his name and asked for her in a voice that inferred he had a right to be there, then he crossed his arms and leaned against the wall by the desk. As he looked around, he thought he spotted Cathy further down the corridor but she didn't head towards him; instead she disappeared through a door with the nurse he'd asked, so he started to walk along the corridor towards them.

'Tell him I'm not on duty.' He could just about make out a whispering voice. 'Tell him I'm away on holiday. Please – I don't want to see him.'

It took a few seconds for Marty to realise that the whispering was coming from Cathy and that she was talking about him.

Marty threw the door open and came face to face with a visibly shocked Cathy and her colleague in the linen room.

'Look, Cathy, I won't disturb you for long,' he said in his most polite voice. 'I just needed a quick word with you about an ex-patient of yours, Eleanor Rivington. As you may recall, I share a flat with her and I'm becoming very concerned about her mental state at the moment.'

The other nurse looked from one to the other, blinking rapidly.

'Can you give us a minute?' Cathy had quickly calmed down; she smiled at her bewildered colleague. 'It's okay, I can deal with this. I remember Miss Rivington well, and I too am concerned about her wellbeing. Perhaps I can help Mr Cornish.

'I'm sorry,' she said to Marty once they were alone in the middle of the linen room that was stacked on three sides with bedding and towels. 'I didn't want to get into trouble for having someone come onto the ward to see me. It's strictly forbidden.'

Marty knew she was lying, but he didn't have the time or the energy to find out why. Without beating about the bush, he said: 'Lennie is missing and we wondered if she was with you or whether you've seen her.'

'Not for a couple of weeks at least. I did tell the other two that I thought Eleanor wasn't dealing with things as well as they thought she was, but they told me to mind my own business.' Cathy was disturbed and not a little guilty at hearing the news. 'If I do hear from her, I'll get her to contact you immediately, I promise. Maybe she's gone off with Jamie?' The nurse sighed. 'Look – good luck. I hope she's okay, poor girl. Now I really do have to get back to work. Goodbye, Marty.'

Despite feeling faint with relief, Cathy stood and watched warily as Marty walked away. The moment she had seen him standing in the ward corridor she had been convinced that he had discovered she was the recipient of the donor sperm and he was about to blackmail her, or, even worse, tell everyone what she had done.

The more she thought about it the more mortified she felt. She couldn't believe she had sunk so low as to inseminate herself with sperm from someone whom she knew nothing about.

As Marty disappeared through the swing doors, Cathy forced herself to walk into the Ward Sister's office. 'Sister, I'm sorry but I feel really unwell. I may be starting the flu. I'm going to have to go home . . .'

Cathy managed to hold it together until she reached her flat and then, as she closed the front door, she slid to the floor and dissolved into huge gulping sobs of shame. Shame at the realisation of what she had done. She couldn't see how her marriage could survive either her betrayal or her guilt and she didn't have a clue what to do next.

# Chapter Twenty-five

Eleanor had been walking around the seaside town trying to get her bearings, but it was proving difficult. She found she couldn't even recall how she had got there – although she knew very well why she was there.

But before she could do what she had come to do, there were things she had to deal with first, rituals to perform, and it was unsettling her that she couldn't get the routine correct. It was all so important to her but she couldn't even find the hotel where the family had stayed the last summer before her mother had disappeared from her life.

The hotel where the three of them had pretended to be a normal happy family.

Eventually, Eleanor found a reasonable-looking hotel and decided it would have to do. This late in the autumn, there were plenty of vacancies. She asked for a room with a view of the sea.

The first night in Eastbourne, as soon as she had checked in, she'd run straight up to her room and stayed there, spending the night hours sitting in a small armchair by the window gazing out over the dark sea that stretched into infinity.

Mesmerised, she watched the red and white lights flickering in the distance that she guessed were small boats, possibly local fishing smacks; for hours she stared at them and wondered what it would be like to be out there in the dark distance looking back at the hotel.

The way her mother was out there looking at her all through the night.

When she really focused and didn't blink, Eleanor could see her mother away in the distance near the fishing boats, smiling and holding her baby. Even though she didn't come in too close, just knowing she was there made everything feel okay.

But the next day, as Eleanor wandered up and down the promenade, she became increasingly frustrated at not being able to recognise her surroundings the way she had expected to. A small voice of reason eventually permeated into her confused brain and told her to go back and start over again at the beginning of the promenade. As she purposefully retraced her steps her stomach rumbled loudly with hunger so she stopped and went into a small sea-front café that was decorated outside with buckets and spades and fake fishing nets. Ordering a pot of tea and some buttered toast she managed to smile and look as if all was right with her world.

'Not seen you in here before, lovely,' the middle-aged woman behind the whirring candyfloss machine stated factually without too much interest as Eleanor waited at the counter for her order.

'No, I'm visiting my mother,' Eleanor responded politely but without making eye-contact.

'Does she live here?' The tone was still flat but at least it was a response.

'No, but she's here now. She's looking after my baby at the moment.'

'That's nice.' The big stainless-steel water drum hissed away and puffed out steam as the woman filled the small pot. 'Good of your mum to babysit and give you a break.'

'Yes, I know. She's been looking after her really well for me. I'm going to meet them later. My mother loves it here by the sea. So does my baby.'

'Very popular holiday town this, even at this time of year. Lots of visitors when the weather's co-operating.'

'I'm looking forward to us all meeting up again very soon. I can't wait, in fact.' Eleanor took her tray and headed over to the vacant windowseat where she could watch the sea and think about where she was eventually going to go. To meet her mother, to see her precious but unfamiliar baby up close, and for them all to be together for ever.

She couldn't wait for dusk to come so she decided to go there early and wait for them. She'd been there before, a long time ago, for a picnic with her mother and father, but something had happened while they were there and she had been hurried back to the car and told not to look.

But she had – and now she remembered.

Before she left her room she carefully gathered the few belongings she had taken with her and put them in a carrier bag and made the bed. Leaving the bag on the bed she wrote a note and left it alongside.

*I've gone to meet my mother and my baby. Here is the money for the rest of my bill. Please forward my belongings to Marty Cornish at the address below and tell him where I am. Ask him not to be sad because I'm so very happy right now. I can't wait for us all to be together.*

*Tell my friends I love them but I have to go.*

Eleanor went down into the lobby and asked for a taxi.

'Beachy Head, please,' she murmured as she climbed in. 'The beauty spot.'

'Not going to jump, are you, sweetheart?' the young man asked her with a wide grin. 'I hope not, the weather's too good and I need the fare off you. It's an expensive trip, you know.'

'I know. I'm going to meet my mother. She has my baby with her. I'm a bit early, but she told me to meet her up there.'

'Phew, that's a relief!' He grinned at her again, this time in the rearview mirror. 'But seriously, it's nice up there this time of year. You been there before?'

'A long time ago, with my parents. We went for a picnic but I think someone drove over the edge and then I was taken home.'

'Happens a lot up there – famous for it, is Beachy Head. Wouldn't fancy it myself. Bit too messy for my liking but

I suppose if I jumped, I wouldn't know anything about it, would I?'

As he chattered away, Eleanor looked out of the car window and could feel her excitement levels rising again as the car sped through the Sussex countryside towards her final destination.

Although they didn't really want him to, Marty had decided to go with the girls to look for Jamie. He didn't have a clue where Jamie was living, but the girls had found out that he occasionally worked at a pub in Earls Court, so together they wandered in there to see what they could find out. The bar was full to overflowing but they couldn't see him.

'Is Jamie Kirk around?' Megan asked the pretty barmaid with an open smile.

'Nope. He's been barred. He was spending too much time with his girlfriend and then he threw a huge wobbly when he got a bollocking so the boss just sacked him. He's a bit of a loon, is Jamie, when he's angry.'

'Girlfriend? Jamie? What's her name?' Megan kept the smile on her face and in her voice.

'Lennie, I think. She'd phone him here and he'd just walk straight out like a puppy every time. He just couldn't resist her. She's a strange one. Funny look in her eye.'

'When was he last here?'

'About a week ago, when he got fired. But he was also boasting how he and the girlfriend were going down to the South of France or somewhere on holiday. I didn't take too much notice, it was probably all talk.' She glanced around nervously. 'Look, I'm sorry but I've got to work, we're so busy and I don't want the sack as well.'

'Did he say when they were going away?'

'No. He just said they were. He did boast about it a bit but as I said, he could have been lying. Jamie does lie a lot. Now really, that's it.' She turned away and started serving again, leaving Marty cut off and fuming.

'Why didn't I see this coming? I should have known a little turd like Jamie wouldn't give up.'

'Well, if Lennie and Jamie are off in St Tropez or wherever, then it's really up to them. Sorry, Marty, but we'll just have to let it go. Deep down, our Lennie is a sensible girl.'

'Yes, but what if something has happened to her?' Marty frowned. 'We have to do something. I can't believe she'd just go off and not tell us.'

'She would if she was with Jamie.' Megan shook her head. 'I think we should just leave it for a few days and wait for Lennie to get in touch with us. And she will – I know she will. She won't leave you wondering for long, Marty. I promise, she loves you as if you were her own brother.'

He sighed. 'I suppose even if she is with that no-mark Jamie she'll be reasonably safe. Even in the South of fucking France.'

# Chapter Twenty-six

Johnny Quentin hadn't been driving a taxi for very long so he hadn't had time to get as cynical about his passengers as most of his fellow drivers were. Being naturally sociable he really loved his job and enjoyed meeting and chatting with the different people he ferried around the town; mostly they were his regulars but during the holiday season there were also the visitors who were entertained by his humorous guided tours of wherever they were going.

His extrovert personality, a necessity for his other job as a stand-up comedian working the local bars and clubs, made him a real favourite with nearly everyone, although experience had gradually taught him that sometimes he had to maintain a tactful silence. He had occasionally been told to shut up by irate businessmen and loved-up couples with eyes only for each other.

The young woman in the back of his taxi en route to Beachy Head was different from his usual fares. She didn't fit into any of the categories that he was used to and he felt vaguely uneasy, although there was nothing in particular he could put his finger on. Her clothes were modern but well made, her hair was shiny and well kept and she gave off a hint of class with her beatific smile as he pointed out all the landmarks and scenery en route. Throughout it all she was scarily serene, and her answers to his questions were very polite but vague. By the time they reached their destination Johnny Quentin knew no more about his passenger than he did five minutes into the journey.

'Right, where do you want me to drop you off?' he asked cheerily as they turned off the main road after the scenic drive through the Sussex countryside. 'And don't dare say over the edge. I really don't like heights and I couldn't possibly oblige because I'd wreck the car and get in bother at the office!'

'Anywhere here will do.' Again in the mirror he could see the enigmatic smile. 'I want to have a walk around before I go to meet my mother.'

'Where are you meeting her? Didn't you say she has your baby with her?' he asked as casually as he could, still unsure of her. Something wasn't right, he could sense it and it bothered him.

'Over there.' She waved her arm in a general direction. 'But not yet, it's too early.'

'What time will she be here then? Not too long, I hope, you'll catch a chill.'

'Later.' Clumsily, she fumbled in her purse, pulled out a handful of random notes and coins and handed them to him without counting. 'I think that's enough.'

'Come on now, that's far too much. Blimey, I'd have driven you to Blackpool and back for that.'

'No, take it. You've been so kind bringing me up here and keeping me company on the way.'

'It's my job; you were my fare. I really can't take all this dosh, my darling.' But even as he was objecting to the wad of notes in his hand the woman was already walking away dreamily with her head down and her hands pushed deep into her jeans' pockets.

His discomfort continued to grow and instead of turning his cab around and heading straight back to his base as he would normally have done, he parked up and continued to watch her warily from a distance. As he studied her, Johnny thought to himself that she didn't *look* like a jumper – she certainly wasn't twitchy or tearful and she wasn't behaving manically – but then again, he knew that one could never tell by appearances. How did someone suicidal really look? How would *he* react if it was him thinking about committing suicide? He mused over the situation curiously as he watched her walk further away from the car.

With his shift almost over, something made him decide to continue watching her for just a little longer. Just until her mother arrived, he thought, hoping against hope that his instincts were wrong.

For the next half-hour or so he wandered around aimlessly and kept looking at his watch, promising himself that he would stay another ten minutes, then another ten minutes;

but as each ten minutes passed he found he couldn't leave. His conscience simply wouldn't let him.

Suddenly, everything changed and he knew without a doubt that she was planning something when she started pacing back and forth, talking to herself and looking out towards the dusky horizon. Each line of pacing took her nearer to the cliff top and Johnny Quentin knew he had to call someone to help. Running back to his cab, he snatched up his radio.

'Call 999 and tell them to send someone to Beachy Head – *now*,' he panted. 'I've got a jumper here.'

Eleanor was completely oblivious to the taxi driver following her and watching her every move. The moment she had walked away from the car she had forgotten him completely. Her focus was the clifftop where she knew her mother and her baby would be waiting for her. All she had to do was wait until the right time and then it would be just a few short steps over the edge and her mother would sweep her up and she would be with them for ever. She knew it. Her mother had told her. She smiled as she anticipated being wrapped in her mother's arms again and then seeing her baby's face for the first time.

She stopped pacing and looked out towards the horizon. Dusk was falling so she screwed up her eyes and concentrated hard. When she looked again, she saw them outlined in the distance. Rosetta was holding the baby in one arm and beckoning to Eleanor with the other.

Eleanor laughed with joy and called out to them. She had known that her mother would come for her.

'Will you catch me, Mummy?' she shouted out across the cool sea-breeze. 'I don't want to fall. Will you catch me?'

Her mother continued to smile and beckon to her from afar, a shadowy figure floating high above the sea. Eleanor looked straight ahead; just another couple of paces and she could step off and be with them both for ever. Her mother and her baby.

Another step . . . and she felt herself falling but it wasn't over the top, it was onto the ground with someone holding her tightly around the waist.

'What are you doing?' she screamed and fought desperately against her restrainer. 'Mummy's waiting for me, I've got to go with her. I want my baby, I want my baby, I want my baby . . .'

The more she fought, the tighter the arms around her became until she had no energy left. Looking up, she could see her mother still there, still beckoning, but she was going backwards, getting smaller and fainter the further she floated back.

Eleanor looked at the owner of the arms and saw that it was her father stopping her from going; his eyebrows were going up and down and his face was purple as he held her tight. He was also laughing madly because he had succeeded in stopping her from going to them.

'You bastard!' she screamed at the top of her voice. 'I

hate you, Daddy. I want to be with Mummy, why are you stopping me? Please, Daddy, let me go! I want my baby . . . Daddy, I want my baby so much. Please let me go to her. *Please*.'

At that moment she relaxed completely in the encircling arms and started howling loudly like a dog caught in a gin trap.

# Chapter Twenty-seven

'I can't thank you enough, mate. You have no idea how much I owe you.'

Unsure how to react, Johnny Quentin smiled sheepishly as, with tears in his eyes, an emotional Marty clamped the man's shoulders tightly in his hands.

'It's okay really, I told you,' he said. 'I was just doing what anyone else would have done. I couldn't drive off and leave her, could I?'

'There's plenty who would have. Without you she'd have gone over the top and it doesn't bear thinking about. I wonder what sent her there, of all places? Did she tell you?'

'She said she was going to meet her mother and that her mother was looking after her baby. She told me she was meeting them at Beachy Head – she knew all about the area.' He looked at Marty questioningly. 'Have you heard of Beachy Head? It's a notorious suicide spot – they come from all over to jump or drive off the edge. I can think of nothing worse, myself.'

'Not really heard of it, but then I don't know this area at all, I'm from Liverpool. God, this is such a mess and I'm a lousy friend.' Marty sighed and put his head in his hands. 'I should have been more aware. We all just kept saying "Lennie's strong, Lennie can handle it, Lennie'll be okay" and so on and so on. We should have realised that no one is that strong. Looking back over it, all I can see is that no one could have gone through everything she's been through and handled it.'

The two young men were sitting opposite each other in the hospital canteen, each of them feeling stunned by the same situation but both in different ways. Johnny Quentin by being an integral part of the drama and feeling proud of himself for saving her; Marty by not being part of it and feeling ashamed of himself for not realising how much pain his friend was really in.

It was two days since Johnny had rugby-tackled Eleanor to the ground and stopped her from jumping to certain death at the infamous suicide spot. After he had forcefully brought her down he had held her tightly as she fought against him, hugged her close when she finally broke down, and comforted her as best he could as he waited for the response to the taxi firm's 999 call. Then, unable to detach himself from the situation, he had followed the ambulance to the local hospital and stayed there.

When Marty had received the call from the hospital asking if he was Martin Cornish and whether he knew Eleanor Rivington, he had naturally been concerned, but once he had got there and discovered the whole truth, a tidal wave of guilt devastated him. Especially when he had been allowed to see her briefly.

Semi-conscious because of the strong sedative, Eleanor could barely move let alone speak. Marty took her hand and spoke to her, but although her eyelids flickered open there was no recognition. She hadn't gone over the edge physically but mentally she was in another world.

Because he felt so personally involved, Johnny Quentin had left a contact number for anyone who came to see her to let him know how she was doing, and a grateful Marty had called him straight after he had seen Eleanor and spoken with the doctors. They had arranged to meet at the hospital canteen.

'Fortunately she doesn't really know what's happening,' Marty said. 'She's spaced out and confused by where she is. She's had a complete breakdown, apparently, so they're going to transfer her to a mental hospital for treatment as soon as there's a bed; I've asked them to send her back to London where her friends are, but I don't know if they will.'

'I suppose they've got to find a specialist hospital that can take her.' Johnny sighed and his forehead furrowed as he thought about it. 'Best she goes to the right place, I guess. You know, it was all so surreal – it seemed to happen so quickly but it was also in slow motion, if you can understand what I mean. I'm still in shock myself over it. She was so normal in one way and yet not in another. I don't even know what it was that made me think she was planning to go over the edge, just something a bit off kilter with the way she was behaving . . .'

'All I can say is, thank God something warned you.'

'Well, I would certainly never have forgiven myself if I had just left her there and she had gone over, that's for sure. Are you and she a couple?' Johnny asked curiously.

For the first time Marty's face brightened and he smiled. 'No, we're just friends and housemates. We've been friends for a while, we just sort of clicked right away. A couple of matching lost souls, me and Lennie – we've both had too much shit in our lives. We share a house in London with two other girls who are also a bit loony.'

'What about the baby she was talking about? And her mother?'

'Ah, long story, mate. Trouble is, Lennie is a good actress and I honestly never ever knew, just how bad she was feeling. I did ask her occasionally, if she was really okay, whether she was overdoing things, but she would always accuse me of mothering her. I should have kept on asking, shouldn't I? I should have *looked*.'

As Marty poured out his soul, he suddenly noticed that Johnny Quentin had stopped listening and was gazing straight over Marty's shoulder towards the canteen entrance.

'Sorry, mate, I *am* listening, I just got a bit distracted for a minute. Here, do you reckon that's who I think it is?' Johnny pointed. 'Look, over there – do you reckon that's the real Saucy Sisters or just two girls pretending and hoping? They look like the real thing to me.'

Marty instantly jumped up and waved as Megan and Venita headed towards them.

'Hi, Marty, how's it going? How is she?' Venita asked with

panic apparent in her voice. 'Is she going to be okay? We got here as soon as we could, all the way from Cornwall, and then the thick-as-two-short-planks driver couldn't find the fucking hospital. Dumb bastard.'

Marty couldn't help laughing at her outburst. Typical Ven. 'Lennie's going to be okay, they said, but it will take a while as she's cracked up completely. She was just about to jump off the cliff when meladdo here pulled her back. Good man, this one. He saved her life.'

'You know them?' Johnny Quentin's face was a picture as he stared at Megan and Venita. 'You know The Saucy Sisters?'

'We're all housemates – me, Lennie, and these two repro-bates here.' Marty grinned as he looked from Johnny to the girls and then back again. 'Girls, this is Johnny Quentin, the taxi driver turned rugby player who saved Lennie.' He smiled and paused for a moment. 'And Johnny, this is Megan and Venita – and yes, they *are* the so-called Saucy Sisters but to me they are just Meg and Ven, dual pains in the arse!'

Johnny stood up quickly but his mouth stayed open as he looked from Megan to Venita to Marty in disbelief.

'I don't believe this. It's a wind-up, isn't it? We've got their photos from the paper pinned up in the office.'

The girls both smiled warmly and then each in turn, kissed him on the cheek.

'We're just so grateful to you. Lennie is our best friend.' Megan settled into a seat and, with a wide smile and doe eyes, looped her arm through his with the familiarity of a friend and pulled him down beside her.

In that instant, Johnny Quentin was done for, he was completely besotted.

The taxi driver was a good-looking young man with lots of shiny brown hair, broad muscular shoulders and an equally broad grin. When he was working the clubs there was never any shortage of females wanting to get off with him, but usually he was the one in control and he could be quite ruthless in a charming love 'em and leave 'em way, and the South Coast was littered with hearts broken by Johnny Quentin.

He was proud of his tally, but this was different. Suddenly, confronted by the page-three icons, he was a tongue-tied schoolboy all over again.

'So how's Lennie right now?' Megan went on. 'Is she really going to get over this? I hate to admit that Nurse Cathy was right and we were all wrong. We should really have listened to the expert. I wonder if she'll come down and visit Lennie? We must let her know what's happened.'

As she was speaking, Johnny was shaking his head back and forth slowly. 'I'm sorry, but I can't believe I'm sitting here with The Saucy Sisters. I've got mates who'd eat their own arms just for a signed photo, let alone a face-to-face meeting.'

'Well, don't you worry, Mr Hero Man. We'll sort those mates and they won't have to eat their arms off, but first we have to see Lennie,' Megan promised.

'Not allowed in.' Marty shrugged helplessly as his eyes welled up again. 'She's under sedation while they figure out where to send her. I've tried to explain to them everything that's happened to her recently, and as I went through it all with them I realised what fucking awful friends we'd been to her.'

'It's okay, Mart,' Venita agreed, 'we feel guilty as well. All of us were so wrapped up in our own lives that we gave that little shit Jamie Kirk free rein to mess with her brain once again.' She paused and looked from one to the other. 'I'm sure he pushed her over the edge with his bloody wacky-baccy and money-grabbing antics, and then of course if you add a touch of boring old Greg into the mix, then I think anyone would want to jump.'

'Okay, guys,' Megan intervened, 'enough guilt. Lennie's going to be all right and we've got Johnny here to thank for that, so let's take him out to celebrate.'

'Good idea, and I'm sure Lennie would approve,' Venita agreed. 'We can leave a message with the nurse. Shall I tell her we'll all be back tomorrow?'

'Yes, tell her that; we'll stay down here overnight. Let's check in somewhere and then maybe Lennie will be a bit better tomorrow and we'll be able to see her.' Megan looked at Johnny and smiled again. 'And of course, we've got a taxi office to visit and maybe even the local pub as well. You okay with that?'

'I'll stay here,' Marty muttered, before Johnny Quentin could untie his tongue and respond. 'I don't think it's right for us to go out celebrating while Lennie's in here on her own.'

'She's *alive*, Marty!' Megan snapped. 'She's not in a heap at the bottom of a cliff, thanks to Johnny, and she's in here getting the right treatment at last. That's a good reason for celebrating, don't you think? Johnny here deserves a good night out on us, and you said yourself she's not allowed any visitors at the moment.'

'I suppose . . . but I do need to warn them about Jamie, just in case. The last thing she needs right now is that little dickhead getting in and turning the screws like he did the last time she was in hospital.'

'Oh, bugger bugger, with all this going on, I forgot to tell you!' Venita smiled smugly. 'I heard that the little dickhead has recently been nicked and remanded. That South of France story was typical Jamie Kirk bullshit to his mates in the pub. My source is reliable and he told me that Jamie was caught dealing to an undercover copper in a pub the other side of the river. He'll get time, I reckon.'

'Now that's a real shame. It couldn't have happened to a nicer person. As he's been done before, they might well keep him in and therefore away from Lennie.' Megan laughed gleefully. 'Now we really do need to get out celebrating!'

# Chapter Twenty-eight

Eleanor was sitting outside the back door in the spring sunshine on the new garden bench that Marty had bought for her homecoming, aimlessly flicking through a magazine that required little concentration when Greg walked through to the yard with yet another huge bouquet, the third in as many weeks.

Four foggy months had passed since her meltdown and she'd been home from hospital for nearly six weeks but was still feeling both physically and mentally fragile. At the same time she was savouring being back in her own surroundings with a functioning brain and being able to make at least some of her own decisions again.

'More flowers? What have I done to deserve all this attention from you?' She smiled questioningly as she took them from him and he leaned over to kiss the top of her head affectionately.

'Yes, Eleanor, more flowers! And it's because you deserve some fuss and attention. How are you feeling today? Marty said you're creeping slowly up the hill back to healthy . . .'

'I'm not too bad at all, Greg – still working in slow

motion but I'm doing as I'm told and not rushing anything. Now I've managed to get my sanity, and my life, back, I'm going to be careful and try to hang on to it. It was a close call and I feel so embarrassed by it all. I can't believe I went so mad.'

She was aware of Greg watching her intently as she shivered involuntarily at the memory of her breakdown and hospitalisation.

'Life is so precious, I know that now, and I really owe it all to Johnny Quentin. He's definitely my saviour and now Megan's pet of the moment, poor man. It'll all end in tears. His, of course!' Again she studied his face curiously. 'How come you want to be involved with the local nutcase, Greg? You could do so much better than a Loopy Lou like me.'

'Please don't talk like that, Eleanor.' Greg was very serious. 'I understand all too well that grief is a strange emotion that can make people do inexplicable things, but then I'm sure your psychiatrist told you exactly that. Just like mine told me when Mom died and I flipped. My mother was my life and then she was gone. At least you have supportive friends. My ex-wife couldn't deal with it and disappeared off with my son.' Pausing, he blinked and then smiled again. 'However, that's all in the past; now the main thing is to get you really well again. How about we go on a vacation? Just you and me and a hotel by the sea, somewhere hot and relaxing. How does the Caribbean sound?'

As his words tumbled out, Eleanor could feel the panic rising in her chest. It felt as if a pigeon was trapped in there trying to get out, and it happened every time the sea was mentioned. She wasn't going to admit to it, but she didn't want to go anywhere near the sea for a long time.

'Sounds good, Greg,' she lied, 'and I'm really grateful for the offer, but if you don't mind I'd sooner not go away just yet. I don't think I'm ready to go anywhere at the moment. Maybe when I've had the all-clear from the men in white coats?'

'Deal. Just tell me when you are ready and I'll arrange to take some time out from the office.'

Greg looked her straight in the eye as he spoke. Eleanor could feel the tears prickling so she blinked quickly and started rustling the Cellophane that enveloped the flowers, feigning interest in the extravagant arrangement.

'Let's change the subject, eh?' she said quietly. 'I'm sure it's getting really boring for everyone, just talking about me and my mental lapse all the time. Tell me about your very latest trip. I've never been to Switzerland. Well, to be honest I've never really been anywhere, but tell me about Switzerland anyway.'

Eleanor watched Greg as he told her all about his recent trip and his job, and wondered if she could ever love him in the same way that she was still in love with Jamie, who was in her mind constantly.

Greg was in his work clothes, clothes that looked ordinary until they were examined; the charcoal-grey suit was hand-stitched and she could see his pale blue shirt was fresh from its expensive packaging. He had taken his tie off but Eleanor knew it would be just perfect when he put it back on. Glancing sideways, she studied his face. He was attractive in an ordinary way. Everything was where it should be and he was groomed to perfection. Gregory Casheron looked like what he was. A perfectly turned out, successful and ambitious businessman who was on his way up to the top.

Eleanor knew all too well that the others thought Greg was boring and staid because he was older than them all and he wasn't a party animal. She knew otherwise, and it was his constant understanding of her illness that had helped her to believe that she would be okay. Of course, he had more experience behind him, including a divorce and a teenage son he hadn't seen since he was a baby, in Canada.

But would she have a future with him? She had thought about it often in the darkest hours of the night when the nightmares still hovered in the background, and she tried to analyse both herself and her mistakes.

Or rather her one big mistake. Jamie Kirk.

Eleanor knew she had to make a choice between a secure future with Greg, who loved her but whom she didn't love in the same way, and an unreliable future with Jamie Kirk, who she would never be able to trust but with whom she was still besotted.

'Are you still with me, Eleanor? I don't think you're listening. You look miles away again.' As the hurt in Greg's voice brought her back sharply and guiltily, she reached out to touch his hand.

'I'm definitely with you, Greg,' she said, 'and I want to carry on being with you.'

He looked at her curiously. 'What do you mean by that, exactly? Are we talking long-term or short-term here? I always have the feeling that I'm maybe just a stop-gap to you. A kind of companion, who you like being with but . . . Oh, I don't know! I mean, I'm not dumb, I know I'm not the love of your life. I know there's someone else always hovering on the edge of everything we do.'

Eleanor's mental comparisons continued. She was aware that her medication was modifying her emotions and reactions, but it also seemed to be enhancing her perceptions.

Jamie Kirk was a no-good, money-grabbing waster who had used and abused her, who had taken advantage of her love.

Greg Casheron was a highly motivated, high-earning grafter who loved her.

It should be no contest. Especially as Jamie appeared to have dropped off the face of the earth after Eleanor had been hospitalised.

'If I told you I was being transferred to the Toronto office shortly, how would you feel?' Greg went on. 'Would you want to come with me, or would you prefer to stay here with your friends? Would you choose to be with me or with the mystery man, whoever he might be? The man who I sense could take you away from me with just one click of his fingers.'

241

Eleanor wondered if she should explain about Jamie, but decided not to; she didn't want to talk about him to anyone ever again. It was over.

'Are you really being transferred to Toronto, or is this hypothetical?' she asked.

'That's not the point. I'd just like to know how you feel. How you *really* feel.'

'Never mind that for a moment, tell me why you don't like my friends, Greg. It bothers me.' Eleanor bypassed his question and returned to the topic that troubled her the most.

'I do like your friends – all of them; we're just different, that's all, and I'm a lot older than them. And you, for that matter. And anyway, be fair, they don't like me, do they?' He smiled. 'It's okay, you don't have to answer that. I'm just wondering where I fit into it all, where I stand in the pecking order of importance in your life.'

Eleanor pondered for a moment and then realised how much depended on her answer. 'I *think* I'd come with you, but then you know that I'm still a bit bonkers so maybe that's not the right answer for you? Not the one you really want.'

'Yes, it is. It's just what I want.' In one swift movement, Greg was down on one knee, 'Eleanor Rivington, I love you, will you marry me?'

This time she didn't want to think, she wanted to feel safe and secure and loved. 'Yes, I will, of course I will.'

'Did you really say yes?' He looked completely bewildered

as if it was the last reply he had been expecting. 'Do you really mean it?'

'Yes, I do, although I'm going to need some time to get used to the idea. As I said, my brain, and everything else, is still working in slow motion. Can we just be happily engaged for the moment? There's no rush, is there?'

With an exaggerated flourish, Greg produced a small velvet box from the inside pocket of his jacket and opened it to reveal a diamond engagement ring with a single solitaire the size of a garden pea.

'No rush! But I want you to have this. If you don't like it, you can change it but I wanted to have the ring here just in case I plucked up the courage to ask you and also just in case you said yes.'

Eleanor jumped up from her seat and flung her arms around his neck. 'Mr and Mrs Casheron. Greg and Eleanor,' she sang out. 'That sounds okay, doesn't it? In fact, I think we'll be okay together.'

Greg's smile faded as he studied her intently. For the first time, Eleanor glimpsed a darkness in his eyes.

'Just *okay*? I'd hoped we had more than that. I don't like words like *think* and *okay*. How about *I love you* or *we'll be wonderful together for ever*?'

'Of course I love you, Greg, and we will be wonderful together for ever. I promise.'

'That's better,' he stated almost sharply. 'You nearly had me worried.'

Eleanor frowned. She wasn't lying as such – she did love

Greg, but maybe not in quite the same way as he thought she did.

His face red, Marty dramatically paced the floor as best he could in the confined space of the kitchen.

'For fuck's sake, Lennie, this is so wrong for you and I know you know it. Please don't do it! How can you possibly be considering marrying someone like Greg? He's not right for you, he's too old and lifeless. You need some fun in your life after everything that's happened.'

'Oh, thanks a lot, Marty. So maybe you think I should marry the funloving and lively Jamie instead? Would *he* be a better choice as a husband?'

'That's not what I meant and you know it. I just don't think you should be deciding to marry anyone right now.'

Eleanor watched as, with tears in his eyes, Marty tried to backtrack on his over-emotive response to her news. She had known he would react that way and that was why she had put off telling him for several days. Marty was her best friend and she adored him, but Greg loved her as a woman and she knew he would be her lifelong security blanket against the world.

'What makes you think you know better than me?' she burst out again, tears in her own eyes now. 'Would you rather I was still with Jamie, supporting him and his habits and being treated like shit? And that's where I will be, if I don't marry Greg and move away.'

'No, you won't, Lennie. You're stronger than that. You

could find somewhere in between hyper and boring, someone your own age. And talking of Jamie, does Greg know about him? Does he know that you and Jamie were sleeping together while he was away working? Have you been honest with him?'

'Oh, shut up, Marty – you sound like a headmaster.' Eleanor carefully sidetracked Marty's question. 'Anyway, Greg isn't boring. He's good company; he's gentle and caring and most importantly, he loves me. You don't have a go at Megan for stringing Johnny Quentin along for as long as it suits her, do you? And you never say anything about Venita and the team of Neanderthal would-be rock stars that she hangs around with all the time.'

'But they're not planning on marrying any of them, and Megan and Venita are different, as you well know. Because of their histories they understand men and they don't need watching out for like you do.'

'Well, excuse me for being a thick-as-shit, mentally incapacitated ignoramus!'

'I didn't mean that either – don't misinterpret me.' Marty realised he'd backed himself up into a corner.

'Well, actually, Marty, I don't give a monkey's arse what you mean or what you think. Greg and I are going to be married and we're going to live in Canada,' she almost screamed at him, before stopping as quickly as she'd started. 'Oh Marty, I want you, more than anyone, to be happy for me. I don't want us to fall out and then we're thousands of miles away and can't make up.'

As her lips turned down Marty smiled and his whole demeanour softened. It was as if a light had been switched back on.

'Oh God, Lennie, I am so sorry. It was just a reaction to the thought of you going away from me. What will I do without you?'

'You've got Jon and I've got Greg and I've a feeling we're both settling, but we'll be fine if we stay in touch.' Eleanor hugged her friend as tightly as she could, knowing only too well that if it hadn't been for him raising the alarm in the first place, she could have been locked away in the house in Hampstead with her father for years.

Or dead and buried under the magnolia tree alongside her mother.

'So much has happened,' she said softly. 'We mustn't ever let that go.'

'I suppose it's not Greg's fault he doesn't dance on tables and tell filthy jokes. Perhaps calm and sensible is what you need after all the traumas you've had. Will you come back and visit?'

Eleanor hugged him even closer. 'Of course I will, and you and Jon can come and visit us. We won't ever lose touch with each other, will we? And I didn't mean it when I said I didn't give a monkey's arse about you.'

'Of course we'll stay in touch. For ever! You're my best friend and you know too much about me for me to ever lose you.' Marty sniffed emotionally. Then: 'When are you going to name the day?'

'Oh, I don't know.' Eleanor pulled a face. 'I think I need time to get used to the idea first. It's different for Greg, he's done it before. Anyway, his stint in Toronto doesn't start for another few months so we've got ages. Do you know yet when our slummy landlord is going to finally chuck us out of here?'

'End of the month, I think. Because we very cleverly didn't go like lambs in the first place he's going to give us all a payoff of a hundred quid each so that we can find somewhere else, but . . .' Marty paused and looked at the floor. 'Now I feel a real hypocrite. I think I'm going to be moving in with Jon.'

'But that's good, isn't it? I thought Jon was the one for you.'

'Well yes, but what about you girls? I feel I'm betraying everyone.'

'We're all grown-ups, maybe it's time to go our separate ways. Even Meg and Ven are drifting apart because of that stuff with Megan's useless father.'

Marty walked over to the window and stood with his back to her. 'Have you told Greg you can't have children, Lennie?'

'Not yet, but I will.' Her reply was defensive. 'Anyway, I don't think it will matter too much. He already has a child, and part of going to Toronto is so that he can try and build his relationship with him. He won't want another child, I'm sure.'

'His decision to make, Lennie. You have to tell him.' Marty

turned round to face her, his expression serious. 'And before you ask me to mind my own business, just remember it's not Greg I'm looking out for. It's you. You'll have to live with this.'

'I'll tell him, I promise. But I'm never going to tell him about Jamie.'

# Chapter Twenty-nine

Like spoons in a cutlery box they were curled up together in bed; Greg was happily enveloped in post-coital drowsiness while Eleanor was enveloped in deep thought. She had learned how to fake it so well that she had almost convinced herself that Greg satisfied her and that everything he was offering her was enough. That *he* was enough. She even managed to get through the occasional love-making session without fantasising about Jamie Kirk and his persuasive words and hands.

No one had seen or heard from Jamie since the day before she had taken off for Beachy Head so she assumed he had moved on to richer pickings elsewhere. Or maybe he had heard that she had been carted off to a mental hospital and decided to bunk off out of it; whatever the reason, she was sure it was for the best if she never set eyes on him again.

The day she and Greg had become engaged, she had gone to her room and ceremoniously thrown all the belongings that Jamie had left there out with the rubbish. That was it, she had told herself fiercely as she tossed his rucksack out. *Jamie Kirk is history.*

Panicked, Eleanor sat bolt upright in the bed and shook Greg's shoulder.

'Greg, let's get married straight away. Let's not wait.'

'Are you serious? I thought you wanted more time.' Greg suddenly came to and took in what she was saying. He leaned sideways on one elbow and gazed up at her. 'I also imagined that as it's your first time down the aisle you'd want the whole wedding confectionery – big white dress, fancy reception, Megan and Venita as bridesmaids . . .'

Eleanor laughed. 'Can you just imagine it? No, we could have a party afterwards maybe, a real celebration, but a quiet secret wedding sounds so appealing. Just you and me and a couple of witnesses. Neither of us have any family to speak of – what do you think?'

'Hey, slow down. I think it sounds fabulous. When are you thinking of?'

'Let's find out tomorrow just how soon we can do it and let's not tell a soul.'

'Sounds good to me – now relax.'

As she leaned back, his hand reached across and cupped her breast, gently stroking her nipple with his thumb. Biting down hard on her tongue Eleanor fought the urge to pull away; closing her eyes, she told herself once again that fantastic sex wasn't the be all and end all. A comfortable love and financial security were far more relevant.

Next day, Greg took the morning off work and they went out together and made all the arrangements, excitedly settling on tying the knot in exactly three weeks' time at the local register office.

Eleanor suffered a constant pang of guilt because she knew she was starting out on her marriage without admitting to her barrenness or to Jamie's part in her life, but she had convinced herself that she was doing so with the best of intentions. It would hurt Greg too much to know that she wanted it over and done with as quickly as possible because she was scared stiff that if she saw Jamie beforehand, she wasn't sure how she would react. She just couldn't trust herself where he was concerned, especially as she was still as weak as a jelly emotionally following the breakdown.

Being married to Greg would be like building a high wall around herself, she thought. He would be her security, and marriage to him would protect her. Jamie Kirk wouldn't be able to get to her if she was a married woman. And Greg would be good for her, she knew that. He loved her and she was totally sure that she would be better off with someone who loved her more than she loved him. That way she was less likely to get hurt.

Although Marty, Megan and Venita all knew about the engagement, they had no inkling that the wedding was to take place so soon. There was even an engagement party being arranged by them all for her and Greg on what would be the day *after* the wedding – but Eleanor hoped they would all understand once it was presented as a fait accompli.

But before any of that could happen, there were some

other loose ends that Eleanor wanted tied up beforehand. Things to do, people to see.

First on her list were Aaron and Hettie Meacham who, because Eleanor had taken off to Eastbourne, had been left with sole responsibility for the funeral of her mother all those years after the event.

'Eleanor! My dear, how lovely to see you – but you look so thin!' Hettie's face lit up and she flung her arms wide as she saw the young woman on the doorstep.

'Now how did I know you'd say that?' Eleanor beamed. Hettie never seemed to change. 'Is Aaron in? I really wanted to talk to both of you, to thank you for everything you've done for me, and of course for my mother. I feel so guilty about the way it all turned out.'

'Well don't, you silly girl. We've already told you that. You were sick, so of course we understand and we were pleased to do it for you and for Rosetta. My oh my, you silly girl, did you really think we minded?'

Hettie tutted loudly as she shook her head back and forth furiously.

'Come and see Aaron, he's in the garden. Now he only works half the week he spends hours out there. Which is good – really, it's good! Otherwise he'd be under my feet more than I could stand. I love him dearly, but . . .'

Eleanor grinned as Hettie's voice trailed off expressively; the tiny woman shrugged her shoulders and held her hands out, palms up.

She followed Hettie through to the large but densely

overcrowded garden that seemed as if it were gradually wrapping itself higher around the house.

'Aaron! Look who's here to see us – it's Eleanor! She looks so well, but still so thin.'

'Oh Eleanor, Eleanor, it's so good to see you. Are you well again now? That was such a difficult business for you, all that . . . I don't know what to say. Are you better, my dear? Are you happy?'

Eleanor made her way over and kissed the wrinkled old man gently on the cheek. Suddenly he looked so much older and she hoped it wasn't because of the added stress she had heaped on him.

'It's okay, thanks, Aaron. I'm fine now though I still have to take it carefully. Anyway, I've got some news for you. Can you keep a secret? You remember that man Greg who was there at the hospital when you visited me? Well,' Eleanor paused and grinned happily, 'we're getting married, just a quiet ceremony, and I want you and Hettie to be our witnesses.'

'Oh, my! Oh my.' Hettie's hands flew up to her mouth and she started crying instantly. 'That is such good news and he seems such a nice young man with a good secure job. Your mother would have been so proud of you.'

'But it's a complete secret, really it is. No one else knows it's going to be so soon. We'll have a big party afterwards to celebrate but we wanted the wedding to be quiet and intimate. Just the four of us. No fuss, nothing fancy.'

'We can keep a secret, can't we, Aaron?' Hettie rubbed her hands together.

'Of course we can, but what do you want to do about your business affairs, Eleanor? Do you still want me to help you out, or will your new husband do that? I won't be offended.'

Eleanor looked at him and fleetingly wished she could have had a father like Aaron Meacham.

'Maybe it's time to think about selling,' she said. 'I don't know when I'll be ready to deal with the house myself, Aaron.'

'I understand that, my dear. It's the right thing to do, but with the history it may take time to find a buyer. It's been empty since . . .' He stopped and carefully studied a tulip. 'People are superstitious.' Suddenly he smiled. 'But I'll do what I can, of course I will. Where are you going to live when you're married?'

'In Greg's flat for a few months, and then we're off to Canada. We're going to live near Toronto where Greg is being transferred, but I'll still keep in touch. It's not really that far nowadays, is it?'

'Eleanor, all we want is for you to be happy and you look as if you will be.' Hettie was becoming tearful again. 'You deserve it after everything you've gone through in your life so far. We both wish you all the happiness in the world and lots and lots of healthy fat babies.'

Eleanor's heart hesitated but she carried on smiling. 'Maybe not too many, eh?'

Leaving Aaron and Hettie's house she felt a comfortable air of finality entering her life. There was just one more person she needed closure from.

Cathy Hart.

She knew the others didn't care for Cathy, but then they didn't understand how much the nurse had helped her in the dark night hours in her hospital bed, and it was because of that intense relationship then that she had become attached to her. So it had hurt Eleanor when Cathy had withdrawn her friendship so abruptly without any explanation. Eleanor still wondered why; she also needed to know if the crazy insemination attempt had been successful.

It all seemed as if that had happened so very long ago, in another life, to someone else. She had been so confused at the time that the actual event was all a bit of a blur, but she hadn't forgotten about it and she wanted to find out. She also wanted to say a final goodbye to Cathy.

Eleanor knew and hated the area where the Harts lived so she marched purposefully through the estate and ran up the stairs to the flat as quickly as she could. When she knocked on the door, Paddy Hart opened it – and his hostility at seeing Eleanor on the doorstep was written all over his face.

'What do you want?' he grunted.

'Hello, Paddy. Long time no see. Is Cathy in,' Eleanor asked pleasantly, ignoring the man's aggressive stance, 'or is she working at the hospital? I'd just like a bit of a natter with her.'

'As you well know, Cathy doesn't live here any more,' he burst out, and she saw how pale he was, unshaven and neglected-looking.

Eleanor felt herself start to panic. She wondered if Paddy had found out about the artificial insemination and that was why Cathy had left. 'I didn't know she wasn't here. I haven't seen her for months, Paddy – I've been . . . ill again, you see. I'm so sorry, I really am, but I certainly didn't know she'd left you.'

Suspicion written all over his face, he focused his watery blue eyes on her face then looked her up and down with a sneer. She could smell the beer on his breath.

'Oh come on now, I'm sure she told you about wanting a baby – she told damn near everyone she met. I swear even the London bus conductors knew about Cathy and her fucking stupid baby urges.'

Crossing his arms he took a step forward, and she couldn't stop herself looking from left to right along the deserted balcony. She got a waft of body odour and unbrushed teeth. This man had really let himself go. Although Eleanor hadn't taken to Paddy, she knew what it was like to feel lonely and abandoned, and she knew he must be hurting.

'Babies, houses in the country, roses around the door – I've never heard such shite. Why couldn't she be happy with what she had? It became an obsession and when I put my foot down and said no more baby talk, no more tests ever, she just packed her bags. I don't even know where my wife is.'

'So she still wanted tests?' Eleanor asked. 'She was still hoping to find a way for a baby?' So the Event hadn't worked.

'Sure she was. On and on about tests, adoption, the lot.

She begged me to keep trying and when I told her I wasn't even going to discuss it again she was gone. The same day. Packed and gone. Without so much as a goodbye she walked out on me and the hospital. Just left a note on the kitchen table.'

'I'm sorry,' Eleanor said sincerely. 'Truly I am. If you hear from her, will you tell her that I'm getting married soon? Then I'm going off to Canada. She was good to me in hospital and I'll always be grateful to her for it.'

'Well, I'm not grateful to you. Just another bloody woman, getting my wife all worked up about babies.'

Eleanor suddenly could take no more of his self-pity. 'Why didn't you just let her try all the options?' she said bravely. It was his own damn fault. Men and their foolish pride! Confusing infertility with impotence, and too stubborn to listen to reason.

'What's it got to do with you, bitch? Shut up!' Snarling, he swung his open hand back to slap her, but before Eleanor even had time to duck she was pushed out of the way and saw a clenched fist land on Paddy's nose, propelling him onto his back in his hallway.

Eleanor turned and nearly passed out. 'Jamie!'

He grinned at her. 'You see? You just can't manage without me, can you, Lennie?'

Eleanor started to palpitate and look around for an escape route. As Paddy staggered to his feet and slammed his front door, her instinct told her to run. To run and not look back. But her legs just wouldn't work.

'How did you know I was here?' she whispered.

'I didn't. It's just one big happy coincidence, Lennie my love. I was just passing. Right time, right place, for once in my life. Now tell me what you've gone and done to upset Nursey-nurse's old man?'

Before she had time to react, he gently took her face in both his hands and kissed her forehead.

'I've missed you so much, Lennie. Please give me another chance. *Please?*'

# Chapter Thirty

Eleanor knew she had to tell Greg. She was constantly aware that she had to, not only because it was the right thing to do but also because she'd promised Marty that she would. But she still hadn't been able to find the right moment and time was running out. She simply didn't know how to do it as she was terrified that once he knew, Greg wouldn't want to marry her.

Then the day before the wedding, while she and Greg were about to have lunch in their favourite restaurant near his office, an excuse not to tell him, an escape route from confession, presented itself to her.

'Eleanor, how do you see our future?' Greg asked, completely out of the blue. 'I mean, in say ten years' time, what do you think we'll be doing? Where do you see us at with our lives?'

'Ooh, what a strange question.' She hesitated and looked at him carefully, wondering if he had a hidden agenda, if he suspected something was amiss. 'I don't know, I don't think my brain is able to work that sort of question out right now. It's a bit deep for my medication. And of course, I'm not clairvoyant.' She forced herself to laugh despite the fear closing her throat. 'You go first.'

Greg screwed his eyes up thoughtfully and looked over her shoulder into the middle distance. 'Well, I'd like to think that we'd be happy and comfortably off, with a nice home, successful . . . Maybe I'll have my own company and you'll be working alongside me. I see us as a partnership in all senses of the word. Together.'

In that instant Eleanor knew it would have to be then. She had to tell him, there was no way she could leave it any longer.

'And children, Greg?' Her voice was quiet as she tentatively pulled open the door to where she didn't want to go. 'Do they fit into your plans? Because if they do . . .'

This time he looked at her closely, his eyes moving over her face as if he expected to see something written there. 'Hmm. I guess we haven't discussed that yet, have we? Maybe we should have. Look, I'm sorry, but they don't feature in my big picture as I see it now. I already have a child that I haven't seen grow up, that I know nothing of.' He paused and frowned slightly. 'Is it something you really want?'

Eleanor sighed with relief and replied weakly, 'No, you see—'

'Good! We're agreed then.' Greg stopped her midsentence, leaned back in his chair and grinned at her, his relief apparent. 'Phew, we'll not have to bother with any expensive, time-consuming progeny then. Now, what wine shall we have?'

With that instantaneous change of subject the door of opportunity closed once more, and Eleanor knew she would never again have the chance to tell him her darkest secret. Greg would continue to think the scar on her belly was from a burst appendix and that she didn't want babies. Her mind travelled briefly to Cathy and Paddy Hart – another childless couple. But at least Cathy still had her womb, even if time was against her. Eleanor wondered what had become of her, and unconsciously stroked her belly, at the place where her womb had been removed, and felt a pang of loss so deep, she nearly cried out with the pain of it.

After lunch, Greg went back to work and Eleanor strolled slowly in the weak spring sunshine back to his flat to check that everything was ready for their early-morning wedding the next day.

Everything was perfectly arranged. They had agreed to go to the register office together despite tradition dictating otherwise. Aaron and Hettie Meacham would meet them there and after the short, formal ceremony they would all go to their favourite restaurant, the one they had just left, for a low-key celebratory breakfast. Then they would go and tell the others.

Deep in thought, Eleanor wandered into the bedroom and gazed at their chosen outfits that were hanging lifelessly side by side on the front of the wardrobe. Greg had selected his favourite pale-grey mohair suit and white shirt, but had bought a scarlet silk kerchief and tie to brighten it up. Eleanor had picked out a beige lace mini-dress by Mary Quant with cutaway shoulders and a pale coffee lining, although she still wasn't completely sure about the red floppy hat that had looked so good in the window of Biba's. The small posy of scarlet roses tied up with trailing beige silk ribbons that she had chosen to match both their outfits was already in the fridge and Aaron, who loved photography, was going to take the photographs.

That was it. Low-key and tasteful. Exactly what she wanted.

Satisfied with their choices of wedding outfits she went from room to room and studied the flat curiously. Although large, it was spotlessly clean and tidy throughout and ultra-modern to the point of being sparse because Greg didn't believe in clutter or ornaments. After the chaos of the shared house the sparseness had seemed strange at first, but now she found it cool and soothing.

After the tour of the flat where she was going to live as Greg's wife, she went back into the sitting room, snuggled up on the sofa and thought over her encounter with Jamie Kirk.

The shock of seeing him, of feeling him beside her, had stirred her in exactly the way she had feared, but she had survived it. She hadn't fallen straight into Jamie's arms and she was going to marry Greg.

She also discovered that she hated Jamie with a passion. She hated him for what he had done to her, for treating her the way he had, and then abandoning her just when she needed him most.

\*　\*　\*

'I don't believe you!' she'd screamed in panic at him as she backed away towards the stairwell. 'You're following me. Why are you following me? I'm getting married on Friday. Go away. Go away!'

'Don't do this to me, Lennie.' His voice had been uncharacteristically calm and persuasive and sounded so very far away. 'I still love you and I know you still love me. I *know* you do. You can't wipe out everything we had together and marry someone else.'

He had reached out to her again but she was ready for him and quickly slid away.

'Well, I don't love you, you selfish bastard. You weren't there when I needed you. You just ran off. Well, now I'm in love with someone else, Jamie, and I'm going to marry him. So just GO AWAY!'

His hands dropped to his sides and he looked at her sadly. The Jack-the-Lad persona that she knew so well suddenly wasn't there. For the first time she noticed that he looked different, that he was actually clean and tidy and his hair was short and groomed.

'I was in jail, you daft bird. I was hung out to dry – set up. Hah. Got six months – out in four for good behaviour. But that's all in the past, forgive and forget. Turned over a new leaf, I have. Only got out a few days ago.'

'How did you find me here then, if you weren't following me?'

'For fuck's sake, Lennie, I was brought up here. My whole family lives here and now I'm sleeping on my nan's

263

sofa-bed. I saw you from the walkway below. It was just a coincidence. A straightforward fucking coincidence.'

'Good. Then off you go, back where you came from, be it your nan's sofa-bed or the gutter, and leave me in peace. I'm going back to my fiancé.'

'But Lennie . . .'

Without saying another word, she focused her eyes on his face and stared as she carried on walking backwards until she reached the stairs. Then, turning sharply, she ran down the steps three at a time and raced back to the road to flag down a passing taxi. The last sight she had of Jamie was of him leaning over the railings and watching her. He had made no attempt to follow her.

Pulling the sleeves of her jumper down over her hands, Eleanor then wrapped her arms around her knees. She was proud of herself for not giving in to him. The moment he had kissed her forehead she had felt herself soften, but the thought of Greg and her impending marriage had stopped her from responding to her feelings. She had been strong enough to walk away and it made her feel good.

But there was no way she could deny to herself that what he said about her was true. The feelings *were* still there. She was still in love with him and she knew that in a way she always would be. He was her first love and her expectations of him had been so high. She hated him for making her feel that way and she hated herself for effectively betraying Greg by loving someone else.

*Tomorrow*, she thought to herself as she pulled her legs up tighter to her body. Tomorrow it will all be over.

In the dark hours just before dawn, Eleanor lay wide awake and as still as stone, a combination of fear and guilt reverberating through her whole body. She desperately wanted to get up, to make a drink and pace the floor, but she resisted because she didn't want Greg to know that she couldn't sleep because then he would stay awake with her; she didn't want him awake and talking to her or, even worse, making love to her because she wanted to be alone with her thoughts.

Without being able to look at the clock she guessed it wouldn't be long before the daylight dawned and the wedding-day plans would swing into action, and they would be rushing around getting ready for their big moment.

Then the pressure would be off her and she would be able to relax.

Wishing it was already over, that she was already safely married, she let her eyes wander over Greg's face as he slept peacefully, completely unaware of her inner turmoil.

Looking at him, she decided that although she had always thought him handsome, his face was actually quite ordinary. Yet everything was just right, as if he had been designed for the cover of a knitting-pattern magazine. Even in sleep his chin was strong and well shaped, and the long, light-brown eye-lashes that she found so attractive, rested on his cheeks. The only flaw in his good looks was his lips, which were a little too thin and naturally curved downwards, giving his face an edge of meanness when he wasn't smiling.

The familiar smell of the previous day's aftershave was very faint, but it was enough to make Eleanor want to reach across and touch his face, but she knew it would wake him.

She wasn't being honest with him, she knew that only too well, but she didn't want to hurt him and risk losing him by confessing the secrets that itched inside her head.

That she had been pregnant with, and then miscarried, Jamie's baby:

That as a result she was infertile, she had no womb.

That she had slept with Jamie whilst Greg was away;

That she was still in love with Jamie.

Jamie Kirk leaned over the balcony and watched thoughtfully until Eleanor was safely around the corner that edged the main road. He knew only too well the things that could happen to strangers on the estate and he wanted to make sure she was safely away from the most dangerous part. It amused him that she hadn't believed him because, for a change, Jamie was actually telling the truth. It really had been just a coincidence that he had caught sight of her from a distance and recognised her instantly.

As soon as she turned the corner out of sight he turned also and headed towards the opposite stairs. Jamie's shock spell in jail had given him time to think and to assess exactly where he was in his life, and as soon as the fug of drugs had cleared from his system he didn't like what he saw. Not only did he not want to be a petty crook dealing in drugs and shoplifting, he was also fed up with scratching a living, never knowing from one day to the next where he was going to sleep or who he was going to screw. Locked up for most of the day and night within the chill walls of a cramped shared cell, the realisation hit him that the life he was leading was a waste of time, energy and his talents.

He didn't want his old life back, he wanted a new one. He wanted to be the boss instead of the lackey. He wanted real amounts of money, a decent lifestyle and a level of respect, and his unexpected incarceration had focused his mind and given him plenty of time to plan exactly how he would go about getting it.

The most important part of Jamie's carefully thought-out grand plan had been to carefully ingratiate himself with a couple of fellow prisoners who were inside for far more serious crimes than himself. They weren't major villains – no one ever got near them – but these were far enough up the chain to be helpful to a budding career criminal. His inherent charm and chameleon personality had made the infiltration a reasonably easy and almost pleasurable task, and when the chips were down there was nothing Jamie Kirk enjoyed more than putting one over on someone.

Once he had done that, he realised he also needed a way of setting up a respectable front for when he was released that would support his official mantra of being a completely reformed character, a good, clean-living member of society. For that end he determined to get round his grandmother.

From the prison that he described to her in exaggerated detail to gain her sympathy, he had written long, apologetic letters, full of remorse and begging forgiveness. He even told her that he was attending the services in the prison chapel.

And it was the truth.

After a few weeks she had softened and agreed that when he was released he could stay with her just until he got back on his feet.

With his head drug free, his acting skills went into overdrive and by the time his release date came around, his new contacts had ensured that Jamie Kirk had a temporary job lined up at a seemingly respectable furniture company operating from a factory unit, and a registered home address at his grandmother's flat.

He had learned that, to be a good criminal, he first had to be respectable – and that was exactly what he had been successfully doing until he had seen Eleanor in confrontation with Paddy Hart and went to intervene. Luckily there had been no one else other than Paddy around to see his fists fly, and Jamie knew instinctively that *he* wouldn't say a word.

As he had watched her running scared, he'd seen instantly that she was still in love with him, even if she was protesting that she was to wed someone else.

Jamie Kirk grinned to himself. Marriage? Nah! He didn't believe it for a moment.

# Chapter Thirty-one

'I can't do this,' Eleanor muttered as she helped Greg get the knot on his tie straight.

'It's only nerves, honey. I feel all fingers and thumbs myself, which is why I asked you to do it.'

'No, not the tie, it's not the tie I can't do! It's the whole marriage thing.' She stepped back and looked down at her feet that were already clad in her new nut-brown patent wedding shoes. 'I can't marry you. I can't go through with it, it's just not right.'

Greg grinned and, comb in hand, he turned to look at himself in the mirror. 'Just calm down, sweetie, take a deep breath and relax. We'll be out of here in a few minutes and in another . . .' he glanced down at his watch, 'in another hour or so it'll all be over and you'll be wondering why you were so nervous. We'll be coming back here as husband and wife.'

'No, we won't. I'm not doing it.' She looked over his shoulder at him in the mirror, hoping he would understand but knowing that he wouldn't. 'There's so much stuff I haven't told you. I'm a fraud – I've misled you.'

She watched in the mirror as he stopped combing his hair and his face froze. Only his eyes moved slowly until they were focused on her.

'What are you talking about, Eleanor? We're getting married at nine o'clock and now you try and feed me a line like that? Come on, you're just being dramatic again. This isn't the time or place for another meltdown.'

Eleanor flinched at his words but carried on nonetheless. 'I'm sorry, but I can't do it to you, Greg. I can't marry you under false pretences. I've got too many secrets. I've kept things from you – important things.' She paused for a couple of seconds and took a deep breath. 'And I've realised I'm still in love with someone else, even though I don't want to be.'

Eleanor was surprised at the wave of relief she felt after uttering the words that had been going round and round in her head for weeks. She knew that she was doing the right thing, but she also knew she had to keep a rein on herself and hold it all together.

Almost in slow motion he turned to face her. 'What secrets are you talking about here? Other than the fact you've just said you're in love with someone else. How much more could there be?'

She couldn't meet his eyes so she looked at the floor.

'I know I should have told you everything before. I wanted to, but I just couldn't find the right words. I'm sorry. You've been so good to me . . .'

'Is that it then? I've been good to you so you wanted to marry me? Nothing else?'

'I'm sorry,' she whispered to the floor.

'Stop saying that! You're not sorry, not at all!'

'I am. I'm sorry because I know I'm hurting you, and I'm sorry I left it till now, but I was hoping it would all be all right, that I could marry you and keep quiet forever. I wanted to do it, but I can't.'

'You said you loved me. Do you? *Do* you love me?'

'Of course I do, but—'

'Enough!' Greg's lips almost disappeared as he shook his head. 'I know exactly what you're going to say next. "I love you but I'm not *in* love with you." Am I right?'

'It's not as simple as that.'

Putting his fingers under her chin, Greg forced her face up and made her look at him. His face was pale and damp as beads of sweat grew on his forehead and upper lip. Greg Casheron was angry but it wasn't a ranting and raving out-of-control anger; it was more a calm and controlled seething. It was the kind of anger she had seen before when she was a child.

'Just answer me this: are we getting married this morning or not?'

'No, I—'

'Then get out. Take your soiled belongings and just get out of my apartment. You can go back to that shithole you came from, go back to your disgusting friends. It seems like I've had a very lucky escape.'

'Please, Greg, listen to me, I'll tell you everything. I'm sure you'll understand when I explain. It's not like it sounds

271

– I *do* want to marry you but not without telling you every-thing first. I have to tell you . . .'

Childlike, she grabbed at his sleeves with both hands as the words tumbled out. She wanted to make him under-stand, but he instantly put both hands up flat on her chest and pushed her away so violently that she stumbled back-wards; as she fell, she rolled over onto her knees away from him, but as she started to get up she felt a sudden fierce pain as his toe connected with her buttock and he kicked her away like a piece of rubbish. The force of the kick sent her headfirst across the room where she hit her forehead on the corner of the wooden fireplace and instantly saw stars.

By the time she came round Greg had gone, leaving his wedding outfit dumped in a heap beside her; on top of the pile was the small velvet box containing her wedding ring along with a short note.

*Be gone when I get back. I never want to see you again.*

As she stood up slowly, her head started throbbing and she could feel dampness trickling down towards her eye. She looked in the mirror to see where the pain was coming from. Raising her left hand to touch the cut above her eye, she immediately noticed that the diamond engagement ring was missing from her finger.

Stumbling to the phone, she forced herself to sound calm.

'Hettie, it's me, Eleanor. The wedding's off. I'm so sorry, I'll explain later.'

She ran through into the bathroom and wrung out a

cold flannel for her head. She knew she had to get out of there as soon as she could, but both her head and body ached.

As she started crying, all she could think about was the frighteningly cold anger on Greg's face and the pain in her buttock that brought to the fore yet another hidden memory of another time, another place.

At that moment she knew she had made the right decision to tell Greg. Now she knew exactly what he was like.

He was like her father.


*'Eleanor, come in here NOW. And bring your explanation in with you.'*

*The child felt the all-too familiar fear that had been gnawing at her for days increase to fever pitch as she correctly interpreted her father's forceful tone of voice. She knew he had once again found fault with her and she knew exactly what it was because it was school report day and her reports were never good enough for him, no matter how hard she worked. Just one seemingly harmless remark or even just a negative word from her teacher, innocently written, would be enough to upset him.*

*She also knew what was going to happen next.*

*When he had come in from work she had dutifully handed the sealed envelope over and then taken refuge in the kitchen with her mother, where they had both waited silently. Each aware that no matter how good it was, it would never be up to scratch for Harold Rivington. But neither mother nor daughter mentioned the inevitable outcome. They never did.*

*Eleanor looked at her mother, silently pleading for help, but all Rosetta said was, 'You'd better go quickly and not make him any angrier.'*

*She stood up and, slowly forcing one foot in front of the other, she made her way through to where her father was standing with his back to the fireplace, waiting.*

*'This is just not good enough. Explain!'*

*Ten-year-old Eleanor looked down at her feet as her father bellowed, 'Come on, girl. Explain!'*

*'I don't know what you mean. I haven't seen it.'*

*His face darkened as she started shivering with fear. 'Don't know what I mean? How dare you! The money I pay out in school fees for your education and you stand in front of me and say you don't know what I mean? Look at this!'*

*Eleanor took the folded piece of card that was being thrust at her but her hands were shaking so much she couldn't focus on the words.*

*'I'm sorry,' she mumbled into her shirt collar without having a clue what she was apologising for, but hoping against hope that just for once an apology would be enough.*

*When her father was in his punishment mode, she would wonder why her mother didn't intervene to help her, to at least stick up for her, but the door would always stay as tightly closed as her mother's mouth; a big fat barrier of solid oak between them as Rosetta Rivington never even acknowledged, let alone talked about, what went on in the family dining room that Harold Rivington used as both an office and a punishment chamber.*

'You know the punishment, Eleanor. You have to learn that I expect only the best from you. The best! You have to be punished.'

'Please, Daddy, no, please don't make me. It's so cold.' Eleanor was already shivering in anticipation of the punishment she knew he was going to mete out, for it was always the same.

'You should have thought of that earlier, madam, when you were playing up at school. This is for your own good – to teach you right from wrong. Now do it!'

Because of her shaking hands it took Eleanor ages to take off all her clothes, ritually folding them and hanging them on the back of one of the chairs as she did so, until she was standing in front of her father, stark naked with her hands by her side.

'In the corner.'

She backed over to the corner and then turned to face the wall. Waiting. He always made her wait, sometimes as long as five minutes, although to Eleanor it felt like hours as she anticipated the inevitable.

Then he slowly removed one of his rigid, rubber-soled slippers and banged it loudly against the palm of his hand a few times.

'Bend over.'

With both hands on the adjoining windowsill she leaned over until her body was angled at the expected 45 degrees and her head brushed the net curtains that hung at the draughty old windows.

Harold Rivington then proceeded to strike his young daughter exactly six times, three times on each bare buttock, pausing in between each thrash to ensure maximum drawn-out fear, before putting the homemade dunce's cap on her head.

*'I'll be back later when you've had time to think about where you're going wrong.'*

*'But it's so cold. Please, Daddy, I'm so sorry, I'll try harder, I promise. Please let me get dressed.'*

*The pain from the beating was always nothing compared to the torture of standing stock still, shivering and trying not to cry. Trying not to wet herself.*

*'No, Eleanor! You have to learn that there is a price to pay for wrongdoing. I don't like doing this but you have to learn. There is always a price to pay.'*

*As she heard the door close, Eleanor knew it would be exactly two hours before he returned, but still she was too scared to leave the corner, just in case. The punishment in summer was bad enough but in winter, in a house with no heating, it was nothing less than torture. Especially as she had to stand to attention with her hands by her side.*

*It never occurred to Eleanor that the punishment was anything other than normal. She just thought that all children had to suffer the same if their school reports weren't as good as expected, if they said a wrong word, if their clothes were grubby or their rooms untidy. Her father told her that all parents punished their children if they loved them. That it was because they loved them.*

*Two hours later, he came back in.*

*'Now get dressed,' he said. 'Your mother wants you. And remember – you must work harder next term.'*

*Later in the evening, the three of them sat down to dinner in the same room as if nothing had happened.*

*At bedtime her mother gave her a sympathetic kiss on the fore-head and an extra cuddle as she tucked her up tightly with two hot-water bottles instead of the usual one.*

*But, as always, neither of them mentioned what had gone on in the dining room.*

# Chapter Thirty-two

'Well, I can't help it,' Venita murmured sideways to her friend as they posed provocatively for the camera that was whirring frantically. 'I think you're being a bit mean. I'm dead chuffed that she dumped him. He's a prat and I don't know what she ever saw in him in the first place.'

'Me neither, but I'm at the point now where I'm getting a bit pissed off with constantly rescuing Lennie from her dramas.' Megan sighed while at the same time looking provocatively into the lens. 'It's just one thing after another, and then of course she rings Marty, and then he rings us. I like her and she's had a shit time of it, but come on, it's getting a bit much. We're not her fucking parents.'

Megan and Venita were at a photo-shoot in a dingy makeshift studio set up in the back room of an East London sex shop; it was several steps further down the porno line than they had gone before, and the photographs were for a dodgy under-the-counter continental magazine, but it was a one-off shoot arranged by Megan's father and it was paying enough cash-in-hand for them to be able to go straight out afterwards and put the deposit down on a decent flat to rent together.

Venita had had serious doubts about the job, which involved full-frontal nude shots, but she had been persuaded by the money which was far more than their usual rate – and tax-free. And, of course, they had been promised that the magazine would never see the light of day in the UK.

'I've just had a thought.' Venita threw her head back and did her best to look orgasmic. 'Now she's not going off to Canada with the dreaded Gregory, do you think she'll be expecting to come and live with us?'

'Oh fuck. I hadn't thought of that. What with Marty going to live with Jon, I can't see that she'd want to be with them . . .'

'Oh, I don't know. Maybe we can persuade her she'd love to share with them now they're going all domestic and talking about an antique shop in Notting Hill!'

'I know,' Megan snorted as quietly as she could. 'That is *so* unlike Marty, but I hope he and Jon are okay. Marty's a good bloke – he deserves for it to work out.'

'Right, girls. I'm ready to move on,' the photographer grinned as he interrupted their *sotto-voce* conversation. 'Spread 'em wide for the camera. I'm coming in for close-ups!'

Venita hesitated but Megan didn't. 'Just show it to the man, Ven, and think of the money. And the flat. Nice flat, nice area, good landlord.'

'That's the idea,' the photographer smiled encouragingly. 'Now take no notice of me, there's nothing you've got that

I've not seen before in glorious Technicolor. Come on, girls, look like you're loving it . . .'

Together they went through a series of choreographed positions until suddenly Venita screamed and reached for the nearby bath towel.

'What's up?' The photographer sighed and lowered his camera. 'I haven't got all day, you know. Time is money for me and me lens.'

'Megan, just look up there, your pervy father is up on a chair or something peering through the glass at the top of the door. Look at him! That is so disgusting. You're his daughter. Oh yuk!' Venita threw a towel at Megan.

As they looked up, Peter ducked down but it was too late, they'd all seen him.

The door opened a crack. 'Don't look at me like that, you lot, I was just looking out for my little girl. I know what some of these snappers get up to when no one's watching.' Peter Longdon sniggered and glanced from one to the other. 'Okay, okay, I promise not to peek again – but any nonsense from Billy Boy, just shout and I'll shove his tripod where the sun don't shine.'

'Just you try and you'll be head first out in the street without any teeth! And if you wanna be a Peeping Tom, then go and do it somewhere else,' Bill the photographer responded grimly.

The independent and normally streetwise Megan had had no family in her life for so long that when her father had turned up out of the blue she reacted totally out of character. Throwing her usual commonsense straight out of the window, she'd fallen completely for his line about wanting to get to know his long-lost daughter.

Her mother had always told her that he had just disappeared off the face of the earth when Megan was two but Peter had told a different, far more sentimental story, and Megan chose to believe him. She really wanted his story to be true because it was better than her mother's version.

Now she looked at her father's face peering round the doorframe and said easily, 'You don't need to do that, Dad. Venita and I have been looking out for each other since the day we met. We're big girls, we don't need minding.'

Wearing his favourite cheeky-boy expression, Peter shrugged and pushed the door closed. None of them had spotted his own camera clicking away through the glass at the same time as Bill's.

'So what are we going to do about Lennie? How can we find out what she's thinking? I mean, right now she hasn't even got a job,' Megan said as they threw their clothes back on. With barely enough room to move in the makeshift changing room, both were keen to collect their money and get away from the so-called studio as quickly as possible.

'I dunno. Maybe we should just keep out of her way for a while, just lie low and not mention it.'

'Or maybe we should just be upfront and tell her,' Megan suggested. 'She'll be okay, I'm sure.'

They walked together over to where Bill was crouched on the floor packing up his equipment and preparing to turn the boudoir back into an ordinary, boring sitting room for the shop.

'Come on then, Bill,' Venita smiled, 'we're done, so splash the cash and we'll leave you in peace.'

He looked from one to the other of them. 'Oh right. I thought I had to give it to Peter.'

He pulled a wad of notes out of his pocket and at that point the door flew open and Megan's father rushed in, his face red with panic. 'That's right, Bill. That's how it is. Now give it to me and I'll divvie it up later. Don't want the girlies here getting themselves in trouble with all that cash on them.'

Venita's hand shot out. 'Not a chance. Megan and I *divvie* everything up ourselves, thank you very much.'

'What about my third then?'

'Not out of this you don't get a third. This is for our new flat.'

Without looking up Bill counted out the notes and with a grin held them out in front of him. 'Come on then,' he said. 'Who wants it?'

In one swift move Venita snatched the money from his hand and stuffed it straight down into the bottom of her bag.

'Thanks, Bill. That's what I like – a good day's pay for a good day's work. And work we did.' She looked at Peter and winked. 'Unlike you, Mr Longdon.'

'I set this up for you,' the man blustered.

'Sure you did. I'm sorry, I forgot that.' Venita pushed

her hand back down and pulled some notes back out, peeling off twenty pounds and offering it to him. 'Here's your cut.'

'Ven, come on. He's my dad. Give him a fair cut.' Megan's voice was unusually childlike as she frowned at her friend but Venita wasn't having any of it. She grabbed her arm and propelled her friend in the direction of the door. 'That is a fair cut for a straightforward introduction that we could easily have done ourselves. Bill's been after us for ages, as you well know. Now come on, Meggie Meg. Let's go and get ourselves a new gaff!'

'You stupid dumb bastard,' Peter Longdon snarled at the photographer who was grinning from ear to ear as he clipped the lids on his cases. 'You knew I was meant to have that fucking money. I told you, I'm their manager and every-thing goes through *me*.'

'You didn't look much like their manager to me; you just got well and truly screwed over. Twenty quid?' Bill laughed and as he did so, Peter put his head down and hurled himself at him as a bull at a red rag. But, still laughing, Bill just moved slightly to one side and the other man flew straight past him and then tripped, landing in a heap on the floor.

'Don't try and mess with the big boys, buster.' Bill held his hand out to help the other man up. 'Now I'll let you off just this once, but try anything like that again and believe it, you will be dead! Got it?'

'Got it,' Peter Longdon gasped, getting his wind back.

'Sorry, mate. Just got carried away, that's all. It won't happen again.'

'Okay. Forgotten already. Now I've got stuff to do, so . . .'

Peter took the hint and, with one apologetic backward glance, he grabbed his coat and was gone out through the front of the shop.

As he left from the front, the back door opened.

'I was watching through the window,' said a voice, 'and that was quite impressive. I think I need to learn how not to lose it when idiots like that are around. I'd have had to smack him one.'

'Yeah? Well, it's just not worth wasting energy on dick-heads like that.' Bill shrugged. 'There's always some loser or other hanging around girls like that ready to fleece them. I've got no time for it myself. It's just one step up from pimping, to my mind.'

'Who is he anyway? Thought I recognised him from somewhere.'

'The father of one of the girls I was shooting. Gross, huh? And he was peeping at them . . .'

'And who were the girls?'

'The one and only Saucy Sisters, but they're on the slippery slope down now. Fame is fleeting if you're all tits and arse and no brains. Shame really, they're nice enough girls, but that's how it goes. This is it for them from now on, unless they find themselves a couple of millionaires real quick.'

'The Saucy Sisters, eh? Well, I never. Good pics? They seemed to know their stuff.'

'Great pics. They're going into a lesbo Dutch mag. But enough of that, I've been told to teach you the alternative side of this business so we'll start right now with the very first lesson. Confidentiality. Nothing goes outside of these four walls – okay? Whatever you hear or see, *who*ever you see, nothing goes any further. There's no way you want to get on the wrong side of the Boss.'

'Who is he, this Boss?'

'Who knows? I've never met him – he goes by the name of Mr Smith. Naturally. As they all do. Could be one person, could be half a dozen different people, but what I *do* know is that if you're working in his business, you do exactly as you're told and ask no questions. As I said. Confidentiality.'

'Well, you can trust *me*, Bill,' Jamie Kirk said, smiling at him. 'Confidentiality is my middle name from now on. My lips are well and truly sealed.'

# Chapter Thirty-three

As Eleanor walked up the path to the old house in Hampstead she surprised herself by feeling quite calm. For the first time she felt as if she was starting to come to terms with how her new life alone was going to be.

With Marty and Jon excitedly planning their new business and Venita and Megan getting ready to move into their new flat, Eleanor had decided that, with no job and no income, the only option was Ashton Gardens. She thought that maybe she could live there until it was sold.

But as she clicked the gate open of number 24, she realised immediately that, despite Aaron and Hettie Meacham's gentle warnings, she had badly underestimated the deterioration that had taken place over the past year or so. Or maybe she had just forgotten how rundown it really was to start with. The garden wasn't too bad because Aaron's sons had kept the grass cut and the weeds down, but the hedges were high and the house itself looked just what it was, abandoned and unloved, a sad empty shell of a building, and Eleanor was suddenly not so sure about living there.

She wandered across the garden looking at the front of

the house, and then stepped back so that she could see the upstairs. A couple of the windowframes were hanging awkwardly on their hinges and most of the paint had peeled down to bare metal. The sills were rotting and the wisteria had taken over, climbing into cracks and crevices and even creeping into the poorly fitting windowframes. Eleanor wondered if the old plant was all that was keeping the house standing.

'Lennie!' a familiar voice called as she was about to put the key in the porch lock.

She didn't even bother to turn round. 'Jamie, I know it's you so just fuck off and stop following me.' She didn't even bother to ask how or why he was there. She had sensed him nearby for weeks, a shadowy presence that she never actually saw, but strangely it didn't bother her. It actually made her feel in control.

As soon as she heard his voice she was irritated that he had also tracked her to the house, but she was nonetheless determined to show only indifference.

'It's all right, Lennie. I'm not going to dance around and make stupid, smartarse remarks, I just want to talk to you. I've grown up since I've been inside, you know. I had no choice.'

'So you call stalking me grown up?' she murmured sarcastically over her shoulder. 'Not that it's of any interest to me, not any more, so you just carry on stalking. I have things to do.'

He moved alongside her but didn't touch her, he just

287

followed her eyes and looked up as she was and studied the exterior of the building.

'I take it this is it, then? This is the house? I thought you said you never wanted to see this place again after everything that happened here.' He paused for a moment. 'Though I guess if you're going to live here with your new husband, that might take the edge off.'

'I thought you were being mature? If you've got something to ask, be my guest, don't pick away thinking I won't notice.'

'Sorry, that was dumb.' Jamie smiled sheepishly and managed to look suitably apologetic. 'But give me a break, I'm still learning how to be a normal human being again. I spent so long off my head that now I'm completely clean, I have to adjust and relearn.' Again he paused. 'So *are* you going to live here with your new husband?'

But Eleanor was no longer listening to him as she walked around Jamie to the porch entrance and turned the key in the first lock and then the second. Suddenly she was standing in the hall, mouth open, and looking around at her childhood home.

'Lennie, you shouldn't be in here.' For the first time he touched her, just gently, on the arm. 'Come on, let's go somewhere we can talk.'

But it was as if he hadn't spoken.

Aaron hadn't told her that the tenants had decorated the house. Sort of.

Where the hall had once been dark and dismal with

ancient wallpaper of faded roses and climbing ivy, now it was the complete opposite. Huge swirls of orange and black decorated the wallpaper that had been pasted onto the walls below the oak picture rail, while above it, lime-green emulsion had been carelessly slapped on all the way up to the ceiling that was covered in peaks and troughs of thick Artex. It looked just like a huge upside-down birthday cake.

Eleanor looked around in horror and then out of the corner of her eye she saw Jamie doing the same.

'Picasso would be so fucking jealous if he saw this masterpiece.' Jamie walked round and round on the spot just staring. 'All I can say is, your old man really did have a problem if he was responsible for this.'

Eleanor started to laugh. It was so horrendous that it didn't even look like the same house she had left on that awful day when her father had killed himself. She had sworn she would never go back there and yet here she was, standing in the hall with Jamie Kirk by her side.

'It wasn't my father who did this, it was the tenants who were here, but no one told me what they'd done or how abysmal it was. Oh my God. This is so awful, isn't it?'

'Well, I have to admit it gives a whole new meaning to the word psychedelic.' Jamie chuckled along with her. 'You know what? It's even worse than the worst of Marty's shirts.'

Suddenly they were in each other's arms, both laughing hysterically.

'I was really thinking about moving in here for a while to get it ready for sale, but how can I live with this paper, even for a day? It is really *bad*,' Eleanor giggled, taking great gulps of air.

'I can't imagine anyone looking at it without being high. Can't your husband decorate over it all?'

Once again, Eleanor ignored the loaded question. 'I'd better look round and see what other horrors are waiting to jump out and shock me.'

Together they walked cautiously through the whole house, and when Jamie reached out to take her hand she didn't object.

'You know full well I'm not married, don't you, Jamie? I know that you know so stop playing games.'

He grinned. It was the old Jamie grin, the genuine wide grin that she had loved so much and she felt her stomach flip.

'Well, I did check out the banns at the register office and yes, I did hang around and I did notice that you never turned up on the day but I wasn't completely sure that you hadn't decided to get married somewhere else.'

'Yes, you did know because you've been on my tail ever since and you knew I was still at the house. But . . . the cancelled wedding was nothing to do with you, in case that's what you're thinking. I just realised at the last minute that it wouldn't work out – we were too different and I just didn't love him enough. I think I'd gone in search of a father figure and considering what a crap father I had . . .' She smiled wryly and shrugged. 'We were going to live in Canada.'

Jamie took her other hand. 'I'm so glad you didn't, Lennie.'

Then: 'I can't imagine who did this or what the fuck they were taking. I thought I was an expert but I never found any drug strong enough to make me want to do something like this!'

Eleanor laughed along again but this time it wasn't quite as hearty. 'The house is one thing but I don't know what to do about the garden,' she said, almost to herself. 'Can I live so close to that – the place where everything happened?'

'Change it completely, I'd say – landscape it and make it unrecognisable. You don't need to be reminded of it all the time.'

'Hmm.' She shivered as she steered Jamie past the dining room. She couldn't bring herself to go in there just yet. 'I haven't got any money, apart from the hundred pounds I got from our landlord, or a job. That's why I'm here,' she explained to Jamie. 'Also, Marty and Jon are setting up in business together in a shop that's got a tiny flat above it. Megan and Venita are leasing an upmarket place in Notting Hill and I know they don't want me with them.'

'Well, I can help you sort this place out – and no, I'm not asking to move in with you, I'll just help out at weekends, whenever I can. We can put this house back together again between us and I don't want anything out of it. I swear to you. I'm doing okay now.'

'I don't know.' Eleanor could feel herself weakening. Jamie definitely seemed different and in a good way. He was clean and tidy and the spitefulness she had so hated was no longer there; without that he was the Jamie Kirk she had fallen in love with in the first place.

She did wonder fleetingly if the clean-cut, smartly turned-out, easygoing Jamie was all an act, but then if he had money and somewhere to live then there was no reason for him to be with her if it wasn't what he really wanted.

All through the thought process her head was screaming at her, *Don't do it!* But her heart was banging away the same as it always had around him.

Maybe she owed it to herself to give it a go, she thought as she studied the orange walls intently. It would either work or it wouldn't, and that way she wouldn't have to spend the rest of her life wondering 'what if'.

'What exactly are you doing for a job, Jamie? You keep mentioning work but not what you actually do.'

'I'm working for a small company on the other side of the river that imports office furniture from Europe. My Probation Officer set it up for me and my job is keeping a check on what comes in and goes out.' He looked at her and crossed his eyes. 'You know what it's like, you can't trust anyone these days!' He smiled directly into her eyes. 'Come on, Lennie, let's give it a very low go, just see what happens. What's stopping you?'

'I've got no furniture,' she said. 'I got rid of the lot. We let it unfurnished, and the tenants obviously took their stuff with them.'

'I saw a secondhand shop on the corner. Next?'

'I've got no job.'

'Doing this place up will be your job. Speculate to accumulate. Next?'

'I've got no real money to speculate in the first place.'

'I have. We can share it. Next?'

'Megan and Venita. And Marty.'

'Just tell them – they'll want you to be happy. Next?'

'They'll be furious.'

'Then don't tell them and if they show up I'll hide in the psychedelic pantry. Next?'

'I can't think offhand.'

'That's it then. Come on, let's go shopping at the weird-looking Alfie's Emporium that I spied at the top of the road next to the station.' He tugged the end of her hair affectionately. 'Don't glare at me like that; you can look on whatever we spend as a loan if it makes you feel better! Pay me back when the house is sold.'

And that was the moment when Eleanor silently threw caution to the wind, took up with Jamie Kirk once again and told herself fiercely that maybe, just maybe . . . it might be a case of *third time lucky*.

The parade of shops at the top of the road was just like every other shopping parade across the country. There was a baker's, a butcher's and a greengrocer's, along with a café and a newsagent that doubled as a Post Office; then at the far end, where two shops had been knocked into one, was Alfie's, a secondhand shop where everything imaginable was packed and stacked to get as much in as possible.

'Let's go and have a cuppa in the café first and then I

can make a list,' Eleanor said as they looked in the window at some of Alfie's goods for sale. 'I think I only need to furnish a couple of the rooms downstairs. I can do one as a sitting room and one as a bedroom and then, of course, there's the kitchen. I can live downstairs and decorate upstairs and then vice versa – what do you think?'

'Sounds sensible but I reckon the outside is a priority. Maybe we should see if Alfie's got some ladders as well. It's a fucking long way up there!'

Eleanor laughed despite herself.

'Can I ask you something, Lennie?' Jamie asked as he watched her face. 'The day I saw you on the Rat-Trap, when I really *did* see you by accident, why was Cathy's old man so angry with you? What had you done?'

'Nothing, thank you very much! Apparently Cathy has upped and left him and he seemed to think it was somehow my fault. I mean, I didn't even know she'd gone. I just went to talk to her, to tell her I was going to Canada.'

'I'm surprised she didn't let you know.'

'I haven't heard from her since—' She stopped and bit her tongue. It was definitely not a good start, trusting Jamie with secrets. 'Ooh, since I can't remember, and I have no idea where she is. I know everyone thought Cathy was a bit weird but she was good to me and I never noticed the age difference that they all made so much of. I wish I knew where she was.'

'I didn't mind her.' Jamie shrugged. 'She worked hard and she survived living on the Rat-Trap for longer than most, so all power to her! Maybe one day, I'll tell you all about life on the estate. Make your hair curl, it will. Now, about this furniture . . .'

With their cases packed, the four friends were in the sitting room, all looking uncomfortable and each waiting for one of the others to speak first. The day they had all looked forward to and dreaded in equal measures had come – the day they were all leaving the shared house and going off in separate directions – and as they hung around for the landlord, no one was quite sure what to say.

Suddenly, Venita jumped up. 'Well, someone say something before I go nuts. This is horrible after so long together, it's almost like a bereavement.' She looked at the others one at a time. 'We've got another thirty minutes before our beloved landlord, or one of his henchmen, is due to show up and pay us off. Shall we play charades while we wait, or shall we just have a conversation?'

Megan smiled sadly. 'Wow, this is so hard, it seems like just weeks instead of a year since we all moved in here expecting a mansion and getting a hovel, and now we're all splitting up. Though me and Ven are still going to be together – Saucy Sisters rule!'

'What about Johnny?' Eleanor asked. 'Is he still your man of the moment? I thought at first that you might be going off to set up with him . . . I would hate to lose touch with him.'

Megan looked sheepishly at her. 'Johnny's okay and I'm

fond of him, but that's about it.' She pulled a face. 'He's good looking and good company, but he's a skint cabbie and he lives in Eastbourne, of all places. I want a famous rock star, like Ven's got! Someone with enough dosh so that I can stop getting my tits out.'

Eleanor shook her head and tutted. 'That's so mean, but when you do dump Johnny, make sure you tell him I want to stay in contact with him, won't you. I adore him – in a platonic way, of course.'

'Well, you have him then! My leaving present to you.'

'Don't say stuff like that, Megan. Now's not the time.' Marty glared at her. 'And anyway, it's not even funny.' He looked over at Eleanor who was sitting cross-legged on the floor. 'He is a nice enough bloke, Lennie. Maybe he can come up to London and help you with the house if old Aaron's sons let you down.'

Eleanor didn't respond; she hadn't mentioned Jamie to them, and she wasn't going to. Very soon, their lives would no longer be intermingled so there really was no need to tell all any more.

'When's the shop going to open, Marty?' she asked instead, to change the subject. 'Are we all invited to the grand opening?'

'Of course! I only found out yesterday that Jon's already got a load of stock – when his grandparents died, they left a lot of their things to him, knowing he would appreciate them. He put it all into storage. Now he's getting it all out to put in the shop to start us off. I can't wait. No more shitty clubs and late nights. We're going to be like a boring old married couple!'

The hammering on the door made them all jump.

'Well, this is it, boys and girls! Oh God, I'm going to cry.' Megan's lip started to quiver. 'We will keep in touch, won't we? Marty? Lennie?'

'Of course we will, you daft cow.' Marty hugged her. 'We just won't be living together any more.'

'And I want to thank you all for helping me through the shittiest of times,' Eleanor said. 'I'm out the other side now and I feel so good. And it's all because of you. Best friends for ever!'

'Best friends for ever,' they all echoed.

The hammering on the door got louder.

'Come on then, everyone. Let's get it over with!' Marty hoisted his case and went to open the door.

# Chapter Thirty-four

A fortnight later, as she looked around the freshly decorated kitchen, Eleanor savoured the new sensation of being happy. Not ecstatic, just comfortable and adjusted to her latest new life. Her third life in as many years.

It was an unusual feeling for her after experiencing only extreme highs and lows for so long, and she was enjoying every second of it. For the first time there was no one watching and analysing her every move in case she flipped again, no one monitoring her emotions for changes and no one to pass judgement on her well-thought-out decision to allow Jamie Kirk back into her life.

It had been a frightening prospect when she knew that, for the first time in her life, she was going to have to live alone and be independent. Everyone had been convinced she was making the wrong decision by insisting on going back to the old house but, despite all the dark prophecies from everyone and eventual offers for her to share with them, she had survived emotionally and now it was working out.

Eleanor Rivington felt she had finally exorcised her

demons and effectively dealt with the past that had haunted her for so long.

She felt as if she was home where she belonged. For the time being, anyway.

'Wake up, Lennie! You're miles away.' Jamie nudged her elbow as he walked through the kitchen to put the empty paint tins in the dustbin in the garden.

'God, you made me jump. Lucky I wasn't actually painting,' Eleanor grinned.

'Well, I don't see how you can paint anyway with your head in the clouds. Penny for them?'

'I wasn't actually thinking anything specific, I was just feeling satisfied with the way it's all going. This is such fun, isn't it? When I first came back here, the thought of doing everything that needed doing and living here at the same time was overwhelming – and yet it's nearly finished.' She picked up the brush and lightly touched the end of his nose with it. 'And it looks great – thanks to you. I couldn't have done any of it without you.'

Jamie smiled at her. 'I've enjoyed it – and anyway, it's good for me. I'm a model citizen now, aren't I? I might even get you to give me a reference as a painter and decorator.'

'The really scary part is that you've actually earned a reference as a painter and decorator and all-round odd-job man,' Eleanor told him. 'Your reputation will be shredded if anyone finds out that Jamie Kirk is a dab hand with a paintbrush and Black and Decker.'

'Well, that's all right by me. My old reputation needed replacing with something respectable,' he smiled at her, 'and you've done that for me, so we've helped each other. It just seems a shame that you have to sell this place after all our hard work. It looks really good, and so different from the *Psycho* palace it was before.'

'Mmm. But my intention has always been to sell it and move on, as you know. This was only ever a money-making exercise for me. Even after all this time there are still outstanding bills of my father's and, of course, I still have to pay Aaron for all his work even though he will try and refuse.' She sighed fondly as she thought about the dear Meachams and their kindness. 'In one way I'd love to stay here, but I also think it would be nice to live in a house that's newer and smaller and far away from London. I fancy the country. A little cottage somewhere . . .'

'You'd be bored witless in the country!' Jamie objected. 'Maybe we can find a way where you could stay right here. We could take out a mortgage on this place – it would be easy enough on a substantial property like this, then we could pay everyone off and start afresh properly.'

Eleanor picked her paintbrush up and went back to concentrating on the skirting board. 'Not a chance! How could I possibly afford to pay a mortgage? I haven't even got a proper job. Working three days a week in the taxi office isn't going to get me a big enough loan. And anyway, you promised not to pressure me into anything. We're just taking each day as it comes, remember?'

'Hey, hey, Lennie, you're being hyper-sensitive again and reading something into nothing. You have to trust me.' Jamie walked over to where she was kneeling. 'I was just trying to figure a way of you keeping this place – it is your home, after all. I wasn't thinking about anything more than that.' Gently, he ruffled her hair. 'You really do have to learn to trust me. I know it's hard for you after the way I behaved before, but I have changed. All that stuff is in the past.'

Whistling to himself, he carried on past her and went out of the room, softly pulling the door to behind him.

Eleanor smiled to herself. Jamie still hadn't realised that she was no longer the naïve and easily manipulated girl he had first met. This time, *she* was in charge. Jamie was trying so hard that Eleanor just knew he was up to something, but she didn't really mind although she had promised herself to stay on guard. She loved Jamie, she always would, but leopards didn't change their spots and, with her emotions working properly, she couldn't see a future for them together. She knew that he was genuinely fond of her, but his declarations of love never quite rang true. She would have to tell him soon, but in the meantime she was content being content, and perfectly happy painting the skirting board.

Only when the kitchen door was firmly closed and he was safely in the hall did Jamie Kirk allow himself a wide, smug smile of satisfaction. Her initial response of panicked refusal had been what he expected but he was certain Eleanor would soon agree to his proposition; it was just a matter of waiting for the right moment to reel her in and then let her think that it had all been her idea in the first place. Then the house would be, at the very least, half his.

His carefully laid plans for the future were all coming together just as he had anticipated. He had a job that was respectable on the surface and a very respectable girlfriend who would soon be his wife, a wife who would know nothing about his alternative career. And because of that he was also well on the way to owning a house in a respectable neighbourhood and then hopefully having a respectable family. Jamie Kirk had carefully constructed the front, just as he had been told to do, so he could safely carry on learning the other more lucrative trade that went on behind the scenes at the furniture unit.

He quickly discovered that all the filing cabinets and other large items at the back of every lorryload of office furniture contained thousands of hardcore pornographic magazines from Denmark or Holland, destined for under-the-counter special collections in sex shops across the country. He also discovered that the company was building its own stable of models to capitalise on the growing market and he knew instantly the direction The Saucy Sisters, Megan and Venita, were going to be forced to go.

During his introduction to the world of porn import, export and distribution he had been told over and over again that respectability was as important as confidentiality, so he wore a suit when he was working and was only casual when he was helping Eleanor with the house. He stayed away from his old haunts and his old friends, and had nothing what-ever to do with drugs himself.

He just hoped that the shadowy Mr Smith, whoever he might be, would receive good reports of his new employee and would be pleased with his progress and adaptability.

However, Jamie wasn't a complete fraud. He really did like Eleanor and he had always known there was something about her that was too good to let go; there was something unworldly and innocent in her nature to which he, given his own chequered history, was deeply attracted.

When he was in prison with plenty of time on his hands he had often wondered about his inability to love. When he thought about it, it bothered him that he had never actu-ally been in love in his life, but once back on the outside he soon stopped thinking about it. Love came a poor third in his life, far behind his burning desire firstly for money and secondly for respect.

From the hallway Jamie heard the expected two toots on a car horn outside.

'Lennie!' he shouted. 'I'm just nipping up the road for some ciggies. Won't be long.'

Before she could answer he was out of the front door, away down the path and heading towards the familiar blue Vauxhall that was stopped further up the road with its engine running.

As he jumped in the passenger seat, the driver pulled off and drove around the block. 'There's new furniture coming in on the Dover ferry tonight.' He spoke quickly and clearly, not wanting to waste time or words. 'Be at the unit for six a.m. tomorrow. Boss wants the lorry unloaded and gone by the time the workers get in at seven-thirty. There'll be an inventory to check.'

'Will do.'

'And he also wants you to keep your eyes on a bloke called Peter Longdon. Here are his details.' Jamie was handed a piece of paper. 'Word is that he has been touting some pirates of our pics, maybe to the papers. You'd better give him a tug and get them back before anyone else sees them. Explain to him gently that he shouldn't really be doing that sort of thing. Copyright and all that!'

'I understand you.' Jamie laughed knowingly. 'And by chance I know exactly who he is. I saw him at the studio a while back when Bill was snapping away at a couple of girls. Looks like a shyster all right.'

'Yeah, well, you can pull him into line. Nothing bad, mind.'

'No, sir. Nothing bad!'

The car pulled up near the house. 'Nice gaff, that – how did you afford it?' the driver asked curiously. 'I heard you were not long out.'

'Long story.' Jamie shrugged. 'Unfortunately, for the sake of the old Probation Officer, I still go between here and Grandma's gaff on the fucking Rat-Trap. But not for much longer. I'm getting married and she's well respectable. Thinks I'm Honest Joe now!'

'That's good. Best not to mix business and pleasure.'

'Will I ever get to meet the Boss?' Jamie asked cautiously. 'I'd like to know who I work for, the bloke who runs the whole outfit.'

'You're kidding me, right? No one ever gets to meet him or even know who he is. Your boss isn't *The* Boss. My boss isn't *The* Boss. No one knows him or anything about him. Known by the name of Mr Smith, of course, but he could be the Prime Minister for all we know.' The driver's words were light but his expression and tone were deadly serious. 'A word of advice, mate. If you want to keep your job, don't go round asking questions, just do as you're told without thinking about it. We're just the programmed robots, the three wise monkeys rolled into one. Hear no, see no, speak no. Best to remember that.'

Walking slowly back up the path, Jamie chewed over the advice and then dismissed it. Keeping your head down equalled anonymity, and that wasn't what he wanted. He wanted Mr Smith to notice him as a talented player.

'Hi, Lennie, I'm back,' Jamie called out as he went back in.

Eleanor ran into the hall. 'Oh, at last! I thought you'd got lost. Hand 'em over, I'm dying for a ciggie!'

Jamie stopped in his tracks and it took him a second to realise. 'Oh shit. Sorry, Lennie, I couldn't get them, I forgot my wallet.'

'Daft bugger.' She raised her eyes to the ceiling. 'When did you realise?'

'I got all the way there and actually into the shop. And

there was a queue. I nearly asked for them on a tab but decided not to.'

'Not to worry, I need the exercise. I'll go this time.' Eleanor slipped her shoes on.

'I'm sorry,' Jamie repeated mournfully.

'It's okay, Jamie, really it is. No need to apologise for just forgetting your wallet, is there?'

Something in her tone alerted Jamie's antennae. 'What did you get up to while I was gone?' he asked casually.

'I was down on my hands and knees getting up close and personal with the skirting board, and now my back's killing me. Why do you ask? Worried I might have put my feet up when you weren't looking or that I was out spying on the neighbours?'

'Don't be daft,' Jamie grinned brightly. 'I was just making conversation.' However, he remained on alert. There was something about her, something almost sly . . .

'Any phone calls while I was out?' he asked.

'Nope. Not a sound.'

'Any visitors?'

'Oh Jamie, don't be neurotic. I haven't spoken to a soul or left the house.' Eleanor touched his arm affectionately. 'Come on, we'll walk up to the shop together.'

'No, you go and I'll open a couple of bottles of beer. We deserve it after all the hard work we've done today.'

# Chapter Thirty-five

'You're going to have to take that chaise-longue out of the window, Marty – it looks strange and deserted without someone reclining on it!'

'Hmm, maybe you're right. Okay, so let's leave it where it is and I'll go and find a very Victorian lady to stretch out full length on it. We could turn it into a feature of the shop. We could have someone perched on the dining chair, another squatting on the chamber pot—'

'Enough already!' Jon leaned forward and laughed long and hard. 'This is a sensible grown-up shop and you have to behave yourself. Now away you go out the back and get to grips with the accounts. Hopefully we've made a few bob at last; it's been three months now, we must be breaking even soon.'

'Yes, sir! Right away, sir!'

Marty was feeling satisfied with his new life and happy that he had let Jon persuade him into opening the antique shop that, after much discussion, they had called *Odds and Ends*.

Without the pressure of working late into the night

rushing around behind a bar, the two men were both more relaxed, able to make the most of their time together. They had both turned their backs on the club scene and were happy just concentrating on their shop and each other. Marty had discovered the urge to nest and spent as much time as he could in the small flat over the shop, furnishing it, decorating it and turning it into a home.

Standing out of sight behind a grotesque but attractive jardinière and planter, Marty watched Jon affectionately as he obsessively arranged and rearranged the knick-knacks inside the display cabinets and then polished every pane of the glass. Whereas Marty was flamboyant in both appearance and personality, at least on the surface, Jon Castle was very low-key and neutral. Unlike Marty, Jon had never kept his sexuality a secret but nor had he shouted it from the rooftops. It had helped that he was from a chaotic and extended theatrical family that had immediately welcomed Marty in exactly the same way as they had their other son's girlfriend.

Jon was not handsome but nor was he unattractive, despite being a couple of stone overweight and paunchy around the middle. At ten years older than Marty, he had one of those faces that improve with age, and the gentle laughter-lines that were accumulating around his eyes and mouth added to his appeal for both men and women. Everyone who knew Jon Castle liked him.

The two men were happy and settled together, and Marty especially loved the security their relationship afforded him. Smiling to himself, he went through into the area they jokingly called the office and started checking through the paperwork that Jon hated but for which Marty had developed a surprising flair.

Because there was just a screen dividing the office from the shop, Marty could vaguely hear the everyday shop conversations between Jon and the customers but they usually washed over him as background noise as he flicked through the invoices and order books and clicked away on the adding machine.

After about an hour of heavy concentration behind the screen, Marty heard the doorbell ping as another customer entered the shop.

'I'm looking for a gift for a friend of mine. A young man who deserves something extra special for his services.'

The voice boomed and registered slightly at a subconscious level with Marty but at the same time he couldn't be bothered to get up and have a look. There were already many regulars who browsed and chatted but then didn't buy, and Marty wanted to get the paperwork finished.

'Is it for a birthday?' he heard Jon ask politely.

'No no no, it's a gift for a young man for some *special services* over and above his usual duties. I'm sure you get my drift.' The disembodied laugh reverberated around the shop and into Marty's space.

At that instant the familiarity of the voice from the past hit him in the gut like a sledgehammer and Marty could feel the bile creeping up the back of his throat. It took all his willpower not to throw up as an all-encompassing terror swept over him. Slowly he forced himself further into the corner away from the stinking presence that he knew was about to defile his and Jon's beloved shop.

Even after all this time, he had known without looking that it was Mr Smith.

'What sort of thing did you have in mind, sir?' Jon asked, still missing, or pretending to miss, the innuendo. 'An ornament? A picture? Or how about this antique wash-stand? These are very popular right now for the bedroom.'

Mr Smith laughed again. The dark, disgusting laugh that had a language all of its own. It was the same laugh that Marty had heard in the background during the most painful and terrifying experience of his life, as time and again he had been debased and tortured by both the sadists and their objects of sexual abuse. Despite the long time-lapse since Marty's ordeal, he again experienced the fear that had accompanied that sound.

'Now explain to me, darling boy, of what use could that be in the bedroom?'

Marty knew that Jon would be feeling uncomfortable but he didn't know what to do to help him. He was frozen to the spot, physically incapable of doing anything. Jon had never been overtly gay. He was comfortable with himself but he never camped it up and he had, over the months, gently persuaded Marty to tone it down. *There's no need, love. We're just Jon and Marty, a couple like any other. No need to deny it, but no need to make a song and dance about it either. We are who we are.*

'They make unusual dressing-tables,' Jon answered sharply,

310

'but maybe this Staffordshire jug would be more suitable for a gift? Or possibly this delicate local watercolour?'

'No, no, darling boy.' The laughter echoed again. 'That's not what I want at all. Let us go back to this interesting wash-stand for the bedroom. I can tell you and I have the same tastes, and I'm sure we could both find a use for something as multi-functional as this.' Again the laugh rumbled ominously. 'Maybe I'll just get my friend a one-way ticket to somewhere instead and you and I can . . . get to know each other better. Hmm?'

'Mr Cornish, are you there?' he heard Jon call to him politely. 'Could you come and help out here? This gentleman is looking for a gift for a friend and your input would be much appreciated.'

Racked with fear and guilt, Marty couldn't even answer, let alone go to help; instead he slid down into the footwell of the old office desk and curled up in a shivering ball, hoping that if Jon came round the corner he would think he'd gone out. No way could he go into the shop and once again see the face of Mr Smith.

Then he heard the bell ping and guessed that someone else had come into the shop.

'The car is outside, sir. When you're ready,' the second most familiar voice from that night muttered deferentially. There was no doubt in Marty's mind that it was Anthony, the Neanderthal minder.

It was at that point that Marty shivered so much he wet himself, but still he stayed where he was.

'I have to go now, darling boy,' he heard Mr Smith murmur, 'but if you can think of anything suitable for my friend, or of course, an *alternative* use for the wash-stand in the bedroom, then here's my card. Ring me, hmm? I'm sure we can come to an agreement on terms and conditions. As I said, I like to pay over and above for good service.'

The bell tinkled again, and although Marty was sure they had left he stayed where he was, petrified and completely ashamed of both himself and his damp trousers.

'Marty! What are you doing on the floor? Didn't you hear me calling you? The biggest dirtbag in the history of the world was just in here making lewd and disgusting insinuations. I thought you'd hear and come and help me out. It was sickening, truly sickening.' Jon shuddered involuntarily. 'He's the sort who gives the rest of us a bad name.'

'Sorry, didn't hear. I dropped my lighter and couldn't find it again. Who was he?'

He watched as Jon looked down at the card as if it was infected. 'Dieter Morgan-Brown . . . I know that name – but where do I know it from? He's someone I've definitely heard of.'

'Is there anything else on the card? An address or something?' Marty slipped back onto the chair behind the desk and reached his hand out casually as if it was really of no interest to him and took the card from between Jon's fingers. 'Well, *I've* never heard of him. Another day, another dickhead. The world is full of them. Just forget it and hope he doesn't come back, eh?'

With a shrug he flipped the card nonchalantly straight into the bin. 'Now you go and make the tea and I'll just finish up here. It's time to shut up shop for the day.'

As soon as Jon was out of the room Marty retrieved the card, put it in his wallet and ran upstairs to shower and change his clothes. At the same time, he instantly started plotting his revenge because, the moment he had heard the name, he had known exactly who Dieter Morgan-Brown was and, because it was also on the card, he also knew where he could find him.

Dieter Morgan-Brown, aka Mr Smith, was a well-known big-shot business agent who was also the father and manager of Allie Brown, a pretty young adolescent singer destined, according to the papers, for squeaky-clean pop stardom.

Mr Smith was actually the alias of a high-profile, long-married, popular character who projected himself as a 'man of the people'. The same man who had dressed up in leather and chains and sadistically whipped and raped Marty to within an inch of his life. The same man who had laughed gleefully as his masked friends did the same.

Then and there, Marty decided that he was going to set this bastard up and then 'out' him to the press. The fuse to his unresolved anger over that night had been relit, and he was determined to get his revenge at last.

# Chapter Thirty-six

For the first time in his life, Jamie Kirk had a job that he was taking seriously and he was loving every minute of it. He could see clearly that the sky was the limit for him financially, so long as he continued to follow every order to the letter. The Boss worked on a bonus system that rewarded success with hard cash, and so far, Jamie was doing very nicely, thank you; he had been earning enough to help Eleanor out with the renovations. Enough to ensure that she was in his debt, so when the time came she would feel obliged to do as he wished.

He went to the factory unit every day and loosely supervised the employees working there but he also went out 'on visits', ostensibly looking for new business. It was a brilliant set-up that operated alongside a genuine working business with only two people in there knowing exactly what was going on.

Marco Dunston, the immediate boss, and Jamie himself.

Jamie had done such a good job impressing the relevant inmates when he was inside that he could see his future as a mirror image of Marco's, and he eagerly anticipated the day when he was powerful, financially secure and could command respect once more on the Rat-Trap.

Jamie Kirk simply loved the feeling of power that surged through him when he was carrying out the Boss's orders, so now he was on his way to visit Peter Longdon as he had been told to do, and was looking forward to flexing his muscles and his authority.

Even Jamie, with his skewered take on morality, couldn't believe that the guy he was going to put the frighteners on was Megan Murphy's father. In his time Jamie had tried it on with both of The Saucy Sisters, and Megan and Venita had knocked him back quite vehemently, but despite that he had got on with them and bore them no ill-will. However, Peter Longdon was a different matter. Even Jamie had standards, and the thought of Megan's own father touting pornographic photos of her and Venita to the highest bidder made him twitchy with anger. He knew that if the photos were published in England the girls and their reputations would be ruined.

The address he had been given was an old three-storey house in the East End divided up into as many individual flats and bedsits as was physically possible. As he walked up the steps to the front door he saw it was ajar so he nipped in and took the stairs two at a time until he found the number he wanted.

He rapped hard on the door and waited for a few moments before swiftly kicking the door in with a centred boot. Quickly he scanned the scruffy bedsit to check that no one was hiding before turning the place over. Flipping the flimsy sofa-bed, he pulled all the bedding out then emptied the chest of drawers and tipped everything from the tiny kitchen area onto the floor. He knew they had to be there somewhere – if not the actual photos, then the negatives.

He could deal with Peter personally at another time, but his priority was finding the photos to keep The Boss happy. However, there was also a part of him that wanted to smash Peter Longdon to a pulp because it made him feel ill just to think of a father doing something like that to his daughter.

'What the fuck—!'

Jamie spun round and snatched at the baton he had laid on top of the small cooker; he was anticipating Peter Longdon behind him but it wasn't him.

'What have you done to my gaff?' The young man stared at Jamie and then looked over his shoulder at the girl behind him. 'Go and call the police, Joyce, quick. Get down to the phone box, tell them there's a burglar.'

In fear, the girl hesitated for just a second then turned and disappeared down the stairs. For a moment Jamie was bemused and wondered if he had got the wrong place; the couple were just kids.

'Don't give me crap,' he said roughly. 'This isn't your place, this is where Peter Longdon lives.'

'No, he fucking doesn't, and I am so pissed off with idiots like you coming here to look for him. We've only lived here for a week and as far as I know, he's in Spain – he left a couple of weeks ago.' The man looked over his shoulder down the stairs. 'You're too late; as I told the other bloke who wanted to batter me, he's long gone.'

Aware of 'confidentiality and respectability' Jamie knew he couldn't afford a run-in with the police so he dug into his pocket and pulled out some notes.

'Sorry, mate, this is for the damage.' Then he pushed him to one side and legged it down the stairs and round the corner to his car, cursing all the way. Not only had poxy Peter Longdon got away from him, he had also got away with the photos.

Jamie knew The Boss would not be happy and he simply didn't know what to do next. Megan! he thought suddenly. She would know where he was — and if she didn't know about the photos he might just be able to blag it enough to get the information he desperately needed.

Eleanor was standing in the kitchen eating a sandwich and looking out of the open door at the newly laid lawn where the magnolia tree had been. A wave of sadness swept over her at the thought of how it could have turned out for her parents if only . . .

Commonsense had told her that it was not right to keep the tree, which was only a memorial to evil, but to avoid any personal involvement, she arranged for a local firm to dig it up and take it away to be burned while she and Jamie were out for the day. They also levelled the ground and matched in some rolls of turf and made it all look as normal as possible.

Now there was nothing to mark the spot but she knew she would never forget; her parents would always be with her in her own memory and that was all that mattered.

She was so far away in thought that it took a few seconds before Eleanor realised that the phone was ringing in the hall.

'Lennie? It's me! How goes it with my favourite girl?' Marty's voice bounced down the phone line.

'Hi, Marty, I'm great. I was just standing here filling my face and day-dreaming. How goes it with you two?'

'So so. I need some advice and maybe some help.'

'Ooh, don't know if I'm any good at that any more,' Eleanor laughed. 'Not problems with Jon, I hope?'

'No, no, everything is fine with Jon, couldn't be better. Look, can we meet up somewhere, preferably at lunchtime when Jon's back at the shop? I need to talk to you face to face. You're the only person I can confide in.'

'What's it about, Marty?' Eleanor asked him curiously.

'Mr Smith, that's what. You remember him? Well, I've found out who he is!'

Eleanor had been off-ish with Marty the previous time he had phoned because Jamie had been there; as she didn't want Marty to know about him being back in her life, she had cut it short and lied to Jamie about who was on the phone.

There was still a part of her that resented being told that Jamie was no good. Marty, Megan and Venita, and then Greg, had always made her feel as if they thought she was too immature and unworldly to make her own decisions. She respected their concern, but no longer wanted their advice, so it came as a relief when she realised that Marty hadn't found out about Jamie and actually wanted to talk about something else.

The small backstreet pub where they had agreed to meet was half-empty, with plenty of free tables, so they took their drinks over to the one in the bay window that looked out onto the street.

'Oh, it's so good to see you, Lennie. I thought you were giving me the brush-off last time I phoned. How's the decorating going? Nearly finished?'

'Getting there. I'm enjoying it actually. Who'd have thought when we first met at the old Regency Hotel that I'd end up having a flair for interior design and you'd become an antique dealer? Maybe we ought to set up in business together! I can decorate, you can furnish.' She laughed loudly at her own suggestion, but when she looked closely at Marty, she saw his face was deadly serious.

'Mr Smith came into the shop,' he said in a whisper. 'He came into our shop and behaved like a disgusting fat pig to Jon. And while he oozed filth I did nothing except cower out of sight under the desk and wet myself.'

'Oh, Marty.' Eleanor sighed and took his hand. 'I'm so sorry, but that was only natural after what that pervert did to you, it's nothing to be ashamed of. What did Jon say? Did you call the police?'

Marty looked down at his hands that were moving

nervously. 'I've never told Jon anything about it. You're the only person who knows. And as for the police, can you imagine having to tell a couple of sniggering coppers what those bastards did to me?'

'You should have told Jon, he of all people would have understood.'

'Well, it's too late now, the moment has passed when I could tell him – but that's not why I wanted to talk to you. I now know who he is. Lennie, you won't believe it, but he's only Dieter Morgan-Brown, the agent and the father of that young singer Allie Brown.'

Eleanor shook her head. 'Never heard of him or her, but then unlike you I was never that into the music scene.'

'He doesn't only deal with music, he's always got a comment on something or other. He's rich and famous and pretends to be such a nice guy. His wife used to be a model and his daughter's a singer. They're the perfect family!'

Eleanor was suddenly concerned for her friend. 'What are you thinking about doing, Marty?'

'Well, I'd like to do the same to him as he did to me and then kill the bastard stone dead, slowly and painfully, but I'm prepared to settle for just making sure everyone knows about him.'

'No, Marty, you mustn't! You're opening a dangerous can of worms,' Eleanor said agitatedly. 'You told me at the time what a thug his bodyguard was. Anthony, wasn't that his name? I mean, do you want to put yourself in the firing line again?'

'I have to.' Marty lowered his voice again as another couple sat at an adjoining table. 'Now I know who he is, I can't just let it go. I mean, I bet I'm not the only victim of him, and his friends. He can't be allowed to do that to people! He can't – I won't let him.'

Eleanor watched as Marty tried to stop himself from shaking violently as the memory of the nightmare came back to him again. As she recalled the way he had been at the time, and how long it had taken him to get over it, her anger bubbled but she knew it wouldn't be good for Marty to try to get revenge on someone like Mr Smith. The man was well out of his league.

'I agree with you absolutely that he should pay, but isn't there a better way? As I said, how about going to the police? They can't all be biased. Surely that would be a safer option,' she suggested.

'No!' Marty snapped. 'It was too long ago for the police to be able to do anything anyway, and if I let it go then I just know it'll happen again. You should have heard the way he was speaking to Jon – it was disgusting.'

'All the more reason to be careful. He knows who Jon is – so if he finds out you're a couple . . . Oh Marty, don't do anything silly.'

'Lennie, I have to, and I'd like you to help me plan it. I don't want to put you in the firing line, I don't want you to actually do anything, just help me plan a strategy that will completely screw Mr Bigshot Morgan-Brown.'

'I don't know, I think it's too dangerous for you. I don't want you to get hurt again, or Jon,' Eleanor replied, but at the same time she knew she would help him. When the chips were down, she'd do anything for Marty.

# Chapter Thirty-seven

'There was a phone call while you were out.' Jamie was waiting by the front door when Eleanor arrived home, the expression on his face dark and angry. It was a look that she hadn't seen for a long time, and she couldn't figure out the reason for its sudden reappearance.

'Who was it?' she asked as she dumped her coat and bag on the table in the hall while simultaneously kicking off her shoes.

'Not a fucking clue. I thought *you* could tell me. Whoever it was hung up when I answered. Twice. Two calls – two hang-ups. Makes me think they only want to talk to you.'

'How strange.' Eleanor shrugged her shoulders expressively. 'Oh well, I'm sure they'll ring back.'

'Oh, I'm sure they will,' he paused and looked directly at her before continuing, 'now that you're home to answer the phone yourself. I mean, it's obvious it's you they want to speak to. Not me.'

Because she couldn't quite understand his anger, Eleanor didn't answer or even react, so Jamie carried on ranting.

'And apart from that, where the fuck have you been? I

came home unexpectedly and abracadabra, as if by magic you'd disappeared without even leaving a note.'

Eleanor smiled quizzically as she tried to figure out his anger. 'And you think I should have left a note? Am I sensing an undertone here?'

'Oh no, Lennie, not at all, no undertone.' He glared. 'I'm asking you outright. What's going on? The one time I come back early, there are dodgy phone calls and you're not in. You've sneaked out while I'm at work—'

'Jamie, if you're going to start being constantly suspicious again . . .' She paused for a second and then said, 'Look, let's get over this, eh? I don't have to account to you and you don't have to account to me about what you get up to when you're out and about doing whatever you say you do when you apparently go out to buy cigarettes.' She watched his face carefully for a reaction and noticed his eyes narrow slightly; she was pleased that he was the first to look away.

Eleanor hadn't confronted Jamie about the day when he had allegedly forgotten his wallet. She preferred to keep what she knew to herself for the time being, especially as there had been other incidents that had raised her awareness. Nothing big, but together it was all adding up to Jamie being deceitful.

He didn't know that, as soon as the front door had closed, Eleanor had run up the stairs and watched him through the leaded-light window at the top of the house that oversaw most of the road outside. There was just one small clear pane in the whole window with a panoramic view, and it was a bit of a mission to get high enough to see out of it; it needed the body at full stretch with one foot on the windowsill for support and a hand on the coving for balance. Eleanor had discovered it when her father had locked her in, and she had made use of it recently whenever she needed to have a good view of the road. And Jamie.

She had watched him as he sprinted down the path and up the road, and then slipped into a waiting car. She had then watched and waited until the car dropped him off again.

And then, of course, he had come back and blatantly lied to her.

'What's up with me is that everything I do here is dead money without any commitment from you. Let's face it, you could be seeing anyone when I'm at work. I'm just the mug doing all the grafting and paying all the bills.' Jamie had started pacing the entrance hall as he carried on ranting.

'That's just plain nasty,' Eleanor said hotly. 'You offered to help and I said I'll pay you back when it's sold. We agreed, no commitment – just take each day as it comes, we said.'

'No!' he shouted ferociously. '*You* said that. I just agreed because I want to be with you. I want us to get married and live here. I want kids. I want money—'

Eleanor cut in without thinking. 'You and I can never have a family, never! I can't have children.' The words were out before she could stop them. She had thought about telling him one day, but she hadn't intended it to be like this, screamed out in anger.

'Bollocks! You got pregnant before, easily enough.' His tone was accusatory as he moved towards her.

'Yes – and I lost it, as you know. Well, just for the record, I also lost my womb in the process. I was given an emergency hysterectomy to save my life. I can never have children because of that. Never, ever, ever.' She broke down and sobbed.

'Why didn't you tell me then? Why keep it to yourself. Nah, I don't believe it. You're using this as an excuse.' She could see Jamie trying to assimilate the unexpected information.

'Because you were off your control-freaking head. You were only interested in this house and the money you thought I had.' She looked at him quizzically. 'And now, have we gone full circle? Have I let myself get caught up in that again? Am I really that stupid?'

'Of course not. This time it's different.' He forced a smile as he reached out to touch her but she moved away. 'Look, I'm sorry, you know how I feel about you, Lennie. I just get so het up when I think you're going to dump me. Marry me? Please!'

Eleanor's own anger faded in an instant. It was déjà vu; she'd been here before. Except this time she was calm about it but she could sense Jamie was irrationally losing control.

'Okay, I tell you what, I'll marry you if we sell this place as soon as possible and move out of London. It'll just be you and me in a cottage in the country. We could start up our own decorating business—'

'In your dreams! I've got a career here, I'm going to be big. I need you here with me, I need to live here, I have to be respectable . . .'

As she watched Jamie fighting to control himself, Eleanor felt sad but not heartbroken; she was pleased she had given it another go with Jamie because now that she knew it would never work out, she could move on from him.

As they faced each other in stand-off, the phone rang and Eleanor went to answer it.

'If that's the shithead who's been hanging up on me, I'll have him!' Jamie shouted after her. 'Tell him I'll break his balls when I get hold of him.'

Eleanor picked up the phone. 'Hello?' she said. 'Oh my God!' she cried out happily after a pause. 'I don't believe it. It's so good to hear from you. How are you?'

At that moment Jamie tried to snatch the phone from her hand.

'Can you just hang on a minute?' She spoke again into the mouthpiece but Jamie continued trying to wrestle the phone from her. 'Look, have you got a number I can call you back on very shortly? I really, really want to talk to you, it's been so long and I've missed you, but I'm in the middle of something right now . . .' Tucking the phone between her shoulder and her ear she grabbed the pad and pencil she kept nearby. 'Okay, I've got it. Just wait there and I'll call you back just as soon as I've sorted this problem out.'

Slamming the phone onto its cradle, she spun round. 'Jamie, I'm sorry but I'm done with all this. We've tried but it's never going to work. I can't deal with this shit again. I'll always be fond of you, but—'

And then she saw him lean towards her with his hands outstretched. There was a rage on his face that was also tinged with fear, and as she tried to figure out what it was that had set him off, she felt his hands tighten around her neck . . . and all hell broke loose.

After she hung up, Cathy Hart sighed with relief. She'd been in London nearly a week before finally plucking up the courage to make the call, and she was thrilled that Eleanor hadn't just hung up on her. Pushing the heavy phone-box door open with her backside, she stepped out onto the pavement just down the road from Eleanor's house.

With hindsight, she knew that at the time she had packed her bags and run away to stay with an old nursing friend in Wales, she had been quite unbalanced. Her hormones had been raging and her baby obsession had completely taken over her life. Nothing else mattered to her – not her husband, her family or her friends, or her job. She had reached her own breaking-point where she was determined to have a baby one way or another, and she couldn't bear the thought of anyone trying to stop her. Especially Paddy.

But now she was feeling sane again and wondering how to resolve all the aspects of her life where she hadn't behaved well. Although she still resented Paddy for his dogmatic behaviour and intransigent views, she could see it had been wrong, after so many years as his wife, to just pen a brief note and go off without saying where or why.

But now she was back and, unable to face Paddy immediately, she had sought out Eleanor first. After dialling the phone number she still had for the shared house and finding it disconnected, Cathy had gone to the old address, only to find it boarded up and covered in Keep Out notices, along with the neighbouring buildings. She very nearly didn't bother any further, for the August heat was driving her mad, but then she thought about it again and, because she knew everything about Eleanor medically, she contacted the girl's original GP professionally and was given the name of her new GP, whose receptionist had easily parted with the address and phone number.

It had shocked her when she'd phoned and she had recognised Jamie Kirk's voice; her instant reaction had been to hang up on him because she wanted to speak to Eleanor herself, not have that little creep Jamie tell her first.

Although Cathy had never been to the Hampstead house, she knew that it was the old family home and wondered what had sent Eleanor back there after everything that had happened. And with Jamie Kirk, of all people.

She waited a while for the phone in the box to ring but when it didn't she started to wander up the road, and she arrived outside the house just in time to see Jamie, with blood all down the front of his shirt, race out, jump into a car parked by the kerb and drive off with tyres squealing.

'Lennie?' she screamed as she ran heavily up the path and

stuck her head round the open front door. 'Lennie, where are you?'

Eleanor appeared in the kitchen doorway. 'Cathy! I was going to phone you back but I got sidetracked.'

Cathy was bewildered; Eleanor didn't seem to be hurt.

'That was Jamie, wasn't it, who flew out of here like a bat out of hell with blood everywhere?' she asked.

'Yes – another big mistake of the Eleanor Rivington variety, but it's over now for good. I've seen the light at last! And he's okay. He's got a bit of a cut on his shoulder and a badly damaged ego. He started a row about nothing and then he tried to bully me again. I don't take bullying any more. Shame about the vase, though.'

Cathy looked down and saw glass all over the hall floor.

'Do you know he actually put his hands round my throat?' Eleanor went on. 'Bastard! I grabbed the vase and hit him. I didn't really hurt him, though. But look – come in, it's great to see you—' She stopped and looked at Cathy, open-mouthed. 'Oh my God! You're pregnant – you're fucking pregnant. Oh my God! How did that happen? Look at the size of you! Does Paddy know?'

'Of course not, you daft girl.' Cathy rubbed her huge belly that was nestling under a vast smock dress and smiled happily. 'Haven't you realised? This here is why I panicked and ran away. This is nothing to do with Paddy – it's all thanks to you! This is my DIY AID baby!'

# Chapter Thirty-eight

Although Eleanor was proud of Marty's tenacity regarding Mr Smith and she could understand how he felt, she was nonetheless concerned for her friend because he was becoming obsessive about the man.

He had even taken to phoning her nearly every day to give her updates. She knew it was because she was the only person who was aware of what had happened to Marty during his time as a prisoner in Mr Smith's apartment, therefore she was the only person he could talk to, but it was wearing her down. Especially as she had the very pregnant Cathy staying with her in the Hampstead house and likely to give birth any day.

Marty told her he had checked out Mr Smith's business address and then he'd set about systematically gathering as much information on the man as he could. Every spare minute of his time, when he could get away from the shop without arousing suspicion, was spent digging for and recording information via any and every source; he wanted to know everything about Dieter Morgan-Brown, his family and his friends.

However, although the dossier he had put together was extensive, none of it was incriminating. There was nothing to connect the man or his Neanderthal minder to anything other than a couple of incidents of illegal parking. Even his apartment in London wasn't the same as the one he had taken Marty to that night.

'What am I going to do, Lennie? I have to find something on him,' he whispered into the phone so Jon wouldn't hear him. 'I can't just give up on it – he could be attacking others every night of the week.'

'Well, I think you're playing a dangerous game but I know you'll not take any notice of me when I tell you to give up on it, will you? So maybe you could phone one of the newspapers anonymously, let them carry on with it?' Eleanor suggested. 'You see, I can't help thinking you're wasting your time. If he can do what he has been doing without ever being caught, then you'll never be able to trip him up on your own.'

'I never thought of the papers – brilliant! I'll phone one of the Sunday rags and tell them all about him, then they can do the work. Why didn't I think of that?'

'Still be careful though, eh? I don't want anything to happen to you,' Eleanor murmured supportively.

'Thanks, Lennie, I love you! I'll be as careful as I can but now I know who he is, I have to nail him, I just have to.'

Eleanor deliberately changed the subject. 'Hey, I know what I meant to tell you! Now, I don't want you going off on one but guess who's staying with me at the moment?'

'Not that little runt Jamie Kirk,' Marty spluttered.

Eleanor laughed loudly. 'No, he's been and gone and you missed him, but that's another story. No – it's Cathy, Cathy Hart the nurse from when I was in hospital? She's back in London for a while so she's keeping me company.'

'Oh great,' Marty sighed sarcastically down the phone. 'Just who you need in your life again. The mad nurse of Notting Hill.'

'Now that's not fair, she's had a pretty rough time of it but I'll tell you all about it another time. Right now I need to buy some really cheap stuff to furnish another room, so can I come to the auctions with you? You can buy the good stuff, the antiques, and I'll buy the leftovers that no one else wants!'

'Okay. I'm going on Monday but I don't see why you have to buy the furniture for her to stay in your house.'

'And also,' Eleanor continued excitedly, ignoring his jibe, 'I'm going to lunch next week at this really posh place in Knightsbridge with Megan and Venita. They're treating me. I haven't seen them for ages, we've all been so busy.'

'Good for you. At least one of us is doing okay then.' Marty's sarcasm echoed down the line.

'Marty!'

'Sorry, Lennie, sorry. I just can't concentrate on anything much right now. First thing in the morning I'm going to phone one of the Sunday rags. Maybe something will happen after that. If I can just bust his balls I'll be satisfied – I'll be able to get over it at last.'

★   ★   ★

Jamie Kirk was knocking on the door and getting no reply so he resorted to kicking it gently with his foot. Then he kicked it a little harder repetitively with the steel toe-caps on his shoes. Despite doing his best to stay clean and respectable, it was becoming harder and harder for him to cope as everything started to unravel around him; he knew he had to find a way to stop it before it all went too far.

Despite Jamie's best efforts to flush him out, Peter Longdon had disappeared without trace but with the photographs and negatives, and Jamie's immediate boss was unhappy because he had screwed up. Jamie felt affronted. It wasn't his fault that the scumbag had got away; he had been looking forward to dealing with him, but that wasn't how it worked in the business.

The first big job he had been trusted with had been to get the photos from Peter Longdon – and he hadn't done it. He had also been told to give the bloke a scare and he hadn't done that either. That had been enough of a failure for him to receive a stern warning from his immediate boss at the unit; then he had been informed that there would be no bonus; then Eleanor had chucked him out and wounded him quite badly on the shoulder. His pride was badly hurt too.

He knew he had been stupid taking it out on her after he had been given the humiliating dressing-down, but he had had to take his frustration out somewhere, and now he was angry with himself for getting angry and right back on the old treadmill. In order to redeem himself and regain his self-respect, he would just have to find Peter Longdon wherever he was and beat the crap out of him.

Jamie heard a noise from inside but as he was about to kick the door again it was pulled back and a very bedraggled and hung-over Venita stood in front of him.

'What the fuck is going on? How did *you* get in the building?' she snarled at Jamie who was standing in the doorway with his hands on his hips and a big phoney smile on his face.

'State-of-the-art security my arse, Ven darling. I just slipped in before the door closed on your neighbour. You really must get that fault looked at, you know!' He wagged his index finger at her. 'I've come for morning coffee with my favourite Saucy Sisters.' Quickly pushing past, he left her standing holding the door back with her mouth agape.

'Oi! Get out of here, you little shit. How dare you just push in here like you own the place?'

'Where's Megan?' As he said it he started going round the square lobby of the apartment, flinging open doors and looking in.

'Jamie! Stop it!' Venita pulled at his sleeve to try to stop him but he brushed her off.

'Where is she? Where's Megan?' he repeated angrily.

'She's not here. She's down in Eastbourne dumping Johnny. Now come into the kitchen and bloody well calm down. I'll make us a coffee and you can tell me what all this shit is about.'

'I don't want a coffee, I want to see Megan. Well no,

that's not strictly true. I want that scumbag of a father of hers, Peter Longdon, and I'll put a fiver on her knowing where I can find him.'

'Why? What's he done to you?'

'I tell you what, Ven – I will have that coffee, and then I'll tell you all about it, as it involves you as well.' He swaggered into the kitchen behind her. 'Nice gaff you got here. Got a spare room for an old friend? I could be your new minder. Like Marty used to be, except I'd be much better.'

Venita couldn't help smiling. 'Yes, we have got a spare room and no, you're not having it. Now come on, tell all.'

Against his better judgement but desperate to find Peter Longdon, he swore Venita to secrecy and then told her all about the photos.

She started panicking immediately. 'Oh God, Jamie, if those get out, Meg and me will be finished in mainstream glamour. No newspaper will touch us! And what about our friends? How on earth did he get them?'

'Not a clue, Ven. I haven't actually seen them but I was told they were pirates from a shoot.'

'The bastard!' Venita was close to tears. 'I bet I know when he took them. I caught him peering at us when Meg and I were doing the scummy shoot that he set up for us. He promised us that they would only go to the European mags. And it was only meant to be one shoot but he persuaded us to do another couple.' She shuddered. 'Oh yuk, Megan is his daughter.'

'Well, I guess he decided to skim a bit off for himself

– and now I *have* to find him. I want to get to him before he does something with them. So where do you think he could be?'

'Dunno. He told us he was going to Thailand on holiday – he's been gone a couple of weeks now. Let's hope he's too far away to do any damage.'

'But I've got to find him,' Jamie snapped angrily. 'My livelihood depends on it. If I don't get those back then I'm in big trouble.'

'Well, you're not going to find him in Bangkok. Mind you, he can't do much harm there so I don't know why you don't just forget about it.'

'Well, of course he can, you daft cow – haven't you heard of Royal Mail? Anyway, I need to find him so I can prove myself to my new boss. Me and Lennie—'

'What's Lennie got to do with this?' Venita interrupted. 'Have you been bugging her again? You know you're not good for her – and vice versa, I reckon. Why don't you stay away from her and find a girlfriend in your own league?'

'Oh, enough going on about Saint Lennie,' Jamie said irritably. 'You're not her mother, none of you are. Now what can I do about Peter Longdon?'

Venita frowned. 'Let me give Megan a call. I suppose we could all do with getting those photos back. What are you intending to do to Peter if you do find him?'

Jamie looked at her intently and then laughed.

'Okay, I get your point,' Venita responded knowingly. 'Let me ring Megan and see what she's got to say.' Picking up the phone she dialled the number but there was no answer. 'No one there – I'll ask her when she gets back tonight. Where can I get hold of you?'

Just as Jamie was writing down the number of the factory unit there was the sound of a key in the lock and then a clattering in the lobby.

'Ven? Are you up yet? I'm back early – couldn't bring myself to stay after I'd given him the news.' The door to the kitchen opened, then: 'What the fuck are *you* doing here?' Megan said.

'Thrilled to see you too, Megan!' Jamie smiled. 'Now where's that delightful father of yours? I need to have a little word with him.'

# Chapter Thirty-nine

A warm breeze travelled up from Hampstead Heath and gently rattled the glass in the newly painted window frames of number 24 Ashton Gardens, signalling the arrival of summer.

Eleanor, who was all alone in the house, was gearing herself up to face her final, darkest demon. Terrified of the consequences of confronting what had happened to her, she had put off even looking in the dining room but now she could no longer delay. The time had come for the house to be put up for sale; Eleanor wanted the money to pay everyone off and start afresh somewhere new and she couldn't sell the house with one room still to be gutted and decorated and, more importantly, with her demons not completely exorcised.

With help from Jamie, Aaron and Hettie's sons and the occasional passing workman in need of some instant tax-free cash, Eleanor had thrown herself whole-heartedly into successfully renovating the house.

She found she could turn her hand to almost anything and once she had got into the swing of DIY, learning as she went along, it had become something of a superstitious mission to her, a project that had to be completed in order for her to be able to successfully move on with her life. It was no longer just the old Rivington family home, it was something that needed fixing and putting back together in much the same way as Eleanor herself did.

Fortunately, the bricks and mortar of the well-built property were sound so there had been no structural outlay but, within the walls, virtually every inch of the old house had had to be repaired, stripped and painted.

However there was still one room that remained untouched. Throughout the time she had been back at the house the dining-room door had remained firmly locked but Eleanor knew now that the time had come to open it.

Gritting her teeth so hard her jaw ached, she stood motionless in front of the closed door for several minutes before taking the key from its hiding place inside the lining of her handbag. Cautiously, she turned the key and pushed the door back wide on its hinges, letting loose the smell of damp mustiness that she remembered so well.

Initially, she took an involuntary step backwards as her subconscious played games with her, but she forced herself over the threshold.

She wasn't sure what she had anticipated but it certainly wasn't to find the room exactly as it was in her memory. The tenants hadn't touched it at all so, despite the lack of furniture that made it seem far larger, nothing had changed. She saw the same flowery wallpaper, the same worn and cracked lino and, worst of all, the same awful curtains that she knew every inch of.

Sometimes, when Eleanor was in the twilight zone of half-sleep, a snippet of memory would come to her but then her brain would suppress it before she could make sense of it. Eleanor wanted to confront that memory, to unlock her mind and move on.

She went over to the far corner and just stood there with her face to the wall and, automatically, she gripped the window sill with both hands.

Closing her eyes, she tried to clear her mind to let the memory back. As the musty smell of the old curtains wafted up her nostrils she wanted to run but she didn't, she couldn't, she was transfixed by the atmosphere.

She could sense her father again, he seemed so close she could almost smell him and she wanted to run. But she didn't.

*'Take off your clothes, Eleanor.' He was angry because her room was 'untidy'.*

*She could hear her father's voice but she couldn't bring herself to look at him. 'I can't. Please don't make me.'*

*'Take them off. Do as I say or you'll stand here until morning.'*

*Slowly, she peeled the top layers off but kept her vest and knickers on.*

*'Everything off, I said.'*

*Sobbing, she pulled off her vest then quickly crossed her hands across her blossoming chest.*

'Everything off.'

'I can't.'

'Now or I'll take them off for you myself and you'll have double punishment.'

Slowly, she slipped her navy serge school knickers down to the floor while still keeping one hand over her chest.

'Stand up straight, hands by your side,' he ordered.

She was sobbing and shivering but still she kept one hand over her chest and the other in front of her pubic area.

'HANDS BY YOUR SIDE,' he bellowed even louder.

Slowly she did as she was told and then to her shame felt the dribble of blood running down her legs.

'I can't. I've got my period,' she sobbed.

'Get in the corner and bend over, you vile child,' he snarled. 'How can you talk to your own father about things like that. You disgust me.'

Crying hysterically she did as she was told and then he punished her as he always had. Six swipes with the slipper with an extra one for defying him.

As always, he took his time and it seemed like for ever before he walked over to the door, but this time, as he turned the key, the door flew open and she heard her mother come into the room.

'You bastard, how can you do this to your own daughter? She's a woman now, can't you see that?'

Eleanor looked over her shoulder and was shocked to see her mother's normally calm face screwed up in a combination of anger and hatred.

Her father turned and raised his hand to hit his wife but Eleanor *saw her mother duck away and then reach out a hand that was gripping a kitchen knife. She pointed it at him. 'Let her out now, let her go and clean herself.'*

*Eleanor didn't dare move. She heard her father roar as he lunged forward and her mother scream out in pain. The couple fell together through the doorway into the hallway and then there was silence.*

*Terrified, Eleanor stayed in the corner and started to count the flowers on the curtains. The silence was eventually broken by a dragging noise and the sound of the back door opening and closing. Then he came back in.*

*'Get dressed, Eleanor, and go straight to your room. I'll take you to school tomorrow.'*

Suddenly, back in the present, Eleanor was shaking and sobbing, in much the same way as she had when she had last been in the room. Trying hard to get her jumbled thoughts and memories into some sort of order, she looked around her. Had her mother really tried to protect her? Had her death been a ghastly accident rather than the cold-blooded murder she had imagined her father had perpetrated?

Feeling exhausted, Eleanor sank down on to the cool lino and cried.

# Chapter Forty

'Lennie!' Cathy called.

'What's the matter? I'm up the ladder on the landing, changing a light bulb.'

'I don't want to frighten you, but I think I'm in labour.'

Instantly panicking, Eleanor clattered down the ladder and then took the stairs three at a time down to the sitting room where Cathy was lying curled up on the sofa looking flushed and uncomfortable.

'What do you want me to do? Is it time to call the ambulance?'

'I'm not sure.' Cathy's breathing was deep and loud as her arms hugged her belly tighter. 'The contractions are really strong but they have only been going a short while and I don't want to go too soon. I know what they do there! A shave and an enema and all sorts of indignities . . . yuk.'

'How long have the pains been going on?'

'Only about an hour.'

'An hour?' Eleanor shrieked. 'Why didn't you tell me then?'

'I wasn't sure then. Don't shout at me. This is bad enough as it is.'

'Do you want a cuppa then? Just tell me what to do and I'll do it.'

'I don't know.'

'But you're the nurse.'

'I know, but this is different. This is me and this is my baby.'

As she sat up and leaned forward, puffing furiously, Eleanor sat beside her and automatically started rubbing her back.

'You're not going to give birth on my sofa, are you?' Unsure of how to react, Eleanor laughed nervously; she didn't have a clue what to do.

'I'm not sure, maybe you *should* call the ambulance . . . I might be further on than I thought. Oh bugger bugger, I wish I'd gone to antenatal classes! *Aaaaaahhhhhhhh*!' she wailed, terrifying Eleanor who was already en route to the phone. 'Lennie, I think it's coming . . . I can't believe this, it just can't be this quick.'

'The ambulance is on its way,' Eleanor said in a voice that trembled.

'I can't wait,' Cathy screeched. 'I've got to push, I've got to *push*!'

'No, not yet – you mustn't. You can't have it here with no doctor or anything.' Eleanor could feel her heart palpitating so hard she thought it was going to explode in her chest. She and Cathy had discussed what would be done when the pains started and she had anticipated a ride in the ambulance followed by lending a sympathetic ear to her friend in the labour ward alongside all the medical staff.

Cathy suddenly hoisted her skirt up to her waist, ripped off her pants and lay back down again with her head on the arm of the sofa.

'Lennie, I think it's here, it's here, I've got to push . . .'

Eleanor froze for a few seconds before her instincts took over. She ran into the hall and then rushed into the kitchen to the washing basket and grabbed a handful of clean towels.

'Okay, okay. Try and hang on for the ambulance, they'll know what to do.'

But Cathy already had her knees up and was grunting and pushing. Eleanor looked down, and to her horror she could see the baby's head emerging.

'Oh my God, Cathy, I can see the head. What do I do?'

'Be ready to catch it!' Cathy screamed. 'Don't let anything happen to my baby . . . *Aaaaaaeeeooowww!*'

The loudest of screams was accompanied by the baby's head forcefully emerging, followed seconds later by the slippery body. Despite her panic Eleanor had one of the towels ready so she gently slid it around the baby.

'What do you want me to do, Cathy? What do I do?'

Still crouched down on the floor by Cathy's feet that were pulled up to her bottom, she looked down in panic at the writhing little thing in the towel then gently lifted it up, aware of the cord that was still connected. Instinctively she wiped its face and mouth with the corner of the towel and then suddenly it spluttered and started to yell.

Eleanor froze for a moment and then started crying herself. Huge gulping sobs as the enormity of the situation hit her.

'Is it okay? Is it a boy or girl?' Cathy asked weakly, her teeth chattering, shaking violently from the shock of the birth.

Hardly able to see through her tears, Eleanor fumbled with the towel. 'It's a girl. Oh Cathy, she is just so beautiful . . . Here, look . . .'

As she handed the baby over, Eleanor heard the bells on the ambulance outside, followed by footsteps in the tiled lobby.

'In here!' she shouted. 'But you're too late!'

A few days later Eleanor was sitting beside Cathy and talking to her, but the new mother's attention was constantly being drawn to the tiny baby fast asleep in the Perspex crib at the end of the bed.

'I can't believe it, Lennie. After everything I went through, I've finally done it. I've got my own baby. I have a daughter!'

'I know, I was there,' Eleanor smiled.

Cathy looked at her intently. 'Are you going to be all right with this? Do you want me to move out? I can see it's bringing it all back to you, all that stuff that happened. I don't want it to make you ill again.'

'It is bringing it back, yes, but in a nice way. Just so long as I can be Aunty and best friend to her I'll be happy, if a little envious. She's so gorgeous and I'm thrilled for you, really I am.'

'Do you think I should tell Paddy? I was going to tell him she was his, I didn't want my baby to be illegitimate, but it isn't fair, is it? She isn't his. But then I have to see him about a divorce. Do I let him think I had an affair? Or do I keep this a secret?'

'I think you should forget about it for now.' Eleanor smiled with her eyes still on the crib. 'You have all the time in the world to deal with all that; just enjoy having your baby. You've waited long enough.'

'I do wonder about the father, you know.'

'Well, don't. He isn't a father, or a daddy, he was just a sperm donor. Now, have you decided on a name?'

'I have. I'm going to call her Hope. After all the years of hoping and hoping . . .'

'Oh Cathy, that is so lovely, now I'm going to cry again.' Eleanor stood up and leaned over the crib. 'Hello, Hope. I'm your Aunty Eleanor!'

'Oh, you should see Hope, she is adorable. I'm so completely in love!' Eleanor confessed as she was telling Megan and Venita the story of Hope's arrival. 'I'm going to be her godmother – I delivered her on the sofa . . .'

Megan and Venita exchanged amused glances and each raised their eyebrows at the same time. The three friends were seated at a circular table in the centre of the up-market restaurant having lunch. Apart from a few short phone calls and a quick café catch-up, they hadn't really talked properly since the day they had all left the shared house.

'Oh, come on,' she chided them. 'I know you thought Cathy was strange and I suppose she was a bit, back then, but it was because she was so desperate for a baby and it sent her a bit loopy. Just imagine yourself in that situation.'

Megan laughed. 'How the hell could I do that? I spend all my time trying not to get pregnant!'

'Yeah, me too,' Venita joined in. 'I'm mid-scare right now.'

'Yes, well, there but for the grace of God and all that jazz.' Eleanor smiled sadly. 'You shouldn't take the piss, you know, it might just be you one day, trying and not succeeding. Trust me, infertility isn't a barrel of laughs.'

Venita looked from Megan to Eleanor. 'Sorry, Lennie, we didn't mean it, it's just our warped humour. Can we come round and see her sometime? The baby, I mean! Though I'm a bit foxed as to why Cathy dumped her husband just as soon as she succeeded. Very strange, I reckon – I bet it's not his.' As Eleanor glared at her she changed tack. 'Okay, sorry!' she sniggered.

'Apology accepted. How about next week?' Eleanor answered brightly. 'Oh, and you must also tell me how gorgeous the house is and how clever I am! Okay, no more baby talk, now tell me what's been going on with you both lately. How's the work situation?'

'We've actually got a bit of a problem at the moment,' Venita grimaced. 'We did a photo-shoot that was a bit porny – well, very porny actually – but really well paid, sort of doing everything, close-ups and all that for a continental lesbo mag, and now someone has copies of the photos. I knew we shouldn't have agreed to do it. I didn't want to and we'd never done anything like it before . . .'

'It was my idea,' Megan admitted. 'It was stupid but that kind of stuff pays loads more than the ordinary tits-out shots. However, Venita should learn to keep her big mouth shut . . .'

'Oh, that's awful. Do you know who's got them? Can't you buy them back?'

'No.' Megan glared at Venita as she spoke. 'He's abroad right now. A friend is tracking him for us, so we should get them back.'

Eleanor listened to what they were saying but knew instantly from their body language that there was more to it.

'Remember me? I'm Eleanor, and I'm not stupid any more. What aren't you telling me? Come on, the whole truth now.'

The instant Megan shrugged, Venita's mouth was up and running, and once she started chattering she proceeded to tell Eleanor everything. As she finished there were a few moments of silence before Eleanor reacted.

'I can't believe your father would do that—' She stopped and smiled sheepishly. 'Though who am I to comment on fathers and their weirdo behaviour! Anyway, how come Jamie Kirk seems to crop up so regularly in our lives? He's like the naughty child under the table at a party who keeps tugging at the cloth so we can't ignore him! And now he's after your dad. Wow. I have to say that I'm stunned.'

'Not as stunned as me,' Megan said sadly.

Eleanor looked at them both again. 'Did he tell you about him and me?'

'Said you'd had a bit of a fling but you'd gone all serious again. I'm sorry, Lennie, that's why we didn't want to tell you that he'd been round. He said you'd be upset all over again.'

Eleanor laughed so loudly the diners at the next table glared at her. 'Oh dear. Good job I can laugh about the lying git now instead of having a breakdown!'

'Lennie, if you were with him, then do you know who he's working for? I know he's into something really dodgy and that somehow it involves those photo-shoots and my dad. He was telling us some of the story but then he started lying, I know he did.' She stopped as the waiter came over to the table.

'Excuse me, is one of you Miss Megan Murphy?' he asked quietly.

'That's me,' Megan replied.

'There's an urgent phone call for you. You can take it at reception.'

Megan frowned as she stood up. 'The only person who knows we're here is Johnny – I told him at the weekend. Why would he phone here? I hope he's not thinking we're going to get back together.' Pushing back her chair she followed the waiter through the restaurant and out into the reception area.

'I can't believe Megan's father would do that,' Eleanor

was murmuring. 'And she was so pleased to have him back in her life. What a shit.'

'Yeah, especially after the crap childhood she had. My parents were – still are – lazy, no-good drunks who should never have been allowed to have kids in the first place, but something like this? It stinks.' She looked over. 'Ssshh. She's coming back.'

Megan looked white-faced and dazed as she sat back down. 'That was Johnny. Dad's been badly beaten up – he's in intensive care in Margate. Bangkok, my arse – he was back in Margate with one of his many slappers. He had my agent's number in his diary, so she phoned Johnny. I'm going to have to go and see him, I suppose.' She looked from one to the other. 'You don't think it was Jamie who did this, do you? He was steaming mad when he was looking for him.'

'I don't know,' Venita sighed, 'but I suppose it's likely, after what he told me.'

'Which was?' Eleanor asked curiously.

'That his great new job is as hired muscle for some local villain. Didn't you know?'

'Well, of course I did. I lived with the bloke, didn't I?'

# Chapter Forty-one

When Eleanor rang Marty to tell him all the news, she knew he wasn't listening. He was just waiting for the gap in the conversation so that he could tell her where he was up to with Mr Smith.

'Why don't you and Jon come round and meet Hope,' Eleanor suggested. 'She is such a gorgeous baby, you'll love her. Please?'

'Okay, okay, don't keep on. Babies don't do anything for me — which is lucky, I suppose. Mind you, Jon is quite besotted with his nephews . . . crazy little sods that they are. I guess he'll enjoy meeting the psycho nurse's baby.'

'Stop saying that,' Eleanor sighed. 'I've told you before . . .'

'I know,' Marty interrupted with a laugh, 'Psych Nurse has morphed into Saint Cathy. I've said I'll visit and I promise I'll drool. What more do you want?'

'That'll do. And now you've agreed to that, I'll let you tell me your news. I know you're dying to!'

'I think I've found the apartment he took me to that night. It looks the same, but according to my spy it's in his wife's maiden name. Wonder if she knows what her Mr Nice Guy tycoon husband gets up to there in his spare time?'

'I thought you were going to hand everything to the paper?'

'I just wanted to make sure there was enough to hook them, and I'm hoping that maybe this is it. Oh Lennie, I can't wait to see his slimy face spread all over the papers, and for him to be publicly disgraced. Jail would be better, but disgrace will do nicely for now!'

Without Marty realising, Dieter Morgan-Brown had twice spotted him hanging around in the underground car park of the block where his secret penthouse apartment was situated. The apartment he kept specifically for his favourite hobby and which had a state-of-the-art surveillance system extending all the way down into the car park itself.

Marty was a stunning young man with perfect features and smooth, almost hairless skin that, combined with his shiny long blond hair, made him stand out in a crowd. It was exactly that which had attracted the older man to him in the first place, and it was those same good looks that unfortunately made sure he was recognised as he stupidly hung around near the doors to the elevator area trying his best to look like a delivery boy.

Much as Dieter Morgan-Brown adored handsome young men and boys, he never used the same one twice for security reasons, and he certainly didn't like them knowing who he was or where he operated from; he enjoyed his opulent lifestyle far too much to endanger it with any scandal. As soon as he had realised it was Marty, he had ordered his favourite pet bodyguard Anthony to follow him, find out everything he could, and then report back before doing anything.

Dieter Morgan-Brown was, publicly, a very jovial character and he was loved by his clients and the media. A churchgoing family man, he always insisted his clients were scandal-free and had no skeletons in their cupboards that could affect his reputation. He was very vocal about keeping up standards in entertainment and was completely open about the fact that, before allowing his sixteen-year-old daughter to go into the business, he had insisted she sign a moral contract promising to not smoke, drink, take drugs – and to remain a virgin.

Dieter Morgan-Brown was seen by everyone as a good, upstanding man in an increasingly immoral business, fighting against the moral decline of the decade.

A couple of times in the past he had used money to silence any young men who tried to cause him a problem, but on one occasion that had ended in a very messy blackmail attempt. Now he just preferred to stop it at source with a visit from the ever-efficient and sadistic Anthony, and it had worked fantastically well because none of the boys that Mr Smith picked up and took home to his pals ever wanted to repeat the experience.

Anthony was Morgan-Brown's secret weapon. The highest

paid and therefore most loyal bodyguard and chauffeur in Britain.

He was sure that a visit from Anthony would be an equally successful lesson for Marty the barman. All the information that the bodyguard had easily gathered made Dieter Morgan-Brown a very happy man; he loved it when he could kill two birds with just the one stone. Or rather, get Anthony to do it for him. He could pull Marty Cornish back into line and ensure total loyalty from the new boy, Jamie Kirk, at the same time.

Every Wednesday afternoon, Jon was always in the shop alone while Marty went to a regular auction in Surrey, and it hadn't taken Anthony long to find that out; so on that particular Wednesday, while Jon was deeply engrossed in buffing a small oak planter at the very rear of the shop, two men strolled casually along the road chatting together just like two friends en route to the pub. Anthony was tall and muscular with shoulders nearly as wide as he was high, Jamie was small and wiry. As they reached the shops called *Odds and Ends*, they ducked sideways into the doorway.

Before they pushed open the door, Anthony's face was expressionless as he stared Jamie straight in the eye. 'Not one word, you understand? Do not make a sound. Not a sound.'

Jamie nodded as the adrenaline started to flow. How hard could it be to issue a warning? He'd happily put the boot in on Peter Longdon. Why not someone else? Only as they got to the door he realised where he was and he guessed it would either be Marty or Jon, even though he couldn't imagine what they had done to warrant a beating.

But Jamie knew that if he bottled out, or even queried what they were about to do, then it would be him instead. That was how it worked.

As he cautiously opened the door, Anthony reached his hand up to a curved piece of brass wire on the door frame and twisted it to stop the bell from ringing. They then easily crept unnoticed into the shop, gently shut the door before flipping over the Closed sign and pulling thick black masks with eye-and mouth-holes down over their faces.

The two men silently approached Jon from behind; Jamie grabbed his arms while Anthony gagged him with a knotted piece of material before pulling a mask down over his face. Then, in one practised movement, Anthony held one of Jon's hands flat down on the desk while twisting the other up his back. No one heard the muffled scream of agony as Jamie did exactly as he was told and smashed the bones in Jon's right hand to smithereens with a cut-off baseball bat that Anthony kept just for that purpose.

As Jon writhed in muffled agony and started to sink to the floor, Anthony grabbed him under the arms and pushed him face down over the desk. Jamie watched in horror as he then pulled Jon's trousers and underpants down, and held the handle of the bat against his anus, twisting it very gently.

Then, after pausing for several seconds to compound Jon's fear, he viciously forced the handle of the bat right up inside him as far as it would go.

He then removed it and casually wiped it on Jon's underpants as the latter slid to the floor. The attack only lasted a few minutes but by the time it was over Jon was already unconscious from the combination of fear, pain and loss of blood.

As they pulled off their hoods and left the shop, Anthony smiled. 'Fucking nancy boys. I hate 'em all.'

Anthony and Jamie then went off in opposite directions.

The day after the attack, while Jon was receiving major surgery for life-threatening internal injuries as well as the damage to his hand, Marty received a phone call.

'Mr Smith and his friend suggest you stop stirring up trouble right now if you want your friend Eleanor to be safe. And Megan. And Venita. And we won't be as gentle with the girls as we were with your friend. Or you.'

It had been a calculated risk but Mr Smith had cleverly worked Marty's fears out correctly. That it would be far more effective to attack his friend Jon than him personally. Mr Smith knew Marty would never be able to admit that it was his actions that had brought the attackers to Jon, and he was sure he would never take the chance of the girls being assaulted because of him.

Another successful silencing operation which, with Jon

unable to identify his attackers and with no witnesses, was swiftly filed under the heading 'sexually motivated'.

Jon was destined to be just another crime statistic.

Jamie was petrified. All he wanted to do was run and hide and never have to go back to the unit where he 'worked' again. Even Eleanor's idea of a cottage in the country was sounding more and more attractive by the moment; any thoughts he had had of a glamorous life of crime had dissolved like the sugar in his tea. He wondered if he felt worse because it was someone he vaguely knew, or if it was because just of Anthony's brutality. The smashing of joints was something that villains liked to do, and in prison there had always been attacks on sex prisoners, but Jamie had never been so closely involved.

When he had been told he was going out with one of the head honchos he had been over the moon. He saw it as the break he had been waiting for, a sign of acceptance, and he had stupidly let his ego be massaged by being told that it was because he had redeemed himself by finding and damaging Peter Longdon and getting the photographs back.

'Good job, Jamie,' he'd been told. 'The Boss is well impressed.'

Without any specific information, he had bounced along enthusiastically en route to the 'job' which was described as 'having a quiet word with someone causing problems for The Big Boss'.

As soon as they turned into the shop Jamie realised what was going on and suddenly felt sick. For an instant he thought the person they were going to 'talk to' would be Marty, but when they grabbed and hooded the man standing innocently in his shop Jamie had realised it was Jon. Marty's partner.

Smashing his hand with the bat that Anthony had secreted inside the sleeve of his coat was one of the hardest things he had ever done, but when Jamie saw what Anthony did to Jon, it was all he could do not to vomit on the spot. He had had no choice but to watch as Anthony happily tortured the man, and suddenly he had a vision of what might happen to him if he fell from grace.

As quickly as he had wanted in, Jamie Kirk now wanted out, but he couldn't see any way that he could escape. He was up to his neck in it, but then and there he decided he would just have to harden up, make the best of it. He could feel the bulging wallet of recompense that was in his pocket as he stretched his legs out in front of him and smiled as his nan tottered towards him with a cup and saucer in her hand.

'Thanks, Nan, I really need that. It's been hard today.'

'You looked a bit bothered when you came in. Are you keeping out of mischief? Only I don't want none of that stuff coming to my doorstep.'

'It's okay, Nan. Everything is great. I've just realised that if I can keep doing what I'm told I'll have a good future with the company. I hope it's not going to be too repetitive though.' Jamie sat up and pulled out the wallet. Taking five twenty-pound notes from it, he said, 'Here you are, Nan, go and treat yourself. You deserve it for being so kind to me.'

'Are you sure this is good money?' the old woman asked hesitantly.

'Absolutely! I earned every penny of it!'

# Chapter Forty-two

It was a mild and sunny late-September morning, and Eleanor was strolling around the garden enjoying the way the light poured in, now that the shrubs and trees had been pruned and the darkness cleared away.

Kneeling down on the new lawn, in the walled garden, her tears fell on the place where her mother's body had been buried.

'I think I know what happened now, I think I remember,' she whispered. 'You tried to protect me, and got killed for it. So much madness, Mummy – but it's going to stop now for ever. Whatever happens, I'll never forget you. I forgive you, I really do, and I even forgive him now.'

Dabbing at her eyes with the sleeve of her sweater, she heard the distant ring of the doorbell, and rising with a last look at the spot where the tree had been, she went back into the house.

'Johnny!' she shrieked with delight, her sombre mood gone in an instant at the sight of Johnny Quentin standing in the porch.

'Hello there, gorgeous. A little dickie bird told me you wanted to keep in touch, and as I was up in London bringing Megan's stuff back to her, I thought I'd drop by and invite you out to dinner. How are you, my darling?'

'Oh Johnny, come in. You don't know how pleased I am to see you,' Eleanor said happily. 'I was scared you'd slink off and then meet someone in Eastbourne, get married and we'd lose touch.'

As he reached forward and kissed her gently on the cheek Eleanor flung both her arms around his neck. Johnny Quentin was the nicest person she knew – and that was quite aside from the fact that he had saved her life.

'Never would I lose touch with you!' He stepped inside. 'So, this is the Hampstead equivalent of the Sistine Chapel I heard so much about.' He looked up and around the spacious lobby. 'It looks great now though. Maybe you should take it up for a living. Eleanor Rivington, Interior Decorator to the Stars!'

'I must admit I'm thinking about it, though maybe not quite to the stars. Come through and I'll put the kettle on then we can catch up. Did you hear about what happened to Jon?'

'I did.' Johnny shook his head. 'That was so awful, and then there was Megan's dad getting beaten up as well. I hate violence, it just seems to be everywhere nowadays. I mean, who'd do something vicious like that?'

Eleanor couldn't quite meet his eye; she didn't actually know anything, but she had bad vibes about the whole situation. Something wasn't quite right about the way Marty had described the attack. She could tell he was keeping something from her. There were so many things Eleanor had been giving thought to just lately.

'Someone with a grudge?' she asked, still facing away from him. 'Although I can't think who'd have a grudge against Jon. He's so mild – unless it really was just because he is queer, as Marty said. It does seem to be happening more and more.'

'So how's Jon doing now?'

'Not very well.' She turned round. 'Physically he's not too bad, although he had a bad beating and his hand still has to have more surgery, but mentally he's a mess.' She smiled wryly. 'And I can relate to that all too well. I've told Marty to keep a close eye on him but he's a wreck himself. He's taken it so badly – he seems to be blaming himself.'

'It must be hard for everyone. Megan's dad is doing okay as well, he had a good battering but he'll live. Let's hope he disappears now, he was so bad for her.'

'I'm sorry about you two . . .' Eleanor said, feeling a bit embarrassed.

'Oh, don't be.' Johnny grinned widely. 'It was no big deal; the relationship had run its course for both of us. I was impressed with a Saucy Sister and Megan was impressed with me being impressed. We both had fun and my credibility went sky high at the taxi office! We'll stay friends though, I hope.'

Eleanor and Johnny chatted together comfortably and

she suddenly found herself looking at him in a different light. He was good looking, hardworking, honest and gentle natured . . . But then she realised where this was taking her and she dismissed the thoughts as quickly as they had appeared.

'Dinner is a great idea,' she said, 'but let me cook it here. Cathy and her baby Hope will be back from their walk soon; we can all eat together.'

Johnny Quentin looked at Eleanor and smiled. 'Sounds good to me.'

As Eleanor was cooking their meal of roast chicken and cauliflower cheese, and Johnny was concentrating on cooing over the baby, she was turning all sorts of things over in her mind in no particular order when she suddenly stopped what she was doing and froze. The words 'someone with a grudge' echoed around and around. 'Someone with a grudge against Jon' was what everyone had assumed. Suddenly it hit her.

*Maybe it was 'someone with a grudge against Marty' who got Jon by mistake.*

One Dieter Morgan-Brown, perhaps. Also known as 'Mr Smith'.

'Megan, Megan, get out of your pit. We're in big trouble. Megan – get up, will you!'

Venita flung her friend's bedroom door open with a crash and ripped off her bedclothes. 'Your fucking father has really done it now. We're all over the papers. Listen to this: "Saucy

Sisters are Dirty Sisters", or how about "They're not Sisters
– Meg and Ven are Lesbians"!'

In shock, Megan sat bolt upright. 'You what?'

'Look at all this! Go on, read it.' Venita chucked the
papers on the bed. 'The phone hasn't stopped ringing, each
of our so-called friends wanting to be the first to break the
bad news.' Furiously, she paced her friend's bedroom, waving
her arms around. 'That's it. Our careers are officially down
the toilet.'

'But I thought that whoever had beaten him up would've
got the photos – why else did my dad get battered? And
Jamie told us it was all sorted, that we were safe.'

'Haven't you ever heard of negatives and copies?' Venita
raised her eyes to the ceiling. 'Megan, can you see what this
means? Our reputations are completely done for.'

'Maybe we can lie low and wait for it all to die down.
Perhaps we could go to Spain or something. It'll blow over.'
Megan wrapped her arms around her knees and shrugged
helplessly. 'It has to, we're not that important.'

'I know it'll blow over but we'll never do mainstream
again. That underwear contract will get pulled *and* the hair-
spray advert. All because of you and your obsession with
having that loser in your life.'

Angrily, Megan sprang off her bed and pushed Venita
hard on the shoulders, sending her stumbling across the
room. 'You are such a bitch. Maybe if you'd been nicer to
him and let him do more for us, then he wouldn't have had
to resort to this.'

Venita held on to a chair to keep her balance. 'Oh, just open your eyes, will you? Why did you fall for it? He only appeared when he realised you could be his cash cow. I just don't understand. You've no interest in your mother, in any of your family, in fact, but then this weasel who did a runner when you were a baby appears from nowhere and you fall to pieces and revert back to an insecure five year old.'

'I needed someone in my life – I needed a father.' Megan stamped her foot in temper. 'It's all right for you . . .'

'No, it isn't. I have fuck all to do with any of my family and I'm fine. He's a con artist, Meg, can't you see that?' Venita's voice was getting louder as she continued her furious rant. 'How can you possibly call him a father? And those photos? That's vile. Just as bad as rape – as if he'd raped you himself.'

'No it isn't, we posed for them. He could have just bought the magazine, like your father could.'

'Most fathers wouldn't want to even look at their naked daughter, let alone take photos and sell them.' Venita rubbed a hand across her face and sat down heavily. 'I am never taking my clothes off again,' she said. 'That is it. No more naked stuff. There must be something else we could do.'

At that point Megan suddenly dissolved. Huge gulping sobs wracked through her as she absorbed the enormity of her father's betrayal.

Instantly Venita softened and, pulling her friend close, she hugged her tightly and murmured gently into her hair, just as she would with a child. 'It's okay, Meg, we'll be okay.

We'll do something – we've got savings and money to come. I'm sorry I shouted at you. I didn't mean it, I know it's not your fault.'

'Yes it is, it's all my fault.' Megan sobbed harder. 'You're right about him. I hate him! I wish Jamie had killed him.'

'You don't know for sure it was Jamie.'

Megan laughed harshly. 'Of course I know it was him – and so do you. But it's Jamie who'll be next when his top-of-the-range thug-boss hears about this. Dad has turned us all over. You, me and Jamie.'

'Yeah, well, I don't give a toss about Jamie, he shouldn't have got involved in it all but then that's him all over. Always an eye for an opportunity to make a fast buck.' She paused for a moment. 'Come on, we'll have some coffee and then decide what we're going to do.' Venita grabbed Megan's hand and dragged her through to the kitchen. 'I've taken the phone off the hook now. We have to try and figure a way out of this mess.'

'And I'm going to have to go to the hospital to confront Dad.'

The buzzing of the intercom made them both jump.

'Ignore it. We don't want to see anyone.' Venita grimaced at Megan. 'God, I hate this already. Today's Sunday, just imagine what it'll be like tomorrow.'

'Perhaps we can get out of the country by then?' Megan replied with a smile.

But someone had their finger on the intercom and it just kept on buzzing.

Megan rushed to the door and pressed the button. 'Give it a fucking rest. We don't want to see anyone!' she snapped.

'It's me – Lennie – you miserable cow. I came to see if I could do anything to help.'

'In that case, have you got two tickets to Malaga and a couple of yashmaks in your bag for us?'

# Chapter Forty-three

When Eleanor got off the bus from seeing Megan and Venita her mind was in a confused whirl. It was as if she had all the pieces to a jigsaw puzzle in front of her but no picture on the box to help her put them together. As she walked down Ashton Gardens, she itemised the pieces. There was Marty and Mr Smith. The attack on Jon. Megan and Venita and the porn photos. The attack on Peter Longdon. Jamie Kirk. They might all be inter-connected – but how?

Eleanor opened the front door and stood inside the porch looking down the path and thinking. She could still picture Jamie bouncing off to work importantly kitted out in an expensive suit. She could also see him in his fashionable jeans and T-shirt walking in through the front door carrying huge bags of expensive wallpaper that he had 'got cheap off a friend'. There was the odd bottle of champagne and flash bunches of flowers. And of course, the day before she had thrown him out, he had come home with a company car . . .

Did all the cash Jamie had to throw around match the income of someone working in a factory, she wondered.

Had she herself colluded in all this by not asking the questions that were always in her subconscious?

Her brain kept shooting back to Mr Smith who, despite all the work he had put in, Marty had decided not to pursue any more . . .

Why had Jamie been so altruistically keen to pursue Peter Longdon to get back the photos of Megan and Venita? And how did he know about the photos, anyway?

Who was the man in the car outside, whom Jamie had twice sneaked off with?

But however much she thought about it all there was nothing on which to base any of her suspicions, other than instinct – and the fact that she knew Jamie wasn't averse to a bit of violence. The pieces wouldn't fall into place.

'Lennie . . . cooeee! You're not hearing me again. What planet are you on this time?'

Cathy was standing behind her laughing, with a wide-awake and contented Hope cradled in her arms. Instinctively, as she turned, Eleanor reached out and gently stroked the baby's cheek. Her face was round and pink with huge eyes and a brush of sandy hair that stood up as if in shock. Hope's strange entry into the world had done her no harm and she was as happy as a tiny baby could be.

'I was thinking that, just maybe, this house has been decorated from top to bottom, inside and out, on the proceeds of crime,' Eleanor said frankly. 'I think the money that Jamie Kirk produced so readily wasn't really his, or that he'd got it by dubious means. With hindsight, Cathy, I reckon that

Jamie Kirk is into something really big and bad, and was using me for a cover.'

Cathy looked at her with a very quizzical smile. 'And? You didn't really think he'd changed that much, did you? A complete about-turn by Jamie Kirk? Come on, be honest with yourself. Did you think he went out and harvested the money tree?' Arranging the shawl more cosily around the baby, she turned back into the house. 'Jamie is, and always will be, a charming toe-rag, but you knew what you were doing with him, didn't you?'

'I suppose,' said Eleanor, following her inside and closing the door. 'The first time I was naïve but the second time I was more aware and it suited me. There's still something about him, you see. I'll always be in love with him – I just can't help myself. But you know, Cathy, there's something niggling at me over the attacks on Jon and Megan's dad. It's driving me crackers, like an itch I can't get to.'

'Best left alone, Lennie, my dear. You have to concentrate on you and what you're going to do now, not worry about the ifs and buts that will never get sorted. Just forget it. As for me . . .' She paused and looked Eleanor directly in the eye.

'And as for you, what?' Although Eleanor guessed what was coming.

'Please, Lennie, I really need to know who Hope's biological father is. I want you to find out for me. I've thought about it and I just want to know. For the future. For Hope.'

Eleanor felt a mixture of sympathy and annoyance. She

loved having Cathy and Hope staying there, it gave her a comforting sense of family. Cathy was becoming more of a mother figure to Eleanor than a friend, and of course there was baby Hope, whom Eleanor idolised. But Cathy kept on returning to the same subject and it bothered Eleanor; it had been a done deal at the time and she didn't want to constantly revisit that awful time in her life.

'Don't try and blackmail me with Hope,' she said, but gently. 'It's just not an option. It was agreed in the beginning and I'm not going to ask Marty to tell all now you've changed your mind. I'm just not.'

'Do you think it was Jon? I look at Hope and wonder . . . she does look a bit like him.' Cathy fished.

'Stop it! Marty has loads of friends – it could have been any one of them. You can't suddenly alter the rules. It's not fair.'

'Supposing she becomes desperately ill and we needed that information.'

'Then of course we could get it. Come on, Marty didn't even know it was for you. He thought it was for someone who worked at the hotel. He'd be furious with me if I brought it up again. Especially now with everything else going on. I'm not going to ask him.'

'You could easily find out without letting on. I don't want the father involved – in fact, I don't want him to know. I just want to know who he is,' Cathy pleaded.

'I won't do it, Cathy. If you'd had the treatment at hospital it wouldn't be an option, would it?' Eleanor turned and went through to the sitting room with Cathy hot on her heels. 'It was done for you as a favour and only because she was going to be your husband's baby, remember?' She hesitated, and changing the subject very slightly she said, 'What are you going to do about Paddy? You're still married to him, aren't you, Cathy? Doesn't he deserve some explanation?'

'I don't know what will happen but yes, I am going to call on him and tell him about Hope. Then we'll see where the wheel stops after that. See how he reacts. I mean, I was completely out of it when I ran off. I'm hoping he'll understand that.'

Eleanor pulled a face. 'Hmm. I wouldn't hold your breath. He was so angry when I went round there to see you, he looked in a right old state. Oh Cathy, I wish you hadn't left it so long to contact him. How will he react to you actually having a baby he knows nothing about, that he hasn't fathered himself? Pregnant would have been dodgy enough, but a baby?'

'I might not tell him about Hope straight away. Is it okay if I leave her with you while I go? I may go tomorrow, if I'm feeling brave enough.' Cathy shivered. 'If not, then I'll go the day after. I have to try and find out his shifts first – if anyone at the hospital is still talking to me.'

'Of course it's okay.' Eleanor smiled, relieved that she had moved the conversation on. 'I love having her all to myself but I do have to visit Jon in the afternoon. I promised Marty. Jon has been told he can go home to recuperate but at the last count he was refusing to go. Jon is absolutely terrified of leaving hospital.'

Eleanor arrived at St Mary's Hospital the next day to find Marty sitting in the corridor with his head in his hands. Jon's family were sitting further down on the opposite side of the corridor and the atmosphere was noticeably frosty.

'What is it, Marty? What's happened?'

He looked up and she could see he'd been crying. 'Jon is going home with his family. They want to look after him. I think they reckon that I'm a bad influence, that he's not safe with me. And they're right, Lennie.' He wiped his eyes. 'It's all over – the relationship, the shop, everything . . . and all because of that . . .' He stopped himself mid-sentence.

'All because of what?'

'All because of this attack. I think Jon blames me for not being there.'

'He'll come round,' Eleanor reassured him with a hug. 'He needs time to accept it. Remember the way I was when I was in shock?'

'This is different. His family, who I thought were my family as well, have turned against me. Look at them, they don't want to have anything to do with me.'

Eleanor looked over at them and smiled but the response was polite rejection. At that moment Jon was wheeled down from the main, long ward by a nurse; another walked beside the chair with his case. His chin was down on his chest and he held his bandaged hand gingerly with the other. He didn't even glance at Marty. Quickly, his mother jumped up and took the handles of the chair and his father took the suit-case; in a split second they were gone from the ward and into the main corridor.

'Aren't you going to say something? Talk to him?'

'No point. He's right to want me out of his life – I'm a waste of space. Look, Lennie, I'll explain later. Right now I just want to go out and get pissed.'

'No, you don't, Marty. I won't let you. We'll go to the flat and pack you a bag and then you're coming home with me.'

'You've already got a houseful.'

'It's a big house!'

While Marty was snatching up a few things from his flat, Eleanor went down into the shop on the pretext of checking it was all safe and secure, but really to ring Cathy and not only warn her that she was bringing Marty back to the house but also warn her off even thinking about mentioning Hope and the AID donor.

As she was talking, Eleanor glanced around the darkened interior of *Odds and Ends* and felt a sadness at seeing Marty and Jon's pride and joy looking dusty and neglected.

The phone was on the desk where the assault happened and she could see the dried blood beside it; it spooked her more than she had anticipated. But even more horrible than that were the dried pools on the floor where Jon had collapsed. She could see instantly why Jon didn't want to go back there and why Marty wouldn't go down the stairs. The police had finished with it, and Eleanor resolved to come back at some stage and give the whole place a thorough clean.

As she replaced the receiver she took one last look around – and that was when she saw a small gold tie stud with the back missing, lying beside a jewellery tray where someone had obviously placed it, thinking it belonged there, that it was part of the stock.

But it wasn't. Eleanor recognised it instantly as the stud she had bought for Jamie last Christmas, the one she had chosen and had delicately engraved with his initials in miniature. A pattern invisible to the naked eye.

Picking it up, she studied it carefully before rolling it round and round between her fingers then dropping it into her pocket. At that moment, the pieces came together.

Jamie had been part of the assault and was therefore working for Mr Smith. There was no other explanation for the tie-stud being there.

'Are you ready, Marty?' she shouted up the stairs, trying to ignore the horror of her realisation. 'If so, I'll go and flag a taxi.'

Because of Jon's attack, Marty hadn't yet been round to Hampstead to meet baby Hope, but it was obvious he wasn't interested in her. He made the right noises to both Cathy and the baby, and then took himself off to his new bedroom.

Eleanor followed him. 'What haven't you told me about Jon's attack, Marty?' she said straight out. 'I know there's something. Do you think it was Mr Smith behind it? Did they get Jon by mistake? You had been tracking him—'

Marty spun round. 'Why can't you leave it alone? You're like a dog with a fucking bone. Haven't you got enough in your life without interfering in mine? Or is that your new role in life, taking in deadbeats? First Jamie, then Cathy and her kid, and now me. Are you after a sainthood as well?'

Stunned, Eleanor shouted back at him. 'Hey! Don't you dare talk to me like that! I know you're upset and if you don't want to tell me then don't, but don't be so bloody rude about it. I'm just trying to help.'

She turned and went out of the room, and as her foot hit the top stairs the door slammed hard behind her. Pausing, she listened for a moment and could hear Marty sobbing loudly. But she didn't go back into him; she was hurt that he'd shouted but she understood that she was simply the whipping boy. Marty just needed some time alone in private.

She also knew from his reaction that she was right. But she didn't have a clue what to do about it.

'There are some letters on the top for you,' Cathy said as Eleanor went into the kitchen. 'How is he feeling?'

'Not good, but then it'd be strange if he was. I've left him to deal with it alone – I think it's best for a man.'

'Mmm. Have you found out what it was all really about?'

'No, not yet, but I intend to – and if it involves Jamie, like I think it does, then I'm going to break his neck. It just seems as if he's managed to cause trauma for all of us. Me, Marty, Megan and Venita . . . though so far, you're safe.'

# Chapter Forty-four

Jamie Kirk was furious when he found out, the way he always found everything out, that Cathy the nurse and a surprise baby had usurped his position in Eleanor's life. Cathy was now living in the house in Ashton Gardens and enjoying the results of all his hard work while he was back on the Rat-Trap. It wasn't fair.

Though he knew he could afford to go and get his own place now, it wouldn't be a big house in Hampstead and he had no chance of finding another classy bird like Eleanor. He almost quite enjoyed the feeling of being hard-done-by, so he wallowed and told a tale to the other lads of dumping her because she was frigid. His bad mood was compounded by being back in disgrace because Peter Longdon had managed to sell the photos and also escape. Not only had he disappeared without a trace, but Megan and Venita were also in hiding.

The truth, that he had screwed it up for himself, ate away at him constantly and fired him up for revenge on anyone.

One chilly October afternoon, he was emerging moodily from his nan's flat when he saw the bent figure of Paddy

Hart, trudging along his outside walkway with two shopping bags. Jamie sprinted down his stairs and up the next flight and just managed to catch up with Paddy as he reached his front door.

'Hello there, Paddywack,' he said as he came alongside the man. 'Remember me?'

Paddy glanced up and then, completely blanking Jamie, he started fumbling in his pocket for his keys.

'Oi! I said hello to you! Where are your manners?' Jamie poked the older man aggressively in the chest. 'You know what happened last time we met, Paddywack. You got a bloody nose. Now say hello nicely.'

Still the other man looked down, still searching in his pocket.

Jamie leaned back against the balcony wall, hooked his elbows onto the edge and frowned theatrically, pretending to chew his lip.

'I see the missus is back. You know the one – Psycho Cathy – she left you and disappeared. Well, I hear she's back, but not with you, of course. She's shacked up with her lesbian lover girlfriend in a fucking great house in Hampstead. And a lovely couple they make too.'

This time Paddy did look up; his eyes were alive with hatred and madness and at the same time he dropped his bags on the ground. Some cans of lager rolled out on to the stained concrete.

'What did you say, you lying little—'

'Oh whoops! Have I put my foot in it?' Jamie sniggered,

delighted at last to have got the reaction he wanted. 'Didn't you know she was being domestic with the adorable Eleanor? Yep, set up home together they have, and even managed to get a baby from somewhere. Regular little family. Is the baby yours?'

Paddy took a step towards him but again, Jamie pushed him with just one finger. 'Oh fuck! Sorry, I forgot, it can't be yours, you only fire blanks! Lennie told me all about it – she and Cathy thought that was a real scream—'

Jamie didn't have time to finish his sentence as, without warning, Paddy let out a roar and hurled himself forward. With one swift movement of unbelievable strength for a man his size, he had Jamie up in the air in a wrestler's lift and pinned down flat on his back on the narrow edge of the balcony.

'Now, Supergob,' he snarled, 'say all that again, slowly.'

Jamie knew he was in real danger. Not for the first time he had over-estimated himself, but he was still sure he could get out of it.

'Hey, come on. I was only joking,' he gasped.

'But it wasn't very funny, was it?' Paddy asked as he leaned down even harder on the much slighter young man, knocking the wind out of him.

'Paddy! What the devil?' a voice suddenly screeched along the walkway. 'Don't be so stupid. Put him down . . . Come on – put him down.'

Jamie didn't move a muscle as he heard Cathy shouting and her heels clunking as she ran full pelt towards them.

Paddy looked sideways along the walkway and watched as his wife got nearer.

'Is it true?' he asked her quite calmly despite having Jamie bodily pinned to a six-inch-wide ledge on the third floor.

'Is what true?'

'That you and that Eleanor woman are lovers, that you have a baby.'

Cathy's mouth dropped open. 'Oh, for God's sake, Jamie, what are you up to? Why do you have to make trouble everywhere you go? I should let him drop you . . .'

Jamie didn't answer, he was all too aware of the sheer drop below him.

She turned her eyes back to Paddy. 'Yes, I am staying with Eleanor – but only because I had nowhere else to go. I'm here because I was coming to see you, to talk to you.' She moved closer, pleading. 'Please put him down, love. I don't really care if he goes over the edge but I care about you, I don't want you being locked up. Put him down and come inside, let me explain.'

'And the baby? Where did this baby come from?'

'Please, Paddy.' Her voice became low and calm as her nursing training kicked in. 'Just let Jamie go and we'll talk about it.'

'And what's this about me firing blanks? You told people that? How could you do that to me? How could you let a scumbag like this know something so personal?'

Petrified, and with every single muscle in his body tensed to its extreme, Jamie was able to see his life flashing before him; he could envisage himself dying on the concrete concourse of the Rat-Trap or, even worse, being crippled for life.

Despite wanting to, his sense of self-preservation told him not to struggle because he knew he was more likely to go over the edge than drop safely back onto the walkway. It would be a huge risk and he wasn't going to take the chance. Instead, he found himself focusing on every sound and movement around him. A cold wind played around his neck, but he willed himself not to shiver. A crowd was starting to gather both on the perimeter of the action on the walkway and also below, and he could hear the buzz of noise. News of a 'bundle' always spread quickly round the estate, where boredom and apathy were the main emotions, and Jamie was getting worried that someone would try to jump Paddy and make it even worse.

He moved his eyes to Cathy, silently pleading with her. He sensed Paddy was just about ready to flip.

'Tell me about this baby. Whose is it? Yours or Eleanor's? Tell me!' Paddy shouted. 'I want the truth!'

'I can't. Not out here, with everyone listening. Just let Jamie go and we'll go inside . . . please. Before you get into real trouble.'

'Not until you tell me about the baby.' Paddy's eyes were moving everywhere as he tried to watch everything at once. 'Whose is it? Is it yours?'

'Yes. Now just come inside and I'll explain.'

'Answer me, you bitch. IS IT MINE?'

'No, it isn't. You know it isn't. But that's nothing to do with Jamie here.'

'Then why was it him who told me? How does *he* know all about it?' Paddy shook Jamie very slightly and the crowd became excited, especially as the police sirens wailed nearby and Paddy became noticeably more jumpy.

'Let me go, Paddy.' In desperation, Jamie spoke for the first time. 'I'm really sorry. I won't press charges. Just let me go.'

Cathy looked at Jamie, her eyes speaking a different language to her words. 'Do you promise not to torment Paddy again? Not to torment any of us?' Silently she pleaded with him to agree.

'Yes, I do. I promise. I'm sorry.' Jamie was shaking now as his terror levels peaked, and he could barely see for the sweat pouring into his eyes; he could sense that Paddy was unhinged.

'Say sorry to my husband,' she went on steadily.

'Look, I was only teasing him, it didn't mean anything, I promise. I'm sorry for everything I've done. I was just jealous, that's all. Eleanor chucked me out,' he gurgled, unable to swallow.

Cathy looked at him in disgust. 'Come on, Paddy, he's not worth it. He's not worth going to jail for life for, is he? Let him go.'

But Paddy was in another world. He loosened his grip, but before Jamie had time to scramble to safety, Paddy smiled and with one push Jamie was over the edge. The crowd gasped in unison as the flailing body landed head-first on the concrete below just as two police cars arrived in tandem.

Jamie Kirk died as soon as his head hit the concrete below, but Paddy didn't witness it. The moment Jamie had gone over the edge Cathy had pushed him through the open front door before quickly slamming it shut. Within the security of her old home she prayed that the estate would protect its own. No one who lived there ever saw or heard anything worth mentioning to the police. Nothing that happened on the estate was ever witnessed or reported.

'Now, you sit down, say nothing and don't move a muscle, Paddy Hart. You're not here. Do you hear me? I'm not here. No one is in.'

She could see he didn't really have a clue what she was talking about but nonetheless he backed up to his favourite armchair and, as his knees hit the cushion, he collapsed into it. As soon as she was convinced he'd stay put, Cathy went over to the kitchen window at the front of the flat and peeked through the nicotine-stained net curtains into the walkway outside. There was no sign of movement and she could see that the crowd had magically dispersed.

It was as if nothing had happened. If it hadn't been for the reflection of the flashing police lights and the sound of sirens she could almost have believed that Jamie Kirk wasn't lying on the concrete below.

Turning she went back to where Paddy was sitting motionless in the chair staring vacantly into space. Her heart went out to him, especially as she knew that the whole thing was her fault.

'Please, God, make the neighbours realise that you are worth ten Jamie Kirks then just maybe we'll survive this. If no one saw anything . . .' she paused and then shook her head. 'I'm not going to think about it. Go and have a wash and a shave and tidy yourself up while I put the kettle on.'

# Chapter Forty-five

Eleanor was at her wits' end. She had a distraught Marty in one room blaming himself for Jon's attack and Cathy in another blaming herself for Paddy and Jamie. When the two of them were in the same room the atmosphere was thick with tension as they each vied for Eleanor's attention and sympathy.

Eleanor was also caring for Hope far more than she thought Cathy should expect her to, still working part-time and also trying to get the house ready for sale. She was worn out with it all.

So when Johnny Quentin turned up early one morning with a big smile and a large pot of rusty-red chrysanthemums, Eleanor almost dragged him inside.

'You have no idea how pleased I am to see you!' she hissed. 'I'm tearing my hair out here. Come on in and talk to me like a grown-up.'

'I guessed you'd be in need of some cheering-up. When Megan phoned and told me everything that had happened, I was really shocked. I know Jamie walked the line, but he didn't deserve something like that. What made Cathy's husband lose it so badly?'

'Jamie was taunting him, apparently, the way he always did everyone,' said Eleanor, taking him into the kitchen and filling the kettle. 'Paddy was down in the depths of depression and Jamie pushed all the right buttons to make him blow. It was a terrible end – a shock to everyone.' She shuddered.

'The girls send their apologies for not making it back to Jamie's funeral but they hoped you'd understand.'

'How are they doing? Still hiding out in Spain? I haven't spoken to them since it all happened.' Eleanor's lips were quivering, but she had herself under control.

'They're still in Spain, but certainly not hiding out. Can you imagine those two checking into a nunnery?' Johnny laughed. 'No . . . they're fine but still licking their wounds, especially now the agency has dropped them, and also their manager, who was really pissed off that Megan let her father set up the porn deal. But life goes on and they're minor celebrities on the Costa del Sol!'

He looked her up and down thoughtfully. 'However, if you don't mind me saying so, you look worn out. You sit down and I'll make a brew.'

'That's the best offer I've had in weeks,' Eleanor said as she sank down onto the pine rocking-chair in the corner of the kitchen, but just then Hope, who was in her pram in the corner, started to cry.

'Oh bugger, bugger,' Eleanor sighed as her shoulders drooped. 'Not again. I was up at five with her this morning. I don't know how much longer I can deal with all this.

There's Marty, Cathy and Hope all here and it's not been long since Jamie's funeral, which was awful. His family were distraught and shouting for vengeance, they didn't have a clue about his dubious dealings, or if they did they were pretending they didn't. Not that they wanted to know him when he was alive. Poor Jamie . . .' With that she started to cry herself. She tried hard not to, but she couldn't help it. 'And on top of it I'm trying to deal with this place single-handed. I've got no money – I just want to run away.' She pulled herself together, smiled weakly. 'Maybe I should go and join the girls in Spain.'

'I don't know about that, but you certainly shouldn't be doing all this on your own.' Johnny went over and pulled her into a tight bear-hug. A simple display of affection between two friends.

'You deal with baby Hope,' he went on. 'I really and truly can't do that, but I'll make us a drink and a sandwich and we'll sit quietly and you can relax for a while. Then you should go and sort those two out. You're not their mother.'

Sitting in the kitchen giving Hope her bottle, Eleanor watched Johnny as he efficiently made a pot of tea and a plate of sandwiches. As he moved around she could see his muscles rippling gently under his white T-shirt that was tight across his chest and tucked in his jeans. He was defin-itely a handsome young man, she thought, but he was also kind. And of course he'd saved her life. So far, nothing nega-tive. Even Megan, who no longer wanted to go out with him, didn't have a bad word to say. Johnny Quentin was his own man and comfortable with it.

'You seem very good at the domesticity thing,' she remarked. 'Very expert in the tea- and sandwich-making department. I guess you've had lots of practice?'

'Oh yes. Well, I live on my own, don't I? My mother still thinks she has to come round and care for me, she thinks I'm incapable of matching up socks, but I can look after myself. I enjoy my independence.'

'Is that why you didn't want to come to London and move in with Megan?'

'Partly. But I also knew deep down that the relationship wasn't going to last. Maybe I was subconsciously saving myself for that special someone?'

The way he said the words questioningly made Eleanor look down and concentrate on Hope. There was a frisson of something in the atmosphere that she wasn't sure how to react to.

After she had changed Hope and put her back into her pram, they sat side by side at the kitchen table.

'Tea, madam?' Johnny asked, lifting the teapot high. 'Milk and sugar?'

Eleanor giggled; it was nice to be with someone who was relaxed and who didn't need looking after.

As they sat in companionable silence, Eleanor's thoughts went back to Jamie. Poor Jamie. Forever trying to prove himself, always letting his need to outwit everyone override his commonsense – and his humanity. She remembered the tie-stud and Jon's wicked injuries, and hoped that Jamie had not been the one to inflict them. She recalled their first meeting, a lifetime ago, when she was a different person. He had been so bad for her in so many ways and it would never have worked, but to her he would always be Jamie Kirk, the first love of her life.

She hoped one day there would be another.

The peaceful mood was broken by Cathy coming down in her dressing-gown.

'Did I hear Hope crying?' she asked.

'Yes, you did, and yes, I've fed her.' Eleanor knew that Cathy was well aware that she had left it just long enough.

Johnny jumped up and smiled openly at her. 'But you're just in time to take over. Lennie and I are going out for the day.'

'That sounds fun. Can we come?' Cathy asked. 'Hope would love to go in a car.'

'Oh Cathy, I am so sorry,' Johnny replied before Eleanor could say anything. 'We're off for a bit of a pub-crawl, socialising with my London mates. I'm sure you'll agree Lennie needs a break?'

'Well, yes of course she does. It's been a bad time for—'

'I knew you'd understand.' Johnny jumped up from the bench and interrupted her mid-sentence. 'And that's why I'm taking Lennie away from it all for a few hours.' With that he kissed Cathy on the cheek and suddenly it was a done deal.

'I feel like a child playing truant,' Lennie fretted as they set off. 'I also feel a bit mean about Hope.'

'Hope is a tiny baby who doesn't have a clue where she is. Don't feel guilty, you've done more than enough for all of them, so let's just go and enjoy ourselves. How about we go for lunch in Camden Town and a walk along the canal? I was joking about the pub crawl.'

'I know, but it worked, didn't it? And although I may feel a bit guilty, I'm still pleased you didn't let me give in. It feels quite invigorating now I've actually escaped!'

The distant sound of a baby screaming forced its way into Marty's confused brain, which had been numbed by two strong sleeping tablets taken the night before. He forced himself awake and then realised that it was Hope; sighing impatiently he got up, threw on the clothes nearest to him and went down the stairs to look for Eleanor so he could grumble about it.

He was becoming increasingly fed up with Cathy living in the house as if it were her own, but he was also worried by the way Eleanor doted on Hope; he was genuinely concerned that Cathy was using Eleanor while it suited her and would then move on with Hope, maybe even go back to Ireland with Paddy, leaving Eleanor bereaved all over again. But he couldn't find Eleanor anywhere; instead he found Cathy in the kitchen frantically rocking Hope's pram as the baby screamed loudly.

'Lennie's gone off with Johnny for the day and I can't do anything with Hope,' Cathy told him. 'I don't know what to do, Marty. Lennie can always soothe her but she just won't take any notice of me. I thought this baby thing would be easy, but I can't do it.' Her voice was getting higher and higher as she spoke and he could see straight away that Cathy was close to tears. Despite his reluctance, Marty felt a small wave of sympathy for the woman.

When Marty had met her again after she'd come back to London he had barely recognised Cathy Hart. She had put on a lot of weight with the pregnancy, and she still hadn't got anywhere near back to her normal slim figure, and her long auburn hair had been chopped short, obviously by an inexperienced hairdresser in a blindfold. Rather than gently wavy, it had frizzed up close to her head and emphasised her newly rounded face that was devoid of all make-up.

Motherhood had certainly made Cathy Hart bloom – but not in any flattering way.

'You're okay, Cathy, go and put the kettle on and let me take her.' Carefully, Marty picked the baby out of the pram and, after tucking her close to him, he started swaying and cooing around the room with her. Gradually the loud screaming eased down to a gentle mewing.

'How did you learn to do that?' Cathy looked at him curiously.

'I live here as well, just in case you've forgotten! Do you really think this is the first time I've ever picked her up?' Marty pulled a silly face at the baby in his arms and then stuck his tongue out. 'She's gorgeous, aren't you, my precious? You're absolutely gorgeous.' The baby gave a loud burp and Marty chuckled. 'There, that's better, isn't it?'

'Sorry. I suppose I hadn't really thought about it. I know you don't like me so I thought you wouldn't like Hope either, and you're a bloke – blokes don't usually have any interest in strange babies.'

'Thanks a lot! So you think I'd be that petty as to blank a tiny baby? How very flattering. And anyway, she's not strange at all, are you, Hope?' The baby yawned.

'Don't you come the old sarcasm with me, young man,' Cathy snapped. 'I know exactly what you can be like.'

'I wasn't being sarcastic, I was just being . . . okay, now how shall I put it? Homosexually witty!' he replied in a silly high-pitched voice.

Cathy managed a smile just as Hope stopped crying completely and her eyelids slowly flickered then drooped.

'See?' Marty shrugged. 'She knows the difference between a happy mummy and a sad mummy.' He paused. 'Look, I know you're under pressure right now, and I'm really sorry about Paddy. Jamie could be such a little shit, I can see how he could easily push someone to the edge. And it'll be hard for Hope without her dad around; I really hope you two can sort things out – Lennie said you're trying . . .'

Marty had been as shocked as anyone about what Paddy did to Jamie. He thought it was tragic that such a lethal collision of temperaments had occurred. It had been a 'wrong time wrong place' accident for both of them.

Unlike the attack on Jon, which had been planned in advance and deliberately wicked. Marty was still crucified by guilt for every single minute of the day, and he hadn't even tried to contact Jon because he knew it had been all his fault.

'I don't know what to tell her – it's too soon yet anyway. Much too soon, but one day I'll figure it all out for her.' Cathy sat down and looked at her fingernails. 'Oh look, you're going to find out one day so I might as well be the one to tell you, even though Lennie's going to kill me.'

'Tell me what?' Marty asked, not overly curious about anything to do with Cathy and her life.

'You know that Artificial Insemination thing Lennie persuaded you to get your friend to do?'

Marty looked puzzled and had to think what she was talking about.

'You know,' Cathy prompted him. 'It was for someone Lennie worked with – just before she had her breakdown? A sort of DIY AID because the husband couldn't have kids?'

'Oh yes, I do remember. Lennie thought it was all such fun, all the ducking and diving and secrecy. God, it must be getting on for a year ago now.'

'Yes. Well, the donation was for me. Hope is the result of your friend's contribution and I'll always be grateful to him. I've asked Lennie to find out which of your friends it is, but she flatly refuses to do so. I reckon it's Jon myself, but she wouldn't ask you. Said it was breaking the agreement. I suppose she's right, but now I've got Hope I feel I have to know.'

Cathy looked him in the eye. 'Please tell me, Marty, is it Jon? Was he the donor?'

Marty felt sick as the room started to spin and he looked down at Hope who was still in his arms.

His daughter. Hope was his daughter.

Like a scalded cat he ran over to her pram and gently placed her inside.

'I can't help you, Cathy,' he said, tucking the little pink blanket around the sleeping child. 'I don't know who it was. Could have been any one from ten.'

Then, taking his coat from behind the kitchen door, he said, 'Just have to pop out for some cigs. Back in a while . . .' and before Cathy could reply, Marty was out of the front door and running as fast as he could.

He wanted to be anywhere that Cathy and the baby weren't.

Cathy sensed that Marty was far more upset than he had let on and she realised Eleanor had been right, she shouldn't have said anything. She had been stupid to bring it up.

Her self-obsession had not only heaped misery on her husband Paddy, she had also indirectly caused the death of Jamie Kirk and now she had upset Marty. Fortunately, for Paddy, the estate had acted true to form and closed ranks so Jamie's death had quickly been classed by the disinterested local police as an unfortunate accident, a common occurrence on the estate. However, Paddy remained wracked with guilt and all too aware of what he had done.

Quietly, she pulled a chair up beside the pram and studied the features of the baby she had so desperately craved. Hope. Her beautiful, perfect daughter. Long eyelashes rested gently on her chubby pale cheeks and a sandy down covered the top of her tiny head. At that moment the wave of maternal love that had failed to materialise when Hope was born suddenly swept over Cathy as she gently brushed her fingers over the baby's forehead.

'Oh, Hope, my darling, I did it all wrong, didn't I? But I can't regret it, can I? I've got you. And who knows? Maybe Paddy will continue to soften; maybe he'll forgive me and you'll have a father after all. He's a good man, you know. Maybe the three of us going back to Ireland and putting the past behind us is a step in the right direction.'

Quickly, she stood up. 'Come on, my precious one, you and I are going out. We're going to see Paddy and make him see sense.'

# Chapter Forty-six

Eleanor and Johnny arrived back home late that evening and both were laughing happily as they went indoors.

'Cathy? Are you here?' Eleanor called out. 'We're back . . . Marty?' She turned to Johnny. 'It's all very quiet, I expected chaos when those two realised they were on their own without a referee in between them.'

As she dumped her bag on the hall table, Johnny suddenly reached forward and pulled her across to him. Before she could react he was up close and kissing her. It was a slow kiss, gentle and very exciting.

'Wow!' Eleanor said breathlessly as they pulled apart. 'What was *that* for?'

'Just because . . . Well, just because I had to. Lennie, I've been wanting to do that for weeks and then suddenly I couldn't help myself. Do you mind?'

'Mind!' Eleanor exclaimed. 'I've been *hoping* you'd do it for weeks. Oh wow! I feel I ought to say "Should we be doing this", but it feels so right. Oh dear . . .' They both laughed together nervously, each feeling a little embarrassed by this unexpected development in their friendship. Their eyes locked and they gazed at each other silently, not moving, until they heard a key turning in the front door. In unison they looked at the door as Cathy came in backwards pulling the pram.

'Cathy! I assumed you were upstairs. Where have you been?'

'To see Paddy. What about you two?' Cathy looked from one to the other.

'We went out for the day and did nothing very much at all. We just relaxed. It was great.' Eleanor moved over to the pram and looked at the baby who was quiet but wide awake. 'How's Hope been? I bet she enjoyed being out and about with her mum. Did you manage okay?'

'Just about!' Cathy laughed. 'Though getting on and off buses with a pram is a challenge I hadn't thought about. I couldn't figure out how to fold the darned thing up! Oh well . . . we live and learn. Now I have to sort out her bottle.'

'Do you want me to feed her?' Eleanor asked.

'It's okay. Thanks for the offer but I have to get used to looking after my baby myself, I've left her to you for long enough. Though I may still need some help to cope until I get fully into the swing of it.'

'I assume it went well with Paddy then?' Eleanor asked.

'Hmm. So so! Fingers crossed anyway.'

Eleanor ran forward and threw her arms around her friend. 'Oh, Cathy, I am so pleased for you and for Hope, I know it's what you really want.'

'Well, I'm not counting my chickens and I think we

may have to move away from here, maybe even back to Ireland. Would you mind, Lennie? I know how much you love Hope . . .'

'Of course I'd mind and I'll miss you both like mad but we'll keep in touch, won't we?' Eleanor smiled brightly but there was a catch in her voice as she contemplated not having Hope around.

'Of course.' Cathy smiled and gave Eleanor a glimpse of the old Cathy. 'We're tied together for ever by Hope, Lennie. You helped me have her and you were there when she came into the world. You'll never get away from us.'

'Even if you're with Paddy?'

'Even if I'm with Paddy. You are an intrinsic part of my daughter's life!'

As Cathy pushed the pram through to the kitchen Johnny looked at Eleanor. 'What's happening here? Do I sense some kind of change in Cathy?'

'It seems like it. I guess she's finally bonded with her daughter!'

'And you and me?' he asked. 'Have we bonded?'

Eleanor looked up to see him staring at her and knew that she would always remember that moment as the one when she fell in love with Johnny Quentin.

'Hey, look.' Johnny pointed at the floor. 'There's a letter.' Picking it up he handed it to her.

'Thanks.' She took it from him and tore open the envelope.

*My dearest Lennie,*

*I don't want to hurt you, but I need some space to myself right now, so I'm going back to Liverpool for a while. I'm sure I'll come back to London some time soon, but right now I need to get away to think. I want to think about Jon, about Jamie and Paddy, about that bastard whose name I cannot bring myself to write, and about everything that has happened in the past, crazy eighteen months. I love you, and I love Jon, and I'm going to find a way to keep you both in my life. I am also going to see that justice gets done.*

*I will be in touch again soon, so don't move too far where I can't find you.*

*Thank you for saving me more than once.*

*Take care of yourself,*

*Love,*

*Marty.*

'He's gone! Marty's gone!' Eleanor cried. 'How can he go just like that?'

'Maybe he needed to get away like we did, but just for longer? He'll come back. You two are like twins – you can't be separated for long.'

'Cathy!' she screamed, 'Cathy, tell me what happened with you and Marty.'

Cathy came through from the kitchen looking sheepish.

'What the fuck did you say to him?' Eleanor demanded.

'Nothing really, we had a chat and I just asked about

the donor, asked if he knew who he was. I know you said not to but I had a right to ask.' Her tone was apologetic. 'Anyway, he said he didn't know and that was it. He put Hope down and went out to the shops, then when he came back I caught him kissing her on the forehead so I told him not to wake her up. He went off upstairs and I haven't seen him since.'

'When did he leave?' Eleanor could feel herself starting to palpitate.

'Leave?'

'Yes, leave. Marty's left, he's gone back to Liverpool.'

'I don't know.' Cathy shrugged. 'I went out—'

*Marty, donor, Hope* . . . Eleanor suddenly knew that Hope was Marty's daughter.

'I *told* you not to say anything!' she cried exasperatedly.

'Hey, I'm sorry but don't blame me because he's left.'

Eleanor suddenly calmed. 'No, you're right, it's not your fault and I'm sure he'll be back. I'm sorry. I was just upset that he'd gone.'

'It's okay.' Cathy turned and went back into the kitchen.

Johnny said tactfully, 'What was *that* all about, or is it something between you and Marty? I don't want to pry.'

'No, it's okay. I'll tell you all about it, but not right now.'

She didn't say anything else because she could feel her throat closing up.

'Okay, well I'd better get back to Eastbourne – I've got an early start in the morning. I'll ring you later.' He kissed her tenderly. 'You deal with what you have to deal with and we'll catch up at the weekend. Then, if you want to, of course, we can start to make plans.'

'I do want to, Johnny. I really do.'

'Okay. See you very soon then!' With a grin and a backward wave he was gone and Eleanor leaned back against the door frame in the porch to ponder exactly what had happened to her that day.

She had fallen in love with Johnny Quentin, the man so interwoven with her past. The cautious part of her brain warned her to take care but she knew that this time her instincts were right. Johnny was right. They knew each other so well and neither of them had any secrets. No more secrets, no more past chances.

'Lennie?' Cathy's voice echoed through the ground floor. 'How about a nice cuppa and a chat? I think we've both got lots to talk about.'

Eleanor grinned. 'Coming.'

# Epilogue

As the church bells pealed out in celebration, the newly married couple slowly exited the portals of the impressive old church in the centre of Eastbourne followed closely by an eclectic mix of friends and family, all jostling to be first out to congratulate the happy couple.

Over the past eighteen months Eleanor and Johnny had moved their relationship forward slowly and cautiously, but nevertheless totally convinced that they were destined to be together. Now their eagerly anticipated wedding day had arrived and everyone could see they were a couple who were perfectly suited and very much in love.

Eleanor's three ex-housemates had tried their very best to persuade her to wear a high-fashion wedding dress, with Johnny in a trendy suit, but the couple had good-humouredly refused and the bride's classic white dress and train stretched far behind her as she stood on the church steps with her husband, smiling widely for the first photographs.

Megan and Venita, who looked unusually demure in peach satin ankle-length shifts, grinned widely as they took it in turns to control an over-excited Hope who, as flower girl, was dressed in a fluffy peach lacy confection that was already grubby from her desire to show off her newly acquired running and falling-over skills to the whole congregation.

Marty, having quickly slipped out of the side door as the service ended, was waiting to greet them at the bottom of the steps.

'Lennie, you look absolutely stunning. Just stunning.' He sighed with tears in his eyes. 'You are truly the most beautiful woman in the whole wide world! I love you!'

Eleanor laughed and leaned forward to receive a kiss on the cheek. 'No need to exaggerate, Marty, but thank you all the same. Today I actually *feel* beautiful. And so happy, of course.'

Suddenly the official photographer and his assistant were ordering everyone back and forth and setting up the poses for the photographs in a way that reminded Eleanor of musical chairs. Family photos, group photos, on and on it went until Eleanor held up her hand. 'I want one very special photograph for the album,' she said with a catch in her voice. 'Megan, Venita and Marty, I want one of you all together with us. My best friends who have stood by me through everything.'

As they lined up, Eleanor looked out at the sea of people milling around in front of them. Amid the crowd she could see Cathy standing with Paddy who had scooped Hope up in his arms as he tried to keep her from running around. Jon was standing slightly to one side looking pale and nervous amid all the strangers and Aaron was standing with one hand on a flamboyant walking cane and his other arm wrapped around Hettie who was sobbing uncontrollably under an enormous lavender hat decorated with more feathers than a peacock. Everyone was there. All the integral people in her life. Except, of course, for her parents.

The morning before the wedding, Eleanor had travelled up to London again and gone back to the house in Hampstead. It was now home to a large happy family whom she had been delighted to sell to. For a few minutes she had stood motionless by the gate looking up at the central leaded window that held so many memories of her beloved mother. Then she had said a silent prayer before whispering her goodbyes and turning away without a backward glance. She knew she would never go back there again.

'Mr and Mrs Quentin, the car is waiting to take you to your reception.'

The crowd parted and amid a shower of confetti the couple walked down the churchyard path to the waiting Rolls-Royce that would take them off to start their married life together.